THE FADED LAND

KEIRAN: THE ETERNAL MAGE
BOOK ONE

D.E. SHERMAN

Timeless
Wind

First published by Timeless Wind Publishing LLC 2024

First edition

Editing by Nicole Amato.

Typography by www.noblecreates.com and Lorne Ryburn.

CHAPTER
ONE

When I first opened my eyes, it was to stare down in confusion at the thin, grubby, dirt-smudged fingers of a child far too old to be a newborn. They should have been the soft, pudgy digits of a freshly born infant, not even an hour old, but instead, I had months and months, maybe even years of memories of my new life.

Something had gone terribly wrong.

The invocations I'd laid into my soul should have sparked my previous life's memories with only the barest brush of mana to trigger them. If not for my new body's memories, my first thought would have been someone had detected my passage through the reincarnation cycle and trapped me in a mana void for years. Just looking around was enough to dispel that line of thinking. The truth was both simpler and stranger, it seemed.

There wasn't a speck of ambient mana in the air around me, not a drop in the dry, dusty earth. I was sitting in a garden, a place that should have been bursting with life, but each row of plants was sadder than the one that preceded it. The pathetic, wilted, shriveled things barely clung to life, starved for the mana they needed to flourish.

It appeared I'd been reborn in a desert, one that had been devastated by some cataclysm that had scarred the land. It had taken my new body years to generate enough internal mana to trigger the soul invocations that would awaken my previous life's memories. There'd been no mistakes, just ill fortune that had seen me reborn on a swath of dead land.

"Gravin."

This was probably a blessing in disguise. If there was so little ambient mana in the environment that it had taken years to trigger the soul magic, I wouldn't have been able to do much during those initial years anyway. At least this way, I'd been spared the tedium of having to live through them. The memories alone were bad enough, fragmented and disjointed as they were.

"Graaavviiin," a voice cooed.

I was going to need to adjust my time frame. Internal mana was going to be my only source of power as long as I was stuck in this mana desert, and I was physically too weak to survive on my own. It would be months before I built up enough mana to ignite my core. Damn. What rotten luck to be reincarnated in a place like this.

"He looks so serious," a different voice said. "Look at that scowl on his face."

"Come here, Gravvy," the first voice said, and suddenly a shadow appeared over me. I looked up just in time to see a plain-faced woman wearing rough home-spun leaning down to grab hold of me. My mother, if the memories of my new brain were to be believed.

"Did you have fun?" she asked. Without waiting for an answer, she whisked me away towards what could generously be described as a hut and said, "Come on, let's get you cleaned up and we'll have dinner."

My mother said her goodbyes to the other woman, a neighbor by the looks of it, and carried me towards a nearby hut, one of dozens lined up next to a dirt street, our home if my new body's memories were to be believed. They were more or less identical, all mud-fired bricks of some sort with woven thatch roofs. I took that time to consider my mana core. The more I thought about it, the more I was sure something had gone wrong. Even in this desert, I should have generated enough internal mana to awaken far sooner than I had. I couldn't recall the exact averages for mana generation rates in babies, but I should have produced enough well before reaching two years of age.

I didn't realize we were inside the hut until I was plopped down on a table and the woman carrying me started tugging at my clothes. "Arms up," she said in a little sing-song voice. My body reacted without my conscious decision, and she pulled my shirt off.

I needed to figure out this mana situation immediately. Otherwise, it was going to be a long few years.

My memory wasn't perfect, but I hadn't been an archmage for nothing. I'd done the math, repeatedly, and the results just didn't make sense. I would have said my mana core was crippled in some way, but I could sense it perfectly. It was as flawless as any other two-year-old's. Even if my math was somehow way off, I could sense it generating mana. It should have only taken about twenty hours before my core had enough mana to awaken my memories, not over two years.

Something was interfering with my mana generation. That was the only explanation that made sense, but I couldn't for the life of me fathom why. Even if someone had found the records of my experiments, it would have been impossible to trace the flow of my soul through the afterlife to my new body. It would take a grand magus invoker to examine my soul here and now to note anything unusual, and judging by the conditions I'd apparently been living in, I doubted there was one within a thousand miles, let alone one bored enough to spot check random babies for soul modifications.

I could only speculate for now. Until I learned more, the best I could do was start working on building up enough mana to ignite my core. Given how pitiful my mana generation was at the moment, that was going to take a month just for the mana to form, and I'd need more than my core was capable of holding. I'd have to invest some time and mana into building a storage crystal to feed my mana into.

Another frustrating delay. I could scarcely picture a way in which I could have started my new life in a worse position. This process should have taken me a few hours at most, not weeks and weeks.

My new family appeared one by one. First, my older sister showed up just as Mother was finishing dinner, followed swiftly by my father. I had memories of both but, perhaps unsurprisingly, a baby's memories didn't provide clear pictures. I wasn't even sure how old my sister was, though she certainly didn't have more than a few years on me. Gravin felt a baby's love for the parents who nurtured him, and perhaps curiosity at his older sister more than anything else. I supposed a bit of acting was in order.

Fortunately for me, Gravin was a quiet child with a tendency to stare at whatever caught his interest. If anything, he seemed a bit timid. That should be easy enough to copy for the time being. Once I'd ignited my mana core, things would have to change, of course. That was several months away, and without an abundant source of ambient mana, my progress was going to be agonizingly slow.

Dinner was a simple affair of humble food prepared with more love than skill, and, unfortunately, no seasonings at all to help the taste. I focused my efforts on fine motor control, which was surprisingly difficult to accomplish and somewhat exhausting. Who would have guessed that eating a meal without making a mess all over myself would turn into such a grueling test? It wasn't even that it was hard to accomplish so much as it was that my stamina was non-existent.

The whole while, my new sister nattered on about what she'd learned that day, which I did my best to tune out. Basic numbers and letters weren't exciting when *I* had been the one learning them thousands of years ago, and they weren't exciting today. More and more, I despaired of how tedious my life was going to be for the next few months. It wasn't until after dinner was done that something interesting happened.

"Good job, Gravin!" my mother said. "You barely need to be cleaned up at all. How about we go to the square early today and you can watch everyone while we wait for the Collectors? We'll be right near the front of the line this time."

"That'll be a relief," Father added. "We can all go to bed early tonight."

My sister's round little face scrunched up at that, but she didn't say anything. At first, I thought it was the early bedtime that she had a problem with, but somewhere in Gravin's fuzzy memories were visions of a group of people all lined up in front of tables, moving forward every few seconds. It was hard to pick details out of it, in part because of Gravin's habit of fixating on things. I had one memory with a clear picture of a man's mud-stained boot in front of me, but no clues as to why we were in line to begin with.

I supposed I'd find out soon enough.

The village was one of those little huddled specks on the landscape, a collection of fifty or so huts surrounded by fields that barely grew enough for the people to survive. Everything was dry, dusty, and hot. I didn't get to see much of it during our short walk to the square at the center, but what I did see was not reassuring. These people were one crop-ruining storm away from being wiped out.

More importantly, at least from my perspective, there was no ambient mana at all. I would have said it was impossible if I wasn't seeing it myself. Everything had mana in it, even the world itself. Living things were the best source of mana, but even in a desert like this, there should have been at least a little. Instead, the whole village was bone dry. Not even the people had any mana coming off them.

They had mana, of course. Each and every one had a dormant mana core, but not a single one of them was full. Maybe it was just that they were all coming back in from a hard day's labor. I could see it being common around here to spend mana on physical invocations to aid in farming. The techniques would be as basic and bare bones as possible, just a simple conversion of mana to energy, but it would explain why not a single person was producing ambient mana from a full core.

While I studied the villagers, they started organizing themselves into four lines that stretched across the square. Families chatted with each other as they waited, though I wasn't able to tell what exactly it was we were all gathered for. Whatever was going on, it was common enough that nobody felt the need to discuss the details.

The north side of the square had a wide, squat building, more than five times bigger than any of the huts the various families had emerged from. It also had a single wooden door, which was the first one I'd seen so far. The huts had all used rough cloth to drape the entryways.

The door opened and eight people walked out in groups of two with tables carried between each of them. Those were lined up in front of the building, and four more people emerged. They were carrying large black rocks, probably about forty pounds or so, close to their chests. Without talking, they all stepped up to a different table and placed the rock down. We were close enough to the front of the line that I could easily make out the details.

Draw stone. Of course. I should have guessed.

The lines started moving, people placing a hand on the stone for a few seconds, receiving confirmation from the attendant and having their names ticked off a list on a nearby sheet of paper, and moving out of the way for the next. Each person's mana core was emptied into one of the draw stones, and within a minute, it was my family's turn.

Father went first, then turned to my sister. "Come on, your turn," he said.

"I don't like it. It makes me feel tired."

"I know, sweetie, but everyone has to contribute so the barrier doesn't come down. The monsters will get in if we don't donate our mana."

My father took her hand and gently pressed it against the draw stone. What little mana she had drained out of her over the next few seconds, and she swayed on her feet. He scooped her up and carried her out of the way so my mother could take her turn. From what I could tell, he wasn't handling the mana drain much better than my sister.

My mother let the draw stone take her mana, then knelt down and boosted me up so I could reach it sitting on the table. "Just put your hand here, like we practiced," she said.

All around me, the other lines were moving forward. Behind us, more villagers were waiting their turns. No one was objecting, at least not beyond some fussing from the smaller children. Everyone thought this was perfectly normal. Had I been reborn inside some sort of cult? And what barrier were they talking about? I would have noticed something like that.

Her hand over mine, my mother guided my hand to press down on the draw stone so that it could steal what little mana I'd managed to generate.

To hell with that.

CHAPTER
TWO

Draw stones were easy to use, so easy in fact that they would passively steal mana right out of the cores of anyone nearby, albeit much more slowly than if someone touched one. It was no wonder it had taken so long for me to awaken if this was a nightly village ritual.

Fortunately for me, anyone with the least bit of knowledge could block the pull of a draw stone. It was a simple matter to keep my mana right where it was. The only question was whether the attendant would realize, but considering there wasn't a single ignited mana core in this entire village, I was betting the answer was going to be no.

I pulled my hand back after a few seconds of pretending to let the draw stone do its business, and the attendant just ticked off a box next to my name. Mother picked me up and said, "There we go. Good job, Gravin! Maybe you should give Senica lessons on how to be brave."

My sister stuck her tongue out at me from our father's arms, and together we walked back to our one-room hut. At least I knew her name now. I was sure Mother and Father would suffice for our parents, and no one would look at me too hard if I forgot the names of anyone else I was supposed to know. No one was even really commenting on the fact that I hadn't said a word yet since I'd awakened. Gravin had always been a quiet child.

Now that I had a better idea of the situation I'd found myself in, I could start forming a plan to get myself out of here. The first step was going to be creating a mana storage crystal. My own core couldn't hold all the mana I needed to ignite it, and there was no ambient mana to draw in. I'd have to hoard it. That shouldn't be too terribly difficult. I just needed a physical object, some mana, and a great deal of patience. The biggest hurdle was going to be how weak my body was. Even without letting myself be mana drained, I was feeling drowsy.

Toddlers slept a lot, and while I could use my own mana to energize myself, I needed it for other projects. A nap wouldn't go amiss right now. Luckily enough, the sun was going down, and it looked like everyone else was getting ready to sleep, too. That led me to take my first good look around the inside of the hut, and I realized almost immediately that there were only two pallets. One was a small, Senica-sized rectangle with a pair of dolls laying on it, and the other was big enough for two adults.

Oh no. Was I still sleeping with my parents? This whole reincarnation was starting to feel like some sort of cosmic joke someone was playing on me. It was bad enough that I was sleeping on an unscented oblong bag of straw, but to have to share the pallet with two other people...

Getting my own place to sleep was right up near the top of my priorities list.

My new family went through their nighttime rituals before Senica crawled onto her own pallet and I was placed between my parents on the larger one. My mother handed me some sort of straw-stuffed doll shaped like what I assumed was a local animal. I didn't recognize it, but that could have been because the quality was lacking or because it was just an animal I'd never seen before. Neither would have surprised me. Wherever I'd reincarnated at, it wasn't a place I was familiar with.

Apparently, it was just expected that I'd want to hang onto "Farnsley," as my mother called the toy. It wasn't ideal for my purposes, but I only needed a storage crystal for a month or two. I could easily empty my mana into the toy every morning once I'd modified it, and no one would think twice about me constantly holding it. It was almost galling thinking about the transference loss, but then again, it wasn't like I had anything better around to work with.

I'd get started on forming the storage crystal inside the toy where it couldn't be seen tonight, and over the next few weeks, I'd slowly fill it. No one would suspect a thing. Perfect.

My eyes cracked open to see sunlight pouring in through the window. Both my parents were already up and preparing for the day, though my sister was still laying on her pallet. I groaned and sat up, then looked around for the toy. It had somehow made its way down past my feet while I slept.

I had not managed to finish forming the storage crystal last night—not even close. I hadn't even managed to use all the mana in my core before I'd fallen asleep. I crawled across the bed, scooped the toy up, and got back to work.

"Oh, you're up early," my mother said. Before I had time to think, she'd crossed the room and picked me up. "Come on, leave Farnsley here. Let's get your morning business taken care of."

With no say in the matter, I was whooshed out of the hut to the nearest communal outhouse. How humiliating.

It was far more difficult than I'd expected to work on the storage crystal. I wasn't allowed to take the toy anywhere, and when I tried, I was told that I was getting too old for that now. Between that and my weak body's inability to stay awake at night, it was hard to get time to even work on the crystal. That was frustrating, but if I was being honest, it wasn't like I was generating mana fast enough that a ton of additional time would make a difference.

It took me a week to finish forming the storage crystal inside the toy. It felt like a rock the size of a grown woman's thumb, and the only way to tell it was there was to squeeze the toy tightly. Its maximum storage capacity was pathetic, and if circumstances hadn't been so dire, I'd be embarrassed to associate myself with its creation.

The storage crystal was horribly inefficient, and I was forced to once again revise my estimations about how long it would take to fill it. At least half the mana I poured into it leaked out before it stabilized, and if the tests

I'd done were in any way accurate, I was going to lose half of it again when I tried to pull it back out.

Two months, at least. That was the best-case scenario. So far, nothing had interfered, at least not in any meaningful way. Mother was intent on monopolizing most of my waking hours, and when she wasn't, Father occasionally took over my evening. The only person who didn't seem particularly interested in me was Senica. At least, that's what I thought.

———

"How come you don't talk anymore?" Senica asked me one afternoon.

I slowly turned my head to look at her and blinked once. It suited my purposes to say nothing, and no one had made any demands otherwise.

"Mom's worried about how quiet you got. I heard her talking to Malra about it while we were gardening the other day," my sister continued. She jabbed a finger in my direction. "So how come you stopped?"

I shrugged my little shoulders and told her, "Nothing to say."

"You'd better start talking again soon. Malra said we should take you to the gover— the govenirer, no, the... to Lord Noctra's house to see if you're possessed."

That was ridiculous. What kind of spirit would waste its time possessing a toddler? What would even be the point? Now, if they were worried about body snatchers or changelings, that would make sense. But a possession? That was just dumb.

Just the same, I didn't need anyone taking a closer look at me before I had the ability to defend myself. Even if they couldn't see the soul invocations I'd woven into myself, that might not stop some third-rate charlatan from pronouncing some suitably mystical sounding garbage to some frightened villagers that ended up with me in even more dire straits than I was now.

"Not possessed," I said.

"Well, of course you're not, dear," my mother said, sweeping me up into her arms. Curse my toddler senses, I hadn't even realized she'd been listening. "Senica is just being mean. Ignore her."

I spent the next half an hour reciting the names of various fruits and vegetables from the garden back to my mother as she told them to me, much to her delight. It looked like I hadn't done as good a job at acting like a normal toddler as I'd thought.

Two more months...

Everything would have gone so much faster if I'd had the ability to cast even the most basic of spells. Mana draining my parents in their sleep, for example, would have increased the amount of mana I could put in my storage crystal. It was too bad I couldn't do it.

Days turned into weeks, and ever so slowly, the storage crystal kept filling. Every evening, I went to the town square with my family and pretended to give up my mana to the draw stone, an event they called the tithe. Every night, I poured it into my storage crystal instead. Soon enough, it technically had enough mana in it to ignite my own core, but with so much being wasted upon drawing it out, it wasn't really close to enough. I needed to fill the crystal to the brim to ensure success.

The whole thing would have been easier if Mother was just a little bit less interested in me. Her constant demands on my time were bad enough, but the amount of energy I wasted appeasing her attempts to play with and educate me were the true problem. It was impossible to keep up without tapping into my mana. Gravin, and no doubt every other baby here, had probably been doing it unconsciously. It was a common enough form of invocation, which itself was by far the easiest kind of magic to cast without realizing it.

If I tried to get out of it, I got admonishments. If I persisted, it turned to concern about my health, which led to greater scrutiny. The last thing I needed was someone like that neighbor Malra snooping around or, worse, going to someone else who might actually be competent. Anyone with a lick of training would notice that storage crystal. I was running a calculated risk not shielding the mana, but it would take ten times as long to fill if I did.

Why couldn't I have gotten an absentee mother, like in my previous life? That woman had been so disconnected from me that I couldn't even remember her name anymore. Thinking about her only brought to mind the smell of burning yamma weed that she'd smoked from a long-stemmed pipe every day and the sound of flesh slapping on flesh, which was how she'd paid for it.

My new mother was nothing like that. It was ungrateful of me to resent her for being such a loving parent, but she was standing in the way of my progress. I played along and did my best to keep my mana expenditure to a minimum while silently fuming about even more delays. Weeks turned into months, and my goal of filling the storage crystal in just two months seemed laughable. Before I knew it, my third birthday had come and gone.

That led to even more expectations, and my mana generation hadn't grown enough to keep up with them. It was now four months of this routine, and every day was an exercise in willpower as I resisted the temptation to tap into the storage crystal, drain it dry, and hope that I could squeeze enough mana out of it to ignite my core.

The day was coming, and soon, too. Even with all the stumbling blocks, I was over three quarters of the way to filling the crystal. Just another two months should do it. This time, I was sure.

"Gravin," my mother said. "I have a surprise for you, sweetie."

I opened my eyes and looked at her. I'd been sitting in the garden while she worked, doing my best to meditate and increase the amount of mana I was generating. With my core in the state it was, there wasn't really much I could do, and I would have normally considered it a waste of effort. In these circumstances, though, anything I could do to shave off a day or two was worth the work.

"This is Cherok," my mother said, gesturing to a man standing next to her. "He's going to be your schoolteacher for the next few months while you learn how to use your mana. Isn't that exciting?"

CHAPTER

THREE

T he man standing at the edge of the garden had a round, soft face
and thick, pudgy fingers. He wore the same rough home-spun as
everyone else in the village, but in his case the fabric strained over
a potbelly. In my former life, I would have pegged him as some sort of low-
ranking noble, high enough up the ladder to not have to do manual labor,
but not so high that he had the time and inclination to maintain a state of
physical fitness. He would be someone for whom appearances weren't
important.

Here, where almost everyone worked the fields, and did so without
much magic to help, finding someone with an appreciable amount of fat on
them was something of a rarity. Everyone else I'd met so far straddled the
line between lean and malnourished. So then, this Cherok fellow must be
important to the village's society, someone in a privileged position. He
represented yet another complication I didn't need.

He advanced through the rows of stunted tomato plants and squatted
down in front of me. "Hello, Gravin. It's nice to meet you."

I had no idea how Gravin would have reacted, but as my sister had
pointed out, I'd developed a reputation for not saying much among my
family. There was no reason to change that strategy now.

"Hello," I said. Then I waited.

Cherok smiled patiently, but after a few seconds of me not saying anything else, he looked back to my mother, who just shrugged in response. "Do you know what mana is?" he asked as he turned back to me.

It was a struggle not to roll my eyes, made easier by the fact that I had a very real fear that this man was going to be greatly hindering my progress. Depending on his capabilities, there were really only two ways to play this. Either I could pretend to be a prodigy and get through the unnecessary lessons as quickly as possible, thus wasting the minimum amount of my precious mana appeasing him, or I could pretend to be hopelessly thick, wasting no mana and deliberately failing all his lessons.

The problem there was that I didn't know if I just needed to prove I could manipulate my mana or if the classes lasted the same length of time regardless. More than that, I didn't know how much he'd be able to detect. There were too many unknown variables to make this decision with any degree of confidence, and of course nobody had bothered to talk to the toddler about what he wanted to do. Why would they?

The only thing Gravin would know about mana was that the draw stones took it. That was a nice, safe topic. "It's what we give to the big rock every day," I said.

Cherok chuckled at that. Perhaps I'd just spent too many months as a small child, but I'd noticed that a lot of adults were very patronizing towards children. It was to be expected to an extent, but there were degrees of difference. My mother, for example, wanted to celebrate every little thing. That was a perfectly valid tactic for encouraging children to grow and explore, but it did get a bit wearing to me personally.

This particular adult was not like that. He clearly looked down on me, probably on all children, and considered me *lesser*. I disliked him immediately. If I'd been on the fence before, that laugh of his sealed the deal.

"That's true, but that's not what mana is. That's just something you do with it," he said condescendingly. I glanced over his shoulder at my mother, but she just stood there smiling at me. Obviously, I wasn't getting any help there.

Cherok was waiting for me to say something again, no doubt intending to lead me through the conversation by the nose while he displayed his intellectual superiority to a literal toddler. I stared back at him and remained silent.

The moment stretched between us, him waiting for me to ask the question he was baiting me into voicing, me more than willing to sit there all day ignoring him. I didn't need to ask him what mana was. I'd known that for over two thousand years, and my original teacher had been an actual mage, not a dull like this guy. All he was doing was interrupting my meditation, which was simply a way for me to pass the time and generate just slightly more mana than I would otherwise.

"Mana," Cherok said, giving up on waiting me out, "is the magic inside us. It makes us strong, and we collectively use it as a community to empower the great barrier that keeps Alkerist safe from monsters."

Almost nobody ever said the name of the village. I'd been here for months before I'd heard it the first time. For a group of people utterly isolated from the outside world, the real surprise had been that they'd named their village at all. I suspected someone who'd died a long, long time ago had come up with the name, and whatever meaning it once had was long forgotten.

Then there was this guy.

"Okay," I said.

Cherok frowned and glanced back at my mother again. She didn't say anything, and I felt a little surge of malicious glee at the whole situation. He looked back to me and said, "My job is to teach children how to sense their mana and, more importantly, how to manipulate their spirit to make more of it. Some of my students are so advanced that they can even use their mana to make themselves stronger or faster. Doesn't that sound exciting?"

It really, really didn't. Also, he didn't seem to know what he was talking about. Presumably, he meant he taught people how to manipulate their mana cores, but I couldn't be completely sure.

"Okay," I said again.

Cherok rose to his full height and walked back over to my mother to talk to her in a hushed voice. I went back to "playing" in the dirt, as my mother had termed my meditation sessions. A bit of mana sharpened my senses so I could pick up their conversation easily. It might have been wasteful, but it seemed prudent to keep on top of whatever they were planning for me.

"Maybe he's just a bit too young," Cherok said, "but he doesn't understand what I'm saying, and he's not interested in learning."

"It sounds like you're saying my son is stupid," my mother said, a warning tone in her voice.

"No, no, of course not. Everyone develops at their own pace, and just because his sister started early doesn't mean he will, too. There's nothing wrong with that. It's just how it is."

"So you don't want Gravin to attend your next class?"

"He can, if you really want him there. But I won't be able to give him special instruction time to help him catch up. It might be best for everyone if we try again in a few months."

Yes, good. That sounded reasonable. It would give me enough time to ignite my mana core. Then whatever demands Cherok made of me would be easily compensated for. As long as the lessons weren't too intensive, I could probably spend most of the time strengthening my core so I could push past stage one quickly.

Considering the utter lack of ambient mana in the village, increasing my own mana generation was really the only way to progress. Once I was strong enough to leave, I could get out of this desert and return to my original plans. I didn't like being vulnerable like this, though there were still a few fail-safes left in my soul if the worst should come to pass.

"Senica wasn't that interested to begin with either," my mother said. "But you'll recall she ended up doing very well."

"She did," Cherok admitted. "But as I said, every child is different. Your daughter was interested in playing and was extremely active. She thought the classes would be boring and a distraction from her games. Once she got a taste of what I had to teach her, her whole attitude changed. Gravin, on the other hand, well..."

"Well what?"

"He's just kind of... sitting there. And from what I understand, that isn't unusual behavior for him. He doesn't do much of anything, isn't curious, doesn't play, doesn't talk. I've been teaching the children of Alkerist for twenty years now, and I've never seen one as disinterested in the world around him as your son. Xilaya, he's not ready, and he might never be ready. There's something wrong with him."

"There is nothing wrong with my boy," my mother hissed.

Cherok held his hands up and took a step back. "As you say. You'd know him best. Regardless, from my conversation with him, I'd recommend waiting a few more months to see if he develops some interest. I can show you a few things to work on with him here at home that might spark something if you'd like."

I hadn't realized I stood out so much. Here I thought I'd just been well-behaved and easy to care for, and instead I'd gotten a reputation as an idiot. I'd be offended if there was even a single person in this whole village whose opinion mattered to me. As it was, I'd take being looked down on if it meant I was left alone for the next few months.

"Our next Testing is in a month," my mother said, her voice quiet and almost desperate. "Gravin needs to be able to show that he's contributing to the barrier."

"Well, I'm sorry, but even if the boy was a genius, it'd be all but impossible to teach him mana techniques in just a few weeks," Cherok said. "Not even I can take a child to that height so quickly, no matter how talented they might be. And your son, I'm sorry to say, isn't."

If only he knew how wrong he was. But no, it wasn't worth it to draw the attention to myself, not when I was still this weak. I had nothing to prove to a bunch of farmers living in the back corner of nowhere and clinging to superstitions about a fictional magical barrier that was keeping them safe from a vague, unspecified threat that never seemed to emerge to prove them wrong.

"What are we supposed to do then?" my mother demanded. "Sellis is already working himself to death. We can't afford for him to be taxed twice a day."

"There is nothing you can do," Cherok said stiffly. "My suggestion would be to keep your legs closed in the immediate future so you don't end up with a third child you can't afford."

It was a good thing I was studiously avoiding looking in their direction, otherwise one of them might have seen my smirk when I felt the mana in my mother's core surge in an unstructured invocation that bolstered her physical prowess. A second later, there came the smack of palm against cheek and Cherok let out a surprised, pain-filled squeal.

It seemed I wasn't the only one who didn't like the village teacher.

"Well then," my mother said, her voice cold, "thank you for the deep insight into my family. Truly, your wisdom is without peer."

I risked a look over and saw Cherok still staggered back a step, one hand clutching at his face. He straightened up, shot me a nasty glare, and said, "My recommendation is that you wait for your son to get older before he begins his schooling. He is nowhere near ready at this time. Good day, Xilaya."

And with that, he turned on his heel and stormed off down the street.

My mother watched him go, her fists clenched at her side and her nose flaring with each breath. Only after he'd turned the corner did she force herself to relax.

"And good riddance," she muttered. When she turned to face me, she'd resumed her normal, smiling expression. "Well then, wasn't that exciting?"

"Mean man," I said.

"People are complicated," she told me. "Do you understand?"

"Mean. Pretends not to be."

My mother paused, gave me a speculative look, and nodded. "Yes, I suppose that's a good way to put it. There's nothing to be done about it, though. Why don't we see about getting this row weeded, and then we can start working on dinner?"

It looked like I'd managed to dodge school for now. With any luck, by the time that particular issue reared its ugly head again, it would be too late to matter.

CHAPTER
FOUR

"Cherok came by to talk to Gravin today," I heard Mother say when Father came home.

There was a silent beat, then, "How'd that go?"

"He implied there was something wrong with Gravin's brain and told me that if we can't afford the mana tax, that I should close my legs more often."

My father's expression darkened. "Did he now?" he said quietly. I would not want to be Cherok when Father caught up with him.

"What's that mean?" Senica asked. I smothered a laugh and turned away from the rest of the family so they couldn't see my face.

"Oh, it's, er, it's just a grown-up thing you won't need to worry about for a long time," Mother said.

"But what's it *mean*?" Senica pressed.

"I'll tell you when you're older."

My sister let out a huff and flopped onto her pallet. "Fine!"

"What do we do now?" Father asked. "There are only a few weeks left."

"I don't know. Even if we pushed the issue and got Gravin into training, this class is just starting too late for it to make a difference, and it's not right to put that kind of pressure on him. He's only three."

"I know, but that's the rule. Everyone contributes mana. No exceptions. We're a family of four, and Gravin is old enough to walk and talk. They're going to start assessing us higher. If we can't produce enough with a daily tithe, we'll both be wearing draw stone pendants for the next six months."

I wondered how many draw stones this village could possibly have. It wasn't like they were rare or anything, but considering these people were out in the middle of nowhere with no obvious way to acquire them, it was strange that they'd have draw stones in abundance.

On a more personal level, if I was understanding this conversation correctly, we were looking at having draw stones literally hanging off our necks. Maybe it would just be my parents, but I still didn't want the stuff in our home. The constant need to resist a draw stone's pull would wear on me, and especially since I still had to sleep in the same bed as my parents, they would be practically touching me all night. It was just a matter of time until they started stealing away my precious mana while I slept. Worse, my storage crystal would have no such protections.

"Hey," Senica said to me. "What's wrong with your brain?"

"I don't know," I said.

"Nothing is wrong with his brain," my mother said. "Cherok was just being a jacka— a jerk. He was saying mean things because he doesn't get along with your father and wanted to take it out on us."

"Cherok's not the problem right now," Father said. "He can be a jerk all he wants. It's the Collector showing up in a few weeks that we need to think about."

"What's a Collector?" I asked.

"They're the ones who administer the draw stones, sweetie. The man at our table is a Collector, and so is the person who will come do our Testing next month."

Of course they were. That made perfect sense. The whole village government was obsessed with harvesting mana from its populace, though I'd yet to see any evidence of what it was all being used for. If I could get my hands on one of those draw stones, my mana problems would be over instantly. Come to think of it, maybe it was a good thing if both my parents ended up wearing one. I could drain the mana out of it, pump it into my storage crystal, and finish igniting my mana core.

It would be better if I was left alone to do it myself. There was less chance of drawing scrutiny that way. I wasn't sure if I could do it in a month, though. I could make an attempt right now, if I wanted, but depending on how bad the loss converting the mana from the storage crystal was, I might fall short. If I didn't have enough, all of my work over the last eight months would be wasted.

"Maybe we're worrying over nothing," Father said. "They might show up, do the Testing, and determine we generate enough mana for a family of four. It'll be Gravin's first time. He could score really high."

"Maybe," Mother agreed, but I could hear the doubt in her voice. "He does spend a lot of time just sitting there. He's probably not using too much passively."

She wasn't wrong. That was a deliberate choice on my part. I didn't move around much because I didn't have enough energy to last all day, and time spent napping was time not spent speeding up my mana generation. If I could just get a few weeks undisturbed, and maybe some better food, I could get this interminable weaning stage over with. I was tired of being a dull.

My parents spent the rest of the evening going in circles about things that were outside of their control and stressing themselves out over them. They only stopped once they realized Senica had picked up on it and was getting a wild look in her eyes. That led to Mother taking a break to soothe her while Father took me outside to sit in the garden together.

"You know, son, I don't think that teacher knew what he was talking about. Plenty of wise men knew to keep their mouths shut when there was nothing important to say," he told me.

I wisely stayed quiet in response, which caused my father to laugh after a moment.

"Yeah, just like that. You know more than you let on, don't you? Well, either way, don't worry about this whole Testing thing. It's not that big a deal. It'll just make for a rough few months, nothing your old man can't survive."

"Will we fail?" I asked.

Father shrugged. "Who knows? It would certainly help if you had some mana to tithe, but you're too young for them to expect very much. A few years ago, we wouldn't even be worrying about this, but right around the time you were born, Lord Noctra let us know the barrier was becoming unstable again, that we weren't tithing enough mana to keep it active all the time. That's when the Barrier Wardens became a thing, to keep a look out for monsters so we can activate the barrier whenever one gets close.

"Supposedly we're building the reserves back up, and soon we'll be able to run it full time instead of just at night when no one can see if there are any monsters out in the dark. Sure has made for a rough few years, though."

Interesting. That might explain why I hadn't seen much of this supposed barrier since my awakening. If they only ran it at night to conserve power, well, it was a rare day indeed that I managed to keep my eyes open once the stars started coming out. I'd yet to spot all six of our moons despite months of looking. It might be worth it to spend a bit of mana just to stay up late and see if I could get a look at this barrier.

"Have you ever seen a monster?" I asked.

Father took a moment to answer. "The Wardens keep us safe when the sun's up, and if they spot something they can't handle, Lord Noctra comes out and fries it to a crisp. Then the barrier keeps everything away at night, like I said. All I have to do is grow food during the day and take care of you at night."

A simple life. I wouldn't say I was jealous, not considering the cost, but I could see the appeal. I did notice that Father hadn't answered the question, though. There was more to that story, but I wasn't getting it out of him, not tonight at least.

That night, I clutched the toy holding my storage crystal tight to my chest and carefully examined it. At maximum capacity, it could hold twenty times as much mana as my own core. I lost about half of the mana I put in, and I'd lose half of it again pulling it out. It was currently three quarters full after six months of work filling it plus two more spent scraping up enough mana to make it in the first place. It wasn't a very good storage crystal, but it was the best I could do under the circumstances.

It took me six days for my mana core to fill all the way naturally, or five if I was given enough uninterrupted time to stimulate my core so it would generate mana faster. I needed eight times my maximum mana to make my core ignite, so in theory, the storage crystal didn't need to be completely full. There was a bit of leeway there in that I could fill my own mana core to the brim prior to starting the ritual, and of course skill counted for a great deal in these sorts of things. If I did it properly, I could get away with as little as seven times my maximum mana in the crystal.

The rest was a buffer, just in case something went wrong. I'd rather spend eight months and ensure I did it perfectly the first time than spend seven and risk wasting it all by failing. The draw stones were a complication, especially if my parents were going to be wearing them at all times. If I did the ignition right before the Testing in a month, I would theoretically still have more mana than I needed, but only a bit under eight mana cores' worth instead of ten. The margins were tight, but I could do it.

If I ignited my core prior to the Testing, I could probably cheat in some way to make it seem like my family produced enough mana to satisfy whatever the requirement was. My ignited core would generate mana twenty times faster than it did in its dormant state. I'd have enough to spare, and it'd be worth the investment to keep draw stones out of our home. I supposed it might also relieve some of my parents' stress as well.

That settled it then. I'd give the storage crystal a few more weeks, then look for a good opportunity to ignite my core. It'd probably be one of the days when Senica was home from school during the day and Mother was visiting with that nosy neighbor who'd thought I was possessed. Senica was supposed to keep an eye on me, but really, who trusted a six-year-old to babysit? Then again, nothing bad had happened, so maybe Mother was right to think Senica could do it.

As we got closer to the Testing, my parents got more and more agitated. From what I gathered, they were convinced they were going to fail, despite both of them doing their best to limit the amount of mana they used during the day. Seeing as to how they weren't really trained at all, at least not that I could tell, almost all of Father's mana usage went towards instinctive invocations to give himself more strength or stamina. Mother pushed most of her mana into our garden to try to help the scraggly plants grow.

There were three days left, and it was Senica's last day off from school before the Testing. If I wanted to do this, it had to be today. We went through the morning routine, breakfast, garden work, play time, and then I was put down for a nap on the pallet I'd been sharing with my parents. Senica played with her two dolls at the table, and Mother went outside to chat with the neighbor, that way she wouldn't keep me up.

Thanks to my own invocation, I was wide awake. I clutched the stuffed animal toy tightly, the better to pinch the storage crystal between two fingers, and with a glance at Senica to make sure she was still ignoring me, I accessed the crystal.

Immediately, I felt the mana inside. It was mostly full, not quite topped off. That was fine. I could do this without a safety net. It would mean months, possibly years considering what kind of setbacks I might see, of work to try again if I failed. But I hadn't gotten to be an ancient archmage without taking a few risks.

I was so sick of being a toddler. It was time to take some control over my life.

CHAPTER
FIVE

I gniting a core was so easy that people did it accidentally in areas with high ambient mana. The only ingredient required is an overabundance of mana, more than a mana core can hold. The smaller and weaker a mana core is, the easier it was to ignite. If not for the fact that there was no ambient mana at all here, I would have done it years ago.

That wasn't the circumstance I'd found myself in, however, so I was forced to use a workaround. My method needed actual skill at controlling mana, since I had to use what I'd saved up in my junky storage crystal to create an artificial cloud of ambient mana. Depending on how quickly I managed to cycle the mana through my core, it would react and reach a critical threshold. The entire core would start producing mana instead of just the one spot where it touched on the Astral Realm.

What I was about to do was in essence what being a mage was all about. Any idiot could channel some mana from their core into a basic invocation to help them hoe the dirt a little harder. Controlling mana that wasn't already connected to them was a whole different skill set. Controlling seven or eight times the total amount of mana my core could even hold was not something the average mage had the ability to do.

But I needed my artificial ambient mana to stay near me where I could use it, so that was precisely what I was going to do. Left to its own devices, it would diffuse and spread until there was nothing left, drunk up by the parched earth of this desert. If there'd been someone I could trust to release the mana from the storage crystal at a steady rate, this would have been simplicity in itself to perform, but I was on my own. It all had to come out at once before I started the process.

I broke the seal on the storage crystal, and mana flooded out of it. Immediately, I started pulling it into my core, packing it in denser, spinning it around. The first core-full was easy; mana in its natural state sat loosely. The second core-full was when things started to get strained, and I had to work to cycle the mana around. When people did this accidentally, it was normally by overexerting themselves casting various spells. That method required far more mana than I had available, and my version was significantly more uncomfortable.

I'd managed to pack in four times as much mana as normal and had it spinning inside my core like a raging vortex when I noticed I was losing more than I'd accounted for. At the same time, Senica had stopped playing and was looking around the hut, far too alert. She'd noticed something. It wasn't hard to guess that some of the ambient mana had been close enough to her that she'd instinctively absorbed it into her own core.

That was great for her. That kind of natural talent was prized, and if she'd been born somewhere else, she probably would have been on the fast-track to full mage status. It was both of our misfortunes to have been born here in this village. Probably one or both of our parents had a similar talent, as such things did tend to get passed down from generation to generation. If I'd been forced to guess, I'd say our mother was the more likely candidate, just given the state of our family garden compared to the neighbor's.

Regardless, it was a problem for me. I needed that mana, and my margins were already thin. If Senica took too much of it, the ignition would fail. I eyed up what was still left in the air, determined that I could still make things work, and stretched myself to take in the ambient mana closest to Senica first. I needed it far more than she did, especially considering anything she took would just end up in a draw stone in a few hours.

I kept pulling in more and more mana, adding it to the collection, keeping it from exploding outward through sheer force of will and the speed of the cycling drawing it tighter. It was like that ride that was popular at mage carnivals, where people would climb into a giant bowl and the operator would use his magic to make it spin so fast that they were pulled to the walls. But in my case, I was doing it with pure mana, and the more I layered in, the harder it was to keep it moving at speed.

I added another core's worth on top of what was already there. That made for seven times as much as normal. One more should do it, but the ambient mana was thin now. Senica had stolen too much of my buffer, and now she was out of her chair and approaching me. "Gravvy?" she said. "Are you sleeping?"

I didn't answer, both because I didn't want her hanging around me soaking up more of my mana and because I didn't have the spare mental capacity to hold a conversation while I spun around more than twice as much mana in my three-year-old core than the average full-grown adult could comfortably hold. Mana kept draining out of the air into Senica, despite my best efforts to snatch it back to myself.

Was there enough left now, or had my sister doomed me to another eight months of slowly building up the reserves in my storage crystal so I could try again? I honestly couldn't tell. An ignition wasn't an exact science, nor was it baking where I just followed a recipe with clearly labeled portions. The only thing I could do was keep drawing in as much of the remaining mana as I could.

"Gravin?" Senica said, climbing onto the pallet next to me. I felt her lean over me, but I kept my eyes squeezed shut and did my best to keep my breathing even. I was asleep, damn it; go away.

"Do you feel it?" she whispered. "All the mana. You feel it too, right?"

The last of the ambient mana disappeared, the lion's share going to me as I actively drew it in, but enough of it funneled into my sister's core through her mere presence and her instinctive desire to claim it that the outcome was far from certain.

I spun my core as fast as I could, and held it for as long as possible. Still, no ignition. I could feel the mana start to escape back out now, too much for me to keep and not held long enough to catch a spark. I needed more, and the only source was Senica. I could take it from her. Right now, my core was so overflowing with mana that was about to go to waste, it would be a simple matter to cast a mana drain spell and take back what she'd stolen. Her own core was full enough that it would still be a net gain.

She'd know, of course. Maybe she wouldn't understand exactly how it had happened, but she'd know I'd drained her mana. Everyone in the village was intimately familiar with the experience of having mana drained from them. There was no way she wouldn't recognize that I was doing it.

Without that mana, I was going to fail. That was a simple fact, so there really wasn't a choice. I gathered up the tattered strands of mana that had fallen out of the spin before they could get away, wove them into the spell, then rolled over and grabbed Senica's hand.

She jerked back, startled, but I didn't let go. My spell touched her core and, just like the draw stone she handled every day, began pulling it out. I took it, all of it, and added it to the maelstrom spinning in my core. And finally, *finally*, there was enough.

My core shifted and the mana began to absorb into it. No longer did the core simply hold and contain the mana; now the mana flowed into the walls. Where before my core had been spongy and soft, an air bladder filled with the building blocks of magic, now it was a ceramic orb, hard and unyielding as mana infused it. The more the mana soaked in, the faster everything that was left spun.

Senica cried out and pulled away from me, but I'd gotten what I needed and I ignored her. The ignition was almost complete, but I could still botch it if I didn't keep the rest of the mana spinning until it was gone. It would only take a few more seconds, three... two... one...

I let out a groan and collapsed down onto the pallet. It was done. My core was empty, but I could already feel it generating new mana. It would most likely be completely full in the next eight hours instead of six days. Finally, I had the spare mana to use magic again. Everything was about to get easier.

"What did you do to me?!" Senica screeched.

Almost everything.

There was no playing dumb here. She already knew. I sat up and looked her in the eyes, then said softly, "I borrowed your mana."

"Give it back!" she demanded instantly.

That was it. There was no question as to why I'd needed it or how I'd taken it. She just knew that it was her mana and I'd taken it without permission, like stealing one of her toys. Never mind the fact that at least half the mana I'd taken from her had been mine to begin with.

Little kids were simple that way. In a few hours, I'd have more than enough mana to give back everything I'd taken from her, but I didn't think Senica was going to be that patient. Besides, giving mana to someone else directly required some knowledge and skill from them. Sure, I could force-fully push mana into her core, but that could damage her, perhaps permanently.

Then again, Senica had shown a surprising and annoying amount of talent at scooping up ambient mana. I could just expel some of mine into the air around her and let her absorb it into her core on her own. Whatever she managed to get would be what she got. It wasn't like she had any way to keep track.

That did bring me back to the first problem, though. I didn't have any mana left, and it would be an hour or two until I had enough. It was time to see how patient a little girl could be. "I can't," I told her. "I used it."

"You can't do that! You're supposed to save it for the tithe."

"I know, but I didn't. It's gone."

"I'm telling Mom," she said.

Little tattletale.

"I'll give you my mana once I make more, but I don't have any right now."

That seemed to appease her. She settled back onto the pallet and jabbed a finger at me. "You'd better. Don't forget."

"I promise," I said.

I was a little bit surprised that she'd accepted the whole mana drain so easily, with almost no questions about what had happened or why. I would have been way more suspicious when I was a kid, but I suppose I'd had a different childhood than Senica did. It might have been nice to grow up as sheltered as she had.

"Did you feel the mana, too?" she asked suddenly.

"No," I lied. "I was sleeping until you woke me up."

"No, you weren't. You had your eyes all scrunched up and you were groaning."

Was I? I hadn't realized.

"You did something with it," Senica said. "Tell me."

"No I didn't," I insisted.

"Tell me or I'll tell Mom *and* Dad you were doing something and that you took my mana without asking first."

Unbelievable. I was being blackmailed by my kid sister. I took back every single nice thought I'd ever had about her.

CHAPTER
SIX

It was time to consider options. I could keep denying it. It wasn't like anyone around here could tell I'd ignited my mana core. If I played dumb, eventually the whole thing would be dismissed as the overexcited ramblings of a child. But it would put me under some immediate scrutiny.

Option two. I could play along, and as soon as I had the mana built up for it, I could hit Senica with a memory erasing curse. It had the benefit of completely removing the problem from my perspective, but with two major flaws. First, I would need more mana than I could hold, which meant relying on a mana crystal again in order to cast such a complex spell. I'd want to make one anyway, especially since my storage crystal had shattered when I'd broken the seal, but that would take time. Second, it would need to be anchored in her own mana core in order to sustain itself, and I wasn't at all sure she could produce enough mana to make that work. There was also the possibility that, even if she could, someone would notice when they came by to do the Testing.

Option three. I could go along with her. I could admit that I'd felt the mana, insist that I didn't know what it meant, and hope she didn't connect my mana drain spell with everything else. Even for a six-year-old, it didn't seem likely that she wouldn't put two and two together.

Option four. Screw secrecy. Senica had a natural talent for sensing mana, and I could work with that. It would mean shedding my disguise, though, at least to my immediate family. That was a big risk. If our parents decided that I wasn't Gravin, that I was an imposter who'd stolen their child rather than actually just being Gravin with the awakened memories of his previous life, they might cause problems for me. I'd just ignited my mana core bare minutes ago; I was still a long way away from being able to take the entire village on by myself.

Plus, even if option four worked out, that would place a huge demand on my time. I'd have to start teaching Senica for real, and while I was sure two grown adults could keep things secret, I was less confident that Senica wouldn't do what all kids do: run her mouth and show off her new abilities. As fun as the idea of sticking it to Cherok with my superior techniques was, it was a bad strategy in the short and long term. Unless my goals shifted radically in the coming months, I didn't see a way coming clean ended well for me.

Options two and four were right out. Options one and three were long-shots, but if Senica was dumb enough, they might work. I'd start with option one and shift gears to three if it looked like it was failing.

"I didn't do anything!" I said, putting a little heat in my voice. It had been made abundantly clear to me over the last half a year that acting was not among my considerable talents, at least not when it came to acting like a toddler. In my defense, it was pretty difficult to lead a life so boring and pretend that it was anything but.

"Did too!" she snapped back. "Fine, I'll just go tell Mom, and you'll get in trouble."

She finished that with a triumphant note, climbed off the bed, and ran for the doorway. I watched her go silently, then laid back down. It took pretty much all of the mana I'd made in the last few minutes, but I put together a basic invocation to sharpen my hearing. Normally, I'd use a spell that enhanced all of my senses, but when starved for mana, beggars couldn't be choosers.

"Mom! Mom!" Senica said as she charged out through the curtain that served as a door to our hut and over to the edge of the garden where our mother sat on a low stone wall next to the nosy neighbor, Malra. "Gravin did something to me."

"He did?" Mother asked. "Did he hurt you? I'm sure it was an accident."

"No, it's not... I..." Senica cut herself off and she shuffled in place. "Can you come see? Inside?"

Interesting. She wasn't ratting me out right away. I couldn't fathom the reason why, and the biggest part of me was sick of trying to figure it out. I was a two-thousand-year-old archmage who'd successfully transferred all of his memories and magical skills to a reincarnated body, damn it. I did not need to dance around the whims of small children and dirt farmers.

Except I was still three years old, and even though I was the most powerful three-year-old in existence, that didn't mean I could brute force my problems. Damn. Just give me a year to advance my core to stage two and become a proper mage again, and I wouldn't have to sneak around hiding anything.

Mother came into the hut with Senica holding her hand. "What's going on in here?" she asked. "You're supposed to be napping, Gravin."

"She woke me up," I said, pointing an accusatory finger in Senica's direction.

"No, I didn't. He was awake already. There was a bunch of mana in the air, and then it all disappeared, and then he took my mana from me, too. He admitted it!"

Her words came tumbling out of her mouth in a rush, so fast that I had trouble understanding what she was saying. Mother just blinked down at her and said, "Try again, sweetie. A little bit slower this time."

I heard footsteps outside the hut, sneaking through the garden and up to our window. No doubt Malra was lurking nearby, snooping around again. This was none of her business, and her knowing anything about it couldn't possibly lead to anything good. The best thing to do was to expose her and let Mother take care of it, but I was still practically out of mana. I could barely power the most basic of conjurations, but then, I didn't really need anything better than that.

Our windows had no glass in them. Much like the doorway, they were just square cut holes in the wall with a thin curtain for privacy. It was so light that a stray breeze would be enough to make it flutter open and reveal someone standing right outside. I could manage half a second of moving air.

I drew every last scrap of mana out of my core and shaped it into the conjuration needed for elemental manipulation, then used it to pull air in through the window. The curtain blew straight out and up, giving Mother a clear view of Malra standing wide-eyed in front of the window. The two made eye contact, and Malra let out a nervous laugh.

"Is there something I can help you with?" Mother asked. She took three extra-long steps over to the window and pulled the curtain off to the side as it fell back down into position.

"Er, no, no. I just thought I saw something in your garden and was going for a closer look. Seems to be gone now. My old eyes playing tricks on me I suppose."

"I see." Mother made no attempts to disguise the disbelief in her tone. "I appreciate you taking a look for me, Malra."

"Right. Yes, anytime. Glad I could help. If you'll excuse me though, I just remembered that I have a thing, I need to, that is..." Malra made some vague gestures towards her own hut and walked off in a hurry.

"Alright, what were you trying to say, Senica?" Mother asked, turning back to look at us.

"There was a whole bunch of mana!" Senica said. "It was... not inside us? I could feel it in the air, and then it went into my core when I tried to touch it. Gravin did it, but he won't tell me how. And then, he grabbed my hand, and he took my mana from me, and now he won't give it back."

I could see just by the look on Mother's face that she didn't believe Senica. Perfect. I'd just play dumb until this whole problem went away. Unfortunately, that didn't mean I'd just get to stay silent on the matter.

"Gravin, did you do something to your sister?"

"No," I lied. "I was sleeping. She woke me up."

"Did not," Senica said.

"Did too," I retorted. I was a veritable bastion of wit here.

"Okay, stop that, both of you," Mother said. "Senica, are you hurt at all?"

"No."

"Gravin, are you hurt?"

"No."

"Then I think we can put this behind us. I sincerely doubt your little brother took your mana, not unless he found a chunk of draw stone in the garden," Mother said.

"But—" Senica started.

"Enough. Nobody was hurt, nothing was broken. Put this behind you and play nice with each other."

"Yes, Mom," Senica said.

"And Gravin, if you did do something to your sister, you'd better not do it again, you understand?" Mother asked. I nodded my head, and she added, "Good. I'm considering this matter closed. Now, I'm going to go out and sit in the garden. Why don't the two of you join me?"

I crawled off the pallet and stretched, then smiled idly as I felt more mana filling my core. Step one was complete. I followed Mother and Senica outside, but made a detour to the outhouse before joining them. It smelled about as bad as it always did, but I supposed I couldn't blame the villagers for not having access to magical plumbing. My experiences over the last half a year had convinced me that as soon as I managed to establish a home of my own, I would be heavily investing my mana in some decent bathroom facilities.

Lost in pleasant daydreams of marble tubs that were basically small pools and cool, crystal-clear drinking water that didn't require a trip to the pump at the end of the street, I didn't notice the sound of a wooden hammer being pounded against a sheet of metal at first. It was only after I'd finished lacing up my trousers and stepped back out of the outhouse that I heard it.

People were running around, shouting at each other and passing out farming tools. My mother appeared out of the crowd, a pitchfork in one hand and Senica held close to her with the other. "Gravin, there you are! The both of you need to go back inside right now."

"What?" I asked stupidly, only partially listening to her as I watched people scurry.

"Inside, I said. That's the alarm for a monster close to the village. I need you two to get somewhere safe while the adults form a line to repel the monster until Lord Noctra shows up to kill it."

With that, we were rushed into our hut, given strict instructions to stay put, and left to ourselves. Mother joined several other women from our street and together they set off toward the western fields.

It was somewhat nerve wracking to be sitting there with basically no mana and my body so physically weak. I didn't even know what kind of monster it was, but the whole village was taking it seriously. That probably meant it was a threat.

Senica had it worse than me, I think. I knew that I could fight if I had to. My options would be severely limited, but they existed. I could make a run for the village square, burst into the building where the Collectors kept their draw stones, and tap into one. There'd be a lot of questions after, but if I had to do it, I could. Senica was still a child, and one I'd mana drained not half an hour ago. She clung to me, hard, and I made no effort to disentangle myself. I was ancient, not heartless.

"It'll be okay," I told her.

"What if the monster kills Mom or Dad?"

"It won't. Lord Noctra will kill it first." Probably. I'd never met the man. I just had to assume he was competent by village standards. Everyone else seemed to think so.

"What if he doesn't get there in time?" Senica whispered.

"He will."

Ultimately, words could only do so much, but I let her hug me close, and that seemed to help. There was nothing else I could do but wait, recover my mana, and see what happened.

CHAPTER

SEVEN

It took me a few months after I first awakened to internalize something important. Intellectually, I understood reincarnation, and if everything had gone according to plan, I would have sidestepped the issue quite neatly. Since it hadn't, Gravin was a real person instead of a mask I was wearing. For about two and a half years, he'd been a normal child who loved his parents and felt mild affection and tolerance toward his sister, who'd been largely ambivalent toward him until he'd started walking and talking. I'd come in before there'd been enough time for any sort of real sibling relationship to grow.

But the thing was, Gravin still existed. I hadn't taken him over or replaced him. I was now both Keiran *and* Gravin, and if it seemed otherwise, well, that was bound to happen considering how few years the Gravin part of me had lived compared to the Keiran part. Gravin didn't give me too many life skills, which was hardly his fault. But he did have connections to his family.

He loved them, and that meant *I* loved them.

It had taken until just now for that to really hit me, now that my parents were actually in danger. A monster was moving towards our village, and they were holding a line to stall it until someone with real power could show up and destroy it. Maybe my parents wouldn't end up getting close to it and they'd be safe. Or maybe they'd be the first farmers to swing a hoe at it and end up dead before anyone else could interfere.

I was afraid for them, but the only thing I could do was sit here and do my best to comfort my sister. I'd gotten used to a certain amount of help-lessness over the last eight months of my new life, but this was on a whole different level. It had been a thousand years since I'd felt so powerless in the face of danger.

Something dense in mana moved into the village, coming from the east. That must be the governor moving in to intercept the threat. He had an ignited core, one that was several times the size of mine. That wasn't surprising; cores grew naturally as a person aged. Most adults had similarly sized cores, though none of them produced more than a fraction of the mana the governor's did.

The governor was moving fast, but not more than a man running might. With the limits in size and regeneration a stage one core had, he'd be smart to save his mana for the fight itself. Even if he had the skills of a master mage, there were only so many spells he could cast before he ran dry. Then again, getting there before the monster killed anyone was also important.

I doubted he was a master mage, not with a stage one core. Maybe at stage three, but not stage one. He'd struggle to hold enough mana to even cast a single spell of the kind masters used. Hopefully, whatever spells he did know would be enough to put down the monster.

The governor's presence passed through the range of my mana sense quickly. It was a good thing he didn't live down in the village proper, or I'd have to worry about him noticing me in return now that I could generate mana fast enough to actually fill my core. Good thing mine was currently only about as full as anyone else's would be after a full day between appointments with the Collectors.

A few minutes later, there was a concussive boom and the roar of rising flames, close enough to hurt my ears and make Senica cry out. A cheer went up from the villagers with that, and people started trickling back in from the fields about the same time I sensed the governor entering the village again. His mana core was far, far emptier now, almost completely dry. If a simple fire blast spell tapped him out that bad, he was even less impressive than my initial estimate.

That was not to say he wasn't still stronger than me. He absolutely was.

But I was three, and he was an adult. There wasn't a dull in the village who didn't have a bigger mana core than me. My advantages were my knowledge, skills, and mana generation speed. Over the next few weeks, I would need to construct a proper crystal to hold mana, with proper shielding to hide it from prying eyes. It was a project that would have taken the me of yesterday at least a year to put together, but I ought to be able to finish it in a few weeks now.

The only question was where I could keep it for easy access. Now that I was making mana like a true apprentice, a once-a-day dump into a junky storage crystal was out of the question. I'd be shedding half of my mana into the air around me if I tried to keep using that, never mind that I'd fill it up in a matter of days now.

A staff would be ideal, but there were a few problems with that. Making one up to my standards would require a lot of time, material, and mana that I just didn't have, not to mention a workshop full of tools with free rein to use them. Then I'd have to carry it around in order for it to be of any use, which would draw all sorts of undue attention. Also, I was a bit too small to be handling a full-sized staff at the moment. No, the whole idea wasn't practical at all.

It was also extremely unnecessary at this stage in my development. There was a reason apprentices were traditionally gifted wands by their masters. I was a long, long way away from needing the sort of force multiplier a staff represented, and there were easier, subtler methods of storing mana. That was the important part right now anyway. Without any ambient mana to fuel my growth, my priority had to be on making sure not to waste any of what my own core generated.

As Gravin, I spent a lot of time in the garden. That was where Mother worked, after all. She gave her energy to the mundane tasks of trying to keep the plants growing in what was one step away from a barren wasteland, and used her mana to encourage growth. Since she spent all day there, working over one thing or another, and I wasn't enrolled in school like Senica yet, that's where I went, too. So I'd build my superior mana crystal there, something that I was properly attuned to and with a hundred times the capacity of my broken storage crystal.

Physical size was a limitation, of course. Even if I made the crystal stationary, which had its own drawbacks, it couldn't be something too big or I wouldn't be able to wrap the spells all the way around it. Building a proper mana crystal with shielding to keep it hidden was a bit like weaving a basket to hold mana, except that each piece of wicker was made out of the mana I could produce in my core. There was an upper limit to how long a piece I could make, simply by virtue of there being an upper limit to my core size.

My musing was interrupted by Senica disentangling herself from me and running for the entryway as Mother pushed the curtain aside. She took a step forward and ducked down to one knee to grab Senica in a tight hug. "There's my girl," she said. "Were you brave? Did you protect your brother?"

"Is Dad okay?" Senica asked, ignoring Mother's questions.

"He's fine. He had to go back to work after Lord Noctra took care of the monster. You'll see him tonight, I promise."

Now that Mother had returned, Senica lost whatever willpower she had that held her together. Maybe she'd been doing it for my sake, or maybe she was just destined to be one of those people who kept up appearances until the crisis was over, then fell to pieces immediately after. Either way, she started crying and sobbing while clutching at our mother's shirt.

Mother did her best to calm her down, mostly with head pats and hugs and whispered assurances, and it took another few minutes before she thought to look over at me. "Gravin, are you okay?" she asked.

"Yes."

"Really? Do you want a hug too?"

"I'm okay."

Mother would probably have made a bigger deal out of it if not for the fact that Senica was practically clinging to her, still quietly crying into Mother's shirt. Instead, I just got a pensive look and a sigh. Belatedly, it occurred to me that this was another one of those moments where I was doing a bad job of acting like a three-year-old. If I was lucky, they'd just take it as me not being old enough to understand what kind of danger my parents had been in.

On the off chance that I wasn't that lucky, maybe it was time to start thinking about exactly how much I should tell my parents and what I'd do if they took the news that their baby boy's previous incarnation had reawakened and had no plans on living the mundane life of a dirt farmer in the back end of a mana desert.

They probably wouldn't take that well. It would be best if I didn't tell them right away.

That evening, a woman showed up to visit us. People in the village didn't have doors, so it was customary to just announce their presence outside the privacy curtain and wait to be acknowledged.

"Sellis? Xilaya? It's Ayaka," she said from outside our home.

My parents exchanged concerned glances, and Father got up from his seat at the table to pull the curtain aside. "Collector," he said. "We weren't expecting you for another few days."

"Don't look so worried, Sellis. I'm not here for the Testing. Do you mind if I come in?"

Father stepped to the side and held the curtain back to let in a woman in her late twenties, about the same age as my parents, actually. She was tall, with short, dark brown hair and a wedge-shaped scar above one eye that cut into the eyebrow. She was also wearing a pin on her shirt that depicted a stylized rock with a bunch of lines bisecting it at the center. It was a rather poor depiction of a draw stone, in my opinion, but it served its purpose.

Why exactly Collectors needed identification in a village that didn't even have two hundred people wasn't clear to me. Probably it was more about pomp and ceremony, a way to make the Collectors feel superior and elite, to grant them a measure of authority. Nobody seemed to hate the Collectors, but the simple fact of the matter was that they were glorified tax men, and I'd never been to any place where they were glorified except here. The village folk seemed to regard mana tithing with an almost religious reverence, and the Collectors were the preachers of that religion.

"Thank you," Ayaka said as she took Mother's customary chair. "I just wanted to stop by for a few minutes to let you know we're pushing back your Testing by another four days. This business with the monster..."

"Why would that matter?" Mother asked.

"It was a mana sniffer," the Collector explained. "As soon as Lord Noctra saw it, he demanded that we go over every single draw stone to make sure none of them are leaking. Every Collector in the village is going to be pulling double shifts to examine them over the next few days."

"Ah, I see," Father said. "And you don't have time to do Testings right now."

"Exactly that. I'm sorry if this throws things off for you, but I thought you had a right to know. I've actually got three more homes to visit to let them know about the revised schedule. We wanted to give you as much lead in time as possible so you can make any arrangements you need to."

"That's much appreciated," Father said. "Four days. Hmm. I'll have to get someone to swap with me. That would normally be my day to do the irrigation on the north field."

Ayaka nodded. "I'm glad I took the time to come let you know then."

"Thanks," Father said. "It would have been a mess if I had to find someone to swap at the last minute."

The adults idly chatted for a few minutes, then the Collector said her goodbyes and left. We continued our evening per our usual routine, but I noticed every now and then I'd get a strange look from Father when he thought I wasn't paying attention.

Whatever he was thinking, I probably wasn't going to like it.

CHAPTER
EIGHT

In the end, the benefits of a wand didn't outweigh the drawbacks. I was a thousand years past the point where it could aid me in directing my magic, and while the typical wand did include a mana crystal, they weren't generally high volume. It was expected that the wand would pull in enough ambient mana to power itself, and that wasn't going to happen here. The storage aspects were minimal compared to its other uses, certainly not enough for the next stage of my own advancement.

Then there was the fact that even if I made a wand that simply looked like an ordinary stick, I wouldn't be allowed to just carry it around everywhere I went. I knew because I'd tested the idea with an actual stick I'd scavenged from one of the few shade trees that grew in the village. Everything had been fine outdoors, but it had been promptly confiscated and discarded when I tried to bring it inside with me.

Nobody would have tried to take my staff from me just because I'd walked into a building with it back when I was Keiran of the Night Vale—not that they could have. I would have found the attempt amusing. Gravin of the village was not afforded the same respect.

What I ended up settling on was a peculiar flat rock tucked into the corner of the garden. It was large enough that nobody wanted to drag it out of the way, but small enough that I could still work with it. Best of all, I could sit on it and pretend to watch Mother while I wove strands of mana through it. It wasn't ideal; I'd need to visit it three times a day to drain the mana I'd generated, which was bound to get awkward. It might be worth it to make a second mana crystal inside the hut later on if it proved to be too difficult to slip outside that often.

Using the garden stone for mana storage meant I had a fantastic amount of space to work with. By my best guess, once I was done enchanting it, it would hold roughly two hundred times the capacity my mana core had. Even with my enhanced mana generation, it would take me close to three months to fill it. It would also be fully shielded from casual detection, and the transference loss would be under ten percent. All in all, it would be a massive improvement from my original storage crystal.

I was practically salivating at the thought. Right now, I was severely limited by the maximum amount of mana I could work with at once. I could cast any novice level spell about once an hour, and if I waited eight hours for my core to fill completely, I could cast most basic spells once. Soon, all of that would change.

I sat on my stone, working quietly while I watched Mother work. Unfortunately, I was still expected to help, and she seemed to think my change of routine to sitting in the corner was some traumatic reaction to the monster coming near the village. It was unexpectedly difficult to get the time I needed.

"Come here, Gravvy," Mother said, holding a hand out to me.

I dutifully climbed to my feet and walked over to her, then looked down at a bundle of leafy stalks growing out of the ground with a trio of pale green squash tucked under them. Each one had a set of jagged yellow veins running down its skin. I had very little interest in gardening, not in this life or any other, but even I could tell there was something wrong.

"What do you think happened?" she asked me.

I shook my head. "I don't know."

I'd released mana into the air to use as part of my ignition, and between Senica and myself, we'd recovered almost all of it. Some of it must have made it outside and been absorbed by the squash. It couldn't have been that much, or the whole garden would be contaminated.

The scarring was probably due to the sudden influx of mana. Something like a normal piece of squash would have a mana core a hundredth the size of a human's. Being exposed to ambient mana like that after growing from a seed in an environment completely devoid of it had likely caused them to physically swell in size. I wouldn't be surprised if they continued to grow into prizewinners.

"To me, it looks like someone tried to help them grow and wasn't gentle enough with them," Mother said. "Did you do that?"

I shook my head again. Technically, it was my mana, but I hadn't been trying to help them, so it wasn't a lie.

"Gravin," Mother said.

"I didn't."

She didn't believe me, but playing dumb had served me well so far. Thankfully, nobody here had the magical education to understand half of what I was up to, and outside of my immediate family, nobody had any reason to suspect me of anything. If not for Senica almost sabotaging my ignition and then running to our mother to tell on me, not even they would be watching me.

"Hmm. Well, we'll keep an eye on them and see if they ripen out of it or if we'll have to throw them out," she said to me.

"Okay," I agreed. I waited a second to see if she was going to draw my attention to anything else. When she didn't, I went back to my rock to sit down and get back to work.

Despite the disturbance yesterday's monster sighting had caused, draw stone tithing continued uninterrupted. We'd gone last night, and we'd be going again tonight. No one was allowed to miss it without a good reason like being old and bedridden. Even then, some Collectors went around with small draw stones to visit the villagers who couldn't make it to the square but weren't so bad off that they were exempt from tithing.

Between dinner and our nightly visit to the square, Mother pulled Father out of the hut and into the garden to show him the squash. "Gravin said he didn't do it," she said quietly, "and I know Senica didn't do it. They weren't like this yesterday. Do you think it has something to do with the monster?"

"I doubt it," Father said. His voice was so soft that even though my back was pressed against the wall under the window, I could barely hear him. "You're sure you didn't make a mistake?"

"Of course not! When have I ever afflicted anything with mana burn?"

"Never," Father said placidly. "I didn't suspect you did."

"Then why'd you ask?"

"Making sure I've got all the facts straight."

Well, that didn't sound good. The fact that they were standing not ten feet away from my partially completed mana crystal—which was not yet shielded in any way, shape, or form—only made it worse. Neither of my parents was likely to stumble across that, not unless they literally touched the rock, but it was right there. It could happen.

"What are you thinking?" Mother asked.

"Nothing I'm sure of, not yet."

"Okay, what are you not sure of then?"

Father didn't answer her, at least not with words. They stayed together in the garden for a few minutes, then came back in to start getting us ready for the evening tithe. Senica dragged her feet, as usual. Perhaps it was some sympathy for her after how traumatic yesterday had been, but Father let her take her time, and when we finally made it to the square, we were at the very back of our line.

The stars were starting to come out by the time it was our turn. Overhead, the moons Tuamar and Felacitous studded the night sky like two great, mismatched eyes staring down at us, one purple and the other green. Usually, Amodir chased after Felacitous, but not tonight. In fact, I had yet to spot Amodir on any of those rare occasions I'd managed to stay up late enough to do a bit of star gazing. Strange, that.

"Evening, Dracken," Father said. "Busy day?"

"Unbelievably so," the Collector groused. "That slave driver Iskara is having us go through every draw stone we have in the next three days to check for leaks."

"Ayaka told us when she came by to let us know our Testing was getting pushed back."

"Oh, right, I forgot it's your month. That's going to cause problems, too. We'll be behind for weeks on that as well. We don't have enough portable draw stones to do extra Testings to catch up. Lord Noctra is going to have to personally pull the mana back out multiple times a day for a week or two, which you know is going to make him cranky. Like he's the one who's got to carry them two miles both ways just to get to his manor."

"Sounds like a pain. Well, let's go ahead and get this over with so you can pack up and get home for the night," Father told him.

"I wish," Dracken muttered. "Soon as we're done, it's right back to checking inventory. Everything we've got here in town has to be gone through tonight so we can start up at the arbor tomorrow morning."

Mother and Senica went first, then Father lifted me up so I could reach the draw stone. Maybe I was imagining things, but there was a look on his face. He was studying me. Whatever he was hoping to see, I had no intention of showing it to him. But just to be safe...

I placed my hand on the draw stone and let it take a bit of mana from me. Last week, it would have taken twelve hours to generate that much mana. Now, it was about ninety minutes of wasted resource. I let my shoulders slump and my hand fell away. Truthfully, I had given up far too little mana to feel any sort of exhaustion, but I'd seen hundreds of examples of other children after they'd completed their tithe. It wasn't hard to mimic that.

Apparently satisfied, Father lowered me back to the ground and gave me a few seconds to make sure I was going to stay upright before removing his hands. "Good job, son," he said. "Ready to go home?"

Silently, I nodded. Whatever he'd been looking for, I hoped he was satisfied with the show. I'd even given up a bit of mana to the draw stone, just in case he was able to feel it. I didn't think it was likely, but he did have physical contact with me at the time. It didn't get much easier than direct contact when it came to sensing another person's mana core.

I didn't *think* Father could sense my mana core, but it was better to be safe than sorry, and it wasn't like it was a real cost to me. Even if I'd emptied my entire core into the draw stone, it was going to be full again when I woke up tomorrow. Until my mana crystal was completed, I was going to be wasting some mana. I'd have to spend it all before I went to sleep so that I didn't end up generating a cloud of ambient mana overnight. I did not need my parents sleeping in that all night and then waking up with full cores. That would just lead to awkward questions. If I didn't have skin contact with them, it would have all safely dissipated, but as close as they were, there was a possibility that some of the overflow would seep into them.

If I'd been able to get my own pallet to sleep on, I could probably have snuck out to the garden at night while everyone else was asleep. That idea hadn't taken off, unfortunately. When I'd tried, I'd been told I might get one for my birthday. Until then, I was stuck sharing. I'd have thought they'd want me out of their bed as soon as possible, but apparently not.

We got home and started getting ready to sleep. It had been an exhausting day and things were getting a bit too tight for comfort, but so far, I was deflecting any suspicions.

"Come on, Gravin," Father said, holding out a hand for me.

"What?" I asked.

"We're going to go for a walk."

"I want to go!" Senica said. She sat back up and started to climb out of her pallet.

"Not tonight," Father said, not taking his gaze off me. "I need some time alone with Gravin."

Maybe I hadn't been as successful as I'd thought.

CHAPTER
NINE

I rode on Father's shoulders as he walked toward the fields. His hands held my legs just below the knees and I rested my arms on his head to help me keep my balance. The village was never a crowded place to begin with, but it was different at night. Everything was quiet, and the only light came from the stars and moons overhead and the candles hidden behind curtains in the windows of our neighbors.

"Do you know where we're going?" Father asked.

"Fields," I said. It was obvious, given that we were practically at the edge of the village and there was nothing left to the west except for the fields. There was an arbor north of town in the mile-wide stretch between the huts and the foot of the mountain, but if we were going there, Father would have cut across the square instead of circling the outside.

"Where in the fields?" he asked.

I shrugged, not that he could see. I had a pretty good idea, but I was going to let this play out before I admitted to anything. Father had his suspicions, but there was no sense in confessing without hearing what I was being charged with first. There was no way he'd guessed the truth of it anyway.

After about ten minutes of walking, we reached a crater. It was ten feet wide and half as deep, and I couldn't help but make a clinical analysis of Noctra's powers. Given how diminished the reserves in his core had been when he returned and the amount of damage his fire blast had done, I placed the man firmly at the apprentice rank. I would have cast the same spell using a third of the mana.

Right now, with a full core, I couldn't quite manage it. Give me another year, and it'd be within my grasp even if I did nothing at all to advance to stage three, where my core would grow in size relative to my body—not that I planned to sit around doing nothing. I wasn't building a giant mana crystal just because I was bored. An external reservoir wasn't ideal for efficiency, but it would do wonders to widen my breadth of options.

"This wasn't here last week," Father said. "It's collateral damage from the magic Lord Noctra wielded on our behalf, to save us from a monster known for its ability to seek out mana. The barrier wardens are especially careful of them, because they're tough and vicious. It's been almost a decade since the last time one showed up."

I was not an expert mana hunter, but I'd picked up more than my fair share of random trivia over the many centuries of my previous life. I had never heard of such a creature. Perhaps if I'd seen it before it had been vaporized, I might have identified it, but a monster that sniffed out ambient mana didn't sound familiar. It was surprising that any monsters survived in an environment like this anyway. One of their defining characteristics was that they needed mana to live, and this part of the world wasn't exactly conducive to fulfilling that need. They must all be extremely weak creatures.

"One of the things the Barrier Wardens do is chart the angle of the approach. It helps us figure out what the sniffer was after, gives us an idea of which draw stone is damaged. Except this time, it was heading right for the southwest corner of the village, where we live. The Collectors are annoyed because there are no draw stones over there, so they have no clue which one they need to find. They have to check all of them now."

Father reached his hands up and lifted me off his shoulders. He set me down at the edge of the crater and looked down at me. "Do you think they're going to find a broken draw stone, Gravin?"

"I don't know," I said. Probably not. That mana sniffer was probably heading straight for me. Given a few hours to generate some mana, I could have protected myself, but I hadn't had that time. Technically, I owed Lord Noctra my life. He hadn't killed the mana sniffer for me, but I'd benefited from it nonetheless.

"When I was a boy, I learned about mana from a woman named Larovi. She was a very good teacher," Father said.

"Better than Cherok?" I asked.

"Hah. Probably. Couldn't be much worse," he mumbled under his breath. I didn't think I was supposed to hear that last part. "Anyway, Larovi thought I was talented, said I could learn to use my mana all sorts of ways. If life had been different, if I'd gotten lucky, I could have been a mage like Lord Noctra."

I knew where this was going.

"I'm not a mage," Father said. "But I still have a feel for mana, and yours has felt weird since yesterday. Senica didn't lie, did she?"

And there it was.

I didn't have a good answer here. I could lie and play dumb, but I didn't think it was going to work as well for me this time. Before, it was Senica's word against mine, and there was no evidence to point towards me. Now, those squash outside the window had mana burn, and that monster had been coming straight for us. Father could feel mana too, though I suspected probably only at a very short range. There were some exercises I could teach him to work on increasing that, even with a dormant core.

No, that would just make things worse for me. I didn't know how the village would react to finding out about me, but there was every possibility it would end badly for me. If I had the time to fill my mana core, I could take on anyone from the village individually, with the exception of the governor himself. I suppose if he had any other mages living with him, they could also be problematic, but I hadn't heard anyone ever mention another person who could use magic there.

The problem with that was my staying power. Sure, I'd win against four or five adults. I might even beat ten. Sooner or later my core would empty out, and then I'd be a toddler and completely at their mercy. I needed my core to reach stage two before I even considered revealing myself to anyone, which meant I needed to convince my father that he was mistaken somehow.

There were some plausible lies that involved magical theory which adequately explained why a mana-hunting monster would be heading in this direction, but no three-year-old would know them. Trying to explain away how Father was wrong would do nothing but cement the fact that I wasn't a normal child in his mind.

What I needed was a partial truth. The issue at hand was that I had ignited my core. No, the issue was that there'd been a cloud of ambient mana, one that Senica had sensed by virtue of being at the outer edge of it, and this mana sniffer had been drawn to because that was apparently just what they did. I wondered how long its sensory range was, considering the mana had only been in the air for a few minutes before I used it up. It must have been close to the village to begin with; the alarm had been rung within half an hour of my ritual.

How did I explain the ambient mana to Father? It had to come from somewhere. More importantly, did I need to explain it? Gravin wouldn't know. It was just there. I was supposed to be napping anyway. There was no need to justify the cloud. I just had to admit that it had existed. Most likely, Father wouldn't understand what it meant anyway.

"No," I said. "There was mana, but she lied about me taking it!"

I felt a twinge of guilt about throwing Senica under the carriage like that, but I'd make it up to her later. Right now, I needed to focus on Father's reaction. I had no idea what the village did when something like this happened.

Father studied me under the light of the night sky, going so far as to squat down to look me in the eye. "No, she didn't."

"She did," I insisted.

"Then why does your mana feel so much stronger, Gravin? Something happened to you yesterday. It's fine. You're not in trouble, but I need you to tell me the truth. How am I supposed to look out for you if I don't know what happened?"

There was a big part of me that wanted to fess up. I wouldn't tell him everything, of course, but I could tell him that I'd ignited my core. I'd have to do it using small, less technical terms, but I could describe it well enough that he'd probably get it. This was my father, after all. He loved me, and I loved him. The part of me that was Gravin did, at least.

The older, wiser part of me squashed that thought ruthlessly. There was nothing Father could do to help me except stay out of my way, and he didn't need to know about my plans in order to do that. If anything, Mother was my biggest issue right now. She made it very difficult to get any work done with all the constant interruptions.

"Gravin, I can feel your mana. You've made more in your core while we've been talking than I do all day," Father said.

Oh, right. That. That was inconvenient. I supposed I did need his cooperation, if only to look the other way. There was no need to tell him I'd reincarnated and awakened my previous life's memories, but there was no getting around the fact that I was generating twenty times as much mana as I was supposed to now.

"There was a bunch of it around me when I woke up," I said. "I didn't do it! It was just there."

Father nodded, like that was perfectly normal. Maybe in this desert, it was. "It filled you up, right here," he said, placing a finger just below my sternum. Mana cores weren't physical objects. If I cut a person open, I wasn't going to find it nestled between two other organs. But they were connected to us, to people and animals and plants, to rocks and rivers and the air itself. It worked a bit differently for things that weren't alive, but they had mana, too. At least, they did in places that weren't here.

The spot Father indicated was right above where my core bridged the Astral Realm and made contact with my physical body. It was as close to a physical location as a human could get. Spells used to attack cores targeted that area specifically, though it took a master of invocation and transmutation to assault a mana core like that. People who could damage another person's mana core were thankfully rare.

"Yes," I said quietly.

"It changed you," Father said. "Were you scared?"

Scared that the ritual was going to fail, maybe. I nodded silently and let him assume what he wanted.

Father pulled me into a hug and said, "It's okay. There's nothing to be scared of. You've been blessed by the spirits."

Just how backwards were these people that they thought an ignited mana core was a blessing from the spirits—ancestral, elemental, or otherwise? More importantly, what kind of expectations would my fictional "blessing" come with? They'd better not think I was going to be the village's personal mana battery for the rest of my life. I had other things to do with my time.

"What does that mean?" I asked.

"It means you're going to be a mage, son. It is a great gift, but also a great responsibility."

"Okay," I agreed.

"I suppose the Collectors will be relieved to know they don't need to check all the draw stones," Father said with a chuckle. Then his voice turned severe. "Now, I understand that you were scared, but you shouldn't have lied about this."

"Sorry," I said. It didn't sound sincere, even to me.

He scowled at me. "Come on, let's go home. You're going to have a busy day tomorrow, so we'd best get you to bed."

"What?" I asked.

"Lord Noctra's going to want to meet you, of course. He'll have to examine you to see how powerful your blessing is. You're still pretty young, probably the youngest mage ever, but that means you've got to learn the basics really soon. Plenty of time for that, and I suppose you'll have to wait until you're older to start learning real magic."

Oh, great. A core ignition wasn't unknown here. And Father was now busy planning out the rest of my life for me. It wasn't his fault, really. A normal three-year-old would have no clue what any of this meant or what to do. He was just trying to be a good parent.

"I guess we won't have to worry about the Testing," Father said. "Mages make mana much faster than us regular folk. You'll be a tithing machine for the next few years."

There it was. Mana battery time. Obviously, I was going to have to be proactive about stomping that idea out before it got out of control.

TEN

"No," I said.

"No?" Father repeated.

"I don't want to."

"You don't want to what?"

"I don't want to give all my mana away," I said. "That's not fair."

I had yet to see any proof that this barrier the village was supposedly powering even existed. It was night. The stars were out. Moons hung in the sky. Where was the barrier? It was supposed to be activated at night, but I didn't sense anything. I had lived inside of and personally powered the barrier surrounding the Night Vale for literal centuries, and while I wasn't expecting much from the village of Alkerist, I could tell if I was inside a barrier or not.

This village had no barrier to keep it safe from monsters, not during the day and not at night. At best, it might come on for a few hours in the very dead of night when I was always asleep, but I doubted it. I'd counted the villagers, calculated the average amount of mana each one gave, and done the math on how long a day's tithing could power a barrier large enough to protect just the village.

With the amount of lost mana using draw stones as a medium cost them, even the most bare-bones ward scheme that did nothing but send up an alert if something crossed it could not run on just the mana the villagers were giving up for more than an hour a day. A true barrier that prevented monsters from crossing it, sized large enough to include the fields and arbor, would run for a few minutes.

There were draw stones up in the arbor that were used to pull in mana from the trees there. I hadn't been able to include them in my calculations because I'd never been allowed near those trees, but a hundred square miles of forest wouldn't be enough to power the barrier full time. We didn't even have a fraction of that size.

The barrier was a lie, and I wasn't going to give my mana away in service to that delusion.

"Gravin, everyone contributes mana, however much we can. It's how we survive. I'm sorry that you'll have to give more than anyone else, but that's your responsibility as a blessed mage. Do you think Lord Noctra wants to drop whatever he's doing and come running whenever there's a problem?"

That might be true, but I wasn't going to live in a manor house bossing people around, and besides, I had my suspicions about him. The mana he was collecting was real, even if the barrier wasn't. Assuming the draw stones were middling quality, the entire village was giving the governor something like three to four times as much mana as he could make on his own every day, plus whatever the arbor was producing. I could think of plenty of things that I would do with that kind of mana, but I suspected most of them were beyond Noctra's skills.

So what was he doing then? More importantly, how did it impact me?

Whatever he was up to, Noctra was lying to the villagers about it. That made it much more likely that he'd try to find a way to use me instead of help me, even if it was just taking more mana from me than anyone else. There was no way I was going to allow that. It would place me under too much scrutiny to allow me to hold anything back for my own projects, and I was not interested in spending time with the one person in this village who could still seriously threaten me and just so happened to have a secret agenda.

My problem was that I couldn't make a reasonable argument as a three-year-old. That just left one solution: magic. I had close to a full core of mana, which meant at best one basic spell. If I was going to forcefully change Father's mind, it would have to be an enchantment. A curse to erase his memory of this conversation wasn't going to work, even if it was feasible. He'd had too much time to think about it and collected too much anecdotal evidence. Without the time or the mana to be precise about which memories to erase, I'd have to wipe out two entire days of memories. That would definitely cause problems once he realized.

That wasn't even accounting for the fact that I didn't have the mana to power the enchantment, and Father didn't have the mana to keep it anchored. As a long-term solution, it fell flat. As a short-term solution, I'd have to pour everything I had into making a new storage crystal tonight, then use all of the mana I regenerated in my sleep plus everything I could get back to just barely have enough mana to make the enchantment.

Once again, I cursed the lack of ambient mana in this region. It was truly unnatural, and if I didn't know better, I'd think someone put me here deliberately. So many of my plans had been derailed due to lack of resources.

Memory wiping wasn't a viable option, but perhaps I could pull off something less delicate. If I didn't make Father forget what he'd learned, but instead nudged him to reach a different conclusion about what needed to be done, that would be both easier and cheaper. It would also be riskier, since he'd still know, and I couldn't predict every bit of outside stimulus that might affect his decisions after I cast the spell on him. I could make him agree that it was best to keep this quiet right here and now, but Mother could easily undo that magic in a single conversation unless I got to her, too. Then I'd need to go to work on the other farmers Father worked with, our neighbor Malra, and, at some point, Senica.

It was an extremely short-term solution that bought me a day or two at most. I needed months to get to stage two. Once I finished putting a mana lattice into my core, then I could afford to take my time while I waited for my body to finish growing so that I could commence stage three. And even then, I didn't want to do it under someone else's thumb. I didn't need their training, and I certainly wasn't giving up my time and mana to advance their ambitions over my own.

"I promise it'll all make sense when you're older," Father said. He must have taken my silence as a lack of comprehension. "Trust me, this is all for the best. You've been given a rare gift, and it's only reasonable to put it to good use. Although... I'm not really sure how it happened. I've never heard of a blessing without the ceremony taking place first."

"What ceremony?" I asked.

"How about I tell you all about how someone normally receives this blessing on the way back home?" he offered. "I'll even let you ride on my shoulders again."

I needed to stall for some more time so I could think of a solution. If I let Father take us home, then he'd immediately tell Mother. Maybe I'd get lucky and Senica would be asleep, but even then, that still doubled the amount of damage control I needed to do.

"I want to stay here," I told him.

He laughed and said, "Alright, just for a little bit longer. Come here and sit with me."

We sat down on the edge of the crater. My legs swung freely, and his heels rested in the dirt below us. "Normally, the only way for someone to be blessed to become a mage is through a week-long ceremony. Everyone rests from their work; we gather together and celebrate. Each evening we pray to the spirits for guidance. No one leaves the temple, Gravin. I don't mind admitting that things can get a bit ripe with so many people gathered together since there's never enough room for everyone to sleep and bathe in peace, but that's part of the ceremony.

"Sometimes, usually on either the sixth day, or the seventh, a spirit will choose one person and bless them with the power to become a mage. Their bodies will generate mana much faster than normal for the rest of their lives. Where people like your mother and I barely have enough mana to keep the strength in our limbs at the end of a long day, a true mage has mana to spare. That's what you'll be like from now on." Father paused. "I guess you won't need so many naps anymore."

It was an effort to control my expression. That whole ceremony was unnecessary. The only part that mattered was that they spent most of a week filling their cores so that the excess would bleed out as ambient mana. Then they just crammed everyone together and hoped someone had a natural ignition from sitting in the mana cloud for about two days. I'd be willing to bet money that it didn't work nine times out of ten. I wondered how much of that mana drained away completely, useless and wasted.

Depending on the number of people involved, I was also willing to bet I could direct the ambient mana to ignite three or four cores each time, assuming I'd had a few weeks to teach them what they needed to do first.

That was an idea, I supposed. If dozens of new ignited cores showed up all at the same time, it would pull a lot of attention away from me.

That was interesting, but not necessarily helpful right now. It might be a long-term plan to keep a significant portion of Noctra's attention elsewhere, or it might backfire and make him start really digging. The ideal solution was still to contain the fact that I'd ignited my core right now before Father started telling people.

"We've never done that," I said, stalling for more time.

"No," Father agreed. "It's not something that happens very often. We've done the ceremony twice in my life. The first time was when Lord Emeto was blessed. He was governor before Lord Noctra. The second, the spirits did not answer our prayers." He reached down to ruffle my hair. "Or maybe they did, just a few years too late for anyone to notice."

I'd been mentally reviewing what spells I could cast right now. Other than various enchantments to modify his memories or behaviors, all of which had the same general drawbacks, the only other solution I had was to physically attack him. Killing him would certainly shut him up, but I wasn't willing to go that far.

Patricide to keep my secrets safe was a level of inhumane I wouldn't have stooped to as Keiran, and I wouldn't do it now as Gravin. Though to be fair, I had never known my father the last time around. There was every possibility he'd fallen to my magic during my wild youth, and I wouldn't know it. But that wasn't the same thing.

What it came down to was that there were plenty of good reasons not to tell anybody about my core. Unfortunately, the only way I was going to convince Father was if I admitted that I was actually an accomplished archmage in a toddler's body and somehow got him to believe me. Otherwise, my credentials were just too laughable for my opinions to be considered.

I loved my father, but I didn't know if I could trust him with this. Best case scenario, he believed me, and I had him backing my efforts. Things would go a lot easier with him and Mother on my side. Worst case scenario, I told him, and he decided I was some sort of monster or devil that had taken over his son. I would have to flee right here, right now, and survive on my own in this weak little body.

I could probably do it now that my core was ignited. I'd have to dedicate the majority of my mana to survival instead of progress, but as long as I made a clean escape and no one managed to track me down, it was viable.

It was a gamble. Either things got easier, or they got immeasurably harder. No matter what I did, everything was going to change after tonight. If I did nothing, I'd find myself under greater scrutiny and with my mana taken from me. If I told Father the truth, there was no telling how he'd react, and I didn't have the mana to reset his memory and try again.

I made my decision.

ELEVEN

"I love you," I told my father.

He smiled back and said, "I love you, too."

I wondered if he'd still say that ten minutes from now. I hadn't truly replaced his son, but the difference might be academic to Father. Gravin was practically an infant when I awakened, far too young to have his own thoughts and goals, to be his own person. His love for his family had mixed with me, but that was the only thing he was capable of contributing to our shared existence.

It wasn't exactly unreasonable to take the stance that I'd stolen Gravin's life from him in order to extend my own as Keiran. This was why I was supposed to awaken immediately upon being reborn, so that there never would have been another person. As usual, life had failed to cooperate with my plans.

"What happens after we die?" I asked.

That took Father aback, and he spent a long moment thinking before he answered, "No one really knows for sure. We have guesses and theories. Some people *claim* they know, but there's no proof. Personally, I think the spirits watch over us in life, and we join their numbers when we pass on. But don't you worry, none of us are going anywhere for a long time. A little ol' monster like this would be no problem, even if Lord Noctra hadn't shown up to take care of it."

I doubted that, considering the size of the crater Noctra's fire blast spell had left behind. Either that monster had been a serious threat, or the governor was trying to make some sort of point about his superiority. Maybe he'd considered it an opportunity to make a statement about how powerful his magic was, just to keep any mutinous muttering against him from going any further.

"Doesn't the afterlife get crowded?"

Father laughed at that. "I imagine they have quite a bit of space to spare. Why the sudden interest, though? You're still little; no need to worry about this anytime soon."

"What if spirits come back to live new lives? What if it's just a big cycle of living, dying, and being born to live again?"

Father finally picked up on the change in my tone. I hadn't been particularly good at talking like a small child to begin with, so it was hard to blame him for not immediately realizing that I'd stopped trying. It was probably the subject matter that had done it. He turned to face me fully and studied me in the moonlight.

"That's an interesting idea, Gravin. I don't think I've ever heard that before. I think we'd know if that were the case, though. Grandpa would have made the effort to come visit again before now."

"Oh, I don't think people remember their previous lives. Things would get complicated in a hurry if that was the case." Then again, if killing someone didn't permanently remove the threat an enemy represented, maybe people would behave better to begin with. "No, I think the only way to keep your memories would be to be an extremely powerful and knowledgeable archmage who'd spent decades preparing to move onto the next step of the cycle and used a powerful lunar convergence to ensure the soul invocations you created didn't fail once you passed on."

I could see the tension in Father's shoulders now. He didn't know what to do or say—not that I blamed him. To the best of my knowledge, no one before me had ever managed to accomplish what I'd done at the end of my life. Outside the uppermost echelons of magical society, knowledge of the mechanics through which souls migrated from one life to the next were little more than guesses and superstition. It wasn't reasonable to expect a dull farmer to know how to handle this.

"I am still your son," I said gently. "Nothing will ever change that. I am Gravin. But I am more than only Gravin. Everything I was in my previous life is still up here in my mind. I know the answers to questions no one here has ever thought to ask. I could tell you down to the minute how long it would take me to generate enough mana to duplicate the spell your Lord Noctra used that left that crater."

"I... Gravin... you. What is this?" Father asked, his voice exasperated. "What do you want me to say here?"

"I'm telling you this because I need you to take me seriously," I said. "Because you are a good father, and no good father would let a normal three-year-old chart the course of his life. That's absurd. But I am not a normal child. When I tell you that I don't need anyone's help to learn magic, you should believe me. When I say that I know best how to use my mana, you should believe me. When I tell you that wherever the mana this entire village tithes every night is going, it's not powering a barrier, *you should believe me*."

"What? That's ridiculous. Of course the mana powers the barrier. Why else wouldn't there be any monsters?"

"Good question. I would go ask the Barrier Wardens. I'm sure it would be interesting to hear what they have to say on the subject."

So far, the conversation was going well. Father hadn't immediately dismissed me as crazy, nor had he attacked me. He was confused, maybe panicking a little, but nobody could blame him for that. The important part was that he was still listening to me, not just looking at me like a three-year-old who was making up stories.

"Something is wrong with this village," I said. "The world isn't like this. Mana should fill the air. It should saturate the ground, so much that you could never use it all. But here, there's nothing. Every single core is dormant, even the core of the world itself. This life you're living, this isn't how things are supposed to be. You're struggling to farm enough food to keep less than two hundred people alive in a barren wasteland. Aren't you all sick and tired of going to bed exhausted and drained of all your mana every night?"

"That's how it's always been, Gravin. This isn't something new. My father lived here, and so did his father."

"But it's not like this elsewhere. This is what my home looked like before I died," I said. I conjured up a living illusion from my memories of the Night Vale in the air.

Trees with bark tinged a dark, velvety blue filled the vale. Their leaves were shades of cool blue and green, tinged with purple veins. I'd chosen my favorite view on the south end, at the edge of a bluff where the entire valley spread out below in all its splendor. Stars gleamed overhead inside my illusion, adorning the night sky while three moons danced around each other, their steps slow and stately and their images reflected in the stream below.

Father stared at it, slack-jawed and eyes filled with wonder. "It's... it's beautiful," he said.

"I know," I said, my voice soft. "I worked hard to keep it that way."

With a tinge of regret, I let the illusion fade away. As much as I enjoyed the view, I had practical concerns and couldn't afford to exhaust my mana holding onto a memory. It had served its purpose, as far as this conversation was concerned.

"I'm not saying the whole world is as beautiful as my old home was, but it doesn't look like this." I gestured towards the dead, barren ground all around us. Even the village's work to make life grow in the fields had produced scant results. "I don't know what happened here or how many centuries it's been this way, but the land here is scarred and dead. This is a wasteland, and it will be the work of generations to bring it back to life. Which leads me to the important question. Why are there people living here at all? Whatever happened here is the kind of event that doesn't leave survivors, so who came in afterwards, took a look around, and decided this was a good place to stay?"

Father chuckled and shook his head. "Those would be good questions to ask at school, son."

I rolled my eyes. "Cherok is an idiot."

"Well, yes, but he knows how to do his job. It sounds to me like it wouldn't hurt you to get an education after all, at least about some local topics."

There was some truth to that idea. When it came to the subject of magic, I wasn't interested in wasting time or mana on children's exercises. But I'd been reborn in a part of the world I'd never heard of, and it wouldn't hurt to learn a little about what had made it this way. It might not end up being relevant to my plans, which consisted mostly of advancing my core to stage three and then escaping this mana desert, but then again, I might just learn something useful if I took the time to look.

"You believe me?" I asked. "About everything, I mean."

Father looked down at me and slowly said, "I don't know. Are you really

Gravin? If you're not, what happened to my son? If you are, what am I supposed to do next? If you're really a mage more powerful than Lord Noctra, there's nothing I can do anyway. So tell me, what do you want?"

"I already told you. I don't want you to tell anyone. I don't need instructions. I just need time to rebuild my mana core so that I can use more magic."

"And... is that going to draw another monster to the village?" Father asked.

"No, not unless we decide to ignite someone else's core, too. Even then, if I didn't have to do it in secret, I could construct a ritual circle to contain the ambient mana and prevent a mana sniffer from sensing it."

Father went stone still and cocked his head. "I'm sorry, what does that mean?"

"What, igniting a core?" I asked.

"That. Yes. It sounds like you're saying you can give blessings to turn someone into a mage."

I snorted. "It's hardly a blessing. It used to happen to people by accident in my previous life. But yes, with a little work on your part and a few weeks of effort on mine to generate enough mana, we could ignite your core. Depending on how well you prepared, you'd start generating mana ten to twenty times faster than you do now, and I could start teaching you novice-ranked spells."

"Me? A mage?"

I smiled at his expression. "Yes, you and Mother both, if you'd like."

"What about Senica?" he asked.

I shrugged. "Not right now. When she's older, maybe. Once a core's been ignited, you can't snuff it back out. You only get one chance to do it right. I would hate to cripple her magical potential for the rest of her life because she rushed into it too young and didn't understand what she was doing."

"She's twice your age," Father protested. "Ah, but... You're not really three, are you?"

"Not quite, no." I took a deep breath and said, "So, that's the decision. This is who I am, and I need to know if you'll keep this a secret long enough for me to do what I need to do to regain my magic."

The silence stretched out between us, but I didn't push him. He'd need far more time than I could give him to come to terms with all of this, but I wouldn't begrudge him a minute to collect himself before he answered. Father was not a nobleman or politician, and I could see his emotions plain on his face. He didn't know the right answer, or even if there was a right answer. He didn't know what to do or where to turn for help.

"Swear to me on the spirits that you really are my son," he said.

"I swear," I told him. "I am your son and have been for my entire life."

With a heavy sigh, he nodded. "I can't abandon my own family, now can I? I won't tell Lord Noctra that you've been blessed." He frowned. "Ignited, I suppose."

I wrapped an arm around his leg and hugged him. "Thank you," I whispered. "I love you, Father."

I hadn't really thought about how scared the idea of having to leave made me. I knew I'd survive, but I didn't want to abandon my family. For now, at least, I didn't need to make that choice.

"I know. I love you, too. Uh, what do you suppose we should tell your mother, though?"

I hiccupped out a little laugh. "I haven't thought that far ahead," I told him truthfully.

"I guess we'll figure that out together. Come on, let's get on home now."

I didn't ride on my father's shoulders on the way back, which I thought we were both a bit sad about, but things were too different now. Growing up was painful for kids and parents sometimes, and it had happened way too fast for him in my case. Things were going to be a bit awkward for the next few weeks, but I was confident that we'd still be a family when we came out the other side.

TWELVE

The next few days of my life were a mixture of awkward tension and peaceful, uninterrupted work. My mana crystal progressed by leaps and bounds, so much so that I had to revise my initial estimates. Mother had been let in on the secret and, while she was initially more wary than Father, she was now allowing me to work without constantly dragging me away. At this rate, I'd finish the mana crystal in well under two weeks.

Part of me wanted to shake my head at how much easier it was to make swift progress now after spending eight months toiling in secret, but the truth of the matter was that if I hadn't ignited my core, I wouldn't have had the proof to convince my parents in the first place. Even with hindsight, I didn't see much of a way I could have reached this point any faster.

Our routine was interrupted on the day of the Testing. Father left in the morning as usual, and Mother had taken to walking Senica to school following the monster attack. I followed along to keep up the pretense that I was a normal child since I was still far too young to be left unattended and we had far too nosy of a neighbor not to go through the motions.

The village's school was a one-room building on the eastern side, and Cherok was usually already inside by the time we got there. Today, he was talking to another parent, but he took a moment to give me a sneer as we approached before returning to ignoring me. I might have been insulted if anyone else had done it, but my opinion of Cherok couldn't get much lower. Only people whose egos ruled their lives let others dictate their actions with such petty displays.

We left Senica behind and left without being forced to interact with the teacher again. "Do you worry about her?" I asked Mother after we'd left. "That Cherok isn't treating her fairly, I mean?"

Mother shook her head. "No. Senica would tell me if she thought she was being singled out. It's just old drama from my generation. Cherok and your father have never gotten along. It spilled over onto me when we got married—not that he liked me to begin with. But as unpleasant as he might be to us personally, he is professional about his job. And besides, anything she doesn't learn at school, you can teach her, right?"

I chuckled. That was true, I supposed. "Only when it comes to magic," I said. "I leave mathematics and literacy lessons to someone else to handle."

"I can already tell you're going to be a headache when you go to school."

"I wasn't planning on going," I told her.

"Everyone has to go. There are no exceptions."

It was interesting that the village placed such a high priority on basic education. I'd seen plenty of small villages just like this one where knowledge was passed down family lines instead of having a centralized learning institution, places where it wasn't unusual for literacy to start and end with a single family or clergyman.

Considering that they did no trade and I'd seen precious few books in the village, the emphasis on schooling struck me as an oddity. If it had just been for the purposes of learning introductory mana usage, it would have made sense. Fortunately for me, I had an easy way to find out.

"Mother, I have a question."

She didn't quite flinch at my calling her 'Mother' anymore, but it had taken a day or two. It really was something she needed to work on before someone noticed. Between the nosy neighbor and my sister, sooner or later she was going to get called out on it.

"What's that?" she asked.

"Why does the village have a school? Specifically, why is it teaching letters and numbers? It's not that literacy isn't a laudable goal in its own right, but there are no books here to read, no paper to write on, and no pens to write with."

"Of course there are. There are dozens of books in Lord Noctra's library. He makes them publicly available for us to read there."

I missed a step. "There's a library?" I asked, flabbergasted. How had I not known this? I'd been living here for close to a year now.

Then again, Gravin couldn't read or write, and Senica got her fill from the school itself. Father spent all day in the fields, and Mother handled the garden and other domestic duties. Nobody seemed to have the time, energy, or desire to read in my home. Mother visited with the neighbors for entertainment, and Father presumably had plenty of friends out in the fields.

It was no wonder no one had bothered to tell me, and I was probably letting my imagination get the better of me anyway. 'Dozens of books' described a single shelf, not a whole library, and there was scant reason to believe it would contain anything interesting or useful.

I was still going to check it out, of course. I would probably need Mother to cover for me and check out any books I deemed worth the time to read, as I doubted whoever was in charge would hand off such an expensive item to a small child. Then I needed to find time to read it somewhere I didn't have to worry about being spied upon. I couldn't do it in the garden while I worked on my mana crystal, and I couldn't do it in the house in the evening when Senica was home.

Completing my mana crystal was very much at the top of my priorities right now, so the books would just have to wait.

"Maybe I'll take you there when you get a bit older... I mean, you know..." Mother trailed off. She really hadn't taken the news about me as well as Father had. It was the eight months of lying that got to her, I think. Rationally, it was understandable. That didn't make her feel any less betrayed by my actions.

On the bright side, I finally got my own pallet to sleep on. That was the first thing they did once it became clear that I didn't have the mind of a three-year-old, and that I was actually something of a stranger to them. That particular change suited me just fine.

The rest of the day passed by in its typical routine. I judged I'd need another eight days just like this one to finish building the crystal and another day after that to properly shield it and attune myself to it. Then I could start pouring mana into it so I'd have a reservoir to pull from for when I needed to do something big.

It was too bad that only I could use it, but that was the drawback to using a mana crystal over a storage crystal. I got better efficiency from it, and it would even generate a bit of mana on its own, but nobody else could contribute to it. There were some ways around that, of course. I could take mana from others and then feed it into the crystal, but there was precious little to give here, and once I did finally ignite another person, they were going to need their mana for their own training.

Without ambient mana to quickly refill their cores, new apprentices were in for a long slog when it came time to practice their spells. As sloppy as they were with mana usage, they'd be lucky to cast three or four spells a day. Any apprentice curriculum designed to work here would need to focus heavily on mana control before even starting to learn a spell. I would probably have to start a theoretical apprentice on a regime of invocations to practice with, since they were both the most cost-efficient and the easiest to keep control over.

I missed my old stage nine core. I'd practically been a god inside the Night Vale, but after so many centuries, the mana upkeep to prevent my heart from failing and my brain from turning to mush had just gotten to be too much. The Night Vale itself had begun suffering for me, which had led me to my reincarnation plan. Other than the terrible location I'd been reborn into, things were working out well. I couldn't wait to see my true home once again.

Father came home early, several hours before Senica, and gathered us inside our hut to talk. "Testing is tonight," he said. "We need to plan for it."

"What's there to plan?" Mother asked. "The Collector will measure how much mana we're tithing, and it will either be enough, or it won't."

"Are they measuring us individually?" I asked. "If not, it would be easy for me to contribute enough mana to make up for any deficiency."

"That's the problem," Father said. "It is individual measurements, so you'll need to make sure your results are close to normal. Can you do that?"

"Easily. I've seen what Senica's tithe looks like hundreds of times. I can match that with about an hour to prepare."

Mother did a double take. "You can produce enough mana in an hour to match what your sister makes in an entire day?"

"Roughly speaking," I said. "To be more precise, it's about an hour and twelve minutes, assuming both our mana cores have equal capacity. Senica's is probably slightly larger than mine, given the age difference, so if I wanted to match her contribution exactly, I'd spend an hour and a half to be safe."

Father just shook his head and laughed while Mother muttered something under her breath about mages and the world not being fair. "It would be better for me to contribute slightly less mana than Senica does if they're going to measure our individual contributions, but with all four of us, I believe we should have no problems with the Testing?"

"I hope not. I tried not to work too hard today," Father said. "Mostly succeeded. Might be... a little bit low."

"Would you like some of mine?" I asked.

Father's eyebrows shot up. "You can do that?"

"Of course. It's not particularly efficient, but it's possible. The question is how much. You're a bit lower than Mother right now. Maybe enough to match her? Close to it anyway, it might be suspicious if you two have identical results."

My parents exchanged glances. "How inefficient are we talking about? I'll probably be fine on my own," Father said.

"It depends on how much I transfer. It's essentially a modified mana drain spell that works in reverse. The basic concept is that I use a spell to create a temporary mana core and place it inside your core. It absorbs mana from you, then returns to me to be harvested for my own use. In this version, I simply reverse the direction and partition off a portion of my own mana, then send it through the connection to you and unravel the shell. The mana will stay in your core, and the amount used in the shell and the connection will be spent."

"I've got to go get Senica," Mother said, standing up. "You two figure this out while I'm gone."

"I hate to say it," Father said after she'd gone, "but it probably wouldn't hurt to get a little more mana. It used to be that when a family did a Testing, everyone took the whole day off. Lord Noctra put a stop to that years ago, saying there was no point in doing it if it wasn't going to show how much mana we had left after a normal day. I'm not technically supposed to even take the few hours off that I did, but nobody'll complain if I cheat a little. It's what everyone else does."

"Take my hand," I told him. I held my own hand up, so much smaller than his that it disappeared inside his grasp. The spell took only a few moments to put together, and I carefully measured out a portion of mana to bring him roughly up to par with Mother. It left me a bit low, but we still had a few more hours before our Testing, and I'd regenerate it by then.

By the time Mother and Senica returned a few minutes later, I'd walked Father through how to break down the artificial mana core and absorb its contents. Mother's face was grim, and Senica was spitting mad. "I told him," my sister said. "I told him! But he wouldn't listen."

"What's this now?" Father asked, looking to Mother.

"Cherok apparently decided to make Senica practice mana control exercises until she'd completely exhausted all of her mana today. He knows our Testing is in a few hours."

It wasn't hard to tell from the grim looks on my parents' faces. This was going to be a problem.

CHAPTER
THIRTEEN

The tension was palpable. My parents had retreated to one side of the hut and were whispering back and forth rapidly while Senica sat at the table and angry-cried. It wasn't hard to guess what was causing that. Cherok had been himself, but our parents were unintentionally making it worse.

I dragged a chair around the table and sat down next to her. "It's okay," I said.

"No, it's not," Senica told me through sniffles. "We're going to fail because of me, and then bad things will happen to us."

"What bad things?" I asked.

"I don't know!"

"I do. Mother and Father will have to wear draw stone necklaces for a few months until the next Testing."

Senica rubbed at her face and looked over at me. "That's it?"

"That's it," I confirmed.

"That's... not so bad."

"Nope."

"Are you lying to me?" Senica asked as she eyed me with sudden suspicion.

"No," I said.

The conversation got our parents' attention and drew them out of their own panic spiral. They understood exactly what those necklaces meant, how much more difficult life would be with their mana being constantly drained. It would be exhausting, almost torturous. Once I thought about it, I suspected I must not have understood what was going to happen correctly. They couldn't wear those necklaces all the time.

Then again, torture was the original purpose of the draw stone. Or rather, it was to keep dangerous people in confinement and unable to fight back, which quite often led to torture. I'd never seen what was happening in this village before, and other than the fact that draw stones automatically stole mana from anyone who touched it, it really wasn't a good material to use in this way. Massive storage crystals would have been much more efficient, but that would require every single person in the village to learn how to interact with them.

Getting mana back out of draw stones was a delicate process, and the amount that would be used up in the process meant that Noctra was only getting a small fraction of the total mana he was harvesting. Even I wouldn't get more than a third of the mana back without some specialized equipment, and I doubted someone at Noctra's level of skill was getting more than a tenth.

"Gravin is right," Mother said. "We're not going to be driven out into the wastelands just because we aren't producing enough mana. Things will just be a little bit harder on us for a few months if we fail the Testing. We would prefer not to have to deal with that, but the world won't end if we do, sweetie."

"I'm sorry I ruined everything," Senica said.

"You didn't ruin anything," Father said. "And rest assured I'll be having words with your teacher about this tomorrow. The only reason I'm not going there right now is that the Collector will be here soon."

"Speaking of which," came a voice from just outside the doorway curtain. "May I come in?"

"Of course," Mother replied.

The Collector slid the curtain to the side and ducked into the hut. She was the same woman who'd come by a few days ago to tell us that the date for the Testing had been pushed back—Ayaka. Her clothes were similar to last time, but now she had a bag created to hold its shape with some clever stitching. It was held by a strap in one hand.

"What's this about Cherok?" she asked.

"He made Senica use all her mana on control exercises," Mother explained. "She's worried we're going to fail our Testing because of it."

"Ah, I see." Ayaka frowned. "I suppose nobody informed the school that the date was changed. I apologize for that oversight."

"Will you be able to take it into consideration?" Mother asked.

"Well," Ayaka said, drawing the syllable out as she thought. "Not as such, no. I will still have to perform the Testing. However, a child's contribution is hardly ever the deciding factor. It's likely that were you going to pass, you'd do so regardless of Senica. If it's that close that a little bit more would be what it takes to push you over the line, then I will see about letting her redo her Testing later this week so that her score can be added in."

The whole atmosphere changed with those words. My parents relaxed immediately, and even though I was pretty sure Senica didn't understand everything that was going on, she latched onto the part about getting a do-over. I was sure Mother would make sure Cherok understood that if he screwed our family over again, she'd make him regret it.

"Thank you," Father said. "I can't tell you how much of a relief that is, Ayaka."

"Collector Ayaka," she told him. It was a gentle reprimand, followed by a soft smile. "I am on duty right now."

"Of course, of course. Sorry about that," he said.

"Very well, let's get started."

My understanding of what a Testing actually consisted of was somewhat hazy. I knew it was a method of measuring our mana output, but it was only rarely done, and Gravin had been much too young to have proper memories of it from the last time our family had been called upon to complete it. I could think of a few different ways I would have measured someone's mana, but I was interested in seeing how someone from the village would do it. Hopefully, it wouldn't involve draw stones.

Ayaka put the bag on the table and began untying the laces that held it closed. I wasn't at a good angle to see what was inside, but it didn't matter. As soon as she opened it, I knew. There was some sort of enchantment on the bag, probably because they didn't want monsters like mana sniffers coming in to investigate the contents.

They were emitters, plain and simple. Each one was eight inches long, shaped like a metal cylinder with a handle on one end. Primarily, they acted to power devices that needed a constant and steady input of mana. More importantly, they were dead simple to use. Anyone with even basic mana control could activate the intake enchantment on an emitter. A sophisticated enough emitter would also have an option to toggle its mana radiation on or off, but these weren't that good. That wasn't surprising; it was an expensive modification that didn't have a lot of practical applications. Most things powered by emitters were done so specifically because the owner didn't want it turned off, ever.

"Sellis, would you like to go first?" Ayaka asked.

"Sure," he said. He took his place across from Ayaka at the table and waited for her signal. Mana snaked out of her in a thin line to connect to the intake enchantment, and she nodded. Father reached out a finger to touch the bottom end of the cylinder—not that it made a difference—and started channeling his mana.

That was the other difference from a draw stone. An emitter wouldn't steal mana from someone just because the intake was turned on. The donor still had to actively pour mana into the device, but anyone who could do even the most basic of invocations on purpose could manage that. It was harder to not give mana to the emitter while it was activated than it was to fill it up.

Even with the reserves I'd donated to Father, he still ran dry over the course of about seven seconds. Ayaka seemed to be able to tell as soon as he was done—perhaps she had developed a sense of mana similar to Father's —and quickly deactivated the intake enchantment while stowing the emitter away inside a cloth sleeve enchanted to seal the mana inside it. That went back into the bag, ensuring that once its own enchantment was reactivated, there'd be no casual sensing of its contents.

That accomplished, she noted down a few numbers on a slip of paper. The process was repeated with Mother, who only managed five seconds before she was finished. Ayaka frowned at that, and both my parents flinched.

"Lord Noctra will have to measure the Testing implement later before I can give you your official scores," the Collector said.

"But you know the unofficial ones already," Father said.

Tight lipped, Ayaka nodded. "It... For a family of four, it usually takes fourteen to seventeen seconds to collect the minimum amount of mana."

"We didn't make it," Mother said. "That seems like a lot. What did it used to be before the kids?"

"Nine to ten, I think?" Father said.

"Those are not official," Ayaka said. "No Collector can accurately measure the amount of mana stored here, but, well... We've all done this enough to get a rough idea. Some people are able to channel their mana faster, though. That can throw us off. It's why only Lord Noctra or Iskara can truly measure the results."

"Come on," Father said. "How many years have you been doing our Testing? You know how fast we are."

Ayaka sighed and looked distinctly uncomfortable. "It doesn't look good, Sellis. I'm sorry."

"Senica took a full second to do her Test last time," Mother said. "If she and Gravin could both contribute that much, we could hit the minimum time."

"Perhaps," the Collector allowed, "but don't get your hopes up. Children always take longer than adults. Her full second is more like half of one of your seconds. And I'm not expecting even that much, considering the circumstances. Your youngest is too young to make up the gap as well."

That was true. I'd given a large chunk of mana to Father, and there hadn't been nearly enough time to regenerate any true amount of mana thanks to how early the Collector had arrived. Besides, even if I had it, it would be too suspicious if I gave it all to the emitter. I'd just touched a draw stone last night. I should have at best a bare twentieth of the mana the average adult had.

Senica went next and, as expected, ran dry almost immediately. Nobody said anything about it, but she still started crying again and mumbled apologies. Mother pulled her into a hug and made gentle shushing sounds.

Finally, it was my turn. I'd already determined how much mana to give to the emitter, which was trickier than it sounded. It was rather like clenching a muscle to stop mid-stream, except it would cut off the mana flowing out of my core instead of... well. Anyway. The hardest part was determining how much mana had already gone out prior to the clench, but I liked to think all those centuries of practice had given me plenty of insight into measuring my own mana.

I touched the emitter after Ayaka activated it and let it slowly take a chunk of my mana over the next second before cutting off the connection despite maintaining physical contact. Ayaka nodded, unsurprised by the results, and packaged up the emitter.

"Good job," she told me. "I was a bit worried about getting a result since you haven't started school yet, but I guess your parents have already been showing you how to use mana."

I smiled and nodded, but didn't say anything. I had a reputation to maintain as a creepy, mute kid who stared at everything, after all. Besides, her words were strained. She might not have the official number, but it was obvious that she thought we'd failed. Even if they retested Senica later, she wasn't going to have enough mana to make up the difference.

We'd just see about that. Ayaka's pessimistic predictions hadn't calculated one thing. I'd noticed something about the emitters that I was betting she didn't know: they hadn't been properly maintained. It might be cheating, but I didn't care if it meant not having to deal with the headache, so I'd cheated just a bit.

I'd wait for the Collector to leave before I told my parents that.

CHAPTER

FOURTEEN

The thing about emitters was that they needed to be regularly cleaned out in order to keep them operating at full capacity. A tiny bit of mana crystallized during the emission process, and if no one ever came along and took care of that, it built up until the emitter was useless.

The emitters the Collector had used had not been maintained, probably not ever, judging by how much mana was built up inside of them. Since there was already a bunch of mana stuck inside the emitters, it was easy for me to break a bit loose to mix in with the fresh mana my parents had donated. I didn't bother to do it for Senica's, and I'd given such a small sliver of mana to mine that it wasn't worth the effort. For my parents, though, it was a good twenty percent increase over what they'd actually given.

I didn't know what the threshold was, but I figured that the extra push should probably do it. If not, then I'd handle that problem when it arose. Right now, I had two parents to let in on the scheme and an older sister who needed to be comforted by the knowledge that she hadn't ruined anything despite her teacher's attempts to screw us over.

Mother was already hard at work on that last part, so I took the opportunity to snag Father's attention and beckoned him closer. "What is it?" he asked, leaning down. Then he thought better of it and shook his head.

"Sorry, it's hard to break the habits. I'm trying not to treat you like a little kid."

"I appreciate that," I told him. And I did, more than he'd ever realize. It was somehow humiliating and infuriating at the same time to be constantly talked down to by every single person I met. "I wanted to tell you that there's nothing to worry about."

"There isn't? The times aren't even close, and Ayaka's known us for years. She knows we're not fast channelers or whatever."

"That may be something you have to deal with soon if she brings it up, because I added more mana to each of your emitters. Sorry, the Testing implements."

Father was silent for a moment as he considered that. Then he asked, "How? I thought you didn't have much left."

"You don't have to actually touch an emitter to manipulate it," I told him. "Once it was outside of the cloth wrapping, I just scraped loose some of the excess mana that had built up inside. It'll mix with the mana you gave it, and whoever looks at it later on will think it all came from you."

He gave a short laugh. "The things you know... You're sure it'll work?"

"I'm sure that whoever measures it will think you put in about twenty percent more mana than you actually did—you and Mother both. I'm not sure that it'll meet whatever arbitrary quota they've decided on, but I couldn't realistically give us much more of an edge than that without it becoming suspicious anyway."

"That's true," Father said. He glanced over to where the feminine half of our family was sitting on the pallet and said, "I should tell your mother, but I don't think Senica is ready to learn all of this yet."

"No," I agreed. "She's too young to have to keep these kinds of secrets."

We'd been speaking softly, but Mother had still noticed us. She shot Father a questioning glance while Senica nestled deeper into her arms. He tilted his head in my direction and waggled his eyebrows back at her. What passed between them in that silent communication, I could not begin to guess. Whatever it was, she relaxed just slightly.

"This has been quite a stressful night," Father announced, "but we don't have to tithe tonight. How about we have dinner, then we can have a quiet night in before bed?"

Maybe I'd get a few more hours of working on my mana crystal done tonight. One bright side about this new arrangement with my parents was that I didn't need to justify myself or invent excuses to hide what I was doing. They didn't know the details, but they knew that sitting on that rock was going to help me. As long as I kept up appearances, it was fine if I wanted to sit on that rock well into the evening.

Yes, a quiet night was just what we all needed.

I was looking forward to things returning to normal so I could get back to work, but I'd forgotten that Cherok had invited the wrath of my parents down on his head. Father did not leave for the fields with the dawn. Instead, he spent time with Mother and Senica while I sat on my rock in the garden and continued weaving strands of mana through it. Progress was good, especially since I had a full core when I woke up in the morning to devote to the task.

An hour after we'd woken up, the whole family moved as one towards the school. We were early, either because my parents wanted a good long while to yell at Cherok, or because Father could only delay his appearance in the fields for so long. Maybe both. Either way, we were the first people there. Cherok himself was still inside, bleary-eyed and working his way through his own morning rituals.

"We need to have a talk." My mother announced her presence in an ice-cold tone. Cherok's back was to the entrance, and he froze as soon as she spoke. When he turned in place and saw both her and Father standing together, his eyes widened, then narrowed in anger.

"Senica, please wait at your seat with Gravin while your father and I speak with your teacher," she said, her voice only slightly warmer.

"Come on," Senica said, tugging at my hand and leading me to the back of the one-room building where a dozen chairs were lined up in two rows. "I'll show you what school is like."

I was only half-listening to Senica as she pointed out her seat in the front row, or when she showed me the papers she'd practiced her letters on. Idly, I noted that I didn't recognize most of them despite the language being similar to what I'd spoken in my previous life. That was something to consider later, but it let me know that if nothing else, school would be useful for learning to write the local dialect. It was an oddity, and I enjoyed picking those apart until I had a satisfying explanation.

It was a frivolous use of mana, but Cherok was the most unpleasant person I'd met thus far in this new life, and I wanted to enjoy my parents taking turns tearing into him. It was petty, yes, but what was life without a little fun every now and then?

"What the hell is the matter with you?" Mother hissed from the outside of the building, her voice pitched low enough that Senica couldn't hear.

"Nothing is the matter with me," Cherok said. "I have a schedule, and it doesn't bend to your whims."

"Is that so? So you just didn't care that our family's Testing got moved to last night because that wasn't on your schedule?"

"Look, Xilaya. Sometimes students lie. You should know all about that, right?"

"Can we not drag up things that happened two decades ago?" Father asked. "I get that you hate us. I'm not even saying you're wrong. We were kids. It wasn't on purpose, but I'd take it back if I could. I'm sorry about what happened, but that does not give you the right to take it out on my daughter."

"You think I give a shit if you're sorry?" Cherok snarled, his voice rising loud enough that Senica jumped and shot a glance at the entryway. "You think that makes it better? That I forgave you because you were both kids? You were old enough to know better. You just thought you were special, and the rules didn't apply to you, and Teno had to pay the price for that. Take your apology and cram it up your—"

"Enough," Mother said. "Your issues with us will remain with us. You knew the Testing had been moved and you deliberately reworked your own schedule to force Senica to spend all of her mana yesterday. Were you trying to ensure that we failed, just so we'd have to suffer for a month or two?"

"I have a schedule for all Testings done by any families who have a student in school. Your daughter's Testing was scheduled for last week. On that day, I exempted her from all mana exercises. Unless a Collector comes and tells me otherwise, I follow the schedule. Kids are always trying to lie to me to get out of doing their schoolwork, and I had no reason to suspect otherwise in this case. If anything, given her family history, I'd assume she was even more inclined to lie than the average student."

I could actually hear Father's teeth grinding while Cherok spoke. I did not think of my father as a gentle man, but in the going on nine months that I'd known him, he'd always been patient and kind. Even when he'd taken me out to the fields to see the aftermath of the mana sniffer's attack, he hadn't been angry with me. He'd just been firmly insistent that I needed to tell him the truth.

So I was a little bit surprised to hear the smack of skin on skin when Father punched Cherok in the face. I hadn't thought my old man had it in him.

There was a stunned moment of silence, then Cherok said, "How dare you! You may rest assured that I will be informing the Garrison about this immediately. Get out now, and take your grubby children with you. I'll look forward to watching you get lashed in the middle of town this evening, Sellis."

"Kids, come out here. We're leaving," Mother said in her normal voice.

I let Senica lead the way. She paused at the door and gasped, but Mother just guided her away from the building. I stepped out into the morning light behind her, saw Cherok wiping away blood from his nose while my father stood five feet away with his fists clenched at his side and a ferocious scowl on his face, and wisely decided that the best place to be right now was not standing between those men.

"You're an idiot, Sellis, same as when you were a kid," Cherok said. "I hope this teaches you a lesson. Better late than never."

"And you never learned when to stop running your mouth," Father said. "Always so full of yourself, sure that your way was the one and only right way, that anyone who couldn't see that was too stupid to realize something obvious. After all this time, you haven't changed a bit. You're more set in your ways than ever."

"Well I won't be the one getting my back torn to ribbons tonight, will I?" the teacher retorted. He gestured across the street, where two women standing thirty feet away were standing next to a hut and watching the exchange silently. "Witnesses. No way to lie your way out of punishment this time. No one else to take the fall for you."

"True enough," Father admitted. "Better make sure it's worth it, then?"

"What?" Cherok asked, right before Father took a step forward and popped him in the mouth.

"I loved Teno like a brother. His death is the biggest regret of my life. I *never* meant for something like that to happen."

"It should have been you," Cherok said, revealing bloody teeth. "If you'd had any decency, it would have been."

"On that we can agree. I don't expect you to forgive me, but you damn well better treat my children fairly. None of what happened then was their fault, and if you think you're going to abuse them to get back at me, well, next time I won't use my fists. Run along now, you'll want to get over to the barracks before the blood dries."

Giving us one last hate-filled glare, Cherok turned his back and scurried off down the street. Father watched him go, then sighed and glanced down at me. "That could have gone better," he said.

Wordlessly, I nodded my agreement.

CHAPTER

FIFTEEN

I t was no surprise to me to see Malra heading our way within twenty minutes of getting back home. Father had left for work, and Mother had started her daily ritual of feeding her mana to the plants in our garden in a doomed attempt to keep them lush and healthy. If the garden had been a third of the size it was, she probably could have managed it, but then it wouldn't have produced enough food for all of us.

Or maybe it would have. Fewer plants with more mana meant more food per plant, but I didn't know the ideal ratio for maximum yield. Gardening was not one of my hobbies, and I'd never been in a situation where I had to conserve mana like this. Maybe the villagers had long since calculated this, or at least had a rough guideline.

Either way, Mother put a lot of time and effort into that little patch of dirt next to our hut, and it was there that we spent most of our time. The addition of Senica to our group was no doubt the clue that drew Malra's attention to us.

"Good morning, Xilaya," she said as she strode out of her hut and made a beeline right for my mother.

"Hello," Mother said. "How are you today?"

"Just fine," Malra said. "Always fine. My garden's a lot easier to care for than yours is."

That was because it was just Malra and her husband now. They were both in their fifties and their children were fully grown, so her garden was half the size. I'd also noticed the village had some sort of social welfare system that awarded larger portions of the field harvests to the elders of the village. To be fair, we also got a larger than normal ration thanks to the family having two children, but it worked out especially well for Malra's household.

That wasn't to say that Malra ever offered to help. No, she was there to gossip and nothing else. I supposed she could make an argument that all the mana she didn't spend helping Mother was going into a draw stone at the end of the day anyway, but since I knew for a fact that there was no barrier being powered by this mana, it was a moot point to me.

I didn't like Malra for the simple reason that she was nosy, and I had secrets to hide. She'd been the one who'd suggested to Mother that I was possessed back when I'd first awoken, and I hadn't ever forgiven her for that. Life was hard enough in this village without my neighbor going out of her way to make it worse.

Her eyes sparkled as they skimmed across our garden and settled on Senica. "No school today? I'm afraid I've lost track of the schedule. It's been so many years since my youngest graduated."

"Something like that," Mother said. "You know that Cherok has never forgiven us for everything... Sometimes he has difficulty remembering that my children are not to blame for that."

"Oh, is that why you all went off together this morning?" Malra asked.

Did this woman seriously have nothing better to do than watch the comings and goings of everyone around her? I'd had dedicated divination wards protecting my sanctum that missed more details than Malra, if only because I'd gotten sick of resetting them regularly when the squirrels and birds started going crazy in the springtime.

"The conversation didn't go well," Mother admitted.

"Oh no, what happened?"

While I personally thought it was none of Malra's business, I recognized that Mother considered her a friend. I also knew that the villagers' entire world was only three or four miles wide and their neighbors were likely the only people they'd ever know throughout their entire lives. Whether Malra found out now or later, everyone was going to know that Father had assaulted Cherok by the end of the day.

In fact, unless I missed my guess, a member of the Garrison was coming down the street right now. I hadn't seen much of them since they seemed to operate as some sort of private security force that loitered around on the grounds surrounding the governor's manor, but they did have a barracks that they worked out of, and they actually acted as a police force if needed.

I always thought of governments as slow-moving machines, and to be fair, they generally were. Bureaucracy was an unwieldy beast at the best of times, but in a village with a population of under two hundred, there wasn't much need for it. It was as simple as approaching someone in charge, asking for them to do a thing, and them deciding whether to agree. If they did, they went and did the thing, usually immediately.

Cherok had probably gone right to the barracks, pointed them at Father, and then walked back out with a vindictive little smirk on his face. From there, it had taken less than an hour for someone to come around.

He was a tall man with sandy brown hair, prominent cheekbones, and a chiseled jawline. Broad shoulders stretched the fabric of his shirt across his chest, and he had arms thicker around the biceps than my waist. Worse, he moved with confidence and poise. There was a short sword hanging from a scabbard tied to his belt, and I expected he knew how to use it. If he had half as much smarts as he did looks, he wasn't someone I wanted coming around regularly.

"Morning, Xilaya," the Garrison man said.

"Karad," she replied, tight-lipped. Mother knew why he was here.

Karad cast a quick glance over at our hut, then asked, "He already in the fields?"

"Yes," Mother said.

"Smart of him," Karad said. "No reason to lose a day's food over this whole mess. Anything you think I should know before I head on out that way?"

"No," Mother said with a sigh. "I'm sure Cherok's report was completely accurate. He doesn't have any reason to lie this time."

"Hmm," was all the Garrison man said.

"Mom, what's going to happen?" Senica asked.

Mother took a breath and said, "Well, the village has rules, sweetie. If you break the rules, you get punished. Your father broke a rule, so Mister Karad is here to talk to him about his punishment."

"Did he get in trouble because of me?"

"No, of course not. He just lost his temper because your teacher wasn't being very fair. Everything will be fine. There's nothing to worry about."

Senica did not look convinced, not with Karad standing right there. Her eyes drifted down to his sword and she started trembling, but Mother folded her up in a hug and said, "It's alright. Don't be scared."

"Sorry to upset the little one," Karad said. "I'll get out of your hair now. Have a good day, Xilaya. Malra."

"You too, Karad," our neighbor said cheerily. She didn't notice the glare Mother gave her, which was probably about the only thing she hadn't noticed considering how much time she spent snooping on us.

Since Mother had everything under control and there didn't seem to be much I could do to affect the outcome of this one way or another, I let her handle calming Senica down and went back to work. This mana crystal wasn't going to build itself, and I still had another week of work before it was stable. I kept an eye on the time as I wove the mana together, though. I was probably going to need a full core tonight.

Father returned home about an hour later than usual and though he tried to hide it, I could see he was feeling tender. He held himself stiffly and gritted his teeth when Senica crashed into his waist to hug him.

"How many?" Mother asked softly from where she was preparing dinner.

"Three," he said.

"Why so many?" she asked, surprised.

"Repeat offender."

"That was eight years ago!"

"Apparently they're keeping track," Father said. He gave Senica a pat on the head and said, "Don't you worry, I'm alright. Just got to take it slow for a few days."

"Karad came through looking for you, gave her a scare," Mother said.

"He told me. Said he was sorry about that."

I waited for him to finish disentangling himself from my sister and send her back to Mother's side, then sat down at the table next to him. I wasn't tall enough yet to use a normal sized chair without standing on it, but that was fine by me. Nobody complained if I didn't eat at the table.

Father looked over and said, "How's it going?"

"It's been an interesting day. I take it you have a history with Cherok."

"You could say that," he said. "It's a painful story, not something I'm too keen on discussing."

"I think I've got the broad strokes of it," I said. "Details would just be gossip at this point, so I won't press."

"Downright decent of you," Father told me.

"Mmhmm. Well, whatever you did or didn't do is your business. I just wanted you to know I've been building up mana for the last six hours to heal you."

Father jerked in place, then winced as his shirt rubbed across his back. "You can do that?" he whispered to me as he cast a glance over at Senica to see her occupied with Mother still. They were chopping vegetables to throw in the stew pot, though Senica was moving considerably slower than Mother and her results were questionable at best.

"Of course I can," I scoffed. "I swear, how much proof do you need before you believe me?"

"Well I'd appreciate it, but you should save your mana for your project," Father said. "This is just the consequences of my actions coming back around to say hello. I'll be fine."

"Call it the village giving back after all that mana you've given it over the years if you'd like," I said. "Now, this will feel hot at first, then it'll cool down. For three lashes, I should have more than enough to patch you up. Here, take my hand."

It wasn't that I couldn't heal at range, but that added to the mana cost once I started including components of conjuration and divination in the spell. At its most basic, healing was an invocation. Most people could do it without thinking about it, and no real structured spell was needed for minor injuries like my father's. Healing somebody else was trickier, since it required a bit of transmutation both to get a feel for what was wrong and to treat the injury itself.

Doing it without being able to touch the subject was substantially more expensive and complicated. That wasn't to say it was outside my abilities—far from it. But, as always these days, I needed to budget my mana carefully.

Father took my hand somewhat hesitantly, and I cast a single diagnostic pulse through him. There were three bright lines across his back that stood out first and foremost, but there were also some smaller injuries in his hands, wrists, and shoulders. One of his knees was slightly swollen, too. I assumed those were the results of twelve-hour days in the fields, but they were well within my capabilities to repair.

Healing spells were slow to cast, even for me. The body was an incredibly complicated piece of machinery, self-repairing and resilient, but at the same time, some parts were so delicate that the slightest nudge was all it took to create a cascading chain of failure. For a job like this, the risk was minimal, but I still took my time.

It was very possible to abridge the process of casting a spell, to drill the formation of its basic components so thoroughly that it came automatically. I did this for most spells I cast, but not healing magic. That always got my full attention for the entire process. It took precisely twenty-five seconds, during which my father started to fidget and made to pull his hand away before my fingers squeezed down around it.

Then the mana took on the shape I needed, and healing magic flashed across his body. The back wounds closed, and the swelling on his knee went down. The nicks and scrapes so common in physical labor sealed themselves closed, and the inflammation on his arm and shoulder cleared up. It took almost all the mana I had, but Father was physically in perfect health again.

"I asked Mother to prepare an extra-large meal for you," I said. "You should eat all of it. You'll need the extra energy."

Father looked down at me with wonder in his eyes, and I smiled in satisfaction. Someday soon, I'd be able to cast spells like that all day long.

SIXTEEN

I'd made something of a promise to my parents—my father specifically. One could argue the semantics, that I'd merely said I *could* help them ignite their cores, not that I would. But I wasn't so petty as that. The real hold up was that I needed to finish constructing my mana crystal before I could do it. The storage crystal had only just barely had the capacity I'd needed, and once I accounted for a significantly lower level of skill from my parents, I expected it would take a much larger amount of mana to spark an ignition.

That day was still some time away, but that didn't mean there was no prep work to be done. After we'd returned from our nightly appointment with the draw stone, Father and I had gone for an evening walk together. There was no privacy to be had in the village, but very few people wanted to return to the fields after their mana had been drained away.

It was interesting, the things the village of Alkerist grew. Most candles were formed from wax, but here, they grew some sort of plant with seeds that hung off of them like pea pods. Those were collected, mashed, heated, and shaped. They didn't last as long as the candles I'd known in my youth, but they burned cleanly and without the harsh odors I remembered tallow candles producing. The plant fibers themselves were processed into the rough paper the village used as well.

There were great patches of vegetables too, of course. The village would not survive on just the humble gardens near our homes—out in the fields, they grew the hardier vegetables in large quantities, the ones that didn't need constant care and an influx of mana to thrive. Corn, beans, carrots, peppers... all in rows and tended to as well as they could. The farmers' mana was spent to keep their bodies moving instead of being invested directly into the plants themselves.

Anywhere else in the world, the ambient mana in the air would have been all that was needed for the crops to thrive. Here, the village had gone to great effort to dig a channel to the river coming out of the mountains a few miles northwest of town. They'd created an artificial stream to irrigate the crops and, not coincidentally, provide a little relief to the people as well.

"All of this," I said. "So much time and effort to replicate what mana would do naturally anywhere else. I cannot understand why you stay."

"Perhaps there's a world such as you've described out there," Father said, "but if so, it's far, far from here. There is another village up here in the highlands, fifty miles or so away, you know. It's the same there as it is here. In the basin far to the west, there's a city with thousands and thousands of people. I can't imagine it, personally. Maybe they have dozens of mages like Lord Noctra to protect them from the monsters. But still, there is no more mana in the air down in the basin than there is up here in the highlands."

If that was true, then the cataclysm that had scarred this land was even more devastating than I'd initially assumed. "What about past there?" I asked.

Father shrugged. "Mountains. Completely impassable, just like the ones to the east and south of us. I've heard if you go far enough north and east, you'll eventually find a lake so huge you can't see the other side, where the water only makes you thirstier the more you drink. It is supposed to be a cursed place."

I barked out a laugh, which brought my father up short. "Do you mean an ocean?" I asked. "They are filled with salt water. There's nothing cursed about them. They are just incomprehensibly vast and deep. It takes a large ship and a good deal of preparation to sail across one, but people have been doing that for thousands of years."

"I have not heard this word before," Father said with a frown. "Ocean. Hmm. I suppose that's as good a word as any. Now, what is a ship?"

"A vehicle used for travel on water," I said, suddenly saddened by the thought of the isolation this village had endured. "Think of a cart without wheels, but much, much bigger, and the gaps between the board sealed with special oils created by alchemists to prevent water from seeping in."

"That sounds like a sight to behold," Father said. "But sadly, not one we're likely to see around here."

"No," I agreed, "I suppose not."

"Enough of that," Father said. "You didn't ask me to come out here just to talk about this."

"You're right. I got distracted. I wanted to check in with you on your progress, to see if you had any questions or if you were ready for the next lesson."

The first thing I'd shown Father was how to resist the pull of a draw stone. Perhaps it wasn't the easiest starting point, but it did seem the most relevant. Everyone in the village had already had some basic mana control drilled into them, even if it was no more than what was needed to use the most basic, shapeless invocations. In order for Father to practice anything greater, he needed to have mana.

"It's a strange feeling," Father said. "But I think I'm getting the hang of it. It's like trying to catch water with my hands, except it's dripping through my fingers. Only it's not just dripping. It's being pulled along."

"One part of it is willpower," I said. "Your mana has to obey you. If you leave places for your mana to slip through, that's what's going to happen."

Father laughed and shook his head. "I know, I know. I'm practicing. Spirits, this is so weird. I'm being lectured by a toddler. Sorry, I know you're not really, it's just... you're so tiny and fierce at the same time."

"I should have waited until after the lesson to heal you," I told him. "That was my mistake for thinking the pain would distract you."

"Alright, alright." Father held his hands up in surrender. "I'm sorry for laughing. Please, oh great and mighty archmage, bring enlightenment to my unworthy self. Ow!"

"Serves you right," I said, smirking. I'd used an act of minor telekinesis to tweak his nose.

"Ought to put you over my knee for that," he grumbled as he held his nose with one hand. I gave him a glare and he shielded his nose with his other hand.

"As I was saying, the draw stone pulls at any loose mana in your core, so you need to actively oppose it with an equal amount of willpower."

"And if my will is too strong, would I take mana from the draw stone?"

I shook my head. "There's more to it than that. If you were talking about a storage crystal, it would be an effort of will to retrieve mana from it, but draw stones are a natural phenomenon. They eat nearby mana to power their vault. It only goes in one way, and getting it back requires some specific magic or tools. No matter how implacable your will is, you'll never squeeze a drop of mana from a draw stone just by opposing its own attempts to consume yours."

Father looked like he was about to say something, but I cut him off. "Besides, it's not worth it. From what I can tell, the Collectors are serious about their draw stones. If one of them starts coming up short, they're going to want to know why. Let's not give them a reason to look in our direction."

"Fair enough. You don't think they'll notice when they're not getting our mana, though?"

I shrugged. "Forty to fifty people per draw stone, and they're not emptying them every night," I said. "That's less than a five percent loss of mana. They might notice if it continues for long enough, but I think we're safe for the next few months."

As near as I could tell, the draw stones were each emptied about once every two weeks on an alternating schedule. I suspected that Noctra was the one to do it, as I'd yet to see anyone else with the sort of skill necessary, but considering how prevalent they were, it wouldn't have surprised me if the governor's manor had a setup to do it without his personal intervention. From what I'd heard, there were a few dozen more draw stones north of town in the arbor anyway. That would certainly be a time-consuming chore to keep them all emptied regularly.

"Anyway, let's go over the exercises again," I said.

"Good thing you're not in charge of a field crew," Father said. "You're merciless."

"If you don't want to have an ignited core, that's fine by me," I told him. "I'm doing this as a favor to you."

"No, no. I didn't say that."

"Good. Now then, let's see you get that mana spinning."

I kept working on my mana crystal throughout the mornings and afternoons. Senica returned to school after two days, but started regularly complaining about Cherok in the evenings. Mother and Father listened to her with grim faces, and I had a sneaking suspicion that Father was going to end up earning a few more lashings before this whole mess was over.

At least it served as a good excuse for why I wasn't in school yet. It was customary for children around my age to begin attending class, if only to learn letters and numbers. Introductory mana control would be part of those lessons, I'd learned, but no one expected children to master much, not even enough to shift mana out of the core and perform basic invocations.

In addition to the lessons with Father, I gently coached Mother on how to sense mana. She was less interested in igniting her core, but she'd confided in me one day that if she'd had Father's ability to sense mana, it would have made her work tending the garden much easier. I didn't agree with her decision, but there was plenty of time to bring her around. In the meantime, learning to sense mana outside of her own core was an excellent first step.

It turned out that while Father might see mana better, Mother was far, far better at manipulating it. That made sense to me, considering that he spent his own mana internally on invocations to increase his strength, and she spent hers trying to nurture the garden.

We'd had a few discussions about the nature of mana, and I'd shown her how to keep track of her own as it left her core and went out into the world. From there, it was a short step to learn how to sense other mana outside of her, one that I was sure she'd make with a bit of practice. My primary fear was that as soon as she got even a few feet of range, she'd give up on improving any further. I had the impression that something about learning magic didn't sit well with her.

We were still weeks away from that being a concern, so I put it out of my mind for the time being. My mana crystal would be finished in the next day or two, and I was looking forward to being able to stockpile enough mana to do some big spells. Specifically, I wanted to start working on the mana lattice I needed to construct in my core to advance to stage two, where my mana generation would more than double again.

As always seemed to be the case, life was not content to leave me in peace to do my work. Four days after our Testing, the Collector showed up one evening with a serious look on her face.

"Sellis, we need to talk," she said. "I don't know why, but Lord Noctra's asking questions about you."

CHAPTER
SEVENTEEN

My parents gave each other uneasy glances, but neither looked over in my direction. I was sure that was what they were thinking, though: that my interference had drawn someone's attention and it had gotten back to the governor himself. It was possible I'd overestimated how much additional mana we needed to pass our Testing, but I didn't think so.

It was also possible Father's public lashing had caught Noctra's attention. Such spectacles didn't happen often, but the fact that a Collector had shown up to tell us made me think it was mana-related. Then again, Ayaka seemed to be friends with Father outside of any relationship related to her work, and she had a somewhat privileged position.

There wasn't much point in speculating on it when Ayaka was just going to tell us in a second anyway, so I pushed such thoughts aside and listened to the conversation. Perhaps sensing that something important was happening, even if she didn't understand what it was exactly, Senica watched silently with me.

"What kind of questions?" Father asked.

"I think it was the public punishment that got his attention," Ayaka explained. Hah, I knew it. "He started asking what the fight was about, and then he got interested in what happened when we were kids. Then he found out about your... talents, and he got very interested in knowing everything about you."

"What could he want from you?" Mother asked Father.

"I guess we'll find out soon enough," Father said, but he didn't sound happy about it.

"Do you think it has something to do with the incident?" Mother asked.

"He knew about the incident already," Ayaka said. "He got the details on that when he first arrived to get the barrier working again."

"Then why now?" Father asked.

"Maybe you brought it back to his mind with your fight," Mother suggested. "When he first got here, he was busy with so much work. Now it's been years, and everything is under control. It could just be that he has the time to properly investigate it now and is finally getting around to it since you and Cherok reminded everybody what happened."

I was going to need to sit one of them down and force this story out of them, and soon. The oblique hinting, the fact that someone had died... I was sure it was a hard thing to talk about, but it was starting to feel like something that I shouldn't just leave alone, especially if it was coming back around to cause problems now. I did not need Noctra looking hard at my family right now, not when I still had months of work to advance my mana core to stage two.

As soon as I got one of them alone, I was going to wring the truth out of them. Until then, my best guess was that Father's ability to sense mana was considered a rare talent here, one that Noctra was now planning to capitalize on.

"Well, this is a mess," Father said. He leaned back in his chair and blew out a long sigh. "I don't suppose I could get so lucky that it's a good thing?"

Ayaka shrugged. "They didn't tell me what their plans are. They just wanted answers to their questions."

"I kind of have a suspicion that Lord Noctra would be asking me these questions directly if it was a good thing," Father said.

"I honestly don't know what his sudden interest is," the Collector told him. "Did you do something recently, besides punch Cherok in the face, I mean?"

"No?" Father said as much as asked. He exchanged a glance with my mother and continued, "Maybe something in our Testing?"

"Oh, that reminds me! The other reason I'm here. Your family passed. If anything, your official measurements were a bit higher than expected."

"Out of the ordinary?" Father asked. I could practically hear his neck muscles straining to hold themselves back from turning his face in my direction, but Ayaka didn't seem to notice.

"No, no. Nothing like that. A bit higher than normal, but nothing unusual. Whenever this happens and we have to investigate, we *always* find out it's a case of someone skipping work that day to conserve mana. It happens all the time."

"Ah. Well, you caught me," Father said. "I couldn't quite arrange things for the job I wanted with the new Testing date, so I ended up just doing a half day."

"You... did. Hmm."

"What does 'hmm' mean?" Mother asked sharply.

Ayaka shook her head. "The results were more in line with a full day off, but I don't think it matters much. The important thing is that you're good for another year or two. And that means Senica and Gravin have time to grow and generate more mana without having draw stones in your home."

"Doesn't seem fair, does it?" Father said. "We never had to deal with this when we were kids."

The Collector gave Father a flat, unfriendly look. "You know exactly why we have to deal with this now."

"Yes, but... now we have the Barrier Wardens, and the barrier is still off most of the time anyway. It just seems kind of... I don't know. What's the use?"

"Why don't you bring it up with Lord Noctra? I'm sure he'd be fascinated to hear your opinion on the subject," Ayaka suggested.

Mother snorted. "Let's not get ourselves in any more trouble than we already are."

"I don't know that you're necessarily in trouble, but it doesn't hurt to know you're being looked into. If you are doing something you shouldn't, I don't want to know about it and I never told you that anyone was interested in you. Understand?"

"I understand," Father said. "Thank you, Ayaka."

"That's Collector Ayaka to you," she said with mock sternness. Then she said, much quieter, "I should get going. Good luck, Sellis. I hope whatever's going on doesn't mean trouble."

"Me too. I appreciate the warning."

The Collector left then, and Senica rushed for the table as soon as she was gone. "What was she talking about? Did you do something bad? You didn't have to give your mana away when you were kids? Why not? That's not fair that we have to and you didn't!"

"Slow down there, kiddo!" Father told her. "I'll tell you what. Let's have dinner, then we'll go do our tithing for the night, and I'll tell you all about the worst day of my life when we get home."

"Promise?"

"I promise," Father said solemnly.

The mood that evening was a unique mix of anticipation and dread—not that I thought Senica picked up on it. Our parents truly did not want to discuss whatever it was that had happened when they were young, but Senica only saw a new story on the horizon. She kept trying to sneak questions into the conversation until Father finally lost his patience and told her she needed to wait until we got back from tithing.

Come dinner time, Father shoveled food into his mouth mechanically without saying a word, and Mother picked at her own plate. I'd never seen anyone not finish their meals, not as hard as they all worked to grow the food in the first place. But that night, Mother gave over half her dinner to Senica, who greedily gobbled it all up. It was only as an afterthought that my sister offered to share with me, and by then she'd already picked out all her favorite parts.

A few months ago, I would have gladly accepted. Food converted to energy in the body and could increase the rate at which mana was generated, but at this point, it was such a comparatively minor boost that it meant nothing to me. Maybe if there'd been a slice of midnight mango I would have reconsidered, but there was nothing that mana dense anywhere near the village of Alkerist. The crops grown here were of the mundane variety with no special properties whatsoever. They were good for keeping a human from starving to death and not much else.

That was too bad, but it was also to be expected. With no ambient mana, of course nothing would grow that could do things like boost mana regeneration or increase focus. I supposed I could spend my own mana to cultivate such food, but it seemed rather futile at this stage. Perhaps when I reached the point where I had more mana than I knew what to do with, I'd reconsider. It might even draw some interest in the mystical arts out of my mother if she learned about the opportunities magical botany could provide.

I wondered if she might excel in the field of alchemy, were she relocated somewhere with abundant resources. I was starting to get the feeling that my parents were not well loved in this little community, and they might be receptive to relocating elsewhere if I could provide the means. Those were plans for a long ways down the road, however.

More immediately, I needed to learn what Noctra wanted with Father and whether I should start preparing countermeasures. For the moment, that meant a choice between hoarding mana in my core, or completing my crystal in the garden. It was so close to done that I wanted to rush back out there immediately after dinner to finish it up, but I restrained myself and dutifully joined my family in walking to the village square to do our nightly tithing.

Father was doing better with holding onto his mana, but in the end, the draw stone won. For as little mana as the villagers typically had, it would take less than a second to drain it all away. Having each person touch the draw stone for a full three seconds was massive overkill, but it wasn't like the mana drain part of the process was actually the bottleneck. Organization and keeping donors moving took far more time and effort than the actual tithing process itself.

Still, he managed to hold onto his mana for a full two of the three seconds. It was only at the end that his control slipped, and the draw stone claimed its prize. Mother, on the other hand, kept hers firmly under her control. She might not have Father's range at sensing it, but once I'd explained how to prevent the draw stone from affecting her, she'd managed to hang onto every last drop. Our garden was already starting to look a bit better, though in truth, the amount of mana she saved was miniscule. Prior to my intervention, she'd only ever given up three or four hours' worth of mana to begin with.

Senica, of course, lost all of her mana, and I gave away nothing. I affected the same wearied shuffle the other children performed when I ended my tithe, and together we returned to our small little one-room hut. Despite her tithe, Senica fairly skipped along.

Father, on the other hand, looked like a man marching to his death. Mother didn't look much happier. I expected this was not a story they'd planned to share with their children so soon, and Senica's attitude was not helping matters. She clearly thought she was getting an exciting new bedtime tale, when in actuality our parents would be picking the scab off of one of their deepest, most traumatic events.

"Story time!" Senica called out in a sing-song voice as soon as we returned home.

"Sweetie... you understand that this isn't a happy story?" Mother said. "It's not made up, either. This is a true story that ended with a little boy dying and our village being in great danger."

"Oh. What happened?" Senica asked, not in the least bit daunted by Mother's warning.

Before we could even get sat down, a voice came from outside our hut. "Sellis? You have a minute? It's Tsurai and Nianta."

Father visibly paled, so much so that even Senica caught on to it. "What's wrong?" she asked.

"Nothing, sweetness. Let me just go see what's going on, and I'll be right back."

I got a glimpse of the two people, one man and one woman, as Father pulled the curtain back from our entryway. Both were wearing Garrison uniforms. Both were armed with short swords similar to Karad's.

It looked like events had outpaced me, and I was nowhere near ready for this.

"What can I help you with?" Father said. I was sure he'd noted their grim expressions just as quickly as I had. We were in trouble.

CHAPTER

EIGHTEEN

Mages had a lot of tools, which could make it hard to know which one was best used to solve the problem at hand. There were a lot of factors to consider, too—things like who and what the target was, whether it mattered if anyone knew they'd used magic, and whether the environment could bear the weight of their spells. Conjuring up fire might be an excellent way to kill a troll, but not if it happened to be in a library the caster cared about preserving.

In my case, my primary concern was cost. I knew how to make the two Garrison members forget they'd ever been here, how to make them wander off in a daze, how to make the ground open up and swallow them whole, and a hundred other things that would make my immediate problem go away. However, I suspected that short of assassinating the governor himself, those would be temporary solutions at best and could very well end up making things worse.

I needed information before I made a choice. For all we knew, this might not be anything bad. It sure didn't seem likely, but the possibility remained. Maybe Father was just going to be told off for fighting and put on notice not to cause any further trouble. That was technically a possibility, however remote it might be.

"How you doing, Sellis? Back feeling better?" one of the Garrison members asked. Tsurai, I thought.

"It's fine. Little sore for a while, but Karad's a soft touch," Father lied.

Nianta snorted. "Don't let him hear you say that. He'll whip you extra hard next time." She paused, then added, "Not that there should be a next time."

"As long as Cherok isn't... himself... to my children, I won't have to punch him in the face," Father said.

"Tall order," Tsurai told him. "Look, everyone knows Cherok's an ass, and normally I'd say to just ignore him, but, well... Can't say that I'd have done it differently if he was being like that towards my boy, either."

"Yeah, but you'd still beat me with a cane if the order came down to," Father said.

"I would, but it wouldn't be anything personal."

"That'll take the sting out of it then," Father said dryly. "Probably wouldn't even feel it at all."

Things got awkward for a second there, but I didn't have it in me to feel much sympathy in my heart for the two Garrison members. I'd seen first-hand the kinds of tragedies people committed when they were "just following orders." The soldier's battle cry, there. All it took was a single monster wearing a man's skin to orchestrate atrocities that would make any demon cackle in glee.

Perhaps I was being unfair to those soldiers. I did not care. As a boy, I'd made arguments for soldiers who were just following orders. I'd believed that excuse. It was their job. They had to do it. Then I'd seen the aftermath of soldiers committing atrocities because someone told them to. Those excuses were small comfort to the broken men and women left behind. I knew that from personal experience.

I shook myself out of dark memories and refocused on the conversation in front of me. Next to me, Senica was watching with scared eyes. Mother was behind us both, silent and tense. We couldn't see Father or the two Garrison members through the curtain that served as our door, but it was easy to imagine Father's defiant posture in his words.

"Hah," Tsurai said. "Ahem. Anyway, Lord Noctra wants to talk to you, so we're here to escort you over to his manor."

"Ah. About what, if you don't mind me asking?"

"You think he'd tell us?" Nianta replied.

Father heaved a sigh. "No, no. Of course not. Alright, give me a minute."

He came back in through the curtain and looked at us. "Hopefully this won't take too long," he told Mother. "I'm sure it's nothing serious. I might not be back before you go to sleep."

I scrambled to my feet and raced across the hut to Mother's sewing kit. "Gravin? What are you doing?" Mother asked, surprise in her voice.

I ignored her as I snatched a button out of the kit. My mana was going to be stretched by this, but I was pretty sure I could make it work if I sacrificed a large chunk of the duration to cut down on cost. I debated on sacrificing other aspects, but decided it was better to have as much information as possible. Quickly, I wove a scry beacon spell into the button, one that would transmit both sight and sound back to me, then encased the enchantment in an aura of untraceability to ensure that Noctra wouldn't notice it.

"Here," I said, rushing back to Father and presenting him the button. "It's for good luck, so don't lose it."

"Good luck, huh?" Father asked as he accepted the button from me and slipped it into his pocket. "Don't worry, I'll take good care of it. I might just need all the luck I can get tonight."

While Mother gave me a shrewd look, she said nothing. Instead, she took my place and wrapped Father in a hug. "Be careful," she said. "Give Lord Noctra whatever he wants and come home safely."

"There are some things I can't give up," he told her, his voice soft. "You know that."

Then they split apart so that Father could give Senica a hug. "I promise I'll be back soon. There's no need to worry," he told her.

"Will you still tell me the story?" she asked.

Father laughed and said, "Sure. How could I not if you're going to be so persistent about it? Besides, I did promise."

Then he was out past the curtain and walking away, flanked on either side by a Garrison member. Mother watched him go from the doorway while Senica pushed a chair over to the window. I sat down on my pallet and started trying to recover my mana as quickly as possible. I was going to need it for this next spell. Scrying was quite expensive, after all.

The governor's manor was about a mile away from the center of town, so I expected I'd have at best half an hour to recover mana. Hopefully Father would be kept waiting for a bit once he got there, because I was going to need at least twice that long.

Technically, it was nearing our bedtimes when the two Garrison members had shown up. Senica had been about to get her good night story from Father before the interruption, and though the excitement had kept her eyes open at the time, now that Father was gone and there was nothing to do but wait, she quickly fell asleep. Once she was tucked in and snoring softly, Mother looked over at me and said, "Are you ready to talk about it?"

"Why don't we sit in the garden?" I offered. "It'll be nice and cool."

We relocated outside the hut and watched the sun dip behind the mountains beyond our village. After getting settled, I said, "To put it in layman's terms, I enchanted the button so that I could look through it with magic."

"To see and hear what your father is doing?" Mother asked.

"As long as he keeps it with him."

"Are you watching now?"

I shook my head. "Not enough mana. In another half an hour, I'll have enough to keep the spell going for about fifteen minutes. Then it'll just be checking in and hoping I don't miss anything important."

"Tell me what you find out," Mother said. She leaned back against the side of the hut and closed her eyes while I settled down on my incumbent mana crystal. I could have finished it first thing in the morning if not for this whole fiasco, but an empty mana crystal wouldn't help here and information about what exactly was going on just might.

"I can share the scry with you if you'd like," I offered her.

She cracked an eye open and peered at me. "You can? Wouldn't it cost more mana?"

I shook my head. "More complicated, but not more expensive."

Mother thought about that for a second before nodding. "I'd like to see, too."

"As soon as I'm ready to start," I promised.

Mana generation being the issue it was, I'd put some thought into the best ways to enhance it. My options were limited without ambient mana, but I could still manually replicate what a stage two core did naturally. It wouldn't be nearly as effective, but with every minute being important, I couldn't leave it on the table.

The difference between a dormant core and an ignited one was that dormant cores only produced mana at the point where they joined the Astral Realm to the physical body. Since there was no physical manifestation of a mana core, that meant the point was singular, somewhat like an island that connected to the mainland through a single bridge. All mana had to pass through that bridge.

Once a core ignited, mana could—and did—pass from any point. With so much more space available, it generated far faster. In stage two, a mage constructed a permanent lattice inside their core. There were a lot of different patterns, some of which worked significantly better than others. Differing schools had spent centuries arguing over which lattice structure would provide the best results, and some clans had their own family lattices that were closely guarded secrets.

This was the point where my advancement was going to differ significantly from my previous life. I'd grown up impoverished and with no one to advise me. Igniting my core had been an accident, and when it had come time for me to advance to stage two, I'd been largely on my own. My original lattice had been decidedly subpar, and some choices couldn't be taken back. Despite my best efforts to modify it as I grew stronger and wiser, there were limits to what I could do.

Now I had a blank slate, and I would construct the lattice I would have made back then if I'd known what I did now. My mana generation would be fifty times faster than a dormant core's, more than twice as fast as it was now. At stage two, my core would go from empty to full in under three hours.

For now, I needed to agitate my core manually with a specific technique I'd developed when experimenting with lattice designs. It allowed me to generate a sort of temporary lattice that required a great deal of mana and concentration to maintain, though if done properly, it would cause my core to generate mana as if it were stage two already.

It would also put a great deal of stress on my core, since it didn't actually have the lattice in place to reinforce it. Doing so for extended periods of time was an excellent way to cripple myself permanently, but for twenty minutes or so, I'd be fine.

I closed my eyes and concentrated on the pseudo-lattice. It formed slowly, each line painstakingly imagined in my core like a picture I was stenciling, just waiting for me to come back to fill in the real colors. My core reacted, and mana started to flood into me.

It was a strain, and I immediately revised my time frame. Perhaps I hadn't properly accounted for my relatively small core properly, but at the rate I was going, twenty minutes might be too long. I'd see where I was at with ten.

The mana poured in, swiftly at first, though a portion of that was immediately cycled into maintaining the lattice stencil. It was still almost twice as much mana as I could generate normally. By the time the ten-minute mark passed, I had enough to cast the scrying spell. With a pained groan, I let the stencil collapse. My poor, battered core almost seemed to throb, though of course such a thing wasn't actually possible.

I moved from my mana crystal to sit next to Mother. "Hold my hand," I said. "It's time."

Her fingers wrapped around mine, and I cast the spell that would scry upon my beacon.

CHAPTER

NINETEEN

Divination was a challenging field of magic. It wasn't just about casting the spell—there was also the result to consider. Good divination spells parsed the information in a way that allowed a mage to experience it the same way we did everything else: with our senses. But sometimes what we saw wasn't something that could be described using those senses, and that was when things got tricky.

Fortunately for me, in this moment, all I wanted to do was see and hear a place that I wasn't. That didn't mean things were easy. I still had to translate the information my mana was sending directly into my mind, but I was more than up to the task. If Father ever truly became my apprentice, though, we would not be starting with a spell anywhere near as demanding as this one.

The vision took shape in my mind, one that I shared to Mother. Father stood in a room looking through a glass window at the mountains east of the village. There was a long wooden table behind him, the kind that could hold ten people at a time with plenty of elbow room, and the walls had wood paneling. There was even a door barring the exit. Considering that all of the huts in the village were made primarily of some sort of clay block that had been fired like pottery and sealed together with a type of mud-based mortar, the presence of so much wood in one place seemed like an obscene display to me.

Two other people were there, both in Garrison uniforms. Neither was speaking, but I thought I recognized Tsurai and Nianta. What I didn't see was the man who'd dragged Father out of town to question him. Typical nobility tactic, keeping someone waiting after summoning them. I recalled a few nobles trying to pull that on me early on in my career as a mage. I'd quickly developed a reputation for breaking things if I got bored. After the third noble tried to take me to task for that, the rest got the message, in smoke signals, if nothing else.

Good times.

Father wasn't quite to the point in his own magical career where he could commit arson to teach someone a lesson, so he occupied his time taking in the view. They were pretty enough mountains, I supposed, but I'd seen them literally every single day of my new life, and they'd lost a lot of their punch to me. Maybe that was just my fault. Compared to the vistas I was used to, the mountain range my village was tucked into just felt rather brown and plain.

Of more interest to me was the room Father was in, but since the man of the hour hadn't arrived yet, I decided to cut the spell short. It was too mana hungry to just look over Father's shoulders while he stared out the window. I'd check back in every few minutes and hope that by the time Noctra did show up, I hadn't missed anything important.

"What happened?" Mother asked.

"The spell costs a lot of mana to maintain. I'll check again in a few minutes to see if anything is happening. We'll probably miss a bit of the conversation, but it's better than burning through all of my mana while Father stares out a window. Then we'd miss everything."

That explanation must have satisfied her, because all she said was, "At least we know he's still alright." Then she sunk back into silence while still holding my hand.

I gave it five minutes to regenerate what little mana I could and told her, "I'm going to check again."

This time, Father had moved from the window to the table, though he hadn't sat down. Instead, he was examining the chairs. We had wooden chairs too, but ours were plain, rough-hewn things that had been sanded more by countless butts rubbed across them than by any carpenter's tools. The abode of Lord Noctra could abide no such crudeness. His chairs were finished, smooth and richly stained, though unless I missed my guess, also quite old and beginning to show signs of wear.

Even being rich was relative, and while I couldn't think of a single nobleman who would proudly display a seat that looked quite so old and shabby, it was still a dazzling display of wealth here. Father didn't look impressed, though. If anything, he looked a little bit sad.

"I don't suppose you know how much longer Lord Noctra will be," Father said with a sigh.

"Sorry," the Garrison guard said. I recognized the voice as Nianta. That would make the other one Tsurai, both faces I'd seen but never been introduced to.

"No need to worry," a new voice said as the door opened between the two guards. A tall man strode through, dressed in what I assumed passed for finery around here. He had long, wavy hair streaked with gray and tied back behind his head to keep it off his face, which was clean-shaven. My scrying spell wasn't powerful enough to report back on mana emanations, but I'd be willing to bet at least one of the three rings he wore was enchanted, and there was no mistaking the wand on a leg holster as anything else.

Idly, I wondered if I'd given his fire blast too much credit. If that had been done with the aid of a wand, Noctra was even weaker than I'd thought. Objectively speaking, that was a good thing for me at least, if not the rest of the village. As the only mage around these parts, he was undoubtedly my biggest threat. He was the reason I was considering making my mana crystal portable, after all. I would have to do it eventually anyway, but ideally, I'd reach stage two before I invested the mana into that project. But with Noctra walking around, having full access to my stored mana at all times became a lot more important.

Of course, if he was really that weak... Well, I'd have a better idea once I was able to get a full measure of the man. That wouldn't happen until I saw him in person, which couldn't happen until I'd grown enough to be able to shield my mana core from casual inspection. It was more important to hide my presence than it was to gauge his abilities right now. Weak he might be, but he was still a fully grown adult, which meant his core by default was many times larger than mine. Somehow, I doubted he was giving all of *his* mana to a draw stone each evening. Or any of it.

"Lord Noctra," Father said, just as polite as he could be.

"Sellis," Noctra said, perhaps a bit more warmly than the situation warranted.

"Oh, he wants something," Mother murmured next to me.

"Mmhmm."

"Come, join me," Noctra told my father as he pulled out a chair and gestured to the one just opposite of it. As he sat down, he said to the two Garrison members at the door, "You're dismissed, thank you."

"Yes, my lord," both said in unison before leaving the room.

Father sat down and said, "Thank you, my lord."

Noctra laughed, not that anyone had said or done anything to laugh at. "You can let your guard down. I'm not going to attack you. I just wanted to get a chance to talk to you."

"What are we talking about?" Father asked.

"Specifically, I wanted to talk about your relationship with Lord Emeto."

"Ah, that. That ended a long time ago."

"Yes, I'm sure the old man's death put a bit of a damper on the whole thing," Noctra agreed.

Father winced, and I couldn't help but agree. I didn't know much about Lord Emeto, but even I could tell the tactless comment had struck a nerve. Mother let out a low, wordless growl next to me, one that I didn't think she was even aware of.

"Something like that," Father said. "Is there something you wanted to know?"

"He was teaching you magic," Noctra said. "Most anyone over the age of thirty in the village knows that. The details of your, ah, shall we say your *accident*, are well-known. What I do not know is what exactly my predecessor was teaching you, and how much you still retain."

"Not much, I'm sorry to say. You know that I can sense mana, yes? It was common knowledge then, and I was so stupidly, foolishly proud of it. I'm afraid I bragged quite shamelessly as a boy. But I was never blessed by the spirits, so you can see it never went anywhere."

"I would say that's more because Emeto died first. Otherwise, you would likely have become an adept," Noctra said.

He was watching Father carefully for a reaction, but whatever he hoped to see, it wasn't there. "I'm afraid I don't know what that is. I'm not saying that you're wrong, but if that was Lord Emeto's intention, he never shared it with me," Father said. "Perhaps he would have, one day, had things been different."

"What's an adept?" Mother asked me.

"Person who knows how to cast spells but doesn't have an ignited core," I said absently while I studied the scene my scry beacon was relaying to me. Noctra wanted something from Father, and I wasn't sure what. Maybe I was missing some context, but it seemed like the governor was taking his time leading up to it.

"You currently work in the fields," Noctra said. "Your talents with mana are being wasted. And I have the results of your family's Testing written down right here."

Noctra brandished a slip of parchment he pulled from a pocket. He unfolded it and slid it over for Father to see. He read it with a blank look on his face, then glanced up at the governor. "Again, I don't know what these numbers mean."

This time, I was with Father. I didn't know what kind of scale they were using, but it wasn't one I was familiar with. I could extrapolate based on my own score, a mere three. Father had scored a twenty-seven, Mother a twenty, and Senica a one. We could thank Cherok for that particular number.

"The average adult in Alkerist scores a twenty," Noctra explained. "Your wife, for example, hits that mark perfectly. You, however, are seven points higher."

That surprised me a bit, considering I'd also doctored Mother's test. She should have scored a bit higher than average, but when I thought about how much effort she put into the garden, maybe I should have expected it. Even knowing we had a Testing that night, Mother didn't have it in her to take it easy.

"I don't know what to say, Lord Noctra," Father said.

"You don't have to say anything yet. I'm not finished." Noctra pulled out another sheet of paper. "These are the results of the Testings of everyone else you share a draw stone with. Now, I know that people take it easy on Testing day and that their scores are always a bit inflated. But I've been here for over a decade, and I also know what the margins look like."

Oh no. I did not like where this was going. Judging by how hard Mother was squeezing my hand now, she'd figured it out, too.

"More importantly, I have the results of every previous Testing you've done. You understand what that means, Sellis?" Noctra asked.

Father wasn't stupid. He knew our tampering had been noticed. I couldn't imagine Noctra had correctly deduced what was going on, but more than a few people had been executed by government officials who knew they'd done *something* wrong, even if they didn't have the specifics of it. I started doing the math in my head for how long it would take to completely fill my core and how much mana I would need to break Father out of a prison.

"What are you implying, sir?"

"You, my friend, have been deliberately underperforming all this time," Noctra said. "I had your group's draw stone brought to me and personally analyzed how much mana was in it. Something has changed. I suspect Cherok's interference caused you to miscalculate."

The governor leaned forward and reached into his pocket again. He pulled out a familiar little device, now dull and empty, and placed it between the two of them. "You're already an adept. You always have been," the governor accused my father. "That's how you knew how to shave off some of the mana built up in this Testing implement to fluff your own results."

CHAPTER

TWENTY

Of all the things Father could do, I thought that bursting out laughing was probably the last thing Noctra expected. The governor did not look as amused, and Father's laugh died into an awkward cough.

Next to me, Mother said through gritted teeth, "Do not antagonize him, you idiot."

"I still don't even know what an adept is, Lord Noctra," he said. "Perhaps if you explain it to me, I can give you a proper answer."

"Why are you insisting on this charade?" Noctra asked. "Sellis, the evidence is obvious. But you're not in trouble. I simply want to put your talents to good use instead of wasting them doing field work."

"I hardly think my time has been wasted," Father said. "My work helps keep the village from starving."

"Oh no, I'm not trying to belittle your efforts. I'm simply stating that we have plenty of people capable of tilling a field. They may not do it as quickly or efficiently as you, but the job will get done. But do you know how many adepts I have in my employ?"

"I don't know what an adept is," Father said, exasperation leaking into his tone.

This conversation needed to hurry up. I had enough mana to hold the scrying spell for another ten minutes, maybe a bit less. I had been hoping to get a look around the manor as Father walked through it, but he'd been dumped in a room and left to wait. Noctra wasn't going out of his way to inform Father of any plans he might have, either, which meant that, so far, this whole exercise had been a waste of time and mana. I hadn't learned anything Father couldn't have just told me when he got back.

"It's a step below mage, someone who can work with mana well enough to cast spells without being a full mage. In this entire village, there is only one single adept, and she came with me from Derro when I first moved here."

"You think I can cast spells?" Father asked, his eyebrows shooting up. "That'd be pretty impressive of me."

"If you can't, it's only because you haven't had a master to show you how, not because your mana-controlling skills aren't up to the task."

"He's actually not wrong about that," I told Mother. "Father is ready to learn some novice-tier spells. I was just waiting until we ignited his core so he'd have the mana to practice with."

Father smiled and shook his head. "While I appreciate how much confidence you have in my abilities, Lord Emeto died fifteen years ago. I promise you his spirit did not visit me from beyond the grave to give me lessons, and nobody else wanted anything to do with me for a long time. It wasn't until a year after you arrived that I stopped being shunned in public, and there are still plenty of people who hate me for being the reason we need to tithe mana to the draw stones every night."

Noctra picked up the emitter and held it up to Father. "How else do you explain this, then?"

"The Testing Implement? I don't know much about them, to be honest with you. All I did was touch it and send my mana in when the Collector told me to."

I had to give it to Father. As far as I could tell, he hadn't told a single lie so far. While I doubted he was being targeted by any sort of truth-seeking spell, the possibility did exist and, if that did turn out to be the case, Father was avoiding telling an outright lie quite cleverly.

Once more I wished I'd had the resources to perform a scry that included the ability to sense mana. I'd have to question Father very carefully when he returned to see if I could learn anything. His mana sense was unrefined, but it was better than nothing.

Noctra sank back into his seat and paused to think things over. "Even if the implement is a coincidence, I've done some research on you, Sellis," he said. "Your talents are too rare to be ignored. If anything, this is my fault for forgetting about you years ago. When I first got here, everything was such a mess that it took years to get caught up. I didn't even connect you with that boy I'd made a note to look into further once I had time a decade ago when you were punished for that attack on the school teacher.

"If that hadn't happened at the same time I was reviewing the Testing implements, I probably still would have missed it. For that, I owe you an apology. Your adult life should have been very different. Adepts are rare, and I should have organized the ritual to seek a blessing from the spirits years ago on your behalf."

"That's..." Father trailed off. Finally, he said, "I don't regret my life, Lord Noctra. I wish things had turned out differently when I was a boy, that my best friend was still alive. And yes, things were bad for a few years there, but I love my wife and my children, and they love me."

"Yes, I am aware. You love your children so much you're willing to take a few lashes to punch out a man who treated your daughter unfairly."

"So you agree that Cherok was out of line?" Father said.

"Of course I do," Noctra said with a snort. "He is hiding behind a technicality to justify his behavior. That's not to say I agree with what you did either, but I understand why you hit him."

"Well... let's just put it behind us. Hopefully, Cherok will stop trying to bully children in the future."

"Hmm, yes. That is something else I'm looking into right now, but it's not relevant to this conversation. Sellis, I need two things from you. First, I need you to stop cheating with your tithes. Believe it or not, we really do need every bit of mana we can get. Second, I need you to seriously consider coming to work for me directly as an adept."

"What kind of work would I be doing?"

"Very little, to begin with," Noctra said. "I would need to teach you a few spells first, but once you're ready, you would help ease my poor assistant's workload. Adepts don't generate the mana needed to cast spells, but they can use it if they get it somewhere else. You would probably start with operating the apparatus that pulls mana from the draw stones, which is an easy—if somewhat boring—task. From there, well, it depends where your talents lie."

"Would it be anything dangerous?" Father asked.

"No, no, of course not. I would never ask you to go face a monster or anything like that. That's my job."

"What's going on here?" Mother said. "Is Lord Noctra really just offering him a job? Why send Garrison members to drag him over there?"

I didn't reply, but I agreed with Mother. Noctra wanted something more than what he was saying. I just wasn't sure what. From a purely selfish perspective, it would be best for me if Father rejected the offer. I could train him far better than some mage born and raised in a land that had never had a whiff of mana in the air anyway, and the last thing I needed was people who could actually sense mana coming around before I was ready for them.

"It sounds like a great offer, Lord Noctra," Father said. "Would it be alright if I spoke to my wife about this first, though? It isn't something I should just rush into on my own, you know?"

Noctra sighed and said, "Are you sure? I would have thought this would be an easy decision for you."

"If I were a single man with no children, I'd have already agreed. I've always loved mana. But this job, well, that's a pretty big change. Xilaya will want to know what's being offered before we just agree."

"I see. Well then, if you're sure, you're sure." Noctra reached down and pulled the wand free of its leg holster.

It was a simple design, just a length of polished wood capped with a metal clip that held a chip of mana crystal. I knew better than anyone that size wasn't everything, but I had trouble imagining that tiny little fragment of crystal did all that much.

"*Nema somno, diadro almus tisago*," Noctra said softly. Father jerked back, but not quickly enough to avoid being tapped by the wand.

I couldn't see the mana, but I recognized those words. "A sleeping spell," I said before Mother could ask. Fortunately for us, the scry spell was linked to the beacon in Father's pocket and wasn't affected by his physical state.

That spell told me a few things. Noctra wasn't skilled enough to cast even basic spells without a verbal incantation to help him control his mana. The fact that he relied on a wand for such a weak spell was also telling. Finally, while that spell technically worked, it really was a roundabout and sloppy way to do it. A simple restructuring of the runes he'd named would have increased its efficiency, and three of those runes could have been replaced with a single, stronger one to lessen the mana cost significantly.

All of that told me that Noctra was not well educated and not that strong. Probably. It was possible this was a one-off spell that he was particularly bad at, and he'd show far more skill with other enchantments. It was also possible that his specialty lay in another discipline. I couldn't underestimate the man just because he'd cast a single sloppy spell.

The door opened and a woman walked in. My first impression was that she was quite tall, though given my relative stature, that was an impression I got from just about everyone these days. She had a severe frown, a scar running down the left side of her face that just missed her eye, and short-cut brown hair.

"That could have gone better for you," the woman said.

"Who's that?" I asked Mother. I'd never seen her, and though I didn't know everybody's name, I'd thought I'd at least seen all the faces in the village.

"Iskara," Mother said. "Lord Noctra's assistant. She arrived with him years ago."

That must be the other adept then. No real mana generation to speak of, but she could have a variety of spells available to her as long as she had a source of external mana to tap into. Depending on what spells she knew and how skilled she was at using them, she might end up being even more dangerous than Noctra.

"These damn peasants never do want to cooperate," Noctra muttered.

"You're sure he's an adept?" Iskara asked.

"As sure as I can be about such things."

"If you're wrong, the cabal is going to add the mana costs to your debt. You know that, right?"

"You don't need to tell me that, Perfidy."

The woman's lips curled up into a grim smile. "I do so love the old names. Don't you, Nocturne?" She said the name with a twist.

Noctra grimaced. "Someday, I'll earn the right to be called that back again."

"Someday," she agreed. "Maybe even quite soon, if you're right about him. What are you going to do?"

"Why, so you can report it all back to Sibilant?"

Iskara shrugged and smiled again.

"I'll do some more tests before I ship him out. I don't need another two years added to my time out here tending this backwater mana farm."

"You've grown so cautious in the last few years," Iskara said. "Be careful, or the cabal might mistake it for cowardice. That's no way for a mage to behave."

"Enough, Perfidy. If you're just here to heckle me, save both of us some time and go away. Or even better, make yourself useful and send in that Garrison idiot I've got total subjugation over. The big one, what was his name?"

"The one with the notch missing in his ear?"

"That's the one," Noctra said with a nod. "I'll have some work for him later."

Iskara left and Noctra stared at Father's comatose form, a pensive look on his face and his wand nervously tapping against his arm. A minute later, the door opened, and a man dressed in Garrison leathers entered.

Noctra started to speak, but at that moment, my mana ran dry and the scrying spell died. Mother jerked next to me and said, "Bring it back! We need to know what they're doing."

"I can't," I said. "I'm tapped out."

"No. No, no, no. What can we do?"

"Nothing for the moment," I said. "That doesn't mean we won't do anything at all, just that I need time to prepare."

"How much time could your father possibly have?"

"I don't know," I said. "I guess we'd better not waste it."

CHAPTER
TWENTY-ONE

I wasn't ready for this, not yet. I could maybe face Noctra next week if I caught him by surprise out in the open without any protections. But I needed to finish my mana crystal and start filling it up before I had enough available mana to cast anything powerful enough to strike a mage down from beyond seeing range.

If the problem was that I didn't have enough mana, there was a solution. I'd written it off the first time I'd considered it because it would draw all sorts of attention and it wouldn't have made a difference, but now I was a day's time from completing my mana crystal. Then I could start filling it. It would still cause problems, but keeping Noctra from doing whatever he was going to do with my father took priority. I'd deal with the fallout later.

"We need the draw stones," I said as I stood up. "I'll take the mana from them to complete my mana crystal."

"What good will that do?" Mother asked, her voice bordering on hysterical.

"The first thing I'll do is shrink it to the size of a marble. Then I'll tap every draw stone this village has to fill it to the limit and take it with me to Noctra's manor. I think I ought to be able to take him with a full crystal to work with."

"You can't!" Mother protested. "What about the barrier?"

"There is no barrier," I said bluntly. "Noctra has been lying to everyone for years. Maybe there used to be one, but it's not there anymore. That mana's being used for something else, something he's keeping hidden from the village."

Mother thought about it for a second, then gave a decisive nod. "We'll need to wait an hour or two for it to get dark," she said. "Do you have something for getting through the door?"

A phantasmal step spell would be the most straightforward solution. It would allow me to just walk through walls or doors, but it was also expensive enough that it would take my entire core's mana to use. I could do it, once. Getting back out would be a different story.

It was riskier to go through the door directly, but far cheaper to use an unlock spell to get through. As long as no one saw me do it, I could be in and out easily enough. The concern there was that doorways were natural places to put wards or other defenses, and while I'd never noticed any on the Collectors' office, I'd also never been within thirty feet of the door. Some spells were small enough or hidden well enough to require close inspection to find, and wards were a prime example.

I could break any ward that might exist in a place like this, but only if I had enough mana in my core. Right now, I was as dry as I could possibly get. If I waited three hours, I'd have about half of my maximum. I didn't want to wait, but it wasn't like I could just walk up to the door in the evening while people were still out and about and force my way in.

"Depends on the defenses, but I should be able to. The lock won't be a problem. If they have magic, it'll get complicated. I can do it as long as I have enough mana."

The Collectors brought out four draw stones every evening. Presumably they had at least eight, since we never missed a day even though the ones they were using had to be sent to the manor to have their contents harvested. Noctra had said his assistant took care of that, and I'd never seen the woman before, so she probably didn't come into town too often. Unless she snuck into the office in the middle of the night to collect the mana and then left as soon as she was done, there should be more than four stones.

If I was unlucky, they'd all be fresh stones with no mana to steal. There was nothing I could do about that except get in there and find out. I'd be out the mana I used on the unlock spell, but that wouldn't set me back too much. If the plan failed, I'd switch from assault to rescue. It would be easy to scry on Father as long as he still had the button, but not impossible without it. One way or another, I could locate him.

There was no point in getting ahead of myself. I knew almost nothing about what kind of defenses Noctra would have set up. Wards were almost a certainty, but he might have mechanical traps as well. From the sounds of it, he'd worked some sort of subjugation magic on at least a few of the Garrison people, though not all of them. That meant I could expect guards that would assist him if it came to open combat.

Beyond that, there could be anything there. I knew I was dealing with at least one mage, but if this other woman, Iskara or Perfidy or whatever her real name was, was an adept and had her own mana crystal, she might as well be a mage, too. I'd be outnumbered and undersupplied for a fight against both of them at once.

But if I looted the draw stones, I needed to be prepared to take out Noctra in the same night. Once that got back to him, he'd tear the village apart looking for whoever had done it. My family was already high-profile to him now; we'd be the first people he'd investigate. I could hide myself from him, but the cost was so great I might as well just leave the village completely.

And I was going to loot the draw stones. Short of walking around mana draining people in their homes in the middle of the night, I didn't see another choice. Maybe if I went to the manor, I might find something I could drain in there, but that would leave me at Noctra's mercy if he caught me. Plus I knew where the draw stones were; the same could not be said about a theoretical mana storage crystal located in the home of the most dangerous person in the village.

"What can I do to help?" Mother asked.

I hesitated to answer that. There were plenty of things she could do—in theory. Breaking in and getting the draw stones to bring to me would help, for example. I just wasn't sure if she could actually do that. There was one useful thing she could do that posed no risk, if she was willing.

"Focus on generating as much mana as you can," I said. "I'll do the same. As soon as it's fully dark, I'll mana drain you and then go for the draw stones."

"What are you going to do about the Collectors?" she asked.

"Hopefully, not run into them."

"What if they're still awake?"

I paused. "Why would that matter? Wait, do they live in that building?"

Mother nodded slowly and I groaned. That was going to make things more difficult if they were awake. If it was just one or two, I could put them to sleep using my own version of the spell Noctra had used on Father. It was far more efficient, but I didn't have enough mana to cast it on too many targets. Besides, the whole point of going there was to get more mana, not waste what I already had.

I could probably pull off a shadow cloak spell, depending on my mana levels. It wasn't as good as true invisibility, but it might as well be in the dark. As long as they didn't shine a lantern on me, it was a last resort hiding spell.

The Collector's headquarters was the same problem as Noctra's manor. I just didn't know enough and didn't have the mana to fix that problem. I would be taking risks either way, but I lacked the ability to mitigate those risks right now. If only I'd had another month or two to finish my work, this would have been much easier.

But that wasn't the world I was living in. This was the best path to saving my father, perhaps the only path with any real chance of succeeding. My body was three years old. Magic was my only advantage, and without mana, I had no magic. I just hoped I could get enough mana from the draw stones to overcome my handicaps.

"Will you check on your father again before you go?" Mother asked.

I hesitated to say yes. I wanted to, of course, but I would need to scry him again later to confirm his location. Checking on him now wouldn't change anything except to leave me with one fewer spells I could cast later.

Slowly, I shook my head. "I can't waste the mana, and I should concentrate on generating as much as I can now."

Mother sat silently next to me, her hand still on mine, and we both did our best to prepare for the night to come.

It was close to midnight now. My core was just under half full, enough for three or four small spells. I studied Mother's core, then sighed and shook my head. Even if I took every last bit of mana, it wouldn't cover the cost of the spell. I'd been hoping, and it was close, but just not quite enough.

"I'll be fine with what I have," I said.

123

"Do you want me to walk with you?" she asked.

I shook my head. It would be more suspicious if anyone saw me walking alone, but once I was there, it would cost me extra mana if I had to hide both of us. Since there was nothing she could do but physically carry the draw stones away, and I wasn't planning on actually moving them anyway, it was best if I went alone.

"Stay here with Senica," I said. "Our family is already in enough trouble without risking you getting caught trespassing too. I'm a precocious child. If anyone spots me, I was just wandering around and it's not my fault they left the doors unlocked. If you get caught there..."

"You're not that precocious," Mother said dryly. "And I don't think Lord Noctra is going to believe it anyway, not with this obsession he's developed with your father."

"No, probably not, but it's not likely to be him that catches me tonight. If I do get caught, I'll just have to move onto the next step with a little bit less mana than I'd hoped to have." Mother had no response to that. After a moment's pause, I stood up and said, "I'll be back in twenty minutes, as long as nothing goes wrong. Maybe thirty if I have to dodge some Collector who's up late."

"Be careful, Gravin."

"I will," I promised.

"There are eight Collectors," Mother said. "Ayaka is the only one who might help you. If you get into trouble, try to talk to her. Explain what happened to your father. She's an old friend from when we were kids. If we're lucky, she'll choose us over Lord Noctra."

"You don't think she would?" I asked, surprised.

"I don't know," Mother said. "I hope so, but you never truly know how strong a friendship is until you put it to the test. It wouldn't be the first time that bond failed."

"More of your mysterious past," I murmured. "You really do need to tell me the full story when this is all over."

"Maybe once your father gets back. It's more his story than anyone else's."

I wondered if Mother realized that I'd be killing Noctra in the process, possibly Iskara as well. She wasn't stupid; she had to have known. But if so, she'd never mentioned it once.

"Be careful," she said again.

With a nod, I set off into the night.

CHAPTER
TWENTY-TWO

The village didn't really have a problem with theft despite the fact that none of the homes even had doors, let alone locks. One part was that people just didn't have much worth stealing, but another part was that the population was so small. Everyone knew everyone, and if someone did steal a bracelet or a shirt or a garden spade, they were going to get caught immediately.

I was sure there were people who would steal just for the thrill of it, but it hadn't been an issue in the last nine months or so. Or, if it had, I hadn't been made aware of it. Regardless, theft wasn't really a problem. People had no need to lock things up, or even to have locks in general.

The Collectors' headquarters was an exception to that rule. It was made of the same mud bricks as every other hut in the village, but its windows had locking shutters and the entryways both had actual wooden doors on them with real locks. I spared a moment to wonder if the village blacksmith had made them; I'd never seen him produce anything more than farming tools, and most of that work was repair jobs. The village had a serious lack of raw metal to work with.

There were two moons out tonight, luckily both small ones. Tuamar the purple moon and Lasrin the red hung in the sky, casting the world into shadows that I moved through. No curtains stirred in the huts around me as

I walked by, and my steps were silent. I was constantly scanning for movement, but came up empty. Perfect.

It took less than ten minutes to make it to the village square, largely because without Senica along to drag her feet the whole way, I was able to move at full speed. I approached the Collectors' headquarters cautiously, wary of any ward lines I might cross. I was confident there weren't any, but it would be foolish not to check, so I took half a minute to confirm there was nothing on the door or hidden behind it.

Most of my confidence stemmed from the fact that while wards themselves might be difficult to see, I would have known instantly if there was a ward stone in the building to power them. At least, I would know if it was active and full of mana. Ward stones weren't necessary to set up a ward, but it wouldn't last very long off just the mana invested in it by a single mage. Considering how starved for mana the whole village was, I doubted Noctra was going to spare some for anywhere but his own manor.

But on the off chance that he was inclined to do that, I couldn't think of a place more likely to be protected than right here. This was where all the mana he stole from the village was stored until he could take direct control of it, after all. Worse, it was all locked into a draw stone, where it could be taken by literally anybody who could lift more than fifteen or twenty pounds. Even if they couldn't get the mana back out, it would be just as lost to Noctra.

My suspicions were misplaced. There was no ward, not outside the door and not behind it. Noctra either didn't think his draw stones were worth protecting in such a manner, or he was just too mana-poor to do even basic alarm wards. Or maybe he didn't know how. I had seen no actual evidence of any wards anywhere in the village, not even the supposed barrier that protected us all from monsters.

I couldn't afford to assume there wouldn't be any defenses ahead of me just because I hadn't seen them yet. It was imperative that my theft of mana from the draw stones go undiscovered until at least tomorrow. Tonight, I'd complete my mana crystal and start filling it. Then just before dawn, I'd break into the manor and find Father. All of this assumed that the draw stones weren't empty.

My unlock spell took a few seconds to finish analyzing the lock and manipulate it into opening, but then I was through. I closed the door silently behind me, but left it unlocked. If I was lucky, I'd be making at least two more trips before my mana crystal was portable and I could finish draining the entire stash, and there was no point in wasting mana on repeatedly unlocking a door. It wasn't like anyone was awake to check on it anyway. At least, I hoped not.

The inside of the building was significantly darker than the outside, illuminated only by the thin strips of magenta moonlight coming in around the outside edges of the shutters. The first thing I saw was the familiar four tables up against a wall to my right, two on the floor and two flipped upside-down to sit on top of them. The chairs were missing, but I spotted them a moment later on the far side of the room as part of a mismatched collection surrounding a dinner table, one which still had dirty plates and what passed for silverware sitting on it.

Apparently, tidiness wasn't a prerequisite to join the Collectors. Hopefully their draw stones were better organized and maintained.

An open doorway behind the table led to a kitchen, which had a back door and no other exits. It was hard to tell with just the slivers of moonlight to illuminate the place, but I thought the kitchen wasn't in much better shape than their dining room was.

Another doorway led to a simple office where the paperwork the Collectors filled out every evening was stored. It had a single desk flanked by shelves on either side, and the chair for it was missing. I glanced back at the table with its mismatched set and shook my head with a smile.

The only other exit from the front room was a hall leading off to the right. It had entryways with curtains hanging from them every ten feet or so on either side of the room, eight in total. These then would be the bedrooms for the Collectors, and the place I was most likely to be caught despite being the darkest part of the building. I paused at the front of the hall to listen.

Soft snores came from behind the curtain to my left. That was one Collector accounted for, seven more to go. I assumed they were all in their rooms, but that wasn't necessarily true. Worse, I could see candlelight coming from underneath the curtain on the third room on the right. One of them could have fallen asleep without extinguishing the candle, but it was just as likely someone was awake in there.

My target was the door at the end of the hall, and it *was* a door, unlike all the privacy curtains. I could barely see it in the dark, but I was willing to bet it had its own lock. Perhaps I could save myself some mana and swipe a key from one of the Collectors, but that meant spending time trying to find it and the risk of waking up whoever was in the room I ended up searching.

I was getting ahead of myself. Maybe the door wouldn't be locked. Before I could find out, I needed to get down the hallway undetected. I moved forward slowly, ears straining to listen for noise. Since this was among the most dangerous parts of my attempted burgling, I even spent a bit of mana to use a sense-sharpening invocation for a few seconds.

As I'd expected, that third room on the right was the problem. There were two people inside, arguing softly, and I couldn't help but laugh to myself when I heard the subject.

"Look," a man said. I thought I recognized the voice as the Collector who oversaw the table just next to the one my family was assigned to. "It's your week to clean the dishes. That means getting the water, too. Just because Tsurai is sweet on you and normally brings it over doesn't mean you get to skip your chores when he's too busy."

"I'll get it done tomorrow," the other Collector snapped. That voice I couldn't place; she was probably one of the Collectors who did Testings and the like.

"You say that, but every time your turn comes up, it's always excuses until Dracken gets sick of looking at it and does it for you."

Roommate problems. A tale as old as time. I remembered back when I was fourteen, just before my core had ignited, I'd had similar fights with the two other kids I was living with. None of us were interested in cleaning anything, and in all fairness, we had very little worth the effort. Our home had been a rundown old shop that had been abandoned for decades. We were just the latest in a long string of squatters hiding from the Sentinels there.

This plan was a bust if I had two Collectors up and moving around. It looked like I was going to have to spend some mana on a pair of sleep spells after all. My core was barely full enough to manage it, and if any other problem cropped up that required magic to overcome, I was going to be screwed. At the same time, I couldn't hide in the building for hours and hope that these two night owls would go to bed.

There was a third option that would only cost me half the mana, but it did leave me open to considerably more risk. I could cast an aura of silence around myself that would prevent any sound I made from traveling more than a foot away from me. With that active, I could walk by the curtain and into the draw stone room and, as long as nobody looked out into the hallway, remain completely undetected.

It would get me access to the draw stones, but I'd need to use it again when I left. It'd still be slightly cheaper than a pair of sleep spells, and it would have the advantage of not giving away that there was somebody in the village who was capable of casting intermediate level enchantments. But if I had to make multiple trips and the two Collectors were still awake when I came back, it would be a net negative on the total amount of mana I harvested.

On the other hand, if the draw stones were empty, I would only be wasting half as much mana to find out since I could simply continue to channel the aura of silence spell and walk right back out. Using aura of silence to sneak past them when I knew I'd have to come back through here several more times was ultimately a losing strategy that only won out if there were wards on the door or if the draw stones were empty. If I didn't come away from this with more mana than when I started, it was all pointless, and Father was likely doomed.

Noctra needed to touch someone to cast his inferior version of a sleep spell, and he needed to verbally chant the runes that went into constructing it. I needed to do neither. All I required was a visible target, and even that could be accomplished through divination magic. But why waste the mana when I could simply pull the curtain aside far enough to peer into the room?

"What the—" one of the Collectors started to say when he saw my eye looking at him. He made it halfway out of his sitting position before collapsing back onto the bed and flopping over.

The other one, the woman, had just enough time to look surprised and turn to face the doorway fully before I finished casting the second sleep spell. I winced when she dropped straight down to the floor, but she'd probably be fine. Based on the awkward position she'd fallen in, I expected her back would be killing her after she woke up. Oops.

With that obstacle taken care of, it was time to find out whether this whole venture was worth it. I crept past the last two rooms and stopped in front of the door at the end of the hallway.

CHAPTER

TWENTY-THREE

F irst things first, I checked for more wards. It wouldn't do to get caught in here after all that. It only took a few moments, and I was sure that opening the door wouldn't trigger any sort of alarms. The most common place to put such a trigger was a sort of trip line behind the door that would be broken by the very motion of the door itself. It was a weak but efficient style of warding, not good for preventing anyone from gaining entry, but excellent for letting someone else know.

This door didn't have anything like that on it.

My hand hovered an inch over the door handle, but I didn't grab hold of it. There were no magical wards, but what about mechanical traps? It would have to be something easily disarmed so that the Collectors could go in and out, if it existed at all. Or it would have to be something magical, keyed specifically to them as individuals or to a token they'd carry with them. If it was magical, though, I'd be able to sense it.

I focused all my attention on that handle as I examined it. Traps were by their very nature designed to be hidden, even more so than normal wards. There could be one on the door, just waiting for someone to touch it in order to activate. I could practically feel the mana hidden in the spell, tingling just below my fingers.

Was there something there, or was my imagination getting the better of me? I was right outside the door of a storage room holding the most valuable thing in the village, and so far, the only defense had been a simple lock on a wooden door that wouldn't have kept out a determined thief willing to put a bit of muscle into breaking in. That couldn't possibly be the only defense Noctra had for his draw stones.

Some wards were designed to go off without the person who'd tripped them realizing it, but I was confident that even if I'd stumbled over such a ward, I would have felt the magic activate. It was far easier to feel active mana than it was to detect dormant wards. So, if there were going to be any defenses, then by process of elimination, this was the last reasonable spot to place them.

I hadn't seen anything in my initial sweep, but I was still hesitant to touch the door. My fingers brushed the door handle, ever so gently, and then I felt it. Hidden away, waiting for someone to wrap their hands around the handle and turn it, was the trap. Turning the handle was the trigger, so as long as I didn't do that, I was safe.

Now that I had a physical connection, I could see it clearly. It was surprisingly advanced compared to everything else I'd seen from Noctra. It seemed like most of his magic fell into the novice or basic categories, but this trap was at least of intermediate difficulty. It was subtle, too, not at all like I was starting to suspect his repertoire consisted of.

What was it he'd told my father? He has an assistant, an adept, who Father would be taking over harvesting the mana from the draw stones for. Iskara, or Perfidy, as Noctra had called her. There was nothing stopping anyone from learning magic as long as they could source the mana to practice. Adepts usually weren't as skilled as mages for the simple reason that the first thing any master did upon taking an apprentice was to ignite their core, thus turning adepts into mages regularly.

But here, in this place, no one knew how to do that. It was entirely possible Iskara was a superior spell caster to Noctra, limited only by her inability to generate her own mana. Would it even matter with this whole scheme they had set up? The village was donating four to five times as much mana as Noctra could produce himself every day.

Regardless of who had cast it, I still needed to get through it. Fortunately for me, the hardest part of disabling any trap was finding it in the first place. After that, it only took a tiny bit of mana to break it. That was good, because a tiny bit was all I had left. What I needed here was basic mana control. There were spells to break traps, but by their very nature, they were inefficient. It wasn't possible to create a spell that would work on every type of trap without some redundancies and wasted effort. Since I didn't have that luxury, I was instead going to perform the equivalent of building a spell live as I explored the trap. It would be good for disarming this trap exactly and nothing else.

I probed the structure of the spell with my senses and sent tiny little strands of my mana into it. I could just lash out wildly and overcome it through sheer damage, and I'd probably be safe from any feedback, but 'probably' wasn't good enough. I spent thirty seconds fully infiltrating the paralysis trap until I understood exactly how it was constructed, then I ripped the mana core right out of the enchantment and added its reserves to my own. No need to waste it. Extra mana was what I was here for, after all. I only got a sliver of the total spell, but it was still enough to recover a third of what I'd spent on one of those sleep spells.

I turned the handle and pushed the door open.

There was nothing but a rack filling the entire back wall and a work bench nearby. The rack had no less than sixty draw stones on it, far, far beyond what I'd expected to find. They were even organized with the fullest ones on the left and the empty ones all the way to the right.

I immediately went to the full side and emptied the draw stone's internal reservoir. Pulling mana from it was a tricky and slow process without the appropriate tools, but my luck had run out when it came to the work desk being fully equipped. Tapping into a basic storage crystal was like opening a drawer and taking what I wanted. Mana crystals were even easier since in order to function properly, they had to be attuned to their users. Nobody else could use my mana crystal, but I would lose almost none of the mana that I moved back and forth and didn't even need to deal with converting it from what was essentially a block of ambient mana to match my core.

Draw stones were more like playing with one of those finger holding puzzles that were given to children. I could pull, but the draw stone pulled back. Too little force and I wouldn't get anywhere, too much and I'd break the puzzle. I had to use just the right amount of pressure to pull the mana back out, otherwise the draw stone would eat the very mana I was trying to take to reinforce its own hold on what was left.

All said and done, it took me about twenty seconds to completely fill my core. Every draw stone was a little bit different in how much pressure it took to tap into it, determined mostly by its size and density, in my experience, but most people who used them took pains to grind them down to a standard size. These weren't exactly uniform, but they were all pretty close.

Most importantly, the draw stones on the full side each had enough mana to top me off twice. By my extremely rough calculations after a minute's examination, I could refill my core forty-two times with the amount of mana in this room. I needed an hour to finish my mana crystal, then another trip to refill my core, half an hour to work the transmutation that would shrink it down to a portable size so I could bring it back, and then another half an hour of work to place the shielding on the crystal and drain the room dry.

Then it would be time to pay Noctra and his maybe-better-than-him adept assistant a visit. With this much mana immediately available to me, I would be able to toss around a few advanced spells and end any fight against them quickly. For the first time since Father had walked away with those two Garrison members, I felt some measure of confidence that I could win this.

With my core full of stolen mana, there was no more reason for me to be inside the Collectors' headquarters. I closed the door behind me, snuck down the hallway, and exited the building. It had barely been five minutes since I'd gone in, and everything was still and silent.

Mother was awake and waiting for me in the garden when I got back. "How'd it go?" she asked when I came around the side of our hut and she spotted me.

"Perfect," I said. "There's enough mana there to finish my mana crystal, shrink it down to a portable size, and burst into the manor with spells firing from both hands if I need to. I just need to finish the prep work first."

"And your father?"

I shook my head. "Haven't checked. I'll scry on him again as soon as I'm ready to go."

I finished the mana crystal in just under an hour while Mother hovered nearby. She didn't say anything, but I could feel the nervous energy roiling inside her. She wanted to move, to do something, but there was nothing she could do right now, nothing except wait and keep generating mana.

"It's done," I said, opening my eyes. The plain field stone I'd spent weeks perched on was now a shard of smooth, glittering crystal the same dark violet as the night sky above. Right now, it was empty, but as my mana filled it, it would look like the stars themselves were trapped inside.

"It's beautiful," Mother said softly.

"Just wait," I told her with a smile. "It'll get better. I need to go steal more mana. I'll be back in a bit."

She nodded, but didn't take her eyes off my mana crystal. With a silent laugh and a shake of my head, I ran back out into the streets to the village square. It was even later now, and the red moon, Lasrin, sat lower in the western sky. The pale violet sliver of Taumar was just barely visible between the crests of two mountains to the north, a good omen if ever there was one.

My sleeping spell was still holding when I slipped back into the Collectors' headquarters, and none of the others had woken during my absence. I quickly finished draining the draw stone I'd started on the first time, then grabbed the next one in line and started on that. Once my core was full to bursting again, I snuck back out and returned to the garden.

"Next step," I told Mother. "Making this small enough to carry."

Stone shape wasn't really designed for what I was using it for, but it would work in a pinch. The spell cost me a little over a quarter of my mana normally, but since I was using it on a mana crystal instead of a random rock, it was almost twice as expensive. I cast it slowly over the next minute, and the crystal shrunk down until it was small enough to fit in my hand.

Unfortunately, the spell didn't change the weight. I now had a hyper dense mana crystal able to hold two hundred times as much mana as my own core, and it still weighed at least fifty pounds. I could fix that too, but it was going to cost me the rest of my mana to do so. The spell was called gravity twist, and its effect was simple: make things lighter or heavier. Like all enchantments, it required me to create an artificial core of mana to serve as a power source, but in this case, I was modifying it to draw its mana from the crystal itself.

If my mana crystal was ever drawn completely dry, the enchantment would break and it would immediately return to its normal weight. As long as the spell was active, though, it would weigh about half a pound. As soon as I was done casting it, I reached down and picked up the crystal. It had one solitary flickering light in its depth, a star about to burn out.

"It's ready?" Mother asked.

"Not yet," I said. "One last trip to the draw stones to fill it full of mana before the weight reducing enchantment starves and breaks. If that happens, I won't be able to move it. Next time I come back, we'll check on Father, I promise."

CHAPTER

TWENTY-FOUR

I had less than twenty minutes to get some more mana into this crystal before the enchantment broke and it became unmovable. Under better circumstances, that wouldn't have been an issue. I would have adequately filled the mana crystal's reserves before casting the spell, or I would have finished the mana lattice my own core needed to increase my regeneration rate.

Tonight, it was just one more time-sensitive issue on top of all the others. I needed to get back to the Collectors' headquarters and steal the rest of the mana from the draw stones. I needed to get over to Noctra's manor and rescue Father before they did whatever it was they were planning on doing. I wasn't even clear on what that might be.

I'd been resisting the temptation to spend a bit of mana to scry on the beacon I'd given Father for the last few hours. It was a cost I simply couldn't afford, not when I might very well need every spell I could cast to defeat a mage and an adept who might just be the more competent of the pair. What little evidence I'd gleaned so far certainly pointed in that direction.

I made my way back across the village for my final trip, slipped inside the Collectors' office on the north side of the square, and paused to listen. As many times as I'd gone in and out, no one had caught me so far, but it only took one incident for this whole thing to fall apart. I did not have the mana left to cast any sort of spells, nor did I have the time to wait for my core to refill.

Luck was not on my side tonight, it seemed.

The two Collectors I'd sent into an enchanted slumber were still out, but I hadn't taken the time to extinguish the candle in the room. My best guess was that someone else had woken up and seen it, then realized they couldn't wake their two colleagues. Several more candles had been lit in the hallway and I could hear the voices of two people in the room, not the original two occupants.

I hid in the shadows of the front room and silently watched the hallway. It didn't seem likely that anyone had bothered to check the storage room, since the door was still closed like I'd left it. Then again, I was making that assumption because I didn't think the Collectors could tell if the trap on the door had been triggered or if anyone had tampered with the draw stones, at least not with a casual inspection.

Still, if they did know someone had done something, it felt like there would have been a bigger scene. Instead of everyone being up and all the candles being lit, it was just a pair of voices in a room discussing the two unconscious Collectors. I couldn't hear the whole conversation, but it sounded like they'd decided the two had eaten some bad food.

Ridiculous, but I supposed a magical attack wasn't the first thing that came to anyone's mind here in this village. There was only one mage, and there was no reason Noctra would show up in the middle of the night and place two of his own employees under an enchanted sleep.

The best way to deal with this situation was going to be risky. Even if I was willing to sap what little mana I had left in my crystal, it wouldn't be enough to throw a sleep spell. I needed more mana in order to have options, and that mana was at the end of the hall behind that door. I didn't have the time to wait for people to leave, and there was every possibility these two might decide to wake up the other four, making my own situation even more precarious in the process.

I started creeping across the floor. It had been a lot of years since my days surviving by stealing things, but I still remembered all the things I'd learned as a boy the first time around. Maybe I was a bit out of practice, but it wasn't like I was trying to slip past trained guards armed with magical equipment. I didn't even have to worry about creaking floorboards here, where every home's floor was just hard-packed earth.

Besides, I weighed less than forty pounds and was barely three feet tall. I wasn't going to be easy to spot in the dark unless I went out of my way to draw attention. Hopefully, the two Collectors would be too focused on their friends to watch the hallway behind them. Unfortunately for me, they had tied the curtain open and let the candlelight spill out into the hall, so there was a spot a few feet wide where all they had to do was look up to catch me. I'd just have to make sure no one was looking when I crossed it.

"What kind of food poisoning does this?" a male voice said, heavily laden with scorn.

"I don't know what else it could be," a second man said. I recognized that voice. It was Dracken, the Collector who manned the table my family was assigned to.

"Damned if I know either, but let's not go attributing it to something stupid like food poisoning."

I made my way down the hallway, pausing at each door to make sure I didn't hear anyone moving inside. There were two with the curtains pulled aside, both empty. Of the remaining six, five were closed and the final belonged to the now-crowded room with four different Collectors in it.

"Do you think we should go tell someone?" Dracken asked.

"Probably, but who?"

"Iskara?"

There was a pause in the conversation there, followed by an emphatic, "No! She creeps me out."

I paused at the open curtain and carefully peered in. I did catch a bit of luck there in that the curtain was tied back on my side, which allowed me to make a sliver of space to peer through by adjusting it slightly. If either Collector had been looking at it directly, they might have noticed the motion, but their attention was on each other and my previous two victims.

One had his back to the doorway, which was just perfect, but Dracken was facing to the side. If I tried to cross by now, he'd definitely see me. The candlelight wasn't much to see by, but it was strong enough to stretch all the way across the hall. There was no way I was going to casually walk past without something in the situation changing.

I had a few options, though none were particularly good. I could extinguish the candle with a bit of elemental manipulation, for example. But if I did that, there was a very good chance the Collectors would start looking around to try to figure out why a candle had just gone out on its own hours before it should have burnt out. Since there were no breezes inside the building, at least not this far away from the windows, that seemed like a temporary solution that would cause more trouble down the line.

Sleep was too expensive, even if I just wanted to get one of them. Shadow Cloak might work if I hugged the far wall, but it would be risky and I'd need to spend time generating some more mana. Maybe I could do it before my mana crystal's gravity twist enchantment broke, but I didn't want to bet on it.

I really just needed a distraction, something that would pull their eyes away from the doorway for a second or two. This was my last trip. As long as I could get into the storage room undetected, I could work in silence to drain away the rest of the mana trapped in the draw stones. If someone interfered part way through, I would have plenty of options to take care of them.

The room was as bare as anything else in the village, just a pallet, a small side table, and a few trinkets sitting on it. The candle was there, next to a quill and ink pot. The pot was ceramic, its top sealed closed with a chunk of wood cut down to size and held in place with wax.

It wasn't that close to the edge of the table, certainly not enough to fall on its own. Minor telekinesis was about the cheapest spell in existence, though, and I could certainly nudge it an inch or two to get it into position. With any luck, the thump would be the distraction I needed.

If either of these Collectors could sense mana like Father could, this plan wasn't going to work. Shielding my own core was possible now that I had the mana generation to accomplish it. Shielding an active working of magic was a whole different skill, one that was considerably more expensive. If I'd had the mana to spare, I would have done it anyway, just to be safe.

With the dregs I'd generated over the last fifteen minutes, I reached out to the ink pot and slid it sideways ever so slowly. Neither Collector noticed, and it was an effort of will to keep myself from breathing out in relief. The pot was halfway over the edge of the side table now, and I readied myself to make my move.

It fell to the ground with a nice thunk. Both men looked over at it, with Dracken saying "What was that?" He took a step over and looked down at the floor.

Perfect.

I took three long steps past the hallway, long for me at least. Any adult who'd witnessed it would probably have laughed at my little legs pumping, but the important part was that I did it quickly and silently. Neither Collector noticed, and I passed through the light back into the darkness. I paused just for a moment at the last set of curtains, then reached up to twist the handle on the storage room door.

I made my way into the draw stone storage room, carefully closed the door behind me to keep it from making any noise, and got to work. With two conscious Collectors less than twenty feet away, I wanted a full mana core immediately. As long as I got that taken care of, it wouldn't matter if they found me. I could handle interference at that point.

With my ears open and trained for the sound of either Collector leaving the room, I got to work. It wasn't a hard job, just time-consuming, and it left me plenty of time to think about my next move. More specifically, I needed to consider what I was going to do with Noctra and Iskara, and what the long-term consequences would be. If I removed them both from power, someone would have to run the village. Someone would have to take care of whatever magical tasks they tended to.

Then again, the barrier didn't work anyway. What exactly Noctra did besides roast the occasional monster that got too close to the village was a mystery to me. If I deposed him, I'd be the one stuck doing his chores until I could train someone else to take over. On the other hand, he was obviously bilking the village in some sort of mana harvesting scheme. It might be a lot nicer place to live if I got rid of him.

There was one serious concern I hadn't put much thought into yet: Noctra and Iskara were part of some cabal, and killing them might bring even more mages looking. Whatever was happening with the mana harvested from the villagers, disrupting that supply was bound to bring more attention down on us. That might not be a fight I could win, so I needed to carefully consider my options before committing myself to it.

Of course, if the choice was between keeping my father alive or keeping the peace with some far-off collection of predatory mages, well, that wasn't much of a choice at all, was it?

CHAPTER

TWENTY-FIVE

T he hardest part of cleaning out the storage room was reaching the draw stones on the top shelves. There was a chair, but even standing on that, it was a struggle to get to the top two rows. I ended up climbing the shelf to sit on the top while I was accessing the uppermost row of draw stones. Sometime while I was working, the two Collectors left the bedroom they'd been standing in. One of them left the building, but the other went and woke the remaining four up.

At that point, I only needed about ten minutes to finish draining the last of the draw stones, and if I was lucky, no one would check the storage room. If they didn't leave me a clear way to escape, I'd waste a bit of mana on a phantasmal step spell to pass through the wall, but I was hoping they'd go somewhere else.

I didn't think I had good odds of sneaking back out through the door, especially since someone was going to realize that I'd left it unlocked. My hope was that the Collectors all knew about the trap on the door to the storeroom and would stay out. Even if one of them went running for Noctra's home, I'd be gone well before they got back.

In that one respect, I got lucky. With hindsight, I should have gone right back out into the hall after I drained the first few stones and cast sleeping spells on the other two Collectors, but I'd let myself become overeager and blinded by all the mana available to me, and in my rush to claim it, I hadn't properly considered the consequences of leaving the Collectors awake.

Now I would deal with an enemy who was on his guard. Oh, he wouldn't know it was me that was coming, but that hardly made a difference. Then again, being on his guard didn't make much of a difference, either. My mana crystal was more than half full. I had enough mana to cast fifty or so spells sitting in there. If I needed to, I could even cast a few bigger ones, though I couldn't imagine a scenario where that was the most efficient use of my limited resources.

I used a basic sensory invocation to sharpen my hearing and confirm that five of the Collectors were still awake and talking to each other. It sounded like they'd all moved to the front room and were sitting around the table out there. Assuming no one had found a way to break my sleeping spell, that left two Collectors snoozing and one unaccounted for. I could do some basic scrying to determine where he was, perhaps try to combine it with a long-range sleep spell to knock him out, but that would increase the cost ten-fold, and the simple truth was that I just wasn't impressed with the village's defenses.

Perhaps it was sheer arrogance, but more likely it was the half-full mana crystal in my pocket that fueled my confidence. It would strain my resources, but I could use a series of shadow leap spells to get to Noctra's base in under a minute and probably still have enough left over to blast him to oblivion. As long as Iskara didn't interfere, I could have this whole threat ended in the next five minutes.

But while it certainly seemed like I'd need to do something about Noctra at some point, that wasn't the goal tonight. He was clearly using the village to farm mana, possibly to pay off some sort of debt, by the sounds of it. I wasn't going to let that just continue to happen, but I wanted to be in a good enough place to deal with the fallout before I made my move.

I glanced around the pitch-black storage room, visible to my eyes only because of my magic. I'd already made my first move, now that I thought about it. The only thing left to do was play it out and see how it went. Given my advantages, I was confident in my odds. Noctra would no doubt have some tricks of his own, and probably many times as much mana available to him as I had, but I'd seen the quality of his spells. There was no way I was going to lose to some apprentice rank mage like him.

Phantasmal step was one of the most advanced spells I'd used since my reincarnation. It took me about three seconds to put the spell together, mostly because I wanted to make sure I'd done it as efficiently as possible, and I walked through the back wall of the room like it wasn't there. The spell only lasted long enough for me to completely step out onto the street bordering the east side of the Collectors' headquarters before it unraveled.

It took most of the mana sitting in my core to cast the spell, and I took a moment to draw more mana from my personal crystal. Then I circled around and hustled down the streets as fast as my short little legs could carry me. Just as I was turning the corner, I heard a door open behind me and a voice say, "Is someone out here?"

If I wasn't mistaken, that would be Ayaka. Fortunately for me, I was already rounding the corner when the door opened, and I doubted she'd seen me in the dark. Even with both the purple and red moons in the sky, there were so many shadows that I blended right into them. Whatever Ayaka thought she'd heard or saw, she didn't take any actions beyond looking out the door and then closing it again.

Mother was waiting for me inside our hut when I got back. She looked up sharply as I slipped past the curtain that served as our front door, then shot a glance to Senica's sleeping form before she asked in a harsh whisper, "You've done it then?"

"I have," I told her. I held up the crystal to show her and added, "There's more mana in this thing now than I could make in three weeks of continuous effort."

"Good. Now use it to save your father."

"Right. First thing is to find out where he's being held."

I gave Mother my hand and focused on scrying on the beacon I'd given Father. A vision of my father lying on his side filled my mind, hands bound behind his back and a gag in his mouth. Other than being bound, it didn't look like he was hurt. Of far more concern was that he seemed to be in some sort of cart, but it was too dark to see without magic.

I pulled the spell back a bit to see that the cart had a blanket thrown over top of it, and a good one at that. The blankets I was familiar with were threadbare, to put it nicely. This one was in fantastic condition and didn't look to have been woven from the cotton-like fibers grown here in the village. It wasn't much of a stretch to assume it had come from Noctra's manor.

A donkey was hitched up to the cart, and walking next to it was someone from the Garrison who was close to seven feet tall and had a series of scars across his face. Part of one ear was missing, and a chunk had been sliced out of his nose.

"That's Nermet," Mother told me. "He, uh, got hurt as a boy."

"It affected his brain?"

"Yes."

That made sense. Subjugating someone else's mind wasn't an easy process, but targeting the extremely young or the mentally feeble made the process easier. Since small children generally couldn't contribute much as a subjugated slave, Nermet was a logical choice to start with. Still, the ongoing mana costs associated with the spell must have irked Noctra, just judging by the average monthly harvest he could expect.

I doubted he had more than one or two subjugations running. Even one wasn't an efficient use of his mana. There was very little need for a muscle-bound slave in this village, not when everyone was obeying Noctra willingly.

I returned to examining the scene. They were obviously moving Father somewhere. Perhaps the manor was too open and Noctra had a secret base hidden away somewhere. If that were the case, it might be better to let them finish transporting Father so I knew where it was. On the other hand, it would be easier to rescue him if I only needed to break the subjugation enchantment holding Nermet's brain hostage. Perhaps I'd follow them until they were close to their destination and step in at that point. Father was in fine shape; he'd survive another hour under the sleep spell.

Mother gasped so loud that I shot a glance at Senica to see if she'd woken up before turning back to Mother to ask, "What's wrong?"

"That's outside the village," Mother said. "They've taken your father down the west road and left the village behind. He's at least five miles away, maybe more."

My heart sank. Five miles was a lot to catch up. I briefly considered my options. A spectral steed could do it, but without ambient mana to feed the spell as it ran, it would fall on me to keep it powered. Five miles at minimum, plus however far they got between now and when I caught up, would take perhaps twenty minutes. If I had any mana left by the time I caught up, it wouldn't be enough to rescue Father with.

Plus, the spell itself wasn't designed for a single traveler. It could make up to three mounts, but the mana cost was the same regardless. Dumb spell. I vaguely remembered thinking that I should find a way to modify it to be cost efficient for a single traveler, but by the time I'd had the knowledge to do so, I'd advanced far beyond ever needing it.

Shadow leap was completely out. I'd run myself dry in under a mile. Flight was a possibility, but it had a lot of the same problems using a spectral steed did in terms of maximum speed, and it had even more expensive mana costs associated with it.

There was a game that apprentice mages liked to play back when I was young. It involved using a novice invocation to temporarily reduce their weight while holding onto a wooden framework with a piece of canvas stretched across it, then using elemental manipulation to blast themselves with air to fly up into the sky.

Steering was difficult, and it required holding two channeled spells at the same time, which apprentice mages sometimes struggled with. A few of them got around it by creating temporary enchantments that would handle the weight reduction invocation. But it did have two things going for it: the spells were fast and cheap

That was exactly what I needed right now. I glanced around the house to find the piece of cloth with the fewest number of holes in it and settled on our front door curtain. "I need to borrow this," I told Mother as I gestured toward the curtain.

"What? Why?"

"I'm going to use it to fly out after Father."

"What! No. Are you insane? You can't go out there, especially not by yourself. The monsters—"

"What monsters?" I asked. "The barrier doesn't work, probably never did. They're already miles out and no monsters have come after them. I think that the presence of monsters outside the village has been severely exaggerated. It took me igniting my core to draw in one single monster, and right now, I could kill dozens of them without running out of mana."

I just needed to get out there, break the enchantment on Father, and get us back to the village. Then I'd do something about Noctra and Iskara. And after that... well, I'd worry about that tomorrow.

I jumped up and started pulling the curtain down, then paused at the sight of three members of the village Garrison walking down the street. Maybe they were just doing a routine patrol. That could be a normal thing that I never knew about because I was always asleep. Prior to igniting my core, this toddler body had required an enormous amount of sleep to function.

On the other hand...

"What do you think Noctra was planning on doing with the rest of us after he kidnapped Father?" I asked.

TWENTY-SIX

Before I could consider any other actions, Mother poked her head out over me and looked at the approaching Garrison members. One raised his hand in greeting, and she hesitantly returned the wave.

"Little late for your little one to be up, isn't it?" the man said. I tried to think if I knew any of them. All three looked familiar, and I knew I'd seen them around the village, but I couldn't put names to any of their faces.

"It's my fault, I'm afraid," Mother said. "I've been up late waiting for Sellis to get back and I woke him up on accident."

"About that," the man said. "We actually need you and your two children to come with us up to Lord Noctra's manor. Sellis is doing some work for him and it's going to be a long-term project, from what I hear, so he requested his family join him."

I wasn't sure if the man was lying or if he was just relaying the lie he'd been told and didn't care enough to examine it, but I wouldn't have believed it even if I hadn't already been spying on Father when Noctra had sent him into an enchanted slumber. There were just too many obvious flaws in that reasoning.

"Sellis wanted you to wake us all up in the middle of the night to walk a mile so we could go back to sleep somewhere closer to him, where we're going to be staying for an unknown length of time?" Mother asked, her voice flat. "Are you going to be sending some people around to keep our garden from being overrun with weeds?"

"Well, that is... No, it's not really what we do... You know, busy with our own jobs and..." the man stuttered through his excuses while Mother stood there, arms crossed.

I waited to see if they'd give up, or if this would turn into a kidnapping once we didn't come voluntarily. Considering that it didn't take three people to deliver a message, I had my suspicions about how this whole thing was supposed to play out. One way or another, their orders were to get my entire family up to that manor, probably so that Noctra could examine us to see if there was any other talent he could exploit in the family.

For a moment, I considered playing along. I needed to go there anyway if I was going to take care of our governor, but with my father being miles out into the wasteland already, I had to prioritize. Beyond that, it wasn't a good battle strategy to let an opponent dictate the terms of the meeting. While I was confident I'd win a fight between the two of us, it would be even easier to do if Noctra didn't realize he was in a fight until I'd already hit him once.

One hit was all it should take.

"I'm afraid I'm going to have to insist, Xilaya," the Garrison member said. "Lord Noctra's instructions were quite clear."

A basic sleep spell, cast by an archmage who knew what he was doing, needed one second to take effect on its target. I started with the one in the back and hoped the other two wouldn't notice, since I'd need to tap into my mana crystal between casts. It took me six seconds to get all three of them, ending with the guy who'd been arguing with Mother right as he was saying "What in the—"

"This is a complication we didn't need," I said, one hand still on the curtain. "I don't think you can stay here now. Noctra is already targeting you. He's going to get much more aggressive when he finds out about all the people I've put spells on."

There would be no denying that there was another mage in town at that point. If we were lucky, he'd think it was a coincidence that was in no way connected to my family. Maybe he'd think someone else from the cabal he'd been talking to Iskara about had shown up to sabotage him. This whole thing was going to put him on his guard, but I didn't have much choice.

I could kill Noctra, or I could go rescue Father. Since they weren't in the same location anymore, I didn't have enough mana or time to do both. I wasn't even sure if I'd have enough mana to get back once I'd rescued him. We could very well end up walking, and since it looked like I'd need to take my family with me now, it was going to be even more expensive to get out there. Fortunately, the elemental manipulation portion of the combo wouldn't cost more just because I had passengers. It was by far the more expensive part to keep going, anyway.

"Get enough food to last us a week and pack it up," I said, my mind made up. "You and Senica will have to come with me. We'll find a secure place to hole up until I can neutralize Noctra and it's safe to come back home."

"You want us to go out into the wastelands?" Mother asked, her voice incredulous. "You have no idea how much danger we'd be in."

"Less than if you stay here?" I asked. "Do you think the man who kidnapped your husband and sold him off is above taking you hostage? Do you think he's going to let you just go on with your day as if nothing happened?"

Mother's lips pressed into a thin line as she glared down at the three unconscious people in the street in front of our house. "Fine," she said as she grabbed the basket near our table and walked out to the garden to start harvesting food.

The weight reduction spell I had in mind was only usable on myself as an invocation, but there was a more expensive version that had looser requirements at the cost of worse efficiency. It would be almost three times as expensive to maintain, but it did have the benefit of a higher maximum weight reduction. I'd be able to make back some of the mana spent on it by needing less mana for the elemental manipulation portion of the combination.

I floated the three Garrison members into the house and left them in a row out of sight of the doorway. Someone would probably find them first thing in the morning anyway when they saw that the curtain was missing, but there was only so much mana I was willing to waste hiding them. Besides, they'd wake up in about eight hours anyway.

The worst of the preparations was waking Senica up. That was a whole chore in and of itself, one I was happy to leave to Mother. My sister did not appreciate being woken in the middle of the night, but I was busy plotting out our course with an application of applied scrying spells. I was no judge of distance, but I thought the five-mile estimate was too conservative. It was probably more like seven or eight.

This was going to be tricky, especially with two passengers, a basket of food, and a sail that had no framework to keep it open. I needed to keep no less than four spells channeled at the same time to make this work, plus repeated castings of another one. I started with the same gravity twist enchantment my mana crystal was under on the basket of food. That done, I could safely banish it from my thoughts and concentrate on the harder tasks.

First was a pair of feather weight spells for my mother and sister, followed by the novice tier weight reduction for me. All three of us combined now weighed less than ten pounds. Then I channeled minor telekinesis to stretch the blanket out across a frame of magic that I held onto. And then I did the hardest part.

I summoned the winds to push us up into the air. It wasn't enough to simply go up high, though. I needed to keep us flying in the right direction, a feat which would have been far simpler by myself, and if Senica hadn't immediately started screaming. In all fairness, Mother let out her own strangled gasp of surprise, but she at least kept the volume low.

The last thing I saw in the cool darkness below was the face of Malra, our nosey neighbor, gawking up at us from her window.

It was far too taxing to keep elemental manipulation going the entire time, so I resorted to sending repeated gusts of air into the curtain to propel us up and give us some speed, then let us drift for half a minute or so before repeating the action. We didn't make the best time, but I saved myself a dozen or more cores' worth of mana over the next few hours.

Part of my task while I was scrying out the route to Father's cart was also to determine a safe place for my family to stay until they could all return home. I'd noticed a few possible candidates, but one spot in particular struck me as completely inaccessible without a pair of wings. It would leave anyone there stranded if they had no magic, but it should also keep any local predators from getting at them.

It was just far enough out of the way that I couldn't easily tell if it would actually save me any mana to take them there first. Luckily for me, there was an easy way to make the decision without relying on mana calculations.

"Mother, do you want me to take you directly to the safe location I found, or should we retrieve Father first?" I asked over the wind.

"We should go to your father first," she said back.

"It will put Senica at risk," I told her.

Mother had both of us in her arms, pressed up against her chest, while the basket of food was held in one hand down by her waist. I'd attached the telekinetic frame holding the curtain open around her chest, and had been manipulating my own weight to help steer and keep us at a good altitude. We were actually flying backwards so that the wind would hit Mother's back, except for the ones I created and sent directly into our sail. It was pretty uncomfortable for everybody involved, and I'd already burned through a third of my mana crystal's reserves.

She took a few moments to consider, then said, "Drop us off first."

"Changing direction," I warned her as I summoned another gust of wind to shift the curtain while simultaneously dropping my weight as low as it could go. We gained another ten feet or so of air and started gliding more north than west. Below us, the landscape had become mostly hills, and I angled us toward one of the smaller mountains at the foot of the range beyond those. There was an isolated ledge there that led back into a wide, shallow ravine. It was all but impossible to reach without wings or magic, and I figured they'd be safe there for an hour while I finished my business.

I restored their weights to normal and broke the enchantment on our food basket after we landed. Senica clung to Mother hard enough that I knew it had to be hurting to have fingers digging into her like that, but Mother just stroked her hair and held her tightly.

"Go bring your father back, Gravin," Mother said. "If... If Nermet gets in your way, you do what you have to do."

"Hmm," I said. "Quite bloodthirsty of you."

"Just get him back," she said grimly. "We'll figure out what to do next after that."

I nodded once. It wouldn't come to that; Nermet was just as much a victim as Father, after all. But I did hope it didn't cost me too much mana to break the mental subjugation enchantment he'd been burdened with.

Leaving him out there in that kind of state was just a slower, more painful way of killing the poor man.

I spread the blanket out with telekinesis, lowered my weight down to a mere two pounds, and let the summoned gust of wind carry me back up into the sky.

CHAPTER
TWENTY-SEVEN

I t took a bit more scrying to pinpoint exactly where the cart hauling my father's comatose body was. One of the drawbacks with low-level scrying magic was that it wasn't good at pulling back from the target to hunt for landmarks, and even if it could, it wasn't like this part of the world had plenty of unique and diverse landscapes going for it. It was a lot of rolling hills covered in patchy scrub grass with mountains to the north and side, curving around to meet each other far to the west.

Presumably, there would be some trails down into the lowlands, but since I planned on catching up to Father long before the cart got to that point, I didn't concern myself with locating them. Eventually, the easier solution became to use sensory-enhancing invocations to sharpen my eyesight so that I could look through the night and the distance while I drifted up in the air.

It was around two in the morning when I spotted the cart. Once I got close enough, it wasn't that hard since it was the only thing moving. I hadn't seen a single one of the supposed monsters that roamed the wastes, but maybe they were all just asleep. Somehow, I doubted it.

The next part was going to be delicate. I had no idea what orders Nermet had rattling around in his poor, abused brain, and I didn't want to have to kill the man in self-defense if Noctra had given him a command like, "Attack anything that gets close to you."

At the same time, trying to do a cerebral deep dive while maintaining three other channeled spells that were only being powered thanks to my ability to pull a constant stream of mana from my crystal didn't appeal to me. The best way to approach the cart would be either by opening with a spell to incapacitate Nermet or by using something to effectively hide myself from his notice.

I was leaning towards a stealthier approach simply because subjugated individuals were notoriously hard to incapacitate if their masters had set things up properly. I wouldn't be able to tell whether Noctra had managed that until I got in there and started rooting around, and that would be much easier to do if Nermet wasn't actively trying to murder me at the time.

The stealthy approach had its own drawbacks, mainly because I was using a curtain as a sail to glide through the air. It wasn't the noisiest way to travel, but it was eye-catching, even at night. It was incredibly rare to get a night without a single moon, and tonight was no exception. Nalicin, the blue moon, would probably set before the sun came up, but that didn't mean another moon wouldn't rise to take its place, and since I was nowhere near an astronomer's conservatory with access to their books and notes, I had no idea where we were at in the lunar cycle. Honestly, things looked so different up there that I wasn't even sure what part of the world I'd been reborn in.

The cart was moving slow enough that I could land a thousand or so feet behind it and spend some mana to catch up. A combination of shadow cloak and aura of silence would keep me unnoticed if I stayed on the ground, though it would admittedly cost me two or three full cores' worth of mana to keep it running for a few minutes.

I shook my head. There was no reason to chase the cart down when I could just land far enough ahead that Nermet wouldn't notice me and I could wait for it to catch up. That would also give me time to regenerate some mana in my core. Ideally, all of my spells would be fueled by my own mana so I didn't lose a fifth of it to transference loss with my mana crystal. That was more of a goal than a current reality, at least until I grew my core to stage three.

I was conflicted about stage three right now. I didn't need to make a decision yet, but I needed a fully grown body to do stage three properly, and I wasn't interested in waiting twenty years for that. When I'd made my original plans, I hadn't factored having a family that I cared about into them. Artificially advancing my body would affect my relationships with them. Reversing that age later was possible, but came with some significant drawbacks that made it dicey. I doubted I could do it without damaging my mana core.

I sat on a rock fifty feet off the trail Nermet was leading the donkey down and considered how far I'd deviated from my pre-reincarnation plans already. Being born into a mana desert had wreaked havoc on my schedule. I should have already possessed a stage two core and aged myself up to at least prepubescence. The lack of ambient mana combined with the bad luck of the village being used as a mana farm really had been just about the worst possible outcome I could have gotten short of being killed as an infant. Even that might actually have been better if it had happened soon enough for the reincarnation magic to cycle again.

But if I hadn't been born as Gravin, I wouldn't have my family now. And I loved my family. Of course, if I'd reawakened my past memories as soon as I'd been born, that might have played out differently as well. The Gravin part of my personality would never have had a chance to grow.

The ethics of the whole situation were murky, to put it mildly. That was bound to happen when pushing the limits of reality, however. As far as I was aware, I was in uncharted philosophical territory. The closest I could think of was body snatching as a form of immortality, but the ethics of that weren't that hard to tease out. When the body I was inhabiting was my own reincarnation, things got a bit hazier.

Or maybe it was just as clear cut. Maybe I was a monster. If I considered my former identity to be separate from my new incarnation, that would mean I'd stolen Gravin's life from him at the tender age of two years and a few odd months. If someone else had done it and I'd found out, would I condemn them?

My musing was interrupted by the creaking of cart wheels and the steady clop of the donkey's hoofs as it pulled my father along. I hopped down from the stone I'd been perched on and cast shadow cloak over me to blend into the shadows before creeping toward the sound.

If possible, I wanted to save some mana and not use aura of silence to cover my approach, but that would depend on exactly how observant Nermet ended up being. I could only make out his towering silhouette without an invocation to sharpen my eyes, but that was enough to keep track of him.

A sleep spell would be easiest, if it succeeded. I was hesitant to try any enchantments that affected Nermet's brain until I got a chance to look at exactly what kind of subjugation magic had been worked on him. A physical restraint would probably be better for his health, though it wouldn't be anywhere near as efficient.

I approached the road, timing my steps with the clopping beat of the donkey's, and I was already within five feet of the cart before Nermet jerked in surprise and peered at me. "Something there?" he asked, his voice dull and slurred.

Surprising, but too late. Magic danced between my fingers as I approached him. Nermet was so focused on whatever sliver of movement he'd seen through the shadows hiding me that he didn't even see me approach. In a fight against a trained warrior, I might have suspected he was baiting me in, but despite his position as a member of the village Garrison, Nermet was the farthest thing from being trained.

I reached out to touch the back of his hand and discharged the paralyzing grasp spell I'd cast into him. His body stiffened mid step and he fell over with a meaty thump. I winced at the sound, hoping I hadn't hurt him too bad, and hopped over him to grab the donkey and slow it to a stop. It obeyed placidly and showed no interest at all in what was happening around it.

The practical side of me demanded I immediately get to work on Nermet. He was a threat and I'd only temporarily neutralized him. The paralysis would last at most ten minutes, possibly less. Considering how big he was, I wouldn't be surprised if he shrugged it off sooner. The spell worked directly on the target's muscles, and the more mass there was, the harder it was to affect all of them.

The sentimental side wanted to go check on Father and break the sleeping enchantment he was under. That probably wouldn't take more than a minute, but it was a minute I wasn't sure I had to spare. I spent a few seconds pulling the tarp off of him to confirm he was alright, then left him sleeping while I got to work.

Nermet's mind was horrifying to behold. Noctra had taken the magical equivalent of a hammer to it and beaten the parts he didn't want until they broke. There was a knot of instructions tying all the broken pieces together, telling Nermet how to react to various stimuli, when to fight, when to run, who to listen to, and who to ignore.

The whole thing was so clumsily done that if Nermet hadn't already had brain damage from whatever accident had happened as a child, there was no way someone wouldn't have noticed. He'd probably had a gradual change in personality when Noctra started working on him, becoming slower and quieter, and the people who knew him just chalked it up to the accident having far-reaching consequences.

Fixing this would normally be the work of days, but with my mana reserves so sharply limited, it would be more like weeks or even months. I could just go in there and smash the spells, but the backlash could very well kill Nermet. If it didn't, it would definitely leave him as nothing more than an ambulatory blob of muscles and organs wrapped in a skin sack.

Nobody deserved something like this to happen to them. Somewhere, buried under all the compulsions, was a person who knew his life had been suborned, that he'd lost control of his own mind, that he'd been turned into a tool for someone else's convenience.

I wondered if the real Nermet had even a single shred of hope that someone would come along and save him, or if he'd resigned himself to his fate. Did he even have enough awareness left to contemplate his own future? Would it be better for him if he did?

I also wondered if his accident had truly been an accident, or if Noctra had orchestrated it to give himself a slave that no one would ever notice had been subjugated. The man obviously didn't have a tenth of the skill needed to perform such subtle magics, and he'd known that he'd be ruining the mind of whoever he chose as his victim.

Maybe I was attributing too much malice to Noctra's actions. Nermet looked to be in his mid-twenties, so it was possible his accident had happened before the governor had come to the village. It was also possible that he had just seen an opportunity and had taken advantage of it.

I found that I didn't much care about the circumstances behind this situation. However it had come about, Nermet was beyond my ability to save right now. The only options I had left were to kill him myself or let him continue on. Maybe he'd live if I let him go. Maybe the people waiting for his cargo would kill him when he turned up with an empty cart.

I wasted precious minutes considering my options, trying to find some other alternative. The only thing I could think of was to usurp Noctra's control and claim Nermet as my own subjugated slave. It would remove him as a threat and keep him alive, but it would be a drain on my own mana that I couldn't afford.

I glanced over at my father, still unconscious in the cart. Maybe there was a way after all. And when I was done with all of this, I was going to return to the village, find Noctra, and kill him immediately.

CHAPTER
TWENTY-EIGHT

reaking the sleeping enchantment on my father took about a minute and a half. Noctra had poured far more mana than was necessary into it, and that ended up working against me as it had been used almost like a layer of blubber wrapped around the enchantment's artificial mana core. What a waste. I could have used the extra mana for myself if it hadn't been so clumsily utilized.

Father's eyes flickered open and he let out a soft groan. "Gravin?" he asked, his voice full of confusion when he noticed me.

"You were put under a spell," I told him. "I just broke it, but give it a minute before you start moving around."

"I... Yeah, okay," he said as he tried to sit up. One hand went up to his head and he winced before relaxing back down. "Where are we?"

"About seven miles outside of the village in the wastelands," I said.

Nermet was fighting his way out of the paralysis spell faster than I liked. It wasn't unexpected, but I'd hoped not to have to waste more mana on keeping him restrained. I watched as he started to twitch his fingers with a pensive frown. Until he got to the point of moving his whole arm, he wasn't going anywhere. I could refresh the paralyzing grasp spell I'd put on him early, but I was still hoping to avoid that.

"Listen," I said, cutting off Father's next question. "The short version, as near as I can tell, is that Noctra is using the village as a mana farm, and sending some portion to Derro in order to pay off some kind of debt. For whatever reason, he thinks that sending you over there will please his debtors, so he's basically sold you into slavery."

"What?" Father sputtered. "That's... what? No, that's ridiculous."

"Are you or are you not in the back of a cart out in your 'monster-infested' lands outside your fake barrier?" I asked bluntly.

Nermet twitched again, this time several fingers at once. I scowled at him and said, "Nermet is under a mind control spell. His whole personality has been subjugated, and he's lost his ability to have independent thoughts. I had a look in his head and things are... they're bad. Really bad. In my current state, it would take a long, long time to fix the damage. I just don't have the mana to spare.

"As soon as he gets free, he's most likely going to try to kill me. Maybe you, too. I'm not sure what his standing orders are if someone discovers what's been done to him."

Father hoisted himself up to look over the edge of the cart at the huge Garrison man lying on the ground. "What did you do to him?"

"Muscle paralysis," I said. "It won't last much longer. We need to decide what to do. I have an idea, but it involves a lot of work on your part. You would need to agree to it."

"What idea?" Father asked.

"We ignite your core. I will help transfer the control nodule of the spell to you, and your mana will feed it. You have to understand that this is a patch job designed to buy Nermet time until we're in a position where we can do something to fix him. He will effectively become your enslaved puppet until I have enough spare mana to properly break the spell inside him or you run out of mana and the control nodule snaps back to Noctra. If that happens, it's very likely he'll try to kill all of us."

Father's eyes got wider and wider as I spoke. He looked back and forth between Nermet and myself, then said, "Lord Noctra did that to him? That's... barbaric. Wait, what you do mean 'all of us?' Who else is here?"

"After he knocked you out, he sent three guys around to collect Mother, Senica, and me. We came out here after you and I left them at a safe spot I found a mile back."

"What!" Father shot straight upright. "You brought your mother and Senica out into the wastelands? Are you insane?"

"I have yet to see a single monster," I said. Near me, Nermet's arm gave a limp flop. "Out of time. You need to decide. Are you willing to ignite your core and spend your mana to keep Nermet alive for the next month or two?"

"We're nowhere near done talking about this, boy," Father said. "I don't care if you are a thousand-year-old mage or whatever, you had no right to bring your sister to such a dangerous place. And then to abandon her on top of it! Your mother won't be able to protect her when something attacks."

"Well, I guess we'd better get this figured out and get back to them as quick as possible," I snapped, out of patience. "Now choose. He's coming out of the paralysis spell. Either we kill him, or we save him."

"Save him, of course!" Father yelled. "What is the matter with you!"

I looked at him and sighed. "I think you are a better person than I am."

I dove back into Nermet's mind and wove my mana around the spiderweb of magic laid on him. The control nodule was buried under the crude subjugation spell, but not so deep that I had trouble activating it. It was a simple version, one designed to accept audible stimulus as a way to update desired behaviors. Basically, it was designed to force Nermet to carry out whatever orders Noctra gave him.

All I had to do was subvert the nodule into accepting my orders instead. It wasn't even that hard, but it was a constant drain on my mana. For now, it was manageable, but it would cripple my growth. And I didn't have a whole village feeding me mana to compensate for it.

By the time I was done, Nermet was able to move again. He regarded me with a bland, vacant expression. "Stand up," I told him. He did so silently.

"That's creepy," Father said.

"It's sadistic," I replied. "The real Nermet is in there somewhere. He knows what's happening to him, but he can't do anything to stop it. His body moves around without his permission, directed by the magic in his brain. Can you even imagine what that would be like?"

Father shuddered and went quiet. After a moment, I said, "We're going to try to help you, Nermet. It... It won't be an easy process, and it won't be quick. It's a lot harder to put something back together after it's been broken, and you... I think you were already broken even before this. As long as my father doesn't give up on you, I promise I'll keep trying, too. I hope that someday you'll forgive us both."

"Forgive?" Father echoed quietly.

"Go sit in the cart," I ordered Nermet. After he'd settled into place next to Father, I started leading the donkey north toward the spot I'd picked out to hide our family.

I was sitting on the edge of the plateau our little hide-away nook was on with my legs dangling over the edge when Mother walked up behind me. She sat down near me, though a foot or two away from the open air, and said, "You know, I knew in my head. You told us the truth, but it didn't feel real until you started throwing around magic so casually."

"Sorry," I said, not really sure what I was apologizing for.

Mother shook her head and said, "It's not your fault. I'm just stubborn, I guess. This is all so big. How could my little boy know so much? Blessed by the spirits, and always with a spell ready to handle every problem. And then the claims about Lord Noctra." Mother paused and her mouth twisted into a grimace. "Just Noctra. He's no lord of mine. Who knows what other things he's been using us for over the years?"

I glanced back at Nermet, who was resting near the entrance to our nook. While Mother and Father had had their reunion and Senica demanded answers, I'd taken the time to look over our new slave. One of the problems with this kind of mind control was that the people who would subject others to it generally didn't care for the health of their victims. The slaves wouldn't report injuries, couldn't, in fact, report them.

Nermet was not in good shape. He was big and he had lots of muscles, and he would keep going until his heart gave out and he died. But he had so many injuries made worse by not being treated, by being ignored and allowed to grow worse. Pain existed for a reason, and when a person wasn't allowed to react to pain, they made their injuries worse.

Both of Nermet's knees were shot. His back wasn't much better. He had a broken hand and torn ligaments. By all rights, he should be on the ground, immobilized. Every second had to be torture to him. At least, it would have been, but Noctra didn't want a slave crippled by his own injuries, so he'd turned off that part of Nermet's brain. It was a small relief that he didn't feel anything whatsoever.

It would cost a relative fortune in mana to heal those injuries, more than I could generate in a month, even if I had no other demands on my precious reserves. That would be one more burden for Father once we ignited his core. If things got much worse, I would need to convince Mother to let me help her ignite hers as well.

"It feels weird asking this, but what do we do now?" Mother asked.

I shrugged. "It's not safe to go back as long as Noctra's still alive."

Mother blinked at that and gave me a sickly look. "You want to kill him? That's a little bloodthirsty, isn't it? Why can't we just expose what he did and run him out of town?"

"Can we prove it?" I asked. "Even if we can, does it matter? You think a mage is going to be intimidated by a bunch of farmers wielding hoes and pitchforks?"

"Then what? You'll just walk up to him and kill him?"

"I'll probably attack him in his sleep," I said, already planning out how best to do it. "No sense in giving him a chance to fight back. I'm not looking for a duel. I just need to kill him and his assistant. And the sooner, the better. I don't think we're in any actual danger out here, but there are at least a few real monsters roaming the wastes. Plus, we've only got a few days' worth of food."

"Are you going to do it today?" Mother asked.

I shook my head and gestured to Nermet. "I need to show Father how to ignite his core so he can feed mana to Nermet. After that, probably, yes. If I don't kill Noctra soon, we'll need to ignite your core too so there's enough mana to grow new food."

I didn't mention it, but there was an issue of water as well. We'd have to relocate soon to deal with that. It was kind of a shame, because this location was remarkably defensible, but we had no containers to haul water back even if I was willing to go find it, and wasting mana transmuting it was far too costly to be effective long-term.

Mother was silent for a while. The sun started to come up, and we sat there watching it together. At some point, she stood up and said, "Come on, let's get some rest. It's been a busy night for all of us."

I rejoined the rest of my family and we laid down in a jumbled pile with the curtain that used to serve as our front door spread out over us. We all needed to recover our strength, but when we woke back up, it would be time to get to work.

CHAPTER

TWENTY-NINE

"I don't understand," Father said.

"Which part?" I asked.

"The why of it, mostly. Why does this ignite a core?"

We were sitting outside our temporary home after our family nap. It was late afternoon, and I was busy lecturing my father on how best to ignite his mana core while staring out at the rolling hills of scrub grass to see if I could catch sight of so much as a single monster. If there were any out there, they were well hidden. I wasn't willing to expend the mana to really seek them out.

"Your core isn't a physical organ in your body like your heart or your lungs," I said. "It's metaphysical, meaning it exists in the mana itself. Everyone's does, to a point. There are some exceptions, but we're a long way from those mattering for the purposes of this discussion.

"Right now, the only part of your core that makes mana is the part where it connects to your physical body. That's a small part of the total core, right? Think of it like a ball that you set on the ground. Only one part of the ball makes contact. But if you were to slice the ball open, you could unfold it so that the entire thing touches the ground.

"You are the ground. Your core is the ball. The more your core connects to you, the more mana it will generate. What this technique does is forges

165

that connection by pushing mana into the wall of your core. Push it enough, and your core will start generating mana on its own."

"That makes sense, I guess," Father said. "But why do you need to spin the mana? That's the hard part."

"Two reasons. First: to guarantee total coverage. It's very possible to miss parts of your core and have a... I wouldn't call it a botched ignition, but a subpar one. Would you rather your core produce five times as much mana as it currently does, or ten? How about twenty? The better you do in this step, the more production you're going to have."

Father considered that for a second, then asked, "And the second reason?"

"It pushes the mana in deeper. As you advance your core, it'll grow bigger, and that process is kind of like stretching it out. The deeper the mana goes into the wall of your core, the better the chances that you'll still be producing mana throughout the entire core as it grows bigger."

Truthfully, that second reason probably wasn't a priority for Father. He was already an adult, so his core was as big as it was going to get naturally, and unless he pursued the path of a mage long enough for his core to reach stage three, he was never going to stretch it any farther. But I'd hardly be a good teacher if I let him cripple his future potential just to skip a step now. There was only so much that could be done to fix a flawed foundation, after all. It was best to just do things properly the first time, a lesson I'd learned the hard way during my first go at life.

"This can't be how the spirits bless somebody," Father muttered. "It doesn't make sense."

"There are other methods to igniting a core," I told him. "The most common one, and I suspect the one that's happening in your mass gatherings, is to just soak up so much ambient mana that your core fills to bursting, and then to move it in an attempt to create some sort of magical effect. It would be random and inefficient and would almost certainly result in a very poor stage one core, but it would technically work."

Senica's reflex to grab at loose mana in the air made her a prime candidate for ignition through a ceremony like that. All she would need to do was consciously try to use the mana in her once she'd gained enough, and the struggle to get the spell working would likely agitate her core to the point that it ignited on its own. I had no doubt that absent any other contenders, she could become a mage at the next spirit worshiping ceremony.

I would have to get to her first. There was no way I was letting my sister start off with a subpar core that could only generate three or five times as much mana as an unignited person's, not when my technique would give her twenty times the generation rate. Of course, it was probably best to wait a few years until she was a bit more mature.

Besides, Father's ignition was going to need significantly more mana than mine had. I had enough left in my mana crystal, but it was going to take the lion's share of it. We wouldn't be defenseless by any means, but it was closer than I liked. But we'd made a choice, and in order to keep Nermet alive, Father needed an ignited core. The drain from usurping the subjugation spell was great enough that I was operating at a net loss, and the farther away from Nermet I got, the more the strain on my mana would grow.

Challenging Noctra now meant taking Nermet with me, which meant giving Noctra the opportunity to break the patch I'd placed on the control nodule. I would mitigate that by not letting Nermet get within a thousand feet of Noctra so that there was no chance of him taking over again.

Truthfully, I probably would have killed Nermet last night and put him out of his misery if not for Father. I was not a good person. I'd accepted that about myself many centuries ago, and while I'd hoped that I might change with a fresh start, I'd known it was foolishly optimistic to think it could actually happen.

I shook my head and said, "Okay, we need to get this done today. Time to practice."

The whole reason we were out here was to get as far away from Senica as possible. She reflexively grabbed loose mana, and we didn't have enough to spare for her. I could get some of it back with a mana drain, but it would be better to just not lose it in the first place. And since we were testing out Father's ability to absorb ambient mana, it seemed easier to avoid complications.

I released some mana from my own core into the air around Father. His ability to sense mana was definitely up to the task of igniting his core, and he immediately started collecting it. It had taken us six attempts to get this far, but there was no getting around it. The spell I'd used to feed Father mana directly for our Testing wasn't going to do anything helpful once his core was full. He needed to push that limit.

When I was first learning to be a mage, we'd used special rooms designed to keep the ambient mana at bay so that we could eliminate distractions and variables. It was only after we learned to properly absorb mana in an artificially clean room that we were allowed to pull it in raw with all the impurities that needed to be filtered out.

Ironically, living in a mana desert meant that none of those impurities existed and every single person I'd met possessed a practically pristine mana core. It did make this part easier, but if Father ever traveled far enough away from home, he'd need to learn to deal with that.

Father finished absorbing the mana, perhaps not as fast as I would like, but at an acceptable rate. "Good," I said, my own core empty. When it came time to do the actual ignition, I'd be relying heavily on the mana stored in my mana crystal. "Now start it spinning."

This part didn't go as smoothly. Father could get the mana moving without an issue, but it more sloshed than spun, and the more he tried to force it, the more it randomly splashed around. "Not like that," I said.

"I. Am. Trying," he told me through gritted teeth.

"Think of stirring a pot of stew. You don't just stick the spoon in and wiggle it around randomly. Start on the outer edges and push the mana in a circle. Don't worry that you don't get all of it. Just keep it going and more will get pulled along as you work up some momentum."

Slowly at first, and then with increasing speed, the mana in Father's core began to spin in place. He got about half of it going properly before he let out a gasp and let it slow to a stop. "That is hard work," he said.

"The faster you get it moving, the easier it'll be to keep going," I said. "And you're going to need to move a lot more than what you've got now. About twenty-five times as much as you currently have."

"Twenty-five!" Father yelped. "That's impossible, and even if I could, we don't have that much mana."

"We do," I assured him. Just barely, but it was there. I'd have enough left to fill my core five or six times after the ignition ritual, assuming there were no screw ups.

I gave Father ten minutes to rest, then had him try again. This time, he got the mana spinning sooner and at a faster speed. Almost everything in his core was moving in sync before his strength gave out again.

My own mana hadn't recovered, so I pulled a bit more from my mana crystal and spread it out into the air with instructions for him to absorb it.

Hopefully, Father got this figured out soon, because I couldn't afford to waste any once his own core was full.

Six hours passed following this cycle. As Father got better at spinning the mana, we started focusing on pure speed, then added keeping the mana rotating while absorbing more. Eventually, we hit the wall.

"Your core is completely full," I said.

"For probably the first time in close to twenty years," Father said.

"Yes, but it also means we can't practice anymore. I wish we could, but it's not in the budget. Normally, I'd have a prospective apprentice do this a few times as I slowly fed more mana to them so they could get used to spinning it with two or three times as much mana as their cores normally hold. In this case, it's not an option. You either get it right on the first try, or Nermet's going to die."

"No pressure then," Father muttered.

"Take an hour to recover," I said. "We'll start then."

That would also give me some time to recover my own mana. Every bit I could feed into the ignition from my own core saved me a bit on waste from the conversion between crystallized mana and personal mana. It was annoying to have to worry about such things, but that was the world I'd been born into.

"Do you think I can do this?" Father asked at the end of his hour.

"By yourself? Probably not. But I'm going to help. It still won't be easy, and while I'm hopeful to get your core going at maximum strength, realistically it's probably only going to be around fifteen times your current output. I'm sorry for that, but we don't have the time or the resources to prepare you properly."

Father glanced over at Nermet, who was still sitting in the same position he'd been for the last few hours, and gave me a firm nod. "I understand why. You've done all you can, and let's be honest here. I was never going to be a mage on my own. However this turns out, even if I have the weakest core you've ever seen, I'll still be better off than I am right now."

"I'm glad you're so optimistic," I said. "Now, let's get that mana spinning."

And together, we started the process of turning my father from an unignited farmer into a mage.

169

CHAPTER
THIRTY

Once Father's mana was spinning as fast as he could get it to go, I started pulling mana through my own core and releasing it into the air. A basic storage crystal would have been better here since I could have shunted the mana directly into a cloud around Father, but it wasn't worth breaking my mana crystal to replicate that effect now. Besides, Father was much slower at gathering ambient mana than I was anyway, and if I'd dumped the entire amount all at once, too much of it would have been lost.

Instead, I let it out in a controlled stream while constantly refilling my own core from my mana crystal. I was paying careful attention to release it only as fast as Father could pull it into his own core, and instead of the immense cloud I'd sat in for my own ignition, he had more of a thin vapor constantly disappearing into him.

About forty feet away, Mother sat with her back against the stone wall outside of our temporary home with Senica on her lap. My big sister started to ask her a question, but Mother shushed her. Near them, Nermet stood with a blank expression on his face. I wasn't sure what he thought of the whole ritual, if anything at all. Did he understand that we were in the process of empowering my father so that he could take over as the one holding Nermet's leash? Even if he did, I wasn't sure he had the capabilities to understand why this needed to happen.

The mana in Father's core was compressed as much as he could get it, but he only had about three times his normal maximum contained inside. There was a small hollow spot in the center where the force of the spin had pulled all the mana away, and he was directing the new mana he pulled from the air around him into there.

That wasn't ideal, but I could see why he'd make that mistake. It was easier to direct mana into a spot it wasn't already filling, and we hadn't had the resources to practice this part. I'd told him not to do this, that the effort to get that still mana to start spinning with everything else was more work than adding it to the mana that was already moving.

Father was rapidly approaching his limit. If he managed to get up to four times his normal maximum, I'd be surprised. I'd also be impressed that he got that far on his first try. Most apprentices topped out between two and three times what they could normally hold. Then again, most apprentices were between ten and sixteen years old when their cores were ignited, and had to deal with various impurities that had built up into their core. Father had a full-sized adult core that had never been exposed to raw ambient mana.

Regardless of how he'd achieved it, four times his core size wasn't going to be enough. Fortunately for him, I was here to help. Normally, a master's job was to help his apprentice prepare for the ignition by giving him the training and tools to manage it on his own. But this was far from a normal situation, and a man's life hung in the balance of a successful ignition here. We were already compromising between Father's future as a mage and saving Nermet's life now.

We could have used an easier method that would result in a dimmer ignition if Nermet's life had been the sole focus, but that would have left Father a crippled mage for the rest of his life. My technique would result in the strongest possible core, and if I had to cheat a little to help Father now, so be it. I could give him remedial lessons later to help him strengthen his control and focus, but I couldn't fix a dim ignition after the fact, at least not to the point where his core would ever be as strong as it was going to be using the spin method.

Manipulating mana inside another person's core was a delicate process. There were a lot of things that could go wrong, resulting in anything from a mild nosebleed due to mana backlash to—in exceptionally rare cases—total core rupture leading to death. What I was about to do was dangerous, but, well, I was an expert and my father trusted me. We'd practiced this as well so that he would understand what he was feeling and not fight me on it.

Admittedly, we'd practiced it with half a core of mana, not one over-stuffed four times over with even more coming in. It would be the same sensation from his perspective, just more intense. He would need to keep absorbing more mana on his own, but tendrils of my own mana, hardened to survive amidst a pool of his, snaked into his core. I saw Father wince at the touch, but he kept the spin going.

I pushed the mana inside his core using my own mana like a paddle, or rather, I shaped my mana into four separate blades and spun them. At first, each section had slits and vents to reduce their effectiveness so that Father would have time to adapt to the increased speed, but as we approached five and then six times maximum mana, I reformed them into solid paddles.

"I... can't," Father gasped out, now leaning forward with his elbows braced against his legs and his head in his hands. Sweat poured off his face and dotted the stone beneath him.

"Don't you dare quit on me now. We're almost there," I said. "A little more. Just focus on keeping the spin going and pulling in the mana. I'll handle speed."

Seven times normal maximum. I could see the reaction starting, the mana starting to seep into the walls of the core to reinforce it. More mana came in, and Father's core... rippled, for lack of a better word. It couldn't tolerate my presence any longer, not when it was ready to ignite.

"That's all the mana. Focus everything you've got left on keeping the speed going. You just need to last a few more seconds," I said, pulling my own mana back out. It broke down almost immediately, disappearing into a mist too fine to be detected, like a drop of water lost to the sands of the desert.

The ignition started, and Father let out a gasp that was one part wonder, one part exhaustion. In a flash, his core became something solid, several times the size of my own, and though it was now empty, it would fill soon enough. Father was officially the first villager of his generation to become a mage.

"How do you feel?" I asked.

"Like a wrung-out dishrag."

"That'll pass."

He started laughing. "That'll pass," he echoed. "Yeah. It's... It's incredible. I don't even know how to describe it. I can feel the mana."

It would take a little bit to confirm, but by my rough guess, we'd achieved somewhere between sixteen and seventeen times his previous generation speed. Not perfect, but acceptable. Once he'd had an hour or so to start generating mana, I'd measure again, but I was confident in my estimates.

"It should take about nine hours to completely fill your mana core," I told him. Even at the lower relative speed, being an adult with a full-sized core had its perks. Adults naturally generated mana about three to four times faster than children to begin with, and could hold a proportionate amount more total mana. All other factors aside, size mattered. That was why so many huge creatures like dragons had enormous advantages in terms of absolute power.

That was also why they were often lazy and relied on brute strength without even a modicum of skill to back their mana up, incidentally. More than a few of them had fallen in duels against archmages of the smaller races precisely for that reason.

As far as Father was concerned, his mana generation would be heavily tied up in maintaining the usurpation of Nermet's subjugation spell. He'd still be generating a net positive, of course, probably even more than I made without the handicap. Hopefully he'd be willing to keep taking direction from me because I'd all but exhausted my mana crystal. It had maybe enough mana left to refill my core another five times, which meant no big, expensive spells and no prolonged fights. My plan was to take a few days to recover some resources while we hid here, then sneak back into the village at night to take out Noctra. Even if I couldn't get any mana from Father, three days would be enough for me to double my current mana reserves.

"For now, you should just rest," I told him. "I'm going to keep an eye out for any monsters like that mana sniffer that showed up when I ignited my core. I don't think we'll have any problems with us being this far up, but we should be cautious anyway. Once you've got your core filled up, we'll start the next step."

"The part with Nermet, you mean?" Father asked.

"Yes, that part," I said, trying not to grimace. That kind of magic was dirty work, and even just cleaning up after it made me feel like I had a layer of sewer sludge coating my soul. No good person should know anything about how mind subjugation magic worked, and Nermet was an ugly reminder that I was all too familiar with it.

Memories flashed through my mind, old ones I'd done my best to put behind me. Katirin discovering my workshop. Goshin confronting me after she told him what she'd found. Stabbing him in the back, literally. The battle with Avry, the fire that burned everything down. The dozens of bodies, the black, charred skeletons.

Lessons painted in the blood of others, innocent people who didn't deserve their fates. Resolving to be better, to atone for my sins, hadn't brought any of those people back. Nothing would. Even if I hadn't broken that oath, it wouldn't have changed anything for my victims.

"You alright there?" Father asked.

I gave him a smile and said, "I'm fine. Do me a favor and keep Senica distracted while I play look out? She looks like she's got about a thousand questions."

Father started laughing as he stood up. "Oh! Wow, that feels... weird. I should be sore, but I'm not?"

"You'll get used to that," I said. "You've been using weak, unstructured invocations your entire life to reinforce your body. Now they've got a lot more mana to work with."

"Amazing. I need to convince your mother to do this. The things we could— er, that is, the health benefits..."

I looked my father straight in the eye and said, "You have no idea how many ways magic can be used to enhance your sex life. The things I could teach you would make your head spin."

"Okay. Well. Now I'm just uncomfortable. I'm leaving this conversation."

I laughed softly as Father ran away from me. My family retreated into the shade of the crevice we were camped out in, leaving me alone with Nermet's silent presence. I could feel him, like an itch in the back of my mind, just waiting for me to give him a new order. That was going to drive Father mad once I transferred the patch I'd applied to the control nodule to him.

It would only be temporary, but even with Father's mana production, we'd lose so much in transference. We wouldn't even have access to his excess unless I built a new storage crystal for him, and those were awful for efficiency. I would need a day or two to gather enough mana to make it, though, and there just wasn't enough time. I would have to use mana draining spells for the time being to take advantage of his surplus.

Movement caught my eye in the wasteland below me. Something big and yellow, covered with shaggy fur and dirt, was making its way toward us. It had a long nose that hung off its face like a twitchy banana as it swayed back and forth. I assumed it was what the locals called a mana sniffer, though that was about as generic a name as it could possibly get. There were thousands of different creatures that hunted down mana to consume, and I was sure hundreds of those did it by smell.

I'd let it get a bit closer, and if it turned out it could climb, I'd blast it right off the rocks. There was no point in letting anyone else know yet, not when it would accomplish nothing but make them worry. I settled down to watch and wait as the mana sniffer got closer.

THIRTY-ONE

The mana sniffer slowly picked its way up the face of the cliff. Considering just how bulky and thick-limbed it was, I was a bit surprised by how much agility it had on display. I wasn't convinced that it was going to make it to the top, but if it made it to the halfway point before giving up, I was going to kill it.

Of more concern was the second mana sniffer that had joined it. Apparently, they weren't as territorial as I would have supposed, considering how scarce food must have been for them in the desert. I'd been almost hopeful that they'd end up attacking each other, but I wasn't that lucky. Instead, one of them had taken the south side of our little plateau hideout and the other was working its way up the north.

"What are you doing?" Mother asked as she emerged out into the sunlight.

"Keeping an eye on the mana sniffers trying to get up here," I said. "I'm almost certain they won't be able to handle the climb once it turns sheer, but I'm going to kill them if it turns out I'm wrong. I didn't think they'd make it as far as they have, but I want to be ready in case they surprise me again."

Mother stiffened slightly at the mention of mana sniffers, but she did a remarkable job of maintaining her composure. After a slight stutter in her step, she joined me at the edge and looked down. "What about on the back side?" she asked.

That was a fair question. The spire of stone we were perched on jutted up out of the ground like a lone mountain, with the next peak miles away. Thanks to the way it was set up, we had a cave-like shelter to stay in. It was a sort of miniature ravine in the side of the mountain, only thirty or forty feet deep and with the two walls angled together so that at the back end they left us with a shallow overhang.

Then the stone continued up another hundred feet or so overhead, leaving us with a wide ledge to overlook the landscape, but only on the southeast side. That meant we couldn't really see if any mana sniffers were coming up anywhere but where our ledge opened up to the sky. Fortunately, it also meant that anything climbing up the back side would go right past us without finding any way to actually reach our camp.

All of that assumed the mana sniffers could manage the vertical climb in the first place, which I wasn't convinced was true. Of course, it also assumed nothing else besides mana sniffers would show up. I was keenly aware that our perch was vulnerable to flying monsters, but so far, I hadn't seen any. It was actually such a nice spot that I figured anything in the area that could fly would already have found it and turned it into a roost.

"I think we're safe, but if these ones managed to get close enough that I needed to intercept them, I'll sweep the areas we can't see from here with a scrying spell," I told Mother. I glanced over the edge again to check on the mana sniffer's progress and felt a hand on my shoulder holding me steady.

"I'm half afraid you're going to fall over every time you do that," Mother said.

"That would be unfortunate. We need all the mana we can get right now."

Far from showing a velvet sky of stars, my mana crystal now had more like a single constellation. It was only about five or six percent full, and I was keenly aware of exactly how quickly I'd gone through what should have been an immense amount of resources saving Nermet's life. Admittedly, that had come with the perk of igniting Father's mana core, which I would have done sooner or later anyway, but the timing was damned inconvenient.

As soon as I finished moving control of Nermet's subjugation spell to Father and refilled my own core, I'd begin the process of siphoning away about a tenth of my maximum capacity into the mana crystal every hour or so, keeping myself close to full but never quite there. It would take about a month and a half to fill it all the way, but every little bit I could store right now would help me when I went after Noctra in a few days.

"How is Senica taking everything?" I asked as a change of topic.

"She is... very excited," Mother said.

"So she latched onto the magic part and you didn't try too hard to explain the deadly risks part?"

"Yes. It's not something a little girl should have to think about. Your father will be able to do magic soon. That's a big enough distraction to get her to ignore what's going on. Although it's becoming a lot of work to keep her away from you. We haven't explained all of your baggage to her yet, but she knows you can do magic too and she is very, very eager to talk to you about it."

"Maybe we'll hold off on that conversation for a few hours," I said. "At least until I know that these mana sniffers aren't going to be a threat."

"I want them gone before I let her anywhere near this ledge," Mother told me.

"I'm not wasting mana to drive them off if they can't actually get up here. It's too important to maintain what little reserves I have left."

Mother glanced over the edge, shuddered, and said, "You'd better be right about this, Gravin. One of those could kill us all, and we've got two."

I had my doubts about that. All things considered, the mana sniffers were remarkably docile toward each other, and though I hadn't gotten a chance to examine them closely, I was willing to bet that they wanted nothing but mana. That meant all the ambient mana I'd released for Father's ignition had caught their attention, and his core was what was keeping them here. My own mana crystal was the largest source of mana in our group, but I'd double-checked to make sure the shielding on that was holding up in addition to making the effort to hide my own mana.

In short, the mana sniffers were here for Father and nothing else. My guess was that those noses weren't for show, and that in addition to tracking down sources of mana, they'd act as some sort of mana draining implement. The only question in my mind was what they'd do to Father after they sucked him dry if they got hold of him. An intelligent monster would know that mana regenerated. It would capture him and keep him alive as long as possible to keep feeding.

Mana sniffers didn't strike me as intelligent from what I'd seen so far. They were more like animals than people. If I had to try to predict what they'd do, my bet was that they'd steal as much mana as they could get before wandering off. If they'd been a bit more aggressive and didn't have such distinctive noses, I would have worried that they'd get their mana by eating people instead, but I knew enough about the biology of monsters to make some educated guesses about how these ones worked.

That was not to say that I was going to let them have a single scrap of the mana up here. Just because Father would most likely survive being fed upon didn't change anything. If it meant killing them with a pair of fire blasts, well, it had worked for Noctra—though I was sure I could do better than an uncontrolled burst of flame if I put a bit of effort into it.

Come to think of it, we didn't get a lot of meat in the village. Most of our protein came in the form of beans. Those pelts would probably make for thick padding, too, even if they were too heavy to use as blankets. Even during the cool months, it was too hot here for much more than light clothing. Most of the children didn't even have shoes, though who could blame them considering that the interiors of our homes were the same hard-packed earth that made up our streets.

"You've gone quiet on me," Mother said.

"Sorry. I was lost in my own thoughts again. This land is so different than what I experienced in my first life. I often find myself wondering where exactly I am and how many years have passed between my death and my reincarnation."

"Can you not do the math?" Mother asked, surprise in her voice. "I would have thought..."

"No, no. It's nothing like that. The calendar used here is simply different. Telling you that I died in the summer of A.N. 3142 doesn't help much when it's now the 408th year of the Galvashian calendar, does it?"

"I suppose that would make it harder to figure out," Mother agreed. "What does A.N. mean?"

"Ascension Naturallis," I said. "We measured it by the founding of the Natular Empire whose first ruler was, well... Naturallis was supposedly his name, though he'd already been dead for centuries by the time I was born, and I was never clear whether it was actually his name or just a title he'd claimed for himself. His grandson took the throne about fifty years before I was born."

"It's so strange to think that you had this whole life already," Mother said.

"You did too. Probably thousands of times. You just don't remember any of them," I pointed out.

"It doesn't feel like they really count, though. If I can't remember any of those memories, I'm really only as old and experienced as I am in this life. For all we know, I could have been a mage in my past life too, but it doesn't do me any good now."

"There are spells to help you draw memories from past lives out of your soul if you're curious," I said. I'd done considerable research on them when I was constructing my own spells for my reincarnation ritual, though I'd never found a use for those spells specifically beyond idle curiosity. It was basically impossible to track who someone's reincarnation was, so there were few practical uses with that kind of magic, though occasionally someone did discover through sheer happenstance that they'd been someone famous or talented and began to delve deeper into their own past life, just to see what they could discover.

I peered over the ledge again and sighed. "These things are persistent, if nothing else. I'm going to have to kill both of them after all. Do you think the meat and pelts are worth anything?"

Mother blinked at that and shook her head. "We've never used any monster parts in the village, as far as I know."

That saved me the need to avoid making a mess or of going down there to harvest usable materials. I focused my mana into a conjuration and sent a searing beam of fire down the side of the cliff to strike the mana sniffer in the face. It started to give an agonized screech, but the flame lance forced it to let go, and it quickly struck the ground below.

The stink of seared meat and burnt fur would no doubt draw in scavengers to take care of the body. Hopefully it wouldn't result in any future problems for me, but I needed to keep an eye out either way. I was already going to have to start scrying around the far sides of our mountain spire anyway, so I supposed looking at a wider area wasn't too much extra work.

"Excuse me," I said to Mother. "I have to go take care of the other one now too."

She nodded mutely and peered over the edge at the remains of the first mana sniffer. "You... you go right ahead, son. I think I'll head back into the shade and see how your father is doing."

THIRTY-TWO

The procedure to transfer control of Nermet to Father went surprisingly smoothly. I kept expecting something to go wrong, some flaw to reveal itself in Father's mana core or some trap in the subjugation spell Noctra had cleverly hidden away, or some monster attacking right as I got to the most delicate part of the job.

Nothing like that happened, and after about an hour's worth of work, I was successfully able to redirect the mana draw from myself to Father. He grimaced with discomfort as soon as it settled onto him, but otherwise said nothing.

"Yes, having a constant drain is annoying," I told him even though he hadn't asked. "Best get used to that feeling. It's not going away any time soon. On the bright side, you have your very own slave to boss around now. He'll do anything you ask, up to and including jumping right off this cliff to his death. I wouldn't advise testing that claim."

I spent a bit more time explaining what the new bond between my father and Nermet meant, what he could do, what he should avoid doing, and the logic behind how orders were interpreted to try to head off any miscommunications before they occurred. Throughout the lecture, both of my parents grew progressively paler.

"This is disgusting," Mother said.

"That is a very common sentiment among those who don't view other people as objects to be used and discarded once they run out of value. Your Lord Noctra does not appear to be one of those people."

"I suppose he isn't," Father said after a moment's hesitation. "All these years, and he's just been using us. Everything we've worked for was a lie."

"Not everything," Mother said. "We're still a family. We still have friends and neighbors back home who are good people. Senica still needs a home to grow up in."

"Nuh-uh," my sister said. "I'm going to be a mage now and use magic to live anywhere I want. Maybe I'll make a new home on one of the moons and you can come visit me."

"Interesting idea," I said. "Which moon do you think would make the best home?"

"Yulitar," she said without hesitation. "I don't want all my stuff to be blue or red or any other color."

Yulitar was the largest of the six moons, and the only one with a pale white coloring. Some necromantic texts referred to it as the Corpse Moon and tracked its cycles for use in clandestine activities. For that reason alone, Yulitar had become my least favorite of the moons. It wasn't that what some busybody necromancers were doing was the moon's fault, but somehow it always meant a lot of work for me whenever Yulitar was in its primacy over the other five moons.

I could just see my sister with her head shaved, in black robes and a matching skull cap, waving around a wand made of some kind of femur and chanting a string of nonsense syllables. She would no doubt think it was a fun game, pretending to be a mage.

I could only hope that when she became one for real, she learned better than that. The last thing I wanted was to have to kill more family members.

"I think we're a long way away from building a house on any of the five moons," Father said. "Maybe we should focus on getting back to the home we already have first."

"Six," I said absently, still half-lost in old memories.

"What?" he asked.

"There are six moons."

"No there aren't."

I blinked. "Of course there are. Tuamar the purple, Felactious the green, Amodir the orange, Nalicin the blue, Lasrin the red, and Yulitar the white. Six moons."

Mother and Father exchanged glances, but didn't say anything.

"What?" I asked.

"Well, it's just... I've never heard of a moon called Amodir. Nor have I ever seen an orange moon," Father said.

"But... you've seen the other five," I said. "I've seen the other five. How could one of the moons just disappear?"

Was it possible that Amodir's orbital path kept it hidden from one hemisphere? It didn't seem likely to me, but if the other possibility was that it had disappeared from the sky, I knew where I'd put my money. "Oh what I'd give to gain access to my vaults right now. I know right where I left an astrologer's journal that includes lunar paths. It was chapter six, right next to that beautiful diagram. What did it say about Amodir?"

Try as I might, I couldn't quite remember. Come to think of it, though, the night sky looked far different than it did in my previous life. And I'd spent a lot of nights looking up at the heavens. There was a reason my home was called the Night Vale, after all. I'd just been assuming the differences were due to being reborn on the other side of the world.

Could I have made a mistake somehow and allowed myself to be reincarnated on a different world altogether? No, that was impossible. The five other moons I was familiar with wouldn't have hung in the night sky. Planets only shared stars, not moons. I had to still be on Manoch, just... on another continent. That was the only explanation that made sense. Amodir's orbital path was just irregular somehow.

"Gravin? Are you alright?" Mother asked.

I glanced up and saw everyone looking at me. My parents both wore worried looks, but Senica was just looking at me like I'd sprouted a second head and started holding a conversation with myself. From her perspective, I supposed it did look like I was going crazy.

"Fine. I'm fine. Just trying to figure some things out that aren't really a priority right now. Sorry."

I had more immediate problems I needed to handle before I started digging into the mystery of the missing moon. My mana reserves were as depleted as they'd ever been, and I was relying on Father to help me recover them in a hurry. It wouldn't be an efficient transfer, but every little bit would help. I gave us maybe three more days before food ran out, less than I'd originally planned since I hadn't accounted for Nermet. Fortunately, we could make it back to the village with a single day's walk, as long as nothing attacked us.

"I'm sorry," I told Mother. "I know this is boring for you and Senica and you have nothing to do right now. I need time to get ready, to generate more mana. It will probably be two days before we go back home, and then it'll be a long walk."

"Why can't we fly again?" Senica asked.

"Too much mana. We only did it the first time because we had to catch up to Father before he got too far away."

I needed to teach Father and Mother elemental manipulation and weight reduction as soon as possible. If something happened to me, I didn't want them to get stranded up here. Fortunately, both spells were perfect for beginning mages and were frequently used to introduce apprentices to structured invocations and conjurations.

Unfortunately, it was going to be harder for them to get Senica and Nermet down. They might be able to fall slow enough with Senica held between them so they could split her weight if she held onto the curtain and they used elemental manipulation to give it a strong up-draft. That had its own set of problems since it meant one of them would need to channel two spells at once, but it was theoretically possible.

Nermet was not getting down without someone able to cast a basic tier spell, also called tier two. Novice, basic, intermediate, advanced, and master tier were the five classifications of spell difficulty, determined both by how complex a spell was and how much mana it demanded. Very few spells that fell under the umbrella of the enchantment discipline were suitable for new apprentices due to the nature of how enchantments worked. Creating and implanting artificial mana cores to power a spell inside something else was not an easy task.

As long as nothing happened to me, it wouldn't be an issue, but I'd still feel better if Mother and Father could get down themselves. "I think I should get you started on your first spells, Father," I said. I turned to Mother and added, "Even though your core isn't ignited, I'd like you to participate as well. It will be more difficult for you to gather the mana to practice with, but the spells I'm going to teach you are the ones you'll need to get down from here on your own."

"But I won't be able to cast the spells," Mother protested.

I shrugged. "Doesn't seem to slow Iskara down. Get some mana from somewhere else. Besides, it's not like we're not going to ignite your core as soon as we can."

"I don't want to be a mage," Mother said.

"Xilaya," Father said. "You really should—"

"Don't you start with me," Mother told him. "Other people have different goals than you. I'm happy for you that your childhood dream fell into your lap through the weirdest and most unlikely twist of fate ever, but don't you dare drag me into this."

"That's not— I mean, it's not like I..." Father trailed off, whatever excuse or rebuttal he'd been trying to make left unfinished.

"We'll see how things go once we're back home," I said. "But I'm going to be honest here. I'm killing Noctra. Probably Iskara too. Father is almost certainly going to have to take on at least the protection duties of your current governor."

"Me?" Father asked. "Why can't you do it?"

"Because I'm three," I said. "I have legitimate concerns like how I'll reach the doorknobs when I get to Noctra's manor house."

"He's got a point," Mother said. "It's hard to think of him as an adult even when he talks like this, even though I've seen him do incredible magic. Every time I look at him, I just see my baby boy."

A hot skewer of guilt stabbed into my gut. I'd taken that from my parents. They wouldn't ever have a chance to watch Gravin grow up now. More than that, all of their current problems were my fault, too. The mana sniffer that had entered the village was because of me. Noctra's interest in Father was because I'd cheated on our Testing. Without my interference, they could have kept living in ignorance like every other family.

To hell with that. Noctra was a pathetic excuse for a human being, and I wasn't going to let him take advantage of over a hundred people any longer. We'd figure out the governmental aspects later, but considering the small size of the village, it didn't really seem like that oversight was even needed. People solved their own problems for the most part.

The Garrison should probably stay in place after Noctra died, but the Collectors wouldn't be needed anymore. The Barrier Wardens could be disbanded as well. Once the lie of the barrier itself was revealed, there'd be no need for them. Or maybe they'd be folded into the Garrison. Someone probably should keep watching for monsters, after all.

Then there were the Arborists. I didn't actually know much about them, but presumably they were somehow keeping the little stand of trees north of the village alive. That would require more investigation to figure out whether they were actually needed or if they were just a part of Noctra's scheming.

That was a problem for next week. For now, I needed to convince my parents to both learn new magic. Before I could get back into that argument, Nermet spoke for the first time. "Someone is coming," he said in a thick voice.

It was so hard to understand him that it took me a second to register what he was saying. Then I raced across the ledge to look out into the wasteland. Sure enough, there was a person down there dressed in loose white clothes and wearing a wide-brimmed hat that hid their face.

"Who do you think that is?" Mother asked as my parents joined me.

"Trouble," I said grimly. It couldn't really be anything else.

CHAPTER

THIRTY-THREE

Whoever the person walking across the dry, dead earth was, they could obviously sense mana from a distance. It was impressive, in a way. Almost no one I'd met since awakening had that kind of skill at even the most basic level. From what I could piece together, Father had been considered something of a prodigy at working with mana as a child, and only the unfortunate accident that I was still missing some details on had prevented him from becoming someone important as he got older.

Instead, he'd become a social pariah, though I hadn't realized it at first. I did not see him out in the fields at work, and when we stood in line for the nightly tithe at the draw stones, he'd always directed conversations inwards toward the family. I'd mistaken it as him being a doting parent at first, but the truth was that very few people could manage anything more than basic courtesy masking subtle hostility.

My father was not well-liked, not at all. One of these days, I was going to have to get the whole story out of him regardless of how painful it might turn out to be. I suspected it was going to be important to know exactly where my family stood once Noctra was dead and gone. Initially, I'd thought that Father might slot into the role since the village seemed to want to have a mage as its head, but I was beginning to suspect they might not accept him in particular.

As we watched the person draw closer to us, I started to get a sense of some mana about them. It wasn't in their core, not most of it at least, and it was shrouded in a way that reminded me of a window with a blanket tacked up in front of it. It didn't fool anybody into thinking there was no light on the outside; it just filtered enough light to keep it from being distracting to someone wanting a bit of darkness.

That was what I felt, a curtain drawn over the mana to mute its presence instead of a shield to hide it completely. I couldn't be certain if the effect was deliberate or not, but I had my suspicions based on what little magic I'd seen in my new life so far that it was more a lack of skill than a lack of choice. Whoever this person was, they were probably trying to cross the wastelands without attracting the notice of any predators that could sniff out mana, and this curtain was the best they could do to reduce the chances of being noticed.

"How do they know we're here?" Father asked.

"Same way the mana sniffers do," I said. "They can feel your mana core."

"From that far away? I can barely feel anything more than twenty feet."

I shrugged. "It's a skill you can get better at, just like anything else. If you'd been allowed to keep your mana growing up, your range would probably be ten times that with minimal effort made on your part. And there are special tools that can have miles-long ranges."

Those wouldn't be in the hands of some random person, though. And since I was sure that was what our uninvited guest was using to track Father's mana core, it narrowed down the possibilities considerably. It was too bad I didn't have the spare mana to shield Father's core for him or the time to teach him to do it himself. Shielding my own core didn't actually cost me any mana; it was just a technique that took some mental effort to maintain, sort of like keeping a muscle clenched. Shielding someone else's mana was a bit more complicated, unfortunately.

The person below us could be a complete stranger, perhaps from Derro. They could have been traveling by, noticed Father's mana, and decided to investigate. None of that seemed likely to me, but it was a possibility. Equally possible was the idea that we'd accidentally settled near some old hermit's abode and made enough noise to get them to come see what was going on. That also seemed unlikely.

The chances that the person under that hat was either Iskara or Noctra were significantly higher. Perhaps one of them had scried on their wagon, only to discover it empty. Perhaps Noctra had felt me usurp control of Nermet and wanted to get a closer look at that. It was even possible that they had some extremely sensitive device hidden away that could detect mana over miles. It would have to be properly calibrated to not go off every time some random farmer invoked a bit of mana to get a quick boost of strength, but if they had something like that, it would most definitely have picked up the magic I'd performed when I robbed the draw stones of their mana.

Then again, three Garrison members *had* shown up at our home an hour later.

Part of me was tempted to confirm my guess with a quick scry, but I squashed that idea with the knowledge that if I was right, I was going to need every bit of mana I could get my hands on to fight. Taking another caster on in a straight fight, even if she was just an adept with no personal mana of her own, was not how I'd wanted to handle the situation. I wasn't worried, not precisely, but no one wanted to get drawn into that kind of a confrontation.

If I were still Keiran the ancient archmage, it would have been different. Back then, I could generate enough mana to suppress dozens of apprentices' magic without even trying. They would simply be so outclassed that it would become a physical impossibility for them to even move mana around. Today, here, I couldn't do that. It would be more like fighting a duel of equals, except we'd both be armed with the mystical equivalent of a thorny switch instead of a mysteel blade.

The person reached the corpses of the mana sniffers I'd killed and halted. The number had grown from two to five over the last day, though they did seem to be getting smaller for some reason. Perhaps they had some sort of social hierarchy keyed to individual size, and the bigger ones got more territory or first feeding rights.

"Retreat back into the crevice," I said. "We'll let them burn some mana climbing up here before I face them."

"If you think I'm letting you deal with whoever that is alone—" Mother said.

"If it comes down to a fight, I don't need the handicap of having to defend you," I told her. "I'm sorry, but you have no mana and Father's barely better off. Neither of you can do much more than basic unstructured invocations. If I have to focus on defending you from fire blasts, I won't be able to fight."

"How do you know it'll be a fight?" Father asked.

"How much do you want to bet that's Iskara down there?"

"It... could be," Father said slowly. "Why are you so sure it is?"

"Because I stole all the mana from the village's draw stones before we came out here to rescue you, and Iskara is the one responsible for them. It could be someone else sensing your mana, but I don't know who else would have the training or equipment to track it over such long distances."

"All the more reason we should be the ones to meet her then," Father said. "We're the distraction. She focuses on us, thinks we're the threat, and then you hit her with the sneak attack."

I started to retort, but then I paused. That plan could actually work, but it did put a lot of risk on my parents. If Iskara didn't stop to talk, I'd have to deflect her opening attack without knowing who it was targeting. As long as the conjuration was physical and we stood relatively close together, I could probably do that without much issue.

If she used something like a stone-shaping transmutation to trap us, getting everyone out of the way would be a lot harder. A mental attack would almost certainly be aimed at one of my parents and would be almost impossible to block without using all of my mana to place mind shields on all three of us beforehand.

"It would be better if you waited as far back as possible with Senica," I said.

"That's not going to happen. You're still our son. We have to protect you," Father said.

There wasn't enough time to argue with them about this. Our uninvited guest was climbing up the side of the cliff now, and doing so at a much faster rate than the mana sniffers had. Now that she had to look up and her hat no longer obscured her face, I could confirm that it was definitely Iskara.

"We only have a minute," I said. "If you're staying, get Senica and Nermet as far back as possible. We'll wait in the open, not in front of the crevice. That way, if she does attack us, there's no chance of her shot going wide and striking anyone in hiding."

Mother ushered Senica back with some whispered warnings about hiding while Father gave Nermet instructions to stay out of sight and to keep Senica safe. As much as I couldn't condone using the subjugation spell to give orders, it was hard to fault Father for that one. Any decent person would have done that anyway, but Nermet physically couldn't unless someone told him to.

Hopefully he was doing what he would have chosen if he still had the ability to make that choice. Hopefully Father didn't die in the next few seconds and cause Nermet to go berserk. I'd warned Father that if something happened to him and the connection ran out of mana to fuel it, or if it snapped for whatever reason, there'd be a backlash that would probably break Nermet's mind the rest of the way.

That was a lot of pressure to put on him, and it was one of the reasons I hadn't wanted to keep the control nodule patch connected to my own mana. I was going to be doing the most dangerous parts soon, and I didn't want the possibility of my death to lead to that backlash.

We assembled into formation, Father and Mother standing close together and me hiding behind his leg, clutching it and peering around the side as I pretended to be a normal toddler. It felt ridiculous, but it should suffice to throw Iskara. As long as our nosy neighbor hadn't run her mouth about seeing us do any magic, we'd be fine. Even if she had, the reasonable assumption was that Mother had cast those spells, not me.

Iskara's hand appeared over the lip of the cliff. I could feel faint traces of mana hanging off her, some sort of climbing spell that made her hands and feet stick to the stone. That was a basic enchantment, something good for practicing with. It might mean that Iskara didn't know many spells beyond that range of difficulty. Or it might just mean that she was used to using the cheapest magic to get the job done. Adepts had to learn to keep careful track of their resources, after all.

Now that was something I could sympathize with. The way my life had been going since my reincarnation, I was starting to feel like an adept, too.

The one who functioned as Noctra's assistant in public and his partner in secret pulled herself fully onto the cliff. She stood up, patted some dust off her outfit, and looked over at us. "Sellis," she said, nodding first to him before looking at my mother. "Xilaya."

"What a surprise to see you out here," Father said.

"Yes, well, when things go wrong, I'm often the one who gets sent to clean up the mess. And this is a big mess. I wouldn't have thought... Huh. That's odd." Iskara paused and studied us intently. "How in the world did you obtain a spiritual blessing, Sellis?"

THIRTY-FOUR

I skara stared at my father, waiting for an answer. I could practically see the gears turning in her head, measuring, cataloguing, and assessing him. She took a step forward, then another.

"That's far enough," Father said, snapping her out of her funk.

"Hmm? Oh. Where was I?"

"A big mess," Mother said dryly.

"Ah, yes. But that was before I realized your husband had been blessed by the spirits. You must tell me how this happened."

There was a hunger in those words. It was well-hidden, but I recognized it. I'd seen it before. Adepts universally wanted to become mages. There was always a reason they couldn't, usually some sort of damage to their mana cores, but occasionally they suffered from a curse or disease that prevented them from manipulating their own mana. In this place, it seemed to be a lack of knowledge as to how to actually ignite a core that held adepts back.

They all wanted to fix that deficiency, whatever it was. I'd seen it dozens of times. Iskara was no exception. Oh, she had her tricks. There was a small wand hidden in her sleeve, probably fastened in place with some sort of wrist strap, that she could draw in an instant to shape the mana inside its crystal into some sort of attack. I also felt no less than six mana crystals around the wrist opposite of the wand, probably strung together on a bracelet. None of them were very big, but all were fully charged.

Iskara had more than enough mana available to her to kill us all. I couldn't let a fight drag out between us, not if I wanted to win. When I struck, it needed to be decisive, so fast that she never saw the spell coming. I needed something I could form instantly and that didn't have any sort of travel time, probably something that would damage her mind.

"I'm not really sure why you'd think I'd tell you anything after what you two did to me," Father said. "If you wanted my help, casting a sleep spell on me, then dragging me out into the middle of the wastes where I could have been eaten by any monster that happened to be in the area wasn't a great way to go about asking."

"That was before you received a blessing. Now you're a mage, and that means you're far too valuable," Iskara said.

"That's why you sent people to kidnap the rest of my family?" Father asked. "To do... what? To hold them hostage?"

"No, of course not," Iskara said. "That was unrelated to you becoming a mage."

I scanned the adept carefully. She was confident, and she had a lot of good reasons to be, but this seemed too much. Did she know something I didn't, or was I just overthinking things? I was used to opponents with monumental resources to draw on, able and willing to spend more mana on simple traps than my new body could generate in a year.

There couldn't be any traps. We'd been camping out on this ledge for days now, and if she'd tried to set something after arriving, I would have sensed it. I couldn't help but be wary of whatever trick she had to use against us. It wouldn't have to be formidable to stop me, not in the state I was in.

"But you realize that it doesn't exactly make me want to help you, right?"

"I don't see why we need to be enemies here," Iskara said with a shake of her head. "It's not like you all have never made mistakes. Last week you were a minor curiosity. Now you're in a position to become a strong asset and get ahead in life. Do you really want to be a farmer until you die? An ostracized farmer that the whole village hates, no less?"

There. When Iskara shook her head, I'd spotted a fine chain hanging around her neck. Now that I had a clue to tell me where to look, I could feel the draw stone amulet hanging under her shirt. That was a nasty trick, right there. A mage would never want to wear something like that; it would weaken them too much, either by stealing away their mana as it was generated or by wearing them out mentally resisting it.

An adept, on the other hand, generated almost no mana to begin with. All the fuel for Iskara's spells was stored in her bracelet, far enough away from the draw stone amulet that it wouldn't be affected until she drew it into her mana core. She'd only need to resist the pull for a few seconds while she cast the spell.

And in the meantime, any spell cast against her would see a majority of the mana drained away on contact. It wasn't perfect immunity by any means, and back when I'd been an archmage in possession of a stage nine mana core, I would have overwhelmed it without even trying. Now, things would be a bit trickier.

"You can't possibly expect me to trust Noctra after this," Father said while Mother nodded next to him.

"To hell with Noctra," Iskara said. "I'll make you a deal. You tell me how you obtained your blessing, show me how to do it too, and I'll kill Noctra myself."

I paused.

That shouldn't really have been a surprise. I'd already gotten the impression that the two weren't on the best of terms. If anything, it seemed like Iskara had been sent by whatever cabal he answered to back in Derro to keep an eye on him and ensure regular shipments of mana made their way back to her masters.

"You'd betray him?" Mother asked sharply. "How are we supposed to trust you if you'd stab a man you've been working with for fifteen years in the back?"

Iskara started laughing. "Oh no, I don't work with Noctra. He's here as a punishment. I'm here to make sure he pays back his debts. Trust me, he hates my guts."

I silently willed my parents to keep Iskara talking, to fish more information out of her, but they both just stared at her mutely. Whoever Iskara's employer was, that was who we would need to worry about after I killed Noctra. The more I could learn about them now, the better off we'd be in the future.

I considered a mental interrogation, but it would almost certainly cost me more mana than I had available. Even if I could break the attunement on Iskara's mana crystals, there was so little in there that it wouldn't be worth the effort. The wand was the same story. They were hand-crafted for the individual who would wield them, though I was curious to see what kind of design changes had been made to compensate for an environment completely devoid of ambient mana.

The short version was that I did not have the budget to go trawling through Iskara's brain for secrets, and I wasn't likely to get much from her anyway. Worse, thanks to that draw stone amulet, I was going to have to be creative with how I put her down. I was considering a transmutation to soften the stone under her feet, but doing it at that range fast enough to trap her would be problematic.

Throwing her off the cliff also had its appeal, but I couldn't trust that she wouldn't save herself with a simple weight reduction invocation. The amulet's location so close to her head also made mental attacks problematic.

A wide burst of fire would probably be effective, though the damage would be far more severe on her bottom half. But really, the best solution would be to cut her off from her tools. An adept without any outside sources of mana was just a regular human with a lot of academic knowledge about how magic worked, after all.

"If it's a punishment for him, why isn't it a punishment for you?" Mother asked.

Iskara shook her head and smirked at my parents. "Now, now. Let's see a bit of reciprocal trust before I go giving away the big secrets. Tell me how you gained your blessing."

"I don't think so," Father said.

In an instant, Iskara's whole demeanor shifted. "I don't think you understand. You're going to tell me. You can do it voluntarily, or I can make you. If you don't want to cooperate, I'll pin the three of... wait, don't you have two kids? Where's the other one?"

Iskara started drawing in mana from her bracelet, and I fought to hold back a grin. There was an angle I hadn't considered once I'd found out about the amulet. In order to cast a spell, she needed to hold off the draw stone from disrupting her mana. I'd assumed she'd be well practiced at it.

She wasn't. Not only was she struggling to keep her mana inside her core while she made the spell, she actually closed her eyes to help her concentrate. Iskara was as vulnerable as she'd ever be, at least for the next few seconds. That was plenty of time.

I conjured up a big block of stone and lobbed it up in an arc to crash down on her head.

Iskara went down in a heap. Blood ran down her face from under her hair, and the mana she'd been working on shaping into a spell disappeared into the draw stone in a flash. She groaned and tried to climb back to her feet, but wasn't able to get past her hands and knees.

Beside me, both of my parents shouted in surprise. I stepped out from around Father's leg and examined my victim. Her head was lolling to one side and blood ran freely to drip onto the stone below. My conjured stone had dissolved right around the same time it had impacted her skull, the mana that formed it disrupted by her draw stone amulet. Most of the spell's mana flashed into the atmosphere where it was drunk up by the harsh environment.

As I approached, I performed a simple act of minor telekinesis to take her wand from her. It was the easier of the two weapons to remove, and potentially the more dangerous if she managed to palm it and used it to increase her offensive capabilities.

I took the bracelet next. It wasn't even something with a clasp or latch, just a plain leather band with six small red stones embedded in them. Garnets, perhaps. My magic tugged it off her wrist and it flew through the air into my waiting grasp.

"You see, the problem is that you'd turn on us even if we agreed to ally with you. If there's one thing people like you are reliable about, it's looking out for your own best interest at the cost of your supposed allies," I said. "Goodbye, Perfidy."

Even in her current state, I didn't trust her enough to get close so that I could remove that amulet. Instead, I used a considerably more powerful version of minor telekinesis, appropriately known as greater telekinesis, to grab Iskara by her foot and drag her backwards thirty feet into the open air. Her body swung loose as it slipped off the side of the cliff, and I let her fall to her death.

My parents watched, slack-jawed. I turned back to them and shook my head. "I thought I'd made it clear that I was killing both of them. I was hoping you'd get a bit more information before I struck, but it wasn't worth the risk once she started casting a spell."

"You just... just like that," Father said. "You're a murderer."

I shrugged. "So was she."

"You don't know that," Mother said.

"What do you think she was planning on doing to us?" I asked. "Why was she asking about your kids? Do you think that was the first time she'd ever used someone's family as leverage? Should I have let her torture Senica until you told her what she wanted to know so that you'd feel morally justified in killing her?"

"No! It's just..."

"The only difference between killing Iskara and killing Noctra is that I don't plan on confronting him first," I said.

I glanced over the edge of the cliff at Iskara's body. She was either very dead or double jointed in every limb, including her neck. I was betting on the former, but I cast a quick scry to confirm it. The last thing I needed right now was her activating some contingency spell with her dying breath.

But no, she was very, very dead. "I have work to do," I said as I walked past my parents into the shade of the crevice.

THIRTY-FIVE

The first thing I wanted to study was the wand I'd taken from Iskara. It wasn't going to be much use to me personally, but it would be an excellent tool to help Father along if I could adapt it to work with him. That assumed I was able to get it working for him without breaking it. Mana crystals were far, far superior to storage crystals in terms of maximum size and efficiency, but they did require an attunement that limited their use to the mage who'd bonded with one. Sometimes it just wasn't possible to recycle a mana crystal, especially one that was so small.

And all of Iskara's had been very, very small. She'd made up for quality with an abundance of quantity, which had its own drawbacks. Foremost among them was access speed. It would be prohibitively difficult to draw from all six mana crystals at once, seven if her wand counted, which meant she needed to pull from them sequentially. That would slow her down a great deal, especially with that draw stone amulet she'd been wearing.

I still wasn't quite sure why she'd come out with that as her defense. She hadn't known she'd be facing a mage, and it wouldn't do much good in hiding her mana from any of the predatory monsters in the wastelands. Nobody would walk around with such a thing hanging off their neck for no reason, though; they were decidedly uncomfortable even to those who had dormant mana cores.

I also hadn't retrieved whatever mana tracking device she'd used to find us. Given the state of her body at the base of the cliff, I had good reason to suspect that it had been damaged in the fall and would likely be useless to me. Even if it hadn't been, I didn't have an immediate use for it anyway. It wasn't like they were that hard to build if I ever changed my mind.

The wand itself was a little thing, finger width and appearing to be nothing more than a neatly trimmed stick. It had been hollowed out and a tiny cylindrical mana crystal slotted inside. That had grown hair-thin connections that burrowed into the wood and spread through the fibers to form the enchantment that helped increase the mage's control of any spells cast through it.

Severing the attunement to a dead woman would be a delicate task, but I thought I could probably manage it without doing any damage to the wand if I had plenty of time to work and wasn't stingy with my own mana. That having been said, I wasn't sure I should. The mana crystal wasn't that big, and the enchantments weren't that complex. I could probably make a better wand from nothing for about the same amount of mana. If I'd had access to my old workshop, I could have done it for a fraction of the cost.

The bracelet of mana crystals was the same issue. First, the stones were so small that they could barely hold any mana. For some reason, whoever had crafted it had used actual gemstones, which anybody who'd made it past the apprentice stage would know was a terrible idea. It wasn't that gemstones were worse than any regular old rock. If anything, they held more mana. But physical size mattered, and it was a lot easier to find a big rock than a big diamond or ruby. The gems barely had any glow at all in them despite being fully charged. Besides, jewelry made for tempting targets for thieves. There was a reason I'd chosen a rock that weighed fifty or sixty pounds as the base object to transmute into my own personal mana crystal.

It was too bad there was no ambient mana here. It would have been nice to build an obelisk to power some big experiments. But without any way to power it, it would be nothing but a big, fancy, dead rock. I had some vague notions of building a bank of mana crystals instead, but in truth, I would probably just leave the area in a few years. The lack of mana was too big of a handicap to justify staying here forever.

"What are you doing?" Senica asked, startling me out of my examination.

"Looking at this," I said, holding up the bracelet of garnets.

"That's pretty," she said. "Where did you get it?"

"From that lady who was here a bit ago. She tried to attack us, so I took it from her. Would you like it?"

Senica's eyes went wide. "I can have it? Are you sure?"

"All yours," I told her as I held it out.

She took it from my hands and peered at it more closely, then threw her arms around me in a hug. "Thanks! I'm going to wear it every day."

"It'll look good on you," I said.

If we'd been anywhere else, I wouldn't have given it to her. It was too valuable, even if I didn't factor in the mana crystal aspect of the gemstones. But there was no one out here, and by the time Senica returned to the village, I planned on having dispatched Noctra and informed everyone about what he'd been up to.

I did not expect that conversation to go over well. The villagers had been taken in by a long con. Fifteen years of believing what Noctra told them was not going to be overcome with a single speech, and most of the evidence I could provide would go completely over their heads. It wasn't like I could prove that Noctra had subjugated the village idiot. He'd always been slow. Nobody but me could measure out how much mana he'd taken from them, and everyone already believed they had a barrier protecting them despite clear evidence to the contrary.

Maybe, weeks and months after the fact when they still had no monsters come sniffing around the village despite Noctra being gone, they might accept that there had never been a barrier in the first place, that their isolation and lack of mana was what had kept them safe. Though without the draw stone harvest, they would start to fill those cores again. That might just mean better harvests as they had more mana to pour into their work. Only time would tell.

Regardless of how the village reacted to it, I was still planning on killing Noctra. Even if I ignored what he'd done to Father, I wasn't about to excuse the torture he'd put Nermet through. That made me something of a hypocrite, but I could live with that. I'd paid for my own sins many times over already, and I didn't care if Noctra didn't get the opportunity to make reparations, not when he was so dangerous to me on a personal level right now.

"What are you two up to?" Mother asked as she walked over to where I was seated.

"Look what Gravvy just gave me," Senica said, holding the bracelet up for everyone to see.

"Oh, that's very pretty," Mother said. "Let me help you put that on."

Senica was distracted by the bracelet and missed the look Mother gave me, one part shock and one part disgust. Apparently, she had some hangups about looting the dead. I supposed that wasn't a surprise, all things considered. Plenty of people new to violence had that reaction, especially those who'd never had to fight to stay alive. If she was lucky, this whole experience would be the first and last time she ever dealt with something like that. It wasn't like I was planning on bringing any of them along when I went after Iskara's partner.

This was probably going to do some long-term damage to my relationship with my parents. I could try to do some damage control, but I couldn't picture that being anything more than cheap lies and justifications. At the end of the day, I was perfectly willing to kill to solve problems when the people causing those problems were evil. That was something my parents would have to accept, or we would quickly grow apart.

Even if they rejected me and pushed me away, they were still better parents than I'd had the first time around, though that bar was incredibly low. Just knowing my father's name was enough to put him ahead of whoever had paid my mother for ten minutes on her sweat-stained bed back when I was Keiran. The fact that my new mother did things like provide food for me had secured her place ahead of the competition. I hadn't even been beaten by anyone yet, not even once.

It was... nice. Different. I wasn't sure how I felt about it. Having any sort of affection for my new parents hadn't been part of my original plan, but I'd found that I was enjoying having a family. I would just have to hope this new reaction to me was brought on by the shock of sudden violence coupled with the fact that I was physically three.

I wasn't sure what I'd be willing to give up to keep them just yet. Would I need to change who I was to be accepted? If so, was I willing to do that? Compromise was a cornerstone to relationships, after all. Nobody got what they wanted all the time, not if they wanted to have true, genuine friends. Down that route lay nothing but sycophants and toadies. That was fine for the man who didn't want or need relationships with other people, but it could be an awfully lonely way to exist, especially for someone who was going to live for thousands of years.

It didn't necessarily mean I needed to hold a relationship with these particular people, who, if I was being honest, were probably all going to be dead in the next century anyway, but I would like to look back on my birth family with some fondness a thousand years down the road.

After she got Senica's bracelet attached, a feat that required it to be double wrapped around her wrist, Mother said, "Can you go find your father for me, sweetie?" and shooed my sister off. With just the two of us, not counting Nermet, who was just lurking in the corner, doing nothing but breathing, she turned to me with a serious look on her face.

"I'm assuming you want to talk," I said.

"Gravin, I... You just..." Mother trailed off. "You understand why this would be hard for us, right? You get that what you did is terrifying?"

"I won't apologize for defending us. She was already gathering the mana to attack."

"I know. Your father felt her doing it, too. He didn't feel yours, however. That's something he wants to ask you about later."

I waved off the question. "Just a matter of speed and practice. There's no trick there."

"Yes, well, you can talk to him about that later. I just... You scared me. This kind of stuff, it doesn't happen here. It's not supposed to. Evil mages and their sinister plots are fairy tales. People don't go around killing each other. We can't. We'd never survive if we did stuff like that."

She wasn't necessarily wrong, but she was ignoring a few facts there, namely that Noctra had been the aggressor in this fight. If he'd left Father alone instead of trying to exploit him, we'd all be sitting at home right now. Though if I was being fair, I would have come into conflict with the village's governor anyway over his exploitation of mana.

"I guess what I'm trying to say is..." Mother trailed off while she gathered her thoughts.

It didn't take a genius to predict where this was going. They couldn't condone my actions. I was disruptive to the community. If they tolerated my presence, society would begin to break down. I'd heard that speech before, a long time ago.

"Doing something like that, it's..."

Here it came.

"Just, your sister isn't like you. She's still a child. You need to make an effort to protect her from being exposed to this kind of stuff. That's important." Mother gave me a hug and added, "Go find your father when you're done here."

Oh. I wasn't expecting that.

CHAPTER

THIRTY-SIX

I waited for Father to finish congratulating Senica on her new bracelet before I stood up. None of us were exactly getting any privacy here, but then again, it wasn't like we'd had a lot back home, either. It was a miracle I'd managed to be born at all, once I thought about it. Then again, considering that most huts held at least two and sometimes three generations, and rarely were they any bigger than mine, I supposed there were some differing cultural notions about privacy and what a couple could do with their kids nearby than what I was used to.

That wasn't to say that I hadn't heard my own mother doing the deed hundreds of times with hundreds of different men during my first childhood, just that we had been so low on the societal ladder that the people I grew up around didn't concern themselves with things like being polite or respecting other people. We couldn't afford to do stuff like that back then.

For all of that, I hadn't shared a bed with my original mother, and I was doubly glad to be out of the bed of my current parents, even if it was early by village standards. If I could get away with it, I'd build my own little guest room in the garden and sleep there. Assuming I gained some nominal form of control over the village after I took care of Noctra, I was going to introduce them to the idea of walls. We had plenty of space; there was no reason those huts needed to all be single-room affairs.

Eventually, I grew bored of waiting. There was very little in the way of entertainment here, which meant Senica was going to be taking up the attention of at least one other person at all times. Right now, that person just so happened to be who I needed to talk to. I was in no rush, but time wasted getting started was time wasted that Father could have been using.

Once I was on my feet, Father got things wrapped up with Senica and sent her off to play, not that there was much to do. I would not be even a little bit surprised to catch her eavesdropping on us in the next few minutes. Considering the subject matter of the conversation, I didn't much mind. I just preferred eavesdropping to including her because if she thought she was being sneaky, she wouldn't interrupt. Hopefully.

"How are you feeling?" Father asked.

"I'm fine. I'm recovering mana at a steady rate, and we should be ready to leave tomorrow evening."

"That's not what I meant," Father said.

"I know," I told him. "I don't regret killing Iskara. She's a long, long way from the first person I've killed, and I sincerely doubt my current life will be so peaceful that she's anywhere near the last."

Father tried to suppress a shudder, but I could see it anyway. It did not surprise me that this kind of talk made him uncomfortable. He was a farmer, like most of the village, and not even one who dealt in livestock. There was very little in the way of fresh meat in our diet. It wasn't entirely absent, but only a handful of people were required to take care of the few chickens and pigs the village owned.

For all his temper and however satisfying it might have been to punch Cherok in the face, Father wasn't comfortable with a display of lethal magical power. There was certainly nothing wrong with that, and it wasn't like I was intending on bringing him with me to Noctra's assassination. If he was a lucky man, he'd never see anyone else die again. I wasn't going to bet on that happening, but it was technically possible.

"I want to start teaching you magic now that you've ignited your core," I said, pushing the conversation along to a new topic. Father hesitated a moment, then nodded.

"Do you think I'm ready so soon?" he asked.

"Why not? Anyone can learn to use magic. The only thing holding you back was a lack of mana. Besides, you've got to start somewhere. You've got some reserves built up. I'm going to get you started today with a brief overview of different disciplines and some simple exercises."

"Ancestors save my soul. I'm back in school," Father said with a laugh.

I flashed him a grin and said, "You've never had a master like me."

"Oh no, what have I gotten myself into?"

He wasn't taking me seriously. That was understandable, given the circumstances. I was three. I was his son. None of the magic I'd used was all that visibly impressive. I lacked the time and resources to put him through some intensive training, for now. But I'd have him cursing my name before my fourth birthday.

"There are seven disciplines, but we are only going to concern ourselves with two of them today. They are: alchemy, conjuration, divination, enchantment, inscription, invocation, and transmutation. The two we are going to work on are conjuration and invocation, but let's go over the rest in the broadest of possible strokes.

"Alchemy is the discipline of extracting mana from raw materials. This is different from ambient mana as the materials filter or alter the mana in some fundamental way, which can be used to a variety of effects. It is a complicated discipline that we will not be spending any time on for the simple reason that it's worthless here. Without any ambient mana for the raw materials to take in, there is nothing here that can be used as a base for alchemy on its own.

"Divination is the act of receiving information through structured magical spells. It can be used to see far-off locations, hear conversations from miles away, find someone or something you have lost, and even predict the future in a limited capacity. There are some novice divinations that we'll study at a later time, but it is one of the more difficult disciplines to start with.

"Enchantment is the discipline we will most likely visit after conjuration and invocation, and it is characterized by its study of spells that rely on artificial mana cores to function. It has nigh-endless applications and mages who choose to specialize in this discipline are almost always highly sought-after and well-compensated. It is also one of the most technically demanding disciplines.

"Inscription—"

"Whoa, hold up," Father said, interrupting me with a raised hand. I felt my mouth twist into a hard frown, but I paused. I hated being cut off when I was speaking.

"You have a question?" I asked.

"If I'm not going to be learning any of these disciplines, why are you explaining them to me?"

"No apprentice of mine is going to be so poorly trained that he doesn't learn at least the basics of every discipline. Given our location, I am inclined to give you some slack when it comes to alchemy, but rest assured, you will learn enough of the other six disciplines to at least perform basic-ranked spells and be able to self-learn intermediate-ranked ones."

"And what if I don't want to do that?" Father said, challenge in his tone.

"Then I will call you a fool and wash my hands of teaching you anything at all. I will not have a student who does not wish to learn." It was clear to me that my father wasn't taking this seriously. Unfortunately, I lacked the means to show off some of the more spectacular spells in my repertoire.

"Gravin, I know you mean well, but I think you are forgetting where we are and who we are. We are simple folk. I work in a field every day, and thanks to you, I'm going to be able to get more done in less time and be in better shape at the end of it. But I don't need a mage's education when I am not a mage."

I stared at him, dumbfounded. "Do you honestly believe I spent the time and resources to help you ignite your core so that you could *remain a farmer* when I was done with you?"

He bristled at that and snapped, "Whether I choose to remain a farmer or do anything else isn't really up to you, now is it? What makes you think you have a say in my life like that anyway?"

This wasn't going at all how I'd expected it to. Perhaps I'd just become used to my former reputation. For hundreds of years, I'd had people begging me, sometimes on their knees with their heads pressed against the floor, to teach them magic. Literal kings and emperors had tried to entice me into tutoring their children. And everyone, *everyone*, understood the inherent power and status of an archmage. There'd seldom been a need to impress upon a prospective student how rare of an opportunity they were being given, not even if they were of royal blood.

And then there was my father, a simple farmer who'd spent most of his life being swindled out of his mana by a con man, born and raised in a desert without a speck of mana in the air or dirt. Not only did he not understand what I was offering, he didn't even care to find out. He was humoring me, the way any parent might when their child told them something they'd learned.

The Gravin part of me was hurt that my dear father, whom I loved so very much, wasn't taking me seriously. The Keiran part of me was coldly furious and seriously contemplating leaving him stranded up here for a few days after we left. I would give him some advice on the invocation he'd need to get down and let him figure it out himself. Maybe he'd be more appreciative of me in the future.

I firmly quashed both of those parts. It was not fair to hold Father to the same standards as students from my past life. He wasn't a mage. He was barely even an apprentice, and only by the most technical of standards. And he was right. He hadn't asked for this. If not for him needing to do this to save Nermet's life, he would still have a dormant core.

"You're right," I said. "It wasn't my place to just decide that you would become a mage. But you still should. There are so many things I can teach you. Even with your core limited to its current stage, you could learn spells to feed a dozen families by yourself. You could learn how to defend the other villagers if a monster appears in the fields. And they're going to need that. Noctra has to go."

"You have a point, but Gravin, I don't want to be the guy who fights monsters. I tried that once. It didn't end well for me. It got someone else killed."

"Not to put too fine a point on it, but if you had known the spells I plan on teaching you, even just the novice-tier ones, you might have saved your friend's life. Someone in this village is going to need to know how to do this, someone who can lead them. I can't do that, not now. Maybe not ever."

"You think I can?" Father was incredulous. "They hate me."

I shrugged. "How many of them do you think are going to follow instructions from a child? I can't even get you to do it without an argument, and you know what I am."

"We could leave Noctra in charge," Father said.

"Is that really what you want? He literally kidnapped you and tried to sell you into slavery. He's been lying to everyone for over a decade and stealing the mana of over a hundred people. We're one bad harvest away from starving to death because of him. He has to go."

Father sighed, but nodded. "I know. It's not ideal. But it might be worse without him."

"That's why I'm trying to teach you what you need to know to replace him. I don't expect you to become a master, certainly not overnight and maybe not ever, but I'm hoping to teach you enough that you can help others ignite their cores and make this village prosper."

"I don't want that responsibility. Twenty years ago, when I was a kid, sure. But not today. Not now."

"Sorry, but you're the only one here. Even if it's not forever, someone needs to step in. Noctra's not going to just leave us alone while I interview the neighbors until I find someone I think is a good fit. It's you or no one."

Father sat there for a minute and thought it over while I waited and pretended I couldn't see Senica's wide-eyed stare from around the corner. Our voices had been raised at some point during the argument, high enough that everyone had heard us. I briefly wondered what Mother thought of my plan.

Finally, Father nodded. "I can't promise I'm going to become a mage. But I'll do my best to keep the village safe until we can find someone who will. You were saying?"

"I believe I'd made it to inscription. Now..."

CHAPTER

THIRTY-SEVEN

I t took me a second to get back into the rhythm of things, and even though I'd given this speech many, many times in my past life, it suddenly felt awkward to be doing it again now. But I'd given magical lectures under worse conditions, and I could do it again now.

"Inscription is similar to enchanting, except that you are inscribing the language of magic onto a physical object. The primary purpose of this is to allow anyone to pick up that object and, assuming a base requisite amount of training, push mana into it to activate it. You might think of it as the other side of enchantment's coin.

"Finally, transmutation. This is the discipline of magic that involves permanently changing one thing into another. Similar to conjuration, the magic is created, it has an effect, and then it ends. The difference is that the temporary effect deliberately alters a physical object. This is different than, for example, conjuring a blast of fire which incidentally leaves the ground scorched."

"That... is a lot," Father said.

"It is," I agreed. "And I'm not going to get into any of those five disciplines beyond what I've just told you. Just knowing their basic purviews is enough information for today. What we're going to talk about instead are invocations, which are the easiest spells to learn, and conjurations, which are the opposite of invocations. The primary difference is that invocations are an internal expression of mana, whereas conjurations are external."

"Okay, I'm with you so far. Invocations are what we're all doing every day to help us work the fields," Father said. "And you can show me how to do it better, I guess? Be more efficient?"

"Technically speaking, I have only observed people using unstructured mana in a way that produces similar effects to an invocation spell. You could classify it as more of a pseudo-invocation than an actual spell. But yes, I'm going to give you some exercises to practice, and teach you how to cast the spell known as weight reduction. It's the spell you'll use to get down from here tomorrow, so it's important to pay attention."

"Wait, do you mean..." Father trailed off as he glanced over at the edge of the cliff. "Are you expecting me to voluntarily jump off of that tomorrow and trust in a spell I don't know how to cast to save my life?"

"I would recommend practicing today," I said dryly. "I've been forced into situations where I've had to use unfamiliar magic on the fly before. It seldom went well."

"But you're going to be watching to save me if something goes wrong, right?"

I shrugged. "I'm on a limited mana budget right now. I'm sure you'll rise to the challenge."

"Spirits guide my path. My son is a monster."

I ignored that. I'd been called worse, and rightfully so. Father's sarcasm aside, I *was* a monster. Just because I'd grown softer in my old age did not make me any less of one. There had been a time in my life when many people had a vested interest in killing me, and in retrospect, they'd been right to make the attempt.

"Let's start with some mana control exercises. You need to be able to direct your mana to do what you want before you can shape it into a spell. It's important to learn and know your own limits here as well. Having access to all the mana in the world does you no good if your mind is so wrung out that you can't concentrate well enough to put together the simplest spell. Additionally, the worse your concentration, the sloppier your spell, which wastes your mana."

In my past life, I would have saved that lesson for after an apprentice had the basics down. Refining mana control was important, but more so at the higher levels of spells where a bleed over effect could ruin the entire thing. Given the situation we were in, though, techniques for conserving mana were going to be some of the most important things I could teach Father.

Fortunately, invocations were uniquely suited to practice this. Since the mana was imbued into the caster's body, it was much easier to recycle excess mana back into the core without anything escaping into the air. That was, not coincidentally, why I started every new apprentice mage with invocations. They were fantastic learning tools for beginners. Everything was easier to control and sense.

"You remember how we spun the mana in your core to pack it down during your ignition?" I asked.

"I do," Father said.

"This will be similar to that, except that instead of keeping it in your core, the goal is to sweep the mana out to the tips of your fingers and toes, and then bring it back to your core without losing any. Think of it somewhat like doing stretches for your mana core instead of your body. The easy part of this will be moving your mana out. The hard part will be bringing it back without losing any along the way."

I watched as Father took his hesitant first steps along the road of magic and offered him guidance where I could. His early attempts often resulted in his mana threading its way down his arms and legs, usually getting close to his goal, and breaking apart when he overextended himself. After the fifth time, I said, "Remember, this exercise is about control. You need to stop trying to give your mana momentum. You're not heaving it in an explosion of strength. You are guiding it with a steady hand to where it needs to be."

Father grumbled something under his breath, but he slowed down and kept a tighter grip on his mana after that. It didn't stretch nearly as far, but he also didn't lose nearly as much when he pulled it back. "I thought you said getting the mana to my hands and feet was the easy part," he said after a while.

"It is."

"Doesn't feel very easy."

"Well, 'easy' is a relative term."

Senica wandered over around then and asked, "Can I try too?"

Considering it had been days since she'd been subjected to a draw stone, her mana core was better than half full. She certainly had enough reserves to perform the exercise, but I had some doubts about her ability to control her mana. Still, it wouldn't hurt anything if she wasted her mana on this and I'd be right here to keep an eye on her if she tried to do anything dangerous.

"Sure," I said. "Do you need any help?"

"Nope!"

She settled down right next to Father, who'd had his eyes closed for most of the last hour in an attempt to increase his focus on the task. He didn't look down at her, but I saw the corner of his mouth curl up into a smile.

It took her twenty minutes to complete the exercise, a bit faster than I'd expected. "I did it!" she said, disrupting Father's concentration again. His eyes popped open to give her a look of disbelief before shifting to me.

I shrugged. "She did. It's not surprising, really. She's smaller, so less physical distance, and she has less mana, so less effort to control it."

"She's six!" Father protested.

"I suppose she's a natural. Maybe we should have ignited her core instead of yours."

Father thought about that for a second, then laughed. "I guess so."

He continued to practice with Senica's encouragement. That wasn't doing much for his focus, but since he might someday need to put together a spell while someone else was actively trying to kill him, I let her keep distracting him. As far as handicaps went, this one was pretty mild.

Surprisingly, not all of her advice was bad. I had to clap a hand over my mouth to keep from laughing when, during one of his attempts, she said, "No, Dad! You have to push it out from the center, not pull on it. That's why it keeps breaking! You're stretching it too much."

Father had been attempting to work the strands of mana winding through his limbs with a sort of gentle pulling motion of his mana, stretching it thinner and thinner the farther it reached. He was pushing more mana in to reinforce the structure, but on Senica's advice, he switched to pushing it out from his core to give it more length and focusing his mental efforts on holding its shape.

There were hundreds of different mana manipulation techniques, and my personal style of teaching was to introduce a student to some base concepts, let them take some time to get a feel for how they wanted to move their mana around, and suggest exercises and training regimens to refine what they were trying to do or alternatives that would be easy for them to transition into. This tended to result in better control as students found what worked best for them before building on it.

But this worked too, and considering how little time we had to actually work on Father's mana control, I couldn't bring myself to object to the interference in the process. It seemed to be helping at least, even if it wasn't the route Father would have naturally gone to on his own.

"Oh, I think I did it," Father said in surprise. His mana had stretched all the way down into his toes while still tightly controlled.

"Now pull it back in without losing any," I said. "Once you can reliably do that, we'll start on the actual spell itself."

The training continued on into the evening with a break for some frankly unappealing raw food from our garden, now several days old. All of us were eager to return to the village, if for no other reason than to have access to the garden and cooking fire again. Despite knowing how I needed to carefully conserve my mana, I had to resist serious temptation to do something to make the meal more palatable.

My father wasn't the brightest student I'd ever taught, not by a long shot, but he was adequate. For the limited plans I'd begun drafting for the future of the village, he would do well enough. It didn't seem like he was interested in a permanent position running the place and defending it, but I thought I could talk him into at least holding the spot until he could find someone to replace him. If I was really lucky, he'd pass on whatever magical knowledge I managed to impart over the next few weeks or months, and I'd be able to go completely hands off with managing the village.

If I were in a better position to do so, I might have considered Senica as a possible student. She was too young still—ironic coming from me—but in five or six years, she would be the perfect age, and I was in a unique position to lay down substantial groundwork with her. As it stood, I just didn't have the mana to devote to helping her yet. Maybe in a year or two, that would change, but I doubted it.

"And that's ten," Father wheezed out as he finished the final stretch of his mana I'd demanded of him. More than half of his reserves had been lost to practice, but that would all refill while he was asleep anyway.

"Alright, time to move on then. Let me show you the weight reduction spell," I said.

"What, right now? I'm exhausted."

"That's intentional," I told him. "You need to be able to cast spells under extreme conditions. A spell you can only use in a test chamber with no outside interference is no use to you. If you find yourself falling from a thousand feet up, you have only seconds to cast this spell before you hit the ground and die. You won't get a second chance if you mess it up."

Father groaned and pulled himself back fully upright. "Okay, okay. You're right. Tell me what to do, oh wise master."

Once again, I ignored the sarcasm, but I did find myself missing my teaching staff. It had that one nifty little inscription to make someone's bottom feel like they'd been swatted with a switch for thirty seconds before the pain faded. I could have used that about now.

There was no sense crying over the loss. I started to pull my own mana out of my core to show Father where and how to use his, being very careful not to actually cast the spell as I demonstrated each part. I was going to need that mana back; there was no reason to waste it.

CHAPTER
THIRTY-EIGHT

"*Raro aevinta temin*," Father said in time with the mana swirling through him.

"No. Not temin. *Temun*," I corrected.

"Does it matter? You said the words were just for the tempo?"

"Not *just* for the tempo, and while you can get away with saying the wrong runes now, being slipshod isn't going to help you in the future. Verbalizing runes has some leeway for novice spells; that's why they're novice spells to begin with. You can make mistakes and still get more or less the result you want, even if it costs more mana and time for an effect that isn't as strong. But it's better to learn it right from the start, especially since when you get to the point where you're inscribing the runes onto physical objects, you can't make even the slightest mistake there."

The mana slipped away from Father's aborted magic while I lectured him, and by the time my explanation had finished, there was no trace of a weight reduction spell to be found. I frowned at that and made a mental note to show Father some exercises aimed at increasing his ability to hold mana into a specific shape for longer periods of time. Sometimes it was important to have a spell completed and ready to be unleashed in an instant, like a crossbow pointed at a doorway, finger on the trigger, just waiting for someone to walk through.

"I need a break," Father said as he flopped down onto the rock he'd claimed as his chair. The frown on my lips deepened, but I forced it away. It wasn't fair to expect Father to be able to handle as much mana manipulation as any of my previous students. Even beginners who'd never done any spellwork normally had the advantage of living in an environment rich in ambient mana. Their bodies adapted to that and provided a stronger foundation when it came time to consciously use that mana.

Becoming a true mage in this desert would be a challenge, but it had its benefits to balance out the drawbacks. Without ambient mana in the background, it would be much easier to practice new spells, at least until Father's internal mana ran out. At that point, he'd have to wait all that much longer for it to naturally regenerate.

Now that I thought about it, his mana core was getting dangerously low. We couldn't afford to let it empty out completely, not with him needing to supply a constant stream of mana to Nermet in order to maintain the subjugation override. I needed to account for that both in terms of his total available mana and how quickly he would get worn down. Maintaining the link while practicing was somewhat like wearing weighted training clothes while lifting weights.

"I suppose we could rest for a few minutes," I said.

"I was thinking an hour or two," Father shot back.

"You'll never get anywhere if that's the limits of your discipline," I told him, to which Father rolled his eyes.

"You're worse than the overseers in the fields," he said. "Half an hour?"

"I suppose, but then we're back to practicing until it's time to eat."

"Deal," he said as he leaned back and put his weight on his hands. "Spirits save me, I can't believe I'm back out in the wastelands again."

"You never did tell me what happened all those years ago."

He sighed and said, "No, I suppose I didn't. It's a painful memory."

"I don't want to press you, but I got the impression that the barrier was real back then, that it actually protected you from monsters."

"Oh, it was. Why do you think the entire village believes in it? The previous governor, Lord Emeto, maintained it by himself. When Noctra arrived, he claimed that it was broken, that he'd repaired it, but it would need much more mana to function now."

That was a reasonable claim in my mind. If something had been broken and the repairs weren't up to standard, mana leakage was entirely possible. It wasn't necessarily a difficult fix, but given what I knew of Noctra's skill level, I would be more surprised that he managed to get a broken ward stone functional at all than that his patch job had holes in it.

"I was... oh, twelve or so," Father said. "My ego was as big as could be, all puffed up because Lord Emeto was teaching me rudimentary mana control. I was special. I was going to learn how to cast spells. I was going to be better than everyone else." He paused and shook his head. "I was an idiot, even for my age.

"I thought that because I could sense mana in others, that it would be fine to go out exploring. If any monsters started coming at us, I'd know they were there. And I was young and strong. I could run for miles without stopping. So I went outside the barrier, and I convinced my two best friends to come with me. Your mother was one of them; the other was a boy named Teno.

"Things were fine the first time we did it, and the second, and the third. We kept going farther and farther away from the safety of the village, spirits bless me if I know why. It's not like there's much to see out here, right? You've seen one patch of barren, scorched earth, you've seen them all. I guess we all thought we'd find some buried treasure or something out here. But we never did."

Father paused to collect his thoughts while I waited. It was hard for me to empathize with that mindset, probably because I'd never had a time as a child where I felt safe and invincible. I'd learned at an early age that I didn't even need to go looking for trouble. In the city of my birth, all I needed to do was stand still long enough and trouble would find me, even in my own home. Nowhere was safe.

Of all the things I regretted in my past, burning down the mansions along Golden Row was not one of them. The only thing that would have made it better was if I could have locked those noble pricks inside while I did it. The way they ran that city earned them death a dozen times over.

"It was a snapmaw that found us. I don't know if you know what those are?" Father shot me a quick glance, and when I shook my head, he continued. "Imagine a lizard as big as a man, brown and orange to help it blend in with the wastes, but able to run three times faster than a human infusing his body with mana. They're ambush predators, hard to spot and quick to close their jaws around their prey, then drag it off to whatever rock they like hiding under to eat it.

"Snapmaws aren't magical, not any more than the rest of us, at least.

And their mana gets spent helping them hide. My oh-so-brilliant plan of just knowing when something was nearby by sensing its mana failed completely, and who lived and who died that day was decided by one simple factor: which of us was standing closest to the snapmaw's hiding spot.

"Teno was probably dead before we even knew the snapmaw was there," Father said, his voice heavy. "Just... snuffed out. Because I was stupid and careless, because I thought I knew better than those boring, stuffy adults. Your mother and I ran for the village. I don't know if it was the fact that we were running that encouraged the snapmaw to chase us, or if it just didn't think Teno was enough of a meal by himself, but either way...

"We ran screaming all the way back, and by the time we crossed the barrier, it was right on our heels. Lord Emeto knew, somehow. He was a mile away at home, probably enjoying his breakfast, but he knew. He reinforced the barrier just as the snapmaw crashed into it, catching the beast halfway. It got stuck there, and some of the farmers rushed it with shovels and hoes to drive it back. I don't know what happened to the barrier. Honestly, you'd probably have a better idea than me, but that encounter broke it.

"The snapmaw must have decided it wasn't worth the fight. It ran off, took Teno as its meal, and disappeared into the wastes. We never found the body," Father said. "Cherok blamed us, rightfully so. It was my fault most of all. He's hated me ever since, and I don't blame him.

"Lord Emeto... I don't know. He was an old man. They said his heart gave out trying to do whatever magic he did, and the barrier broke. In one morning, I got my best friend and my mentor killed. And then Noctra came a few years later, and told us he needed mana from everybody. He set up his draw stones, and the whole village hated me for that, too, because it was my fault they had to do it."

"You were a child," I said quietly. "You made a mistake, but they've been hanging that over your head for fifteen years now."

"I was old enough to know better. I was supposed to have a bright future ahead of me. If things had gone differently, I might have been the next governor once Lord Emeto felt I was ready. But that wasn't good enough for me. I had to go see all the scrub grass and sand with my own eyes."

I didn't have any words to refute that. At least, there weren't any that I hadn't already said. He'd made a mistake, the kind that in my old life would have gotten someone ostracized and resulted in them packing up to move somewhere where no one knew their name. That was an impossibility here, where exile was just an extended death sentence. So he'd lived with it, with the daily reminder to the entire village that he'd cost them a measure of peace and security that they couldn't get back, not ever.

I imagined that cold civility was probably about the warmest a conversation got for my father, at least among those who remembered the time before his mistake. In all fairness, the loss of the barrier was completely Emeto's fault. It sounded to me like he'd overwhelmed the ward stone by trying to push too much mana through it in an attempt to strengthen the barrier. He should have known that what he was doing would have consequences.

I doubted the villagers saw it that way. There probably wasn't a single person within a hundred miles of here who understood enough about magic to grasp how a ward stone even functioned. All they knew was that a child had gone beyond the barrier, which apparently wasn't strong enough to keep out monsters in the first place, and brought trouble back with him.

I had my suspicions about the purpose of the barrier. It seemed to me that it was probably more to deflect casual interest away and hide mana usage that might draw in monsters than a hard wall that prevented anything but humans from crossing it. That would have required far too much mana to keep running in this environment.

Somewhere near the end of Father's tale, Mother had heard what he was saying. As he fell silent, she moved in to wrap her arms around him and hold him tightly. There were no words between them, but something in that hug seemed to comfort him. Maybe it was their shared experience, or maybe it was just knowing there was one person in the world who loved him anyway.

An archmage had many talents, but in my case, comforting others wasn't among them. I could only watch as Father took a minute to pull himself together, give Mother a quick kiss, and then turn back to me as if nothing had ever happened. "So, there you have it," he said. "That's the story of how I broke the barrier, got a child killed, and became a pariah."

CHAPTER
THIRTY-NINE

"I don't want to do this," Father said.

"I'm sure you'll be fine," Mother told him.

"You can do it, Dad. You practiced a lot," Senica added.

He turned to look at me. I shrugged and gestured for him to get going. We were going to need at least three hours to travel, probably more considering Senica and I were both children with short legs and low stamina. The sooner we got started, the sooner we'd be done.

"I really don't think I'm ready," Father tried.

"Just go," Mother said, giving him a shove. He took a step forward, windmilled his arms to keep his balance, and shot her a glare. The tip of one foot hung in open air, but he'd managed to stop short of going over the cliff.

"I cannot believe you just did that!" he told Mother.

"What happened to all the enthusiasm you had this afternoon?"

"That was before I had to jump off a cliff!"

Bored of the banter Father was trying to drum up to stall, I wrapped the rest of the group in my magic. Three applications of feather weight to Mother, Senica, and Nermet, and one slightly cheaper weight reduction for myself later, I summoned a gust of wind to blow us all out into the open air, where we began drifting down to the ground below while Father stood there, slack-jawed and gawking at us.

"A little warning would have been nice!" Mother snapped as Senica clung to her like a wet cat trying to claw its way out of a tub.

"Sorry," I said, though my voice was carried away by the wind. That was fine. It was a lie, anyway.

Above us, I felt Father's mana twist into his own weight reduction spell a moment before he jumped over the side. It wasn't perfect, being both inefficient and at only about two-thirds full strength. He started catching up to us rapidly, and we all landed about the same time. Father hit significantly harder than our own gentle touchdowns, but he didn't say anything about it.

"Which way is it back home?" Mother asked. "It all looks so different down here."

I silently pointed ahead and to our left. There wasn't really a road this far out from the village, but I'd confirmed that the cart's wheels had left a trail in the dirt and dust. It was faint after days of exposure to the wind, but it would still lead us back home. If for some reason it failed, well, it might mean wasting some of my mana, but one way or another, we were getting back tonight.

"We should get going," Father said. He glanced around the wastes and added, "Before something finds us."

We had good odds of walking back without encountering any problems, but since Father was not able to hide his mana, I wouldn't be surprised if I ended up having to kill an aggressive monster that sniffed him out. As long as it was only one or two, it probably wouldn't be a problem.

Our speed was hindered by Senica the most, and my parents took turns carrying her to help speed things up. Father offered me a ride, but I declined. I might be taking two or three steps for each of theirs, but I had a basic invocation keeping me going. Senica didn't have that option, and sooner or later she would become the person holding us back as my parents' strength flagged a few hours into the march.

I didn't complain about the frequent breaks. As much as I wanted this to be over, I wasn't willing to spend mana to speed up our progress, not tonight. It was a gamble, and I was betting that we wouldn't encounter trouble on the way, at least not so much trouble that it would have been more mana-efficient to help.

I spotted the beast stalking us on our third break. It was a few hundred feet back with a shaggy pelt the same brownish-yellow dust color as the rest of the wastes. About the only thing I was sure of was that it wasn't a mana sniffer. Those had quite distinctive faces. This looked more like a badger, or maybe an overgrown mole. It might not even be a monster at all, though I'd need to get closer to examine it if I wanted to know for sure.

Mindful of my mother's admonishments to keep Senica protected when dealing with trouble, I caught Father's eye with a slight wave of my hand and tipped my head toward the beast. He glanced past me, following the direction I'd pointed him in, and I saw a brief surge of unfocused mana course up to his eyes.

He tensed for a moment when he saw the creature, but then relaxed almost immediately. I took that as a good sign that he recognized it and that it wasn't all that dangerous. He confirmed that a moment later when he said, "Arbor gopher. Territorial, but it won't follow us, and it won't attack as long as we stay away from its home. Probably has young'ins nearby."

"Nothing to worry about, then?" I asked.

"Not by itself, no. We shouldn't linger, but we weren't going to anyway."

"That makes it sound like there could be a problem if we stay."

"It's not about the gopher so much as what it shares territory with. If there's one gopher, then there are twenty more you don't see, and where there are families of gophers, there are dust jackals."

His words conjured up a mental image of lanky, long-limbed dogs the same color as the gopher, but I had a sneaking suspicion that they wouldn't be normal animals. At the very least, they'd be magic-using animals. Possibly, they'd be monsters instead.

The primary difference between an animal and a monster was its relationship with mana. Specifically, the defining characteristic was whether the creature's physiology could function without mana to keep it going. An animal might use mana, often in instinctive and unstructured ways, but a monster *needed* mana the way people needed food and water. I'd made a study of monsters at one point, and I'd found that often the simplest way to contain or control a monster specimen was to put it in an environment where I controlled its access to the mana it needed.

Undead were a prime example of a monster that couldn't survive without access to mana. Take away the ambient mana, and the average zombie would collapse within hours unless it could find another source to feed on. One second, they'd be vicious flesh-eating abominations. The next, they were nothing but a moldering corpse on the ground.

Plenty of seemingly-animal creatures were actually monsters in disguise. False hares looked just like their mundane counterparts, except that when a predator tried to catch and eat one, they found themselves being eaten instead as the animal in their mouth suddenly morphed into a blob of grasping tendrils and razor-sharp teeth.

But crippling their cores would cause them to destabilize into a mound of writhing flesh and teeth with no way to pull themselves back together. If they stayed that way for a few hours, they would literally fall to pieces. Not once had I ever had a sample last more than three hours after they lost access to mana. Without it, their physiology just broke apart.

"And what exactly is a dust jackal?" I asked.

"Pack hunters that manipulate the ground and air to blind prey in clouds of dust. They don't seem to have a problem seeing in it, and they love to hunt in areas arbor gophers inhabit. All the burrows the gophers dig provide them with plenty of loose dirt to use."

"Fascinating," I said. "Are they smart enough to leave the gophers alone? Or perhaps the gophers just know how to avoid them?"

Father watched as the gopher, rather larger than I'd initially given it credit for, trundled out from behind its rock and farther away from us. "I don't know," he said. "I just know if you find arbor gophers, beware of dust jackals."

That was an interesting, but hopefully pointless bit of information. It still wasn't entirely clear where dust jackals fell on the animal to monster spectrum, but I was leaning more toward animal with magical abilities. If it did come down to combat with a pack of them, mana draining would not be my go-to opener.

As anemic as everything that relied on mana in these parts was, it probably wouldn't be worth it anyway. Mana drain was fine as an offensive spell when the goal was to take mana from the target, but not when I needed to shore up my own mana reserves, not unless the target was my sister who'd just accidentally absorbed a full core's worth of the mana I desperately needed.

There were other options that were more mana-efficient, but really, the best strategy was to start walking again and hopefully avoid the fight altogether. Father must have agreed, because he overruled Senica's whining protests and got the whole group moving again. I noticed Mother and Father both keeping much more of a lookout than they previously had, and after some whispered instructions, even Nermet started watching around us.

Something I hadn't considered before beginning my plans to reincarnate into a new life was that it was much harder to see things that were far away as a toddler. Up close, my vision wasn't bad, but the farther away something got, the harder it was to focus on it. I'd done my best to compensate with magic, but it always came back to resource management. In some situations, like this trip, it was worth it to use a sharpened senses invocation periodically to look around for trouble.

I was relying on the adults around me to give me advanced warning between uses of the spell, which I only had active for a few seconds every minute or two. I might spot an ambush, or something watching us like that arbor gopher, but anything fast enough could very well get in range in that gap time between spells.

I just kept telling myself that we'd be fine, that it was only a three-hour walk that had turned into something closer to five hours. The wastes weren't thick with monsters like the villagers seemed to think. We'd barely seen a handful for all the days and nights we'd been camping out here, and only then because the mana sniffers were attracted to Father's ignition.

But knowing my luck, I fully expected to deplete a portion of my mana crystal's reserves on the journey. If it wasn't the dust jackals finding us, it'd be something else, be it monster or emergency. Someone would fall and break a leg, requiring expensive and difficult healing spells to get them moving again. Or we'd stumble upon some natural phenomena like an illusory maze and become trapped in it.

Once I thought about it, that last one might actually be a blessing in disguise. It would be well worth the time to harvest the mana powering something like that. Of course, that all but guaranteed we wouldn't ever encounter one, not that it made much sense to find a pocket of natural mana in a desert like this anyway.

Or it could just be the damned dust jackals after all. I grabbed Father's shirt and pointed down at a set of paw prints clearly visible in the dusty ground. His jaw tightened and he nodded, then scanned the area for more paw prints, touched Mother's shoulder, and pointed off towards a dry gully not a quarter mile away from us.

"Probably holed up in there," he said when she shot him a questioning glance. "No big deal as long as we keep walking."

But he didn't sound like he believed it, and now that I had a target to focus on, my sharpened senses spell revealed to me that Father's guess at their location had been perfectly accurate. His optimistic suggestion that we'd be able to walk right on past them was less so.

"They're coming," I said. "Six of them."

CHAPTER

FORTY

My first impression of a dust jackal was that it looked like a dog with stork legs that were far too long for its body. It had dark brown earthy-colored fur on its back, and lighter dusty brown, almost yellow patterns on its legs and face. Everything about it was squished, like it had been pressed flat. Its muzzle was long and narrow, and its ears were long and pointy, so close together that they practically touched at the base.

All in all, it was a rather ugly creature. Judging by how similar it looked to the other five coming in right behind it, I suspected it was a typical example of the species. I'd certainly seen worse in my time, but I couldn't imagine anyone wanting to take one home and keep it as a pet.

More surprising, however, was the amount of mana I sensed coming off the group. It rolled off the animals in waves, catching hold of the dust they kicked up in their run and spreading it out into a blinding screen that flowed in front of them toward us.

"Run," Father demanded as he rushed to place himself between the jackals and us. "Nermet, carry the kids. I'll stall them."

I had to admire his bravery even as I rolled my eyes. Father had no weapon and was barely competent at a single utility invocation. There was very little hope that he could do anything to save himself, and he knew that.

He was just trying to buy us time to run while he distracted them by sacrificing himself.

"Oh, move out of the way," I said, pushing at his leg as I stepped past him. "Honestly, it's getting a bit tiresome having to remind you of this constantly."

The dust was a form of elemental manipulation, almost evenly split between earth and air. Other than the magical manipulation to keep it billowing in the air, I didn't detect anything special about it. My guess was that it would blind us the same way a good old-fashioned dust storm would: through the physics of having small dirt particles hitting our eyes.

If the jackals could see through it, that would likely be through enhanced senses or some sort of elemental feedback from the dust, or possibly both. That whole plan relied on the dust cloud reaching us and the jackals swooping in while we were blinded, though. It was simple enough to stop just by killing them before they got that close.

I was about to do just that when a thick, muscular arm scooped me off my feet and started pulling me away from the fight. I blinked and glanced up to see Nermet running with Senica held in his other arm. Her eyes were wide with fear as she clutched at the man, though I couldn't say whether it was from the abrupt abduction or from the predators closing in on our position. Nermet himself, well, he didn't look determined or scared or confused. Really, he didn't have much of any expression on his face, just like always.

"Call him off please. He's interfering," I yelled back at my parents.

But Father wasn't listening. Mother noticed what was happening, and she tried to grab Nermet and get him to release me, but he shrugged her off and kept running. If I wanted free, I was going to need to use a bit of magic. I hated to do it because Nermet hadn't really done anything wrong, but if I let him carry me away, it would probably be the death of both my parents.

No spell that caused pain would make a difference. I'd need to escalate to the level of maiming Nermet to get out of his grasp that way. Fortunately, there was a more elegant solution. The human body had plenty of interesting reactions when touched with lightning. Most living things did, I'd found. For this situation, I needed a simple shocking touch spell. I sent it down his arm, causing his muscles to spasm and allowing me to slip from his temporarily weakened grasp.

That would ache for hours, but it needed to be done. I tumbled to the ground, stunned for a second by a blow from Nermet's moving leg as I fell.

Before he could swerve around and scoop me back up, I recovered, climbed to my feet, and rushed back towards my parents.

The leading edge of the dust cloud obscured Father's form, which meant that my original plan of a single arc lightning spell to wipe out the whole pack was off the table. The spell didn't discriminate between friend and foe, and I couldn't risk it hitting Father now that the jackals were so close. I'd need to resort to targeted and more costly spells to resolve the situation.

First, I needed a way to find the dust jackals through their concealing cloud. The most direct method would be to use elemental manipulation to contest their control of the dust, but it would be me against a whole pack. I could likely do it, but the mana costs to fight back so many others at the same time would be prohibitively expensive.

A much cheaper, if more complicated solution would be to rely on the divination discipline of magic to learn what I needed to know. Life sense was a spell that gave the caster the ability to feel the location of any living things within a certain range. The jackals would stand out to me no matter how they chose to hide with that. It was a bit expensive to keep running, but I should only need it for a handful of seconds.

I cast the spell while I fled from Nermet. By the time it was done, I was inside the dust cloud myself, with Father about ten feet to my right. The jackals had spread out into a semi-circle in front of us, the closest one no more than fifteen feet away and moving to trap us while its counterpart did the same from the other side. If we stood there and let them, they'd cut us off from all sides and fall on us all at once.

I needed a spell strong enough to kill a jackal in one hit but precise enough not to worry about injuring my own family. I needed it to be quick enough to cast that I could kill all six jackals in seconds or versatile enough to kill multiple targets without sacrificing precision. In addition to all of that, I needed it to be cheap.

That last condition limited my options severely, but I had a spell in mind that I thought fit the situation. My only concern was that the jackals had what appeared to be two elemental affinities. Against a sapient caster, I would have hesitated to use an elemental conjuration that they'd shown proficiency in lest they counter the spell.

Against animals and dumb monsters, it was less of a concern. I pulled mana through my mana crystal and let it stream out from my core into the shape of the spell I wanted, a relatively cheap conjuration known as stone needle. If it had been a permanent transmutation, it would have been costly. But as a conjuration, I was able to cast one each second for about a quarter of my total reserves, with my mana crystal making up the difference.

Every second, a four-foot-long needle of sharp, black stone jutted up from the ground and punched through a jackal's jaw into its brain. It remained in existence for precisely three seconds before breaking back apart into mana and vanishing. By the time the jackals realized something had gone wrong with their plan, three of them were dead. None of them thought to flee before I killed the last one.

Without their power holding the dust in the air, it was a simple act of air manipulation to sweep the cloud away and reveal the results of my handiwork. An arc lightning spell would have been about a third less mana, but this was acceptable.

Before I could examine the corpses more closely, Nermet grabbed me again with his injured arm. "No," Father said, snagging his shoulder as he turned to run again. "It's fine, you can put them down now. Just wait here with us."

Nermet gave no response but to set Senica and me back on the ground. I suppressed a sigh that was one part annoyance and one part sympathy and walked forward to look at the corpses I'd made. Mother reached out a hand to stop me as I passed by, but she paused before actually touching me and turned to Senica instead.

"What are you doing?" Father asked as I approached the first body. He followed me over and eyed the single bloody entry wound visible below the jackal's jaw.

"There's something off about these creatures," I said. "Their magic was more powerful than I expected."

"Didn't seem to slow you down much," Father told me. "All I saw was the dust blinding me and then a few seconds later, it blew away and they were already dead."

"Mmm," I agreed. "The dust was the giveaway. For what should be six creatures of animal intelligence working with almost no mana, it was far too well coordinated an effort with far too much mana put into it. I expected something half the size of what they created, and that it would be patchy or thin."

Mana cores could be tricky things to harvest. They weren't physical organs, and anyone thinking to cut open a freshly killed monster and scoop it out was in for a disappointment. It wasn't really even possible to harvest the core itself, barring some extremely unlikely scenarios and a lot of specialized equipment. What I *could* do was harvest the leftover mana and get a feel for the core's structure in the process.

This wasn't normally a worthwhile procedure. The mana would leak out on its own and join the rest of the ambient mana in the world without me having to do anything at all. For obvious reasons, that didn't work here. If I wanted to take the mana directly and refine it with my own, time was of the essence.

I extended my senses into the body and found the jackal's mana core. It was surprisingly robust for an animal that size, and more importantly, it wasn't a perfect, flawless sphere like I'd been expecting. Instead, I could detect faint ridges and folds along its surface, almost like...

"This core is partially latticed," I muttered to myself. "Impossible."

Had someone been experimenting on the animals? There was no way a wild, dirt-wielding dog had managed to ignite its core and then begin the process of transforming it with a stage two lattice. Someone or something had to have been helping it along.

I quickly harvested the mana from it—more than I'd used to kill it, so this encounter wasn't a total loss—and moved on to the next. I found the same thing there, though this one hadn't been quite as far along in the latticing process.

When I was done, I stood up and regarded Father with a frown. "Something is wrong with these jackals. I can't believe they would have developed mana cores like this naturally. It's far more likely someone was experimenting on them."

"Who would do that?" Father asked.

"Who knows? My first guess would be Noctra, but only because he's the only one I can think of with the means. I can't imagine why he would do this, and what his experiments would be doing way out here, miles away from the village."

The silver lining to the encounter was that the dust jackals had so much mana, I'd actually come out ahead by a good amount. But still, the mystery of it worried me. I couldn't think of any good reason to experiment on the local wildlife, especially not in a region so starved for mana to begin with.

Maybe that had been the point, though—to alter animals to produce more mana so they could be regularly drained of it. Maybe them being all the way out in the wastes was an accident.

I didn't know, but I suspected I would need to find out sooner or later. I couldn't ignore the signs of another mage in the area if it turned out Noctra had nothing to do with it.

For now, there was nothing to do but keep walking toward home.

CHAPTER

FORTY-ONE

W e were about a mile from the village when Mother abruptly stopped in place. Father, who'd been walking next to her, glanced over and halted as well. "What's wrong?" he asked.

Dusk was upon us, and our shadows stretched out before us, courtesy of the setting sun at our backs. My own shadow was engulfed by Nermet's massive, steady presence behind me, leaving only four shadows darkening the scrub grass on the trail leading home.

"I thought... No, sorry. It's nothing," she said, her eyes locked on the hill to the north of us.

I hadn't noticed anything myself, but I wouldn't be surprised if someone was there. There were four organizations in the village. The Collectors who worked with the draw stones were responsible for the nightly tithing. The Garrison were a small police force that responded to things like drunken—or not so drunken, in Father's case—brawling or cases of theft. The Arborists were responsible for the arbor north of the village.

The final group was the Barrier Wardens, whose job it was to patrol the outskirts of town to help provide an early warning system during the day when the barrier was supposedly turned off. I hadn't met one personally, and knowing that the barrier itself was a lie, I suspected they were deep in Noctra's pockets.

If there was anyone wandering this far out into the wastes, it would be a Barrier Warden. So Mother had either seen one who was watching us, possibly as a sentry deliberately posted there by Noctra, she'd seen a monster or animal of some kind, or she'd seen nothing and it was her imagination playing tricks on her with the shadows.

Did I need to know the truth bad enough to spend mana to find out? On the one hand, I wanted the element of surprise when I got to Noctra's home, and a Barrier Warden running ahead could give him time to prepare some defenses. Certainly, a mage on his guard for an attack could be more difficult to kill. On the other hand, I had a decent supply of mana in reserve, enough that I could probably beat any Barrier Warden near us to the destination.

Even if I couldn't, I had yet to see any magic from anyone since I'd awoken that I could classify as impressive. The only thing holding me back was the need to be stingy, but if I wanted to go all out, I could cast a personal barrier, walk into the manor, and smite Noctra with any number of spells he'd have no defense against.

It turned out to be a moot point. A few seconds later, a young man just approaching adulthood rushed out from around the base of the hill. He was wearing thick boots and a light cloak which only partially covered the sword hanging from his belt. "Sellis! Xilaya! You're alive!"

"So it would appear," Father said dryly.

"When your whole family disappeared a few nights back, we thought something had managed to sneak into the village and drag you out of your beds," the man said. I noticed a pin on his cloak, that of a blue circle with a wavy line pattern on it.

"Why did you think that?" I asked. It was out of character for Gravin, but I wanted to know if Noctra had planted evidence to suggest something like that, or if people had just made some assumptions based on a total lack of evidence.

"Well, what else could it be?" the guy asked, blinking down at me. He only focused on me for a second before dismissing me and turning back to my parents. "Gave the whole village a scare, though. The Barrier Wardens have been working double shifts all week to make sure whatever it was didn't get back into the village again. Lord Noctra's been locked up in his manor for days going over the barrier stone trying to figure out what went wrong with it."

Father opened his mouth to speak, but the man talked right over him. "So, what was it? I can't even imagine what kind of monster could carry off a whole family. And why's Nermet with you? Did he chase after it and save you guys? I can't believe no one's even injured."

"Lilo," Father said, cutting the Barrier Warden off. "There was no monster. Noctra used his magic to kidnap me and was selling me to someone in Derro because he thought I could do magic, too."

Lilo's jaw dropped. He looked back and forth between the adults in our group for a second before letting out a weak chuckle and saying, "Very funny, Sellis. Come on, what really happened?"

Father looked Lilo dead in the eye and said, "Noctra used his magic to kidnap me and sell me off. My family came after me to rescue me."

"Hah. Hah. It's not as funny the second time."

"I didn't think it was that funny, Lilo. Why are you laughing?"

"Well come on. It's absurd! Lord Noctra wouldn't do something like that, and even if he did, you're telling me a housewife, two children, and the village simpleton ran off to rescue you? Excuse me if I don't believe you. I don't know what game you're trying to play here, but trying to drag Lord Noctra's name through the mud isn't going to work out well for you. Come with me. I'll take you to the Garrison and you can wait there while someone lets Lord Noctra know you're back."

For a moment, I considered doing just that. Really, the only thing keeping Noctra alive was that we weren't face to face. But if I killed him in the middle of the village with witnesses everywhere, there was going to be a lot of fallout to deal with. It would be better to present all the evidence of his wrongdoings before I got outed as his murderer.

Besides, giving up the element of surprise just to have Noctra come to me was pure laziness. It would be far better to let the rest of my family go to the Garrison while I ambushed him en route. That way, I'd find him away from whatever defenses he'd set up in his manor *and* I could still ambush him.

Now I just needed to get Father to agree to go with Lilo. Our original plan had called for them to either return home or wait on the outskirts of the village, depending on how things looked. Technically, this fell more into the 'stay outside the village' scenario, except I hadn't accounted for the possibility of using my family as bait. I'd expected that in the worst case, we'd be captured by loyalists who were in on Noctra's scam and taken directly to his manor.

In all fairness, that could still happen. Our stay with the Garrison could be an incredibly brief one before we were marched right back out onto the streets. I doubted Lilo had any measure of authority at all, let alone enough power to counteract any order that didn't come from Noctra himself. The Barrier Warden struck me as young and impressionable, a fresh recruit still learning how to do his job.

"No. I'm not going to be marched over to the Garrison building like a criminal caught raiding his neighbor's garden. I'm certainly not going to do that to my family." Father folded his arms across his chest and added, "And I'd like to see you try to make me."

"Come on, Sellis. Don't make this more difficult on yourself," Lilo said, dropping one hand to the sword hidden beneath his cloak. I wasn't sure if anyone else had noticed the weapon when the Barrier Warden was approaching us, but if he moved to draw it, I'd be expending some more of my mana to stop him.

Father glanced back at Mother, then down at us. I gave a twitch of my shoulders to let him know it was his decision. I wouldn't kill Lilo– that would only earn me ill will with the village where I planned on spending the next several years consolidating my power—but I had no qualms about a bit of non-lethal magic. Really, Father knew the Barrier Warden better than me. If he decided to cooperate, I'd go along as long as it didn't jeopardize my own plans.

Seeing that Father wasn't backing down, Lilo threw back his cloak and started to draw his sword. A second later, he collapsed to the ground as my sleep spell hit him. Father was so surprised that he let the Barrier Warden fall without making any effort to catch him, and the loud thump elicited a wince.

"So I guess that explains why I woke up sore after Noctra did that to me," Father said.

"You actually fell across a table," I said absently as I approached Lilo to examine him. Rolling him over was out of the question, but I wasn't particularly interested in making him comfortable. I just wanted to confirm he was alive and see how much mana he had in his core. The answers to those questions were 'yes' and, unfortunately, 'not much.'

It would still take me a few hours to recover from that sleep spell unless

I tapped into my mana crystal. I wanted to hold off on that as long as possible to avoid the conversion loss. I'd top my core off when I got close to the manor, but until then, I would generate as much mana naturally as I could.

"You should probably stay out of the village if this is how people are going to react to us coming back," I said.

"Agreed," Mother added. "But for how long? We need to go home at some point, if only to assess how bad the garden's gotten while I was away."

"I think we have more important considerations," Father started to say.

"Than our food?" Mother asked. "Really? You don't think starving is an important consideration?"

"That's not what I meant, and you know it. Your garden will be fine. I'm more concerned about people like Lilo deciding it's fine to draw a weapon on us. What lies has Noctra told people? How many of them think we're criminals now?"

"Lilo's always been an idiot. Getting that badge just made him worse." Mother sighed and rolled him onto his back. "He's going to be difficult to deal with once he wakes up."

"It'll all be over by then," I said.

I noticed the pinched lip grimace Mother gave me, but Father backed me up. "It's us or him. Even if we ignore all his lying and how he's used the entire village, we personally aren't safe as long as he's in charge. And it's not like we can lock a mage up."

Technically, we could, but I'd never been in the habit of sparing my enemies, and I wasn't about to start now. Leaving Noctra alive would just mean more problems down the road, not to mention the ruinous mana costs. Even a locked cell full of draw stones wouldn't be enough to ensure his captivity, not when it was just a matter of willpower to resist them. A few hours of meditation to hold onto his mana would be all he needed to fill his core and work some sort of magic to escape.

Truly locking him up would be time consuming. I'd need weeks to create the inscriptions and more mana than I could generate to power them. It just wasn't worth the effort for a man who would no doubt prove an uncooperative prisoner. And while I had a lot of questions he might know the answers to, none of them were all that pressing. First priority was advancing my mana core to stage two. After that, I'd worry about whatever plans Noctra was scheming, assuming they outlived him.

"I'm going ahead now," I said. "What are you going to do?"

"I suppose it would be best to wait near enough to the village to not have to worry about monsters, but not so close that our neighbors try to arrest us," Father said.

"It's risky," Mother added. "And your magic isn't going to be enough to protect us right now."

"I know, but... What else can we do?"

"Go to the manor with Gravin."

"No," I said. I shifted my eyes toward Senica for an instant. "It's not a good idea."

"Ah. Right. We'll keep ourselves safe. You can find us when you're done?" she asked.

I nodded. Father still had the scrying beacon button in his pocket, and I'd renewed the enchantment on our way here.

"Then take care of yourself. Stay safe, and don't do anything risky."

"I'll do my best," I promised.

Then I walked off alone into the deepening night.

CHAPTER
FORTY-TWO

I had never been near Noctra's manor, and my first impression was that it was far bigger than necessary. It was still rustic by my standards, but compared to the rest of the village, the manor was beyond luxurious. In terms of sheer size alone, it dwarfed every other building. The manor was easily five times bigger than the Collectors' headquarters, and that had eight people living in it in addition to the administrative rooms. As far as I knew, Noctra shared the manor with Iskara and no one else. A few conference rooms and meeting halls did not account for the massive amount of space it took up.

That wasn't even looking at the materials. A lot of lumber had gone into the place, though it still featured the same mud-fired bricks used in the village proper to fill that wooden framework out. The roof was made of clay tiles, something that would be impossible to replicate in my home without adding a wooden framework to mount them to. I even spotted glass windows through a few of the open shutters. I hadn't seen glass anywhere else in the village. Noctra had probably made them with magic.

All things considered, the manor felt like a monument to vanity and waste. The space itself wasn't the problem; mages needed plenty of room for workshops, after all. No, it was everything taken as a whole and then compared to the village struggling to survive barely a mile away.

I wondered what secrets were hidden inside those walls, and how much of the mana that had been stolen away had been used to enrich one man. I supposed I'd find out soon enough, given that I was planning on murdering said man and going through his house to check it for traps and research notes. I wanted to know *everything* Noctra had been getting up to recently, especially since it seemed obvious that he had a partnership of sorts with at least one other person in another city. The more I could find out about that person, the better.

I approached carefully, wary of both wards and guards. It didn't seem likely to me that Noctra would have people patrolling the grounds around his home normally, but I had to assume he was expecting some sort of trouble if he had bothered to send Iskara out to find us when we were still camping in the wastes. It was entirely possible he'd enlisted extra Garrison members to temporarily guard him on the assumption that someone, probably Father, would show back up.

Really, it would all depend on how exactly Noctra had discovered his plans had been derailed. My best guess was that he'd scried the route and discovered we weren't on it. Possibly he'd scried the cart directly, which was the big reason I'd insisted on leaving it behind. The donkey that had pulled it was long gone anyway, left untethered and hopefully living free in the wastes, but probably dead and inside some monster's belly.

There weren't too many other possibilities. Wards on the road were technically possible, but a ward stretching over that kind of distance, even if it was nothing but a trip wire to let someone know that a certain part of the path had been crossed, was prohibitively mana-intensive. It was possible that Noctra had a secret familiar that was spying on us, but that was advanced magic, and I just couldn't credit him with having the knowledge or skills to form a familiar bond.

I wasn't planning on taking any foolish risks, but in my estimation, Noctra didn't know about me. I'd been on the lookout for any scrying around my general location, and once again, I didn't think he had the magical chops to pull it off without me noticing. Most likely, he'd scried the road itself and Iskara had narrowed down the location by feeling Father's ignition ritual. The worst-case scenario should be that Noctra's magical gaze was firmly pointed at Father, leaving me free to sneak in and ambush him.

I gave it ten minutes to sweep the grounds around the manor, even going so far as to spend a bit of mana to heighten my senses while I looked for any guards. If there were any, they were stationed inside and probably near the entrances. I wasn't planning on entering the manor through any doors or windows. This was important enough to spend a bit of mana on a phantasmal step spell to keep my strategic advantage. With luck, I wouldn't need anything more than that before I found Noctra.

While I was studying the outside of the house with my physical eyes for guard patrols, I used my own scrying magic to sweep the interior. Scrying wasn't great for finding magical traps, at least not at the level I was currently using it, but it would let me figure out the layout of the house and look for any guards stationed on the inside.

My mystical exploration answered some of my questions about the size, at least. It seemed like at one point, the manor had actually been used as a sort of town hall, though not in my lifetime. The huge room was empty now save for rows of dust-covered chairs and tables. Anyone entering would quickly find themselves choking and coughing without some sort of mask to protect themselves.

The manor had a large dining hall as well, nowhere near the size of the town hall, but still with a table big enough to seat twenty, just judging by the number of chairs placed around it. It was at least kept clean, but it was obvious which side of the table had seen regular use just from the difference in wear. A separate kitchen had two hearths to cook in, alongside a large sink and ample counter space.

We had nothing but an old cauldron my mother had inherited from her grandmother that was hung over a fire pit and an old, rickety table that didn't have enough chairs surrounding it for a family of four. From my understanding, that was a common setup in the village. Certainly nobody had a setup like this. It wasn't exactly extravagant so much as it was serviceable, but compared to the people Noctra ruled over, it was a significant upgrade. Considering literally nobody lived in the manor except Noctra and Iskara, it was also complete overkill.

Perhaps the village had been different under the governance of Emeto. I could see plenty of signs that the manor had been designed to house not only the governor, but his staff as well. There were offices and meeting spaces to suggest that the village's business had been taken care of at the manor, too. None of them were in use now, for some reason.

Lord Noctra was a mage who valued his privacy, it seemed.

I restrained myself from giving the manor a thorough exploration with my magic. As much as I would have liked to, it was possible that Noctra had woven wards into his labs and experimentation rooms that might detect my magic and alert him to my presence. Until I knew for sure, or more realistically, until the man was dead, I limited myself to what I would consider public rooms. Those often had too much foot traffic to effectively ward, at least not if the mage powering them was on a budget, and there was very little chance I'd trigger anything there. Nobody wanted a ward that alerted them a dozen times a day every time the maid came through the kitchen.

That did limit the odds that I'd successfully scry out Noctra's location, but I'd at least be able to eliminate the majority of the manor before I set foot inside, and once I was there, I could start manually searching the rooms likely to be warded to find Alkerist's governor. Considering how dark everything was inside and that I still hadn't seen a single sign of any guards, I felt that I had good odds of entering and exploring undetected.

I might not even need to waste the mana on phantasmal step if all it took was an application of an unlocking spell to get in. I'd counted four different doors leading into the manor already, though I'd be avoiding the ones leading into what I'd mentally dubbed the meeting hall. The kitchen entrance was probably the best one since it led into a public room and wasn't likely to be warded or trapped. It was also on the south side of the manor, which was convenient for me since that was the direction I'd approached from.

My preliminary mapping complete and my mana core all but empty, I decided I'd done enough investigation from afar. Either Noctra was a mage so far beyond my current abilities that I had no chance of winning, or he'd actually taken no steps beyond locking the doors and windows to keep people from entering his house in the middle of the night.

That wasn't quite true, as I discovered when I approached the kitchen door. Noctra, or more likely Iskara, had made some effort to arm the door with the same paralysis trap that had guarded the draw stone storage room. Having already seen it once, it was much easier to spot this time around, and I swiftly claimed the artificial mana core that powered the spell.

Even with the paralysis trap removed, I took my time examining that door. I absolutely could not afford to make any mistakes at this point. It was hard to take Noctra seriously as a mage, but I was keenly aware that arrogance could be my downfall. I'd nearly been caught by this exact same trap a few days ago because it was too advanced for what I'd judged Noctra capable of casting. He had connections with other mages, though, and if there was any place he'd use that resource to protect himself, it was here in his home.

I spent a full minute crouched in the shadows near that door with the mingled lights of three moons casting purple, green, and blue light down on me. It was only after I was positive that there were no more wards or traps on the door itself or the room it led into that I dared to cast unlock and turn the handle.

There was a point when caution turned to timidness, and I'd run out of ways to ensure my own safety. I needed to either advance or retreat, and if I chose to retreat, I might as well abandon the village and start working on setting up a sanctuary out in the wastes so I could hide and take the time I needed to regain my lost power.

I'd be damned if I let some two-bit mage whose every spell cost four times as much mana as it should and who couldn't manage anything in the intermediate tier of magic chase me off. That wasn't even considering what he'd done to the village, stealing immense—by my current standards, at least—quantities of mana, and trying to sell my father into slavery to pay off some sort of debt.

No, I wasn't going to run. If anything, I was eager to finish my business with Noctra and begin pillaging his labs and equipment to see just what he'd been up to over the years. If there was one thing I needed just as desperately as I needed time, it was knowledge. There was no better place to get it than inside this building.

I reached up and twisted the handle, then pushed to let the door swing open on silent hinges as I stepped into Noctra's manor.

CHAPTER
FORTY-THREE

I did not have the luxury to explore all night. If nothing else, it was significantly darker inside the manor than it had been outside, requiring me to expend a steady stream of mana to maintain sharpened senses just so I could see. I had a decent idea of where I needed to go already, thanks to my scrying efforts, but it would be slow going since I needed to check for wards in every room and at every doorway.

My goal was a hallway on the east side of the manor. It had four doors on the west wall and three more on the east, and my first thought was that those were living quarters for the family of the governor. Theoretically, they'd have been refurbished into libraries, offices, and studies. Judging by the spacing, the center door in the east wall would be the master suite where Noctra was currently sleeping.

To get there from my current location, I needed to pass through a dining room and a parlor to access what I assumed was supposed to be the servants' quarters. In addition to a dozen rooms so small they could barely fit a bed, there was a laundry room and a pantry there. I'd seen no sign of anyone living in that section of the house, which just reinforced my belief that Noctra lived here alone in order to conduct his experiments in private.

There was a main hallway that bisected the manor, but my reason for avoiding it was simple: it had no less than three doors separating different sections of the house. By contrast, the servants' quarters had only a single door separating it from the hallway I suspected contained the master suite, and I'd spotted the key for it hanging from a hook just inside the pantry. Noctra probably didn't know about that and, as security conscious as he was, I doubted he'd be happy to find out that the servants were not only circumventing all his locks, but they'd left the key to the one door that did separate him from them lying out.

People, as always, were the weakest link in any security system. If they needed access to anything on a regular basis, it was a sure bet that someone somewhere was circumventing a protocol or defense in the name of convenience. And since servants needed to go practically everywhere, it was generally a safe bet to start looking at them when breaking into a place one wasn't supposed to be.

I made my way through the kitchen to the dining room and paused at the threshold to check for any wards or traps. Here at least, there was nothing, but that didn't mean I could afford to be careless. The dining room itself lacked any exterior windows, and I was left with memories of my scrying to get through without tripping over anything. I turned right and followed the wall, one hand trailing it lightly until I came to the small servant's cart stationed in the corner. That was my signal to skip four feet of wall where a display cabinet of ceramic dishes stood, then proceed another ten feet to the doorway leading to the parlor.

Once again, I paused to search for traps and, once again, there were none. Had I been breaking into a mage's home back in my old life, I would have suspected I was walking into a trap at this point. It was criminally easy to ward a home and power it with ambient mana to anyone who'd reached the status of full mage. Not finding them in areas that were heavily trafficked by the servant staff was one thing. Not finding any at all was something else.

The logical answer was, as always, that living in an area with no ambient mana required a mage to make sacrifices. No matter how many times I encountered it, it left a bad taste in my mouth. Whatever had happened here must have been horrific to leave scars in the world so deep that they still hadn't healed after generations.

I needed to confirm for myself how wide this mana desert was. If I only needed to travel twenty or thirty miles to escape it, I'd leave tomorrow morning. But what little conversation I'd overheard about Derro made me think it was more widespread than that. Noctra was making regular shipments of mana to associates there, which meant that at the very least, it was in the same situation as Alkerist.

I needed maps and history books. I'd never heard of a mana desert this big in my previous life, and it seemed like something I would have known about. Wherever I was, it was considerably hotter than it had been in the Night Vale, so I could make some assumptions about being much farther south than I'd been in my previous life. This area wasn't quite a literal desert, but it wasn't far off. Trees were scarce. Livestock was practically nonexistent, and there wasn't much in the way of plants to feed them anyway. What food we did grow here was the result of hard work and spending mana.

Water was abundant, strangely enough. There was enough at least that the village had a communal well and no rules about rationing it. If I didn't know any better, I would have suspected some magic in play there. But no, it was just another mystery to throw on the pile. Hopefully Noctra's library would give me some answers.

I made a brief stop in the pantry to swipe the key there, then crept down the hallway, ears straining for the sound of anybody up and moving near me. I already knew the servant rooms were deserted. It didn't look like they were ever used except as storage, despite being kept clean. Whichever villagers came to the manor every day to work, they went home to their huts nestled together in the village proper in the evenings.

When I got to the door at the far end of the hall, I stopped and gave it the same careful examination I'd given to the one leading into the manor. If there was any door that Noctra was going to spend some effort on, it was this one. I was expecting some wards that could only be bypassed by use of the proper key at minimum, possibly even wards that required individual attunements with only certain staff members allowed beyond the door. A few traps wouldn't have surprised me, either.

I examined the handle. Nothing. I looked at the hinges. Blank. I peered up and down the door frame, even going so far as to spend some extra mana to sharpen my eyes so I could look at the top. As far as I could tell, this was in every way a normal door, remarkable only in that it was made of wood, which was in scarce supply outside of the manor.

There was no way the man was this lax about his interior security. He'd put a paralysis trap on a servant's entry door! Well, he'd had Iskara do it, anyway. That was not the kind of precaution a man who didn't value his privacy took. I'd been expecting traps on every door and wards in every room. Maybe I'd just expected him to spend too much mana on magical defenses.

Or maybe he hadn't done it because he couldn't. Maybe Iskara was the only one who knew how to cast the spells. Functionally speaking, she wasn't at much more of a disadvantage than Noctra was here. Adepts generally relied far more heavily on ambient mana than mages did, but in this case, they were both functioning off the backs of the villagers themselves. It was entirely possible that the reason there were no traps or wards anywhere was that Iskara wasn't here to renew them.

But if that was true, why was there still a paralysis trap on the door I'd come in through?

Things weren't adding up, and considering I was breaking into the man's house right now, I didn't like the mystery of it all. Was he incompetent, or was he incapable? At this point, I had to question every assumption I'd ever made about Noctra. Was he even a mage?

I'd felt his mana when he'd killed that mana sniffer, and I'd seen him cast a spell through a wand to make my father fall asleep. The enslavement spell on Nermet was also tied back to Noctra. Whatever else he might be, he was at least able to cast spells. But what if I'd been wrong about him being a mage? What if he was an adept, just like Iskara?

It didn't matter much in this scenario. Mage or adept, I already had a good grasp of his skill level, and if it came down to a fight, I had to assume he had more than enough mana due to his stockpiles from the village. Any spell battle we fought wouldn't last more than four or five spells anyway. If I did everything right, the battle would begin and end with a single spell: mine.

First, I needed to find Noctra, and this door was in my way. I inserted the key, twisted it, and turned the handle. The door swung in about two inches before I grabbed it and pulled it to a stop. There, a half foot up from the floor, was a ward line that I could only just barely see the edge of. I hadn't sensed it during my examination of the door because it hadn't actually been attached to the door itself.

This was far more nerve-wracking than I'd expected it to be. Normally, I'd be casting all sorts of divinations to spot this kind of stuff before I ever made a move. I probably wouldn't even bother to show up in person unless my opponent was another archmage. Right now, I had none of my safety nets, and it had been over a thousand years since I'd been so vulnerable. I could remember the fear I'd felt during some of my first close brushes with death, the knowledge that the line between my life and death had come down to just one decision being made the other way, one step taken slightly differently.

That's what I was feeling now, except it was all the more galling because the enemy mage was a man I had absolutely no respect for. His spellcraft was laughable. And yet he could still kill me, as weak as I was. Now was no time to be stingy with my mana, but I couldn't maintain a fraction of my normal defenses for even ten seconds before I ran dry. If I wanted to have enough mana to fight with, I would have to rely on my reflexes to bring a shield to bear if I needed it.

And I was relying on luck and caution to sense traps like this ward line. Now that I knew it was there, I could disable it, but there was no guarantee that the mere act of disrupting the ward wouldn't alert Noctra. This could very well be my last chance to move about undetected, and I'd feel a lot better about that if I knew for sure where Noctra was.

The ward itself might give me some desperately needed clues. By examining it, I could get an idea of what style of ward scheme the manor had, and, more importantly, whether they were sensitive to scrying. Being able to scry out all the areas in the house I hadn't touched before would be hugely beneficial.

I looked it over and felt the tension drain out of me. It was a simple alarm ward, designed to activate if anyone walked through it. In this case, it would trigger when the door opened far enough to touch it, which I'd almost done inadvertently before spotting the ward line. I could suppress it long enough to get through without it activating, and with no chance of warning the caster by breaking it.

It wasn't definitive proof that I could safely scry the rest of the manor, but it was an obstacle I could easily overcome so that I could continue my search. I got to work, and within thirty seconds, I'd redirected the ward line to scan across the ceiling, well above the door's clearance, and passed beneath it into the hallway.

Now, I just needed to see if my guess about Noctra's bedroom suite being behind the center door was correct.

CHAPTER
FORTY-FOUR

I t was the moment of truth. I'd snuck down the hallway, made sure my mana core was topped off, checked every single doorway for wards and traps, removed yet another paralysis trap on the handle, and now was standing on my toes with a finger hooked around the handle, ready to turn it. If I was right, Noctra was sleeping not twenty feet away from me. This could all be over in the next five seconds.

I turned the handle. It twisted partway, then stopped well short of unlatching the door. Of course it was locked. After all the efforts I'd gone through to make sure I wasn't walking into a trap, I hadn't thought to check the mechanical lock itself. I could tell at a glance that the key I'd swiped from the pantry wasn't going to fit in this lock, so I was forced to resort to magic to get through.

I didn't really want to on the off chance that Noctra could feel it. Conjuration was among the hardest disciplines to hide from other mages, right up there with transmutation. Even I could only limit it so much, and against a mage just a few feet away, I'd be relying on blind luck.

As I saw things, I had four options. The first was to burn some mana on a phantasmal step spell, almost seven times as much mana as unlock. But phantasmal step was an invocation, which meant it was extraordinarily easy to hide its use since all the magic was internal. It would practically guarantee me an easy, unnoticed entry into the room at the cost of almost my entire core of mana.

The second was to go look for and find a key, but that would take precious time and there was every possibility it was inside the very room I was trying to get into. I could end up searching the entire manor and coming up with nothing, which would drastically increase my chances of getting caught if I needed to worry about every possible ward.

The third option was to use unlock and hope that Noctra was asleep or otherwise occupied. I couldn't hear anything through the door, even with sharpened senses active, but if I didn't catch him unaware, it would take several seconds for the spell to work. I could be walking into a fire blast as soon as I opened the door.

Finally, I could risk scrying the other side of the doorway. It would only take a few seconds, but if I set off a ward with it, I could be alerting Noctra that someone was here even if he wasn't physically in the room. Of course, the same thing might happen if I walked into the room, but I'd at least get a chance to look for wards if I was careful when I opened the door.

Every strategy had its drawbacks, depending on whether Noctra was awake or asleep. To make the best decision, I needed more information than I had. There was a spell that could scry for wards, but it would drain about two days' worth of mana generation for thirty seconds of use and it would only detect the existence of wards, not their function. I was confident it would remain undetected, unlike the intermediate ranked scrying spell I'd been using.

Ward scanner would leave me low on mana, but it was the least risky of my possible moves. I'd still have enough mana to throw out four or five spells, but if Noctra wasn't in there, I would effectively be crippling myself. If Noctra was in bed, it was the best move. If he wasn't, it was probably the worst.

Well, I had a simple solution for that. I could just use life sense to determine if he was there or not. It wasn't likely that his wards would be powerful enough to cloak him from an intermediate divination. If he was in bed, I'd burst in and kill him. If he wasn't, there was no reason to even bother going into the room.

Sometimes I just got so far ahead of myself with over-engineered solutions that I forgot that simple spells could provide just as much utility with a dash of cleverness added to them. I was far too used to having virtually

unlimited mana to throw at problems and far too dismissive of easily countered basic spells when my opponent probably didn't rank as greater than
an apprentice himself.

A few seconds later, life sense confirmed for me that the other side of
the wall had no human life in it. Given the state of the wards and traps I'd
encountered so far, I had very little reason to believe that my spell was
being tricked, which meant I'd probably wasted my time and mana coming
here. To be thorough, I'd check the other rooms and hope Noctra was
working on something somewhere else. It wasn't as good as catching him
asleep, but it was better than him not being here at all.

I only had to go eight steps down the hall before someone came into the
edge of life sense's range. They were in the farthest room away from me on
the west side of the hall, upright in a chair, from what I could tell, with their
head lolled to the side. Perhaps I'd gotten lucky after all and Noctra had
passed out in the middle of working on a project.

I spent the mana to keep life sense active as I approached the door.
Whoever was inside showed no signs of moving or reacting—not that I
made all that much noise to begin with. I stopped in front of the door,
mentally prepared myself to cast a sleep spell just in case whoever it was
that was in there was actually awake after all, and reached up to test the
handle. It turned easily, and I slipped inside the room.

There was a man sleeping in an overstuffed chair in the corner, softly
snoring and with drool coming out of the corner of his mouth. He looked
like he was in his early forties with black hair going gray at his temples,
wrinkles starting to form around his eyes and on his forehead, and deep
bags under his eyes.

If I hadn't already known what Noctra looked like from scrying him, I
would never have connected this man to the con artist governor of Alkerist.
He looked exhausted and worn out, like he had none of the vitality he'd
displayed when he'd met my father. His clothes were wrinkled from
sleeping in them, and his hands were liberally stained with ink.

He also appeared to be living in this room for some reason. A pile of
clothes had been built up in the opposite corner of his chair, the bookshelf
behind the desk was stuffed with every sort of personal possession and no
books, and even his mud-stained boots were placed neatly against the wall
next to the door.

It was hard to reconcile the man before me with the one who'd kidnapped my father and sent him to be a slave in another town. Based on the ceramic mug and the empty jug near his feet, Noctra had drunk himself to oblivion. What could have caused him to descend to such a state? Was everything else just an act?

Most importantly, did it matter?

I'd come here to kill Noctra. If I'd had the mana for it, I might have captured and mentally interrogated him first, but that wasn't a realistic possibility, and keeping him alive was far too dangerous. It was better to end this now.

I took a few steps back, then conjured a basic force bolt. At the same time, I used a mana manipulation technique known as spell shape to alter the force bolt's composition to make it harder and sharper. I studied Noctra one last time, committing his current state to memory, then I let the force bolt fly.

Humans were, as a general rule, fragile creatures. There were many, many monsters with skin so tough a spell as simple and weak as a force bolt couldn't even scratch them. There were monsters that regenerated from injuries so quickly that a hundred force bolts cast by a hundred apprentices wouldn't be enough to overcome them.

For Noctra, governor of the village known as Alkerist, the force bolt's sharpened tip entered his eye and passed through into his brain so quickly that he gave a single jerk in place and stilled. He didn't even slip out of his chair. If not for the ruined eye and the blood running down his face, nobody would even have suspected he was dead.

Just like that, his hold over the village was broken. I should have been elated, or at least grimly satisfied. I'd accomplished my goal. There'd be some fallout to deal with, sure, but my family was safe. I had time to devote to myself so that I could form my lattice and graft it to my mana core. I had time to figure out where I was and what had happened here.

I should have been happy, but I couldn't shake the feeling that this was only the beginning. There was something else out there that had its sights on Alkerist, something that wasn't going to give it up just because the puppet it had installed here had been dispatched. The mysterious cabal based out of Derro had an interest in Noctra. He was connected to them in some way and in their debt.

Someone would come calling, probably soon.

Maybe that was what had gotten Noctra into such a state. He'd been in debt; perhaps selling my father was a desperate move and he'd known that it had failed. If so, I needed to start digging through any and all records in the manor. If I was lucky, I'd find some storage crystals that I could harvest for my own work.

I glanced back at Noctra's corpse and shook my head. I should have been relieved it was over. Instead, I was already preparing to tackle another problem. "One thing at a time," I said.

First, the body needed to go. It should be incinerated for good measure, just in case anyone in this mysterious foreign cabal was scrying on Noctra directly, though it seemed far more likely that there was some sort of scrying beacon in the manor. Tracking that down was going to be a nightmare.

Actually, going through everything was going to be a nightmare. I hadn't looked around much, but unless every room was empty and Noctra was doing no research whatsoever, there was a lot of space to fill here in the manor. I couldn't credit the idea that he was sending all of the mana he stole to the cabal without keeping even a little bit for himself.

There was no point in getting ahead of myself. With Noctra dead, I was now free to properly explore his manor without worrying about alarm wards. The first thing to do was get a proper inventory of what I was working with, then start figuring out what needed priority. Gathering evidence of Noctra's misconduct was bound to be near the top of the list, or else to the villagers I'd just be a murderer instead of a savior. I wouldn't say that I cared much about their opinions, but it would be difficult to live here if they were constantly trying to arrest me or kill me.

I gave the room one last disgusted glance. The rubbish, the stink of booze, the piles of dirty clothes... It all reminded me far too much of the last time I'd been three years old. At least there wasn't the stale smell of yamma weed and sex overlaying the whole thing. That would have completed the mental picture.

I'd search somewhere else first.

FORTY-FIVE

I started by doing a quick lap around the manor. There were six alarm wards and two more trapped doors, both of which I marked for further investigation. I'd come back and see what was behind them as soon as I finished my initial circuit.

The manor was, for the most part, a big, long rectangle made up of connected rooms. There were exceptions, like the servants' hall and the governor's loop at the end, but the majority of the layout was room after room. There were several small rooms that sat in the middle of the rectangle with no exterior wall and thus no windows to brighten them up, but now that I was no longer worried about being discovered, a simple light spell, usable by any novice, lit the way for me.

Most of the manor was about as interesting as I expected it to be. Large parts weren't in use and were sealed off to collect dust, especially the west side of the building where most of the space had been devoted to public works. From the looks of it, Noctra hadn't had much of an interest in that. After I'd confirmed my mental map and filled in the spaces I hadn't dared scry into previously, I returned to the trapped rooms.

First up was Noctra's suite. I was operating under the logic that he'd keep the most valuable and sensitive objects nearby, and the most potentially dangerous safely locked away in specially prepared chambers, though at this point, I wouldn't be surprised if his labs had no reinforcements at all. Nothing else seemed to. A proper mage, Noctra was not.

A simple unlock granted me access to the suite, and I sent my little ball of light ahead as I opened the door. It swooped into the center of the room and I paused, unsure exactly what I was seeing. There was a bed, unused. That made sense, considering where I'd found Noctra. A small and somewhat ragged cloth doll sat there, perched on one of the pillows.

Next to that was a small vanity with a circular mirror. Several cases sat organized on its surface, and it had no less than three drawers built into it. That wasn't a piece of furniture I typically associated with men, but perhaps Noctra simply enjoyed cosmetics as a hobby. He'd hardly be the first man I met who did. It was hard to reconcile that with the man I'd seen in my scrying, let alone with the state of his corpse in the other room. I was no expert on the finer arts of makeup, but I didn't think he'd been wearing any.

By the time I found the dresses hanging in the closet, I was starting to think I'd come into this room under a mistaken impression. Noctra hadn't been a big man by any means, but there was no way he could possibly fit into any of those clothes. The simplest explanation for that was that this wasn't Noctra's suite. It was Iskara's.

This was without a doubt the master suite of the manor. There were other rooms, but they were all far smaller and lacked the connected closet and personal lavatory. There was even a private office accessible via a door on the south wall. That one was locked too, but I forced it open easily enough.

The inescapable conclusion was that Iskara had the master suite, and Noctra lived and slept elsewhere. That painted their relationship in a very different light, and as I thought back to the conversation I'd spied on between the two of them, I became even more sure that I was on the right trail now.

Noctra was here to work off some kind of debt to a cabal. He'd presumably been stripped of his rank and lost the right to his codename, Nocturne, when he'd been banished to Alkerist. Iskara had come with him, not to assist him, but to oversee his work. That was probably why she personally handled the draw stones. She was the one who was keeping track of how much mana the whole operation provided because she was the one in good standing with their cabal back home and she didn't want him skimming off the top.

The draw stones were probably also her responsibility. There were an awful lot of them in one place, especially a place otherwise so poor. They probably belonged to the cabal and were here on loan to assist with their tithing scam. The more I thought about it, the more it made sense. I'd just assumed the relationship because Noctra was a mage and Iskara was an adept, but I should have known better.

She was his taskmaster. With her dead, he could very well have panicked the first time he tried to scry her or communicate. Whether he realized I'd killed her, or more likely thought that Father had done it, or that someone from this cabal had come after her, he'd seen the writing on the wall.

The man was a coward as well as a con artist. Rather than make an attempt to defend himself, he'd hidden himself away and started working through his stashed liquor. I was vaguely annoyed that as low of him as my opinion had been, the reality had turned out to be even worse.

Other than confirming the owner of the suite, the only room of interest was Iskara's office. There was a box in there, locked of course, that had been designed with about fifty compartments full of storage crystals. It made sense, in a way. The mana was destined to go to Derro, and they needed to get it there somehow. Draw stones were by their very nature too big and heavy to conveniently move around, and I'd already known that Iskara was draining them here in the village.

This, then, was where all the mana was going. About a third of the storage crystals were full, but all of them were extremely low quality. Part of me itched to take the mana from them, but they'd serve as evidence of what Noctra and Iskara had been up to.

While it would have been convenient to find some letters or a personal journal detailing all their dastardly deeds, no such evidence existed. Presumably, Iskara hadn't been a total idiot and any correspondence she had received like that had been promptly destroyed. There were various tools for transferring mana around, including a channeling lock used to lessen the transference loss when using a storage crystal. One of those would have been nice to have had eight months ago.

Once everything was cleared up, I was going to claim this office-turned-workshop and refine or replace the tools to bring them up to something approaching my standards. This would be an excellent place to start working on my lattice. The design I had in mind was going to be somewhat modular to account for the natural growth of my mana core over the next twelve to fourteen years, which would cause some inefficiencies in the long run. I'd be able to rebuild it properly later, and in the short term, I'd enjoy a vastly increased rate of mana generation.

Hidden away in her desk was a ledger, one that I assumed was keeping track of how much mana she'd stolen from the villagers, and how much was left after being pulled from the draw stone into her little setup in here. When I opened the book, however, I found myself in for a rude surprise.

I couldn't read this language.

It was ridiculous. I spoke it just fine. Sure, I'd had to use Gravin's memories merged with mine to adjust for the regional variances, but it hadn't been an issue. Somehow, they were using an entirely different alphabet, one that I'd never come across before. Once again, the disturbing question of where exactly I'd been reborn reared its ugly head.

I was definitely still on Manoch. Of that much, I was certain. It was a part I'd never been to or even heard of before, but there couldn't possibly be another world with one of the same languages I'd learned back home. Even if there was, it didn't matter. I'd reviewed the soul invocations after I'd awakened again and confirmed they were working correctly. I was still on the same world I'd left. Somewhere out there, my sanctum in the Night Vale was waiting for me to return to it.

The only reasonable explanation was that this book was not written in Enotian. I couldn't picture a way that an entire language would have its alphabet replaced, so Iskara must have instead been bilingual and filled out her ledger in another language. Alternatively, the whole thing could be some sort of cipher using made-up symbols that no one but her would know. That seemed like a lot of work to go through for a simple ledger, though, especially with all the other tools serving as evidence of exactly what had been happening inside this work room.

There were spells to translate unfamiliar languages, though they could easily fail to crack coded messages. That would be a project for another day, once I'd solved my mana issues permanently. There was probably something important in there, but unless I failed to find any evidence at all of

Noctra and Iskara's guilt, I wasn't going to waste my time and mana trying to translate it.

The very next room I stopped in was a small study. It had a single desk with a chair behind it and two more of those over-stuffed chairs that I'd found Noctra sleeping in in either corner of the room. Behind the desk was a shelf lined with cubby holes for various scrolls. At the top was a small row of books, no more than ten.

I used minor telekinesis to pull the first one down and frowned at it. The more I flipped through it, the deeper my frown got. This book appeared to be written in a foreign language as well. So was the next one, and the one after that. By now I recognized many of the symbols, even if I didn't know what they meant. It still might not mean anything. Noctra and Iskara had come from somewhere else. Perhaps they'd brought books with them that were written in the dominant language of wherever they'd lived before.

I checked the rest of the books anyway and several of the scrolls. Everything appeared to be written in a language I couldn't read. If this was how it was going to be, I would have to consider reorganizing my priorities to push learning whatever tongue this was to the top.

It wasn't all a waste of time. One of the scrolls revealed a map when I unfurled it. It displayed an island, circular and ringed with mountains except for one spot near the northern tip. There were five towns on it, and the map made it clear that the entire island was one with very little rainfall. Even being unable to read the labels, I felt confident that I was looking at the place I was living on. Alkerist had to be one of the three villages on the east side, tucked away in the mountains, which probably made Derro the bigger town in the center of the flatlands in the middle.

I didn't recognize the shape of the island, and unfortunately, the map didn't display anything else. I still didn't know where I was, but it was nice to have an idea of how to leave this place and hopefully get out of this mana desert: west, then north.

I continued my exploration of the warded rooms and found mostly what I'd expected. There was a room that was being used as storage for various mana tools and included a workbench to repair them. There were three more bedrooms, one of which showed signs that it might have belonged to Noctra despite him not having been sleeping in it.

And in the center of the house, behind a locked door, was a room with a dozen different books left open and scattered across the floor. Stone carving chisels and files were pushed into the corner like so much debris and refuse, all of it centered around a single pedestal with a top about two feet wide.

Set on top of that, looking like nothing so much as a fang of blue granite with a series of cracks running through it, was a ward stone bigger than I was.

CHAPTER
FORTY-SIX

This whole time, I'd been thinking of the barrier as something of a myth. The village obviously functioned fine without a barrier and had been for years. Based on Father's story, I'd made some assumptions about local history that were seemingly incorrect.

It didn't take more than a glance to confirm that this ward stone was designed to project a huge barrier, though figuring out exactly what kind would require a few minutes to read the runes inscribed on its surface. That was largely irrelevant right now anyway, since it had met some sort of unfortunate fate and cracked. It was nothing but a conversation piece now, though I assumed someone had been trying to fix it.

If my understanding of the timeline was correct, it probably hadn't been Noctra's predecessor who'd been working on it. He'd died during the incident that had killed Father's friend, and it looked like the magical backlash from the ward stone might have been what had done it.

That left Noctra himself, though he'd obviously failed after spending a great deal of effort. Just judging by the few diagrams he'd left open in various books, it was obvious that he didn't understand the first thing about how ward stones operated. It looked like he'd been trying to apply the principles of a static ward field to the stone when he should have been looking into transmutation to patch up the damage and inscription to fix the runes that had been destroyed.

The confusion was understandable, given the name, but ward stones had much more in common with enchantments than they did with traditional wards. There was, admittedly, some overlap, but whoever had been working on this one had gone in completely the wrong direction trying to fix it. I couldn't read any of the labels on the diagram, but it appeared to me like they were trying to create some sort of patch made of pure mana that would hold the shape of the destroyed runes.

That would never work, of course. It was a temporary solution at best, and completely missed the point of the ward stone being a physical object to anchor the spells to. The ward stone itself was the work of a master scribe with a solid foundation in transmutation, far too complex for someone who barely qualified as an apprentice to repair.

I'd have to examine the runes more carefully—I could still read those, at least—to confirm what exactly the ward stone was meant to accomplish, but I couldn't see any good reason that I wouldn't be able to fix this thing. For now, I was going to leave it alone as more evidence of Noctra's lies. Between this and Iskara's workshop, I had plenty of proof of what they'd been up to. The problem was that it might not be so apparent to someone who didn't understand magic.

Hopefully, someone in the village could read that ledger. That book was probably my best option for proving that the mage who'd been protecting their town was actually scamming them and stealing their mana. On the off-chance that its contents proved completely indecipherable, it was probably a good idea to keep looking.

Of the few remaining rooms, only one of them proved to have anything interesting in it. Other warded rooms were being used as storage, and I might repurpose some of those raw materials in the near future if it proved to have any quality, but for the moment I only wanted to take a general inventory with an eye for things the villagers could understand.

The exception to that was a room with a map pinned up on the wall. It clearly showed the town and the surrounding wastes, no labels needed. It also marked twenty or so spots in a rough circle around the village, though focused heavily on the west and northeast portions where the land flattened out. If I didn't miss my guess, one of those marked spots was near the trail we'd returned on.

Noctra knew about the dust jackals. I thought back to their mana cores, so unusual to find in nature. Animals almost never had a stage two core.

They might have a pseudo stage three, as that was far easier to accomplish, if ultimately weaker, when done out of order, but it took a degree of intelligence to create and graft a lattice to a mana core. Dust jackals did not have that intelligence, not unless the pack I'd killed was exceptionally stupid. Assuming they were indicative of the species as a whole, someone had been experimenting on them.

I briefly went through the diagrams in the notes before nodding to myself. Most of them looked like ideas for constructing a lattice, meaning Noctra was at least aware of the concept, even if he hadn't managed to refine it enough to do it to himself. I would have noticed if he'd possessed a stage two core when I finally encountered him, and from what I could tell, he'd only had a decidedly mediocre stage one.

Good on him for practicing, I supposed, though I could think of a few organizations from my past who would have balked at him using animal test subjects. Given the nature of making changes to a mana core, I couldn't personally blame him for wanting to make sure he had it right before he grafted a lattice into his own core. Making suboptimal choices due to a lack of knowledge was how I'd ended up in the position I had in my previous life. Doing things right this time was one of my major goals.

Of course, I knew how to repair the lattice I was going to build, including how to swap out a few modular pieces to increase overall efficiency later on once my core grew to full size. I'd be weaker for the next decade or so than if I used a permanently fixed lattice, but I wasn't willing to sacrifice long-term power in exchange for a small advantage now.

When I finished looking around, I took a moment to gather my thoughts. I had sufficient evidence that any mage could understand that Noctra had been bilking the village for years, but there were no mages besides myself. Father might technically be an apprentice, but he was too new to know what he was looking at, and his standing with the village wasn't good anyway. I had a lot of written material, but I didn't expect anyone to understand a word of it since it wasn't in the language we were all speaking.

The cracked ward stone was a damning piece of evidence, assuming no one tried to blame me for it. But again, it was something a mage would easily understand and anyone else might not. I could only hope that the villagers would recognize what it was and that it had been like that before

I'd gotten here. It seemed to me that seeing a few big cracks in what was obviously magical writing would be enough proof to say that it didn't work, but some people didn't think like that. To them, a shovel still worked even though the handle was splintered and the blade was chipped. Worn-down magic should still work too, just maybe not as well.

If only it was so easy.

I had some proof that Noctra had been using mana to do experiments, though not any proof that it was anyone's mana but his own. That might not fly by itself, but if I could translate the notes, I could prove his experiments had been used to modify local wildlife to make them dangerous and, if I wanted to lie about the technical definitions, turn them into monsters. He hadn't done that, but claiming that their governor was making monsters would have a lot more impact than saying he was doing magical experiments on animals to refine his technique.

I had Nermet, but he'd already been slow before Noctra had gotten ahold of him. Fixing him was a goal, but it probably wouldn't have an effect on whether anyone believed me over the next few days. Unfortunately, I lacked the equipment to keep records of what I scried. That would have made things much easier if I could just cast out an illusion of the conversation between Father and Noctra.

Those were easy enough to tamper with and there was always someone crying foul whenever a mage tried to submit an illusion as evidence, but it might work in my favor here. These people didn't have a clue what was and wasn't possible with magic, and if they were going to doubt the factual evidence I had, I wasn't above presenting them with some fabricated evidence that I couldn't prove was actually true.

The biggest problem with this whole situation was that I did not have the kind of mana reserves I'd need to protect myself from the entire village if they turned against me. Extracting myself was achievable. Getting the rest of my family to safety with me was a far more dubious prospect. I could take the mana from those storage crystals now, I supposed. It wasn't like anyone except for my father would be able to feel the mana in them.

Even if I did all that and went scrounging for every bit of mana I could pull out besides, like from cleaning out those emitters they used as Testing devices, it wasn't going to be enough to fight off the entire village without killing people. It was far, far easier to kill than it was to restrain, especially in large numbers. Three or four arc lightnings could kill a third of the village and was well within my means. For the same amount of mana, I'd get six or seven paralyzing grasps, and those would last only minutes.

Taking the mana held in the storage crystals wouldn't make a big difference, and on the off chance that someone could read the ledger, I wanted it to match up properly. If things went sideways, I'd find an alternate solution. For now, I probably had enough proof to at least merit a closer look at things.

I needed to talk to Father about all this. With Noctra gone, the village was without his dubious protection. Yes, they'd be able to keep their own mana again, and that should make life significantly easier for them if they wanted to keep on the way they'd been going, but there should be someone around to drop a fire blast on a roaming monster should the need arise. I didn't want that person to be me, nor did I expect the village to want me for the role. I was three. I still had to stand on my toes to reach door handles on occasion.

The sun would be up soon anyway. It was time to go retrieve my family and walk Father through what I'd uncovered. Senica should probably be kept away from the room with the body in it. Really, it wouldn't be smart to let her near any room with anything expensive and valuable in it. I'd gone out of my way to deliberately keep everything as close to how I'd found it as possible, and I didn't need anyone messing that up. I could trust Father to look, but not touch. I did not trust Senica to follow that rule.

I locked the side door leading into the kitchen behind me, not that I expected anyone to come rummaging through before dawn. But I'd found the keys to the place while I was poking around and there was no reason not to take precautions, so I did it anyway, then set off at a jog hastened by a simple invocation to find my family.

Assuming they hadn't been caught, they would be waiting south of town. When I hadn't found them after about ten minutes of looking around, I grew worried that something had gone wrong. Perhaps another Barrier Warden had run across them and captured them without my magic there to assist. Perhaps they'd run afoul of some creature lurking out in the dark.

Perhaps Father had just given in to Mother's badgering and they'd returned home. I doubted it, but it was possible. There was an easy enough way to find out, though I did feel I was being a bit too free with my mana even as I cast a scry spell.

It snapped into place immediately and I saw my whole family in the village's one and only holding cell in the Garrison barracks. *Damn*. That was going to be a pain.

CHAPTER

FORTY-SEVEN

T he good news was that nobody was hurt. The bad news was that I recognized two of the people standing outside the cell as Collectors. It wasn't much of a stretch to connect the night we all disappeared with the theft of all the mana from their storage room. Even if they didn't think we were involved in it, they'd likely want to know as much as they could about what went on that night.

But in all likelihood, they did suspect us. I'd put those Garrison villagers to sleep as well when they'd come to take us to Noctra's manor, just like the Collectors who'd been in my way. Now that I thought about it, I was pretty sure one of the Garrison members standing there was part of the trio I'd hexed.

"You've brought trouble down on the village before," one of the Collectors said. "Why should we believe it's any different this time?"

"I was a child who made a mistake," Father said hotly. "And why are you putting my daughter in a cell with me if you think I'm the one who caused this whole mess?"

"Shut up," the Garrison man snapped irritably, giving Father and the Collector a glare. "Lord Noctra will sort this out as soon as he wakes up. I've already told Tsurai to go let him know we caught you skulking around out in the fields. Until he gets here, all of you, be quiet. I'm sick of hearing you all bicker."

I recognized that man, Karad. He was the one who'd shown up looking for Father after that incident with the schoolteacher. He'd been a lot more polite back then. Now he looked harried and exhausted, not unlike Noctra himself. I wondered if he'd been in on the whole scheme and was even now expecting some sort of retaliation from the cabal that had secretly controlled our entire village.

I needed to get ahead of this somehow. Tsurai was presumably going to find Noctra's body soon, if he hadn't already. Father was likely to be blamed for the murder, all things considered. These people had already made up their minds that my family was guilty of something. They were just waiting for someone else to decide exactly what.

Was there a way to handle this without revealing myself? I could probably do it if I established a telepathic link with Father and just used magic while he acted as if he was doing it. I was more than practiced enough to cast even advanced spells without needing a focusing chant or any sort of ritual gestures, and I doubted there was anyone sensitive enough to mana to detect me if I was actively trying to hide my spell usage.

On the other hand, the amount of mana that would take was a lot more than I was prepared to spend. Even if I was willing, I would have at most two minutes of conversation before I was completely tapped out. Spreading it out to give simple instructions without allowing for Father to reply might give me enough mana for thirty commands, but if I cast a single spell with each instruction, it was going to be less than half that.

The other option was to come out into the open. I could probably convince people I wasn't insane. Magic has a tendency to impress those who didn't know much about it, even cheap, flashy, low-strength spells. But I'd already seen how hard it was for people to connect the idea that I wasn't a normal child with the concept that they should listen to me. Adults had a hard time taking orders from toddlers, even if they knew in their heads that the toddler wasn't actually a toddler.

My real issue was that I just didn't believe it was worth exposing myself to danger by revealing my existence. I'd left plenty of enemies behind as Keiran, maybe not nearly as many as I'd buried, but even a single one finding me in my weakened state would be enough to end things. It had already been a risk to tell my parents, and I still wasn't convinced giving Senica a memory wipe was a bad idea. I didn't think she'd spread the knowledge maliciously, but anyone who'd ever had kids knew exactly how bad they were at keeping secrets. It took a special breed to keep their mouths shut, ones who'd grown up having no one but themselves to depend on and who'd learned the hard way not to give an advantage away.

Senica hadn't had that kind of childhood, thankfully.

I could break my family out of the cell and evacuate them back out of town. We'd need to steal enough food to survive for a few weeks at minimum and find a place I could fortify into something we could live in, but it was theoretically possible. Somehow, I doubted my parents would go for it. Their goal was to get everything back to normal. They'd only gone along with getting rid of Noctra because he was preventing that from happening.

I retreated from the town to make sure no one in any of the fields spotted me, then spent the next hour periodically scrying on the beacon Father had carried. It was in a pile with the rest of the supplies we'd had left upon returning to the village. The spell didn't require the beacon to be held by anyone in order to function, so that wasn't a problem unless they decided to move it somewhere more than fifty feet or so from Father. At that point, I wouldn't be able to manipulate the scry to keep an eye on them.

Eventually, Tsurai burst into the Garrison yelling for Karad. "Boss! Boss! You're not going to believe this." Everyone froze and peered at the man, who was breathing hard and looking around. As soon as he spotted Karad sitting at a table near the cell, he rushed over. "Lord Noctra's dead."

Karad shot to his feet. "What?"

"I waited an hour, but when he didn't come out, I started knocking on doors. He didn't answer, but I remembered the latch doesn't work right on that door near the atrium, so I poked my head in and found him dead in his study. It looks like someone stabbed him in the eye with a knife."

"Spirits protect us," Karad muttered. He gave my parents a suspicious glance, but they were just as wide-eyed as everyone else. "This mess just keeps getting more and more complicated. Go get everyone who's not already on duty and bring them here. You've got ten minutes before we set out."

"You got it, boss," Tsurai said before running off.

Karad turned to face the cell and stomped up to it. "How are you involved in this?" he demanded.

Father glanced over at Mother, then replied, "You've been sitting next to us most of the night. How are we supposed to have done anything?"

"Maybe we caught you on your way back out," Karad said. "You got in to do the deed, then bungled the escape."

"Let me get this straight. You think that my wife and I snuck into Lord Noctra's manor with our six-year-old, murdered him in his sleep, and then got caught as we were leaving? Where do you think we were going in this scenario?"

"I don't know. Why don't you tell me?"

"Would it make a difference?" Father asked. "You don't believe me anyway."

"Because your story is that Lord Noctra, who's lived here for fifteen years, suddenly decided that you were magically gifted, and that he was going to sell you off to some associates of his back in Derro. But you somehow managed to escape, your family came looking for you, and you all survived for a week out in the monster-infested wastelands. And you just coincidentally happened to get back in town the same night the man who supposedly wronged you died."

"You can't have it both ways, Karad. If you think I'm lying about Noctra's actions toward me, then what would be my motivation for trying to kill him?"

"Oh, I know you went to see him. It was two of mine who took you up there. What I don't know is what happened while you were there. Did you want something and he refused to give it to you? Did you swear your revenge on him, then flee with your trouble-making wife just long enough for him to let down his guard? Maybe you lost your boy out in the wastes? Nobody seems to know where he is. Iskara disappeared a few days ago, too. You have anything to do with that?"

"I already told you what he did," Father said. "Both to me personally and to the village as a whole. Come on, you know what that barrier looked like when we were young. Haven't seen that in a while, right? So what's all the tithing been for?"

"Lord Noctra told us it wouldn't look the same after he fixed it," Karad said. "I remember being gathered up in the town square when he made the announcement. You were standing not five feet away, over by Remat's parents' place, all by yourself because no one wanted anything to do with you after you got Teno killed."

"He lied to us. He's been lying to all of us for years."

Karad laughed at Father and said, "So that's it? That's your whole argument? Lord Noctra's a liar and we should all believe you instead? Do you think they'll exile you or just kill you now and save you the walk into some monster's belly?"

I'd expected some amount of pushback to the idea that Noctra hadn't been the man he'd portrayed himself as, but this behavior went far beyond that. Either I'd seriously underestimated Noctra's influence with the Garrison, or something else was going on here. Noctra had already outright subjugated Nermet. It was possible he'd used mental manipulation to make everyone in the Garrison view him far more favorably than was reasonable.

It was also possible Karad was in on it. I couldn't see a good reason Karad would need to know, but just generally keeping the captain of the village guard on his side was a smart move for Noctra. If that was the case, it was likely that the Collectors would have an equally strong reaction. And I'd already assumed the Barrier Wardens had to know that the barrier was fake and were somehow okay with it.

With so many of the villagers who were in a position of authority already compromised, convincing everyone else that Noctra was a bad person might be even more challenging than I'd initially assumed. If I needed to dispel some mental compulsions on better than thirty people, I was going to need more mana. Maybe I could be more strategic than that and just target the ones at the very top. Noctra probably spent more time and effort on them, anyway.

This was all just speculation. I had no proof that anyone other than Nermet was under any sort of compulsion. Father was not well-loved in the village, and a respected man who'd been protecting the villagers—at least as far as they knew—for fifteen years had been very obviously murdered with what was extremely suspicious timing. If it had been safe to leave my family out in the wastelands for even one more night, I'd have done it just to avoid linking them to Noctra's death.

The proof to exonerate my family was back in the manor, but someone with some magical expertise was going to be needed to explain to the Garrison members what they were looking at. I tried to think if there was anyone like that in the village, and immediately came up with the one person who was respected, knew about mana manipulation, and had absolutely no reason to lie to protect Father.

It looked like I was going to go to school after all.

CHAPTER

FORTY-EIGHT

O ne thing I'd learned over the years was that the more moving parts a plan had, the more attention I had to give it to make sure that those parts were going in the direction I wanted, at the time I wanted them to move. Simple plans were better, but not always practical. My plan here had a few holes in it. For example, I didn't know if Cherok would actually know enough about magic to identify anything in Noctra's manor. For another, there was no guarantee he could read whatever language those books were in. But he was the most likely candidate I could think of out of a very small pool of possibilities.

I couldn't talk to Cherok myself, of course. For one thing, I didn't think he'd listen to a child. For another, if he knew he was doing my father a favor, I was sure he'd decline. But then, I didn't need to. It was still early enough in the day that very few people were out and about. Mostly the streets had Garrison or Collectors staff rushing around. I snuck into town and waited for an opportunity for one of them to pass near the school.

In my hand I held one of the keys I'd taken from the manor, the one that unlocked the kitchen door. I spent a bit of mana to enchant it into a scry beacon while I kept watch, and as soon as I noticed one of the Garrison members walking by, I tossed it out onto the street.

"Huh?" the guy said as it landed in front of him. He blinked down at the key, then looked up at me. "Hey, aren't you—"

Mind magic was one of the most abused sub-disciplines. One part divination and one part enchantment, its primary purpose was to make other people do whatever the mage wanted. Nermet's total subjugation was an extreme example of this, and I found it abhorrent to do something like that. It was a fate worse than death.

Perhaps that made me something of a hypocrite, because I had no compunctions against using a lesser version of that spell to keep myself safe. The version I was using was called command, and it used divination to connect to the subject's mind in a manner similar to telepathy, then implanted an enchantment that directed them to perform a certain action.

The primary difference was that a command would last for minutes, maybe half an hour, before the target broke themselves out of it. This Garrison member was going to deliver a message for me and then go on with his life, while Nermet remained a literal slave, a mind trapped inside a body he could no longer control.

"Deliver this key to Cherok and inform him that Noctra has been murdered. Tell him they need his expertise in identifying and handling the specialty equipment discovered in the manor. The key will let him in through the food delivery door in the kitchen," I ordered the Garrison man.

Nodding absently, he picked up the key and ferried it over to the school a block away. When he was done, the enchantment would unravel, and he'd have no memory of ever performing the service I'd pressed on him. It would take a skilled mage to even detect that I'd ever cast any spell on him, and they'd have to examine the man in the next hour or two if they wanted to find even that much.

My mission accomplished, I retreated out of the village and back to my hiding spot to watch events unfold. If things went the way I was hoping, Cherok would discover the evidence and understand it well enough to speculate on what Noctra and Iskara had been up to. He would exonerate my family without ever realizing who it was he was helping, though I fully realized the evidence was only of the "it was justified to murder him" sort, not the "we didn't do it" kind. It was a bit harder to work around that since I had, in fact, done it.

If things did not go well, I'd need to extract three people from that cell in the Garrison barracks by force. The easiest way would be to just use a transmutation spell to make a hole in the back wall so they could walk out, possibly with a handful of sleep spells to stop any pursuers. Mana would be tight, especially if I used too much of it scrying, and I didn't have a good plan for our family to survive after fleeing.

It would be much more convenient for me if the villagers just accepted that they'd been duped and that they were better off without Noctra and Iskara around, especially since I was almost positive someone from that cabal would show up eventually to find out why the mana shipments had stopped. The more time I had to prepare for that, the better.

I gave Cherok twenty minutes to walk over to the manor before I scried on my new beacon, only to find it sitting on a table, the schoolteacher nowhere in sight. Had he left it behind? It wasn't impossible to scry directly on the manor itself, but I'd been counting on the added efficiency of using a beacon to reduce the mana burden.

Just as I was about to switch targets, Cherok walked into sight. The man hadn't even left the school yet! The village governor was dead and instead of rushing over, Cherok had taken the time to dress and groom himself and was even now eating breakfast. There wasn't a shred of urgency to his actions, either. A murder in the village was not enough of an abnormality to stir him out of his morning routine, apparently.

Unbelievable.

Half an hour and three check-ins later, Cherok was finally on the move. By that point, the sun was fully up, and I could see people heading out to the fields to start their day. Cherok made his way east of the village at a leisurely stroll, stopping often to chat with anyone he happened to wander past, though he kept the details of what he was doing vague. At no point did I catch him ever saying anything more than that he had some business with Lord Noctra.

It was possible I missed it since I was limiting myself to checking in on him every five or ten minutes instead of watching him continuously, but it seemed to me that he knew not to spread information around until the authorities were ready to make an official announcement. Considering how long it had taken him to stir himself out of the school, I was somewhat surprised that he'd take that stance.

At least, I was until he arrived, and I realized he'd still somehow beaten the Garrison there. How exactly the wheels of bureaucracy could turn so slowly in a village of less than two hundred people was a mystery to me, but I doubted this was the first time. Cherok had known he didn't need to hurry, and even taking his time, he was still the first one on the scene. He'd already been inside the manor for five minutes before Karad showed up with six other people.

"Cherok, what are you doing here?" Karad asked after finding him in the room Noctra had devoted to altering mana cores.

"Helping with your investigation," the teacher replied as he peered around. "Ganor stopped by and said you needed someone with some expertise to look over all the magical stuff in the manor."

"Did he?" Karad asked, his eyebrows going up. "Huh... Not a bad idea. I didn't think he was that smart."

Cherok snorted, but didn't reply. He just kept flipping through the book with all of Noctra's notes on different possible lattice shapes. "This is fascinating," he murmured. "If I'm reading this correctly, Lord Noctra was trying to figure out how to make it so he could generate even more mana than a normal mage's core would."

"Great. Does that have anything to do with why someone killed him? You wouldn't believe what Sellis and Xilaya are trying to sell me on."

All that effort to keep my family out of it, gone just like that. Now I needed to worry about Cherok's grudge against my father causing problems. On the bright side, it did look like I'd managed to get someone who could read the books in the manor over there, so it wasn't a total loss. This was a prime example of my earlier thoughts about having to control moving parts, though.

Cherok froze for an instant, then said, "Oh? I thought their whole family was gone. What do they have to do with this?"

"Who knows? Caught them and their girl skulking around in the dark a few hours ago. Can't just be a coincidence that they show back up on the same night someone sneaks in here and murders Lord Noctra."

"Just them and the girl? What about that dimwitted son of theirs?"

"No sign of him, and none of them will talk about him. We found Nermet with them, too, but you know he's not going to be able to tell us anything. Just between you and me, I can't figure any of this out. I wouldn't have said Sellis had something like this in him, but they managed to survive for near a week outside the barrier, even if they did lose their boy. Who knows what else he's capable of?"

Cherok remained silent as he flipped through the pages for a few more seconds, then asked, "Is there anything in particular I should be looking at?

As interesting as this all is, it's obviously a project Lord Noctra worked on for a long time, and I don't see how it relates to his murder."

"I couldn't tell you," Karad said. "Wasn't even my idea to bring you up here, though I'm sure I would have once I'd gotten a chance to see what was in these rooms."

"I'm sure," Cherok agreed pleasantly, though I caught him rolling his eyes behind Karad's back. "Let's just get a quick look around and see if there's anything you need me to identify, and then I can get out of your way so you can do your thing."

"Good idea. I haven't had a chance to look around myself yet, though, so I'm not sure exactly where you're needed. I think Tsurai knows better than I would right now. Let's go see if we can find him first."

I let the scry spell drop and frowned. Things hadn't gone as close to plan as I wanted, but we weren't out of the game yet. It would all depend on what Cherok made of the broken ward stone and the storage crystals. As long as someone came to the right conclusion about that, we had a shot at getting my family out of trouble.

If not... well, I'd be draining those storage crystals and probably breaking back into the Collectors' draw stone room again. It wasn't like the village had much use for the mana they'd already tithed anyway. If they cooperated, I'd probably use it to ignite a few other cores, maybe fix their ward stone for them.

Come to think of it, that was probably a good bargaining tool. I needed to talk with my parents, since Father would have to be the face of this. I did not want to be the target of whatever assassin the cabal sent to take control of their investment again. Nor did I want to be any sort of person of interest that they tried to kidnap and use for their own gain.

As much as it pained me to watch my supply of mana continue to dwindle, I needed to see what Karad was thinking about all of this so I could determine my next move. I recast the scry spell and resumed my spying on the manor.

"What's all this?" Karad said as he and Cherok peered into Iskara's in-suite workroom.

Perfect. Now I just needed to see if I'd given Cherok too much credit, or if he'd actually be able to figure out what was going on.

CHAPTER
FORTY-NINE

Cherok peered at the storage crystals intently. "Yes, I recognize these," he said. "These are crystallized mana, which means…"

Karad snorted impatiently. "I'm not one of your students. Don't try to tease the answer out of me."

"Which means these are the final form of a draw stone after it's been completely filled with mana," Cherok finished, shooting Karad a waspish glare.

I pinched the bridge of my nose and resisted the urge to groan. This plan had been a mistake.

"Sure, and why are there so many of them? Sellis claimed Lord Noctra was hoarding our own mana for his own personal use or selling it to Derro."

"Preposterous. Lord Noctra wouldn't do that. No, I'm sure he was using them for exactly what he's always told us he was: powering the barrier. There should be a device somewhere on the grounds that they slot into to provide mana."

"Fascinating," Karad said flatly. "Why are there so many if the barrier hasn't been working right for years?"

"How would I know? Maybe he was saving them for emergencies?"

"Possible, I suppose. What about the rest of these tools?"

"Yes, that. Hmm, well," Cherok said as he peered at the workbench. He picked up the channeling lock and turned it around to study it. "I'm afraid

I'm not actually a mage, so I couldn't tell you what these all do. I believe this one is a housing for the crystallized draw stone after it's been inserted into the barrier generator."

I couldn't tell if Cherok was incompetent and trying to bluff his way through this, if he actually believed what he was saying, or if he was malicious and deliberately lying to get Father in more trouble. Either way, things were not going the way I wanted them to.

Cherok hadn't recognized that the experiment Noctra had been performing had ringed the village with dangerous predators. He didn't know what the storage crystals were or how they worked. My only hope was that he wouldn't be able to deny that the ward stone was busted. A couple of giant cracks running through them were obvious, but with my luck, Cherok would tell Karad that it wasn't a ward stone, it was a thermal regulator for Noctra's bath water.

Karad picked up the ledger and started flipping through it, his eyebrows going higher and higher with each page. "How sure are you about the purpose of these crystallized draw stones?" he finally asked.

"Reasonably certain. Why?"

"Because this appears to be a tally of how much mana Lord Noctra owes something called the 'Wolf Pack,' and according to the last entry, he's only paid off about half of the total."

"You're not saying... you believe *Sellis*?"

"I don't know what to think, Cherok," Karad said, brandishing the ledger. "There were obviously things Noctra wasn't telling us. Like, why was Iskara living in this suite instead of him? She's his assistant. For that matter, where is she?"

Cherok flinched back and said, "I don't know. Stop yelling at me."

"Cut the posturing. I don't need your wild guesses, I need facts. I've got a family in a cell right now telling me that Lord Noctra was actually an evil bastard who was scamming us, and I'm starting to think they're right. I need to know what the repercussions are going to be to this. Is the barrier going to fail? Did it never work to begin with? Are these Wolf Pack people going to show up wanting to know where Noctra is? Will they take it personally when I tell them he's dead?"

Karad was smarter than I'd given him credit for, which wasn't necessarily a good thing. I needed him to comprehend what was going on without getting any stupid ideas about manipulating the situation to set himself up as the new governor. But if he was smart *and* willing to work with me, well, that could be useful. The more I thought about it, the more I was sure things could work out well.

It would mean revealing myself to him, but it would allow Father to get away from the whole situation. He'd made it clear he didn't want to be in charge. He didn't even really want to be a mage, surprisingly. As far as he was concerned, his core ignition was going to make him a damn fine farmer, and not much else. What a waste.

As satisfying as it was to watch Cherok get chewed out, it wasn't an efficient use of my limited mana. I'd learned what I needed to know. Karad had accepted that Noctra had been up to something. He might still think Father had killed the governor, but I didn't think I'd have to work too hard to convince him that Noctra had needed killing.

I had a basis to start negotiations. The hardest part would be overcoming Karad's initial prejudices. I needed to convince him that I was not a normal child and that, more importantly, I had the solutions to a lot of problems the village had. There was a severe mana shortage. I could fix that by igniting a few cores and teaching those people how to ignite more. They might not be the highest quality like mine, but they'd be ten times better than what they had now.

This little village could be an oasis in the desert if every single person had an ignited core. Things would be green again, and if they really wanted that barrier, an entire village of mages could easily afford it. They were already used to tithing their mana. If everyone gave five times as much as they did now, it would still only be half of what they'd be capable of making.

Alkerist could be an investment, my own personal safe haven. I just needed to get the first generation going, and they'd spread my teachings. A hundred apprentice mages with access to five or six utility spells and fire blast would be more than enough to repel a rogue agent, and if a mage of sufficient caliber to defeat them did show up, I could step in.

I wondered where Karad lived. I needed to have a chat with him, preferably alone.

The next six hours were a bore for me. I focused mostly on generating as much mana as I safely could while keeping an eye on my two scry beacons. My family was securely detained, but they weren't mistreated. They were given a meal, privacy to use a chamber pot, and otherwise left alone.

At the manor, various Garrison members, Collectors, and Barrier Wardens cycled through, as well as two people I thought might be Arborists, but I wasn't sure. I recognized them by face, but not name. Almost nobody stayed that long, and Karad's orders to everyone were the same: maintain business as usual. They'd make an announcement when everyone gathered for the nightly tithe; no need to cause any panic before then.

I had, sadly, missed the examination of the ward stone. Then again, if Cherok's identification of everything else was indicative of his skill, it no doubt would have only served to annoy me even more to listen to whatever ignorant theory he sprouted off with there. Perhaps it was for the best that I hadn't caught that particular moment.

The way I saw it, I had two options. I could force an early meeting with Karad, which probably wouldn't be the one-on-one I wanted and would put me at a disadvantage, or I could let him make his announcement and work to spin it in my favor afterwards. That way, I'd have more time to generate mana and I could surprise him with the meeting on my terms.

The only good thing about my Cherok plan was that Karad had taken the key from him after dismissing him. Since Cherok had practically done more harm than good, I wasn't sorry that the scry beacon was staying with someone interesting to me. Karad didn't have absolute authority like Noctra had, but it seemed like in the absence of Noctra or Iskara, he was steadily taking over. No one had challenged him yet, but I'd overheard talk of a meeting between himself and the heads of the other organizations.

I'd considered crashing that as well, and I still might. If I did, though, I wanted to have as much mana as I could at my disposal first. A day of spying had left my reserves dangerously low, and at minimum I needed enough for a mass sleep spell. It was slightly more mana efficient to drop four people with mass sleep than individually targeted sleep spells, though it did take significantly longer to cast. If the four leaders had assistants with them, though, I'd need something that hit many people at once to ensure I could escape if things went sour.

I waited until late afternoon when children were all over the place, free from the day's schooling but not yet home for dinner. The adults were all busy working, and with no one paying much attention to one more kid running around, I ran across town to the Collectors' building, then used phantasmal step to go right through the wall into the draw stone storage room.

The stones weren't nearly as full as they'd been last time I was here, but it was still close to a week's worth of tithing from the villagers. Draining them dry and adding the mana to my personal mana crystal was well worth the time and risk I'd taken. I used a second phantasmal step to get back out, blinked against the transition from dark room to sunlit street, and started off toward Noctra's manor.

There were plenty of people there, but this wasn't like the crime scenes I'd seen in my first life. The village didn't have nearly enough Garrison members to cordon off the area, and I honestly didn't think they had the training to realize they should even try. Most deaths in Alkerist were the result of accidents or predation, not murder. I imagined the few murders that had occurred had probably been much more straightforward.

It pained me to waste mana on a third phantasmal step, but I didn't see a way to sneak through the manor with it being occupied now, not unless I wanted to burn mana on a full invisibility spell. With my pitiful reserves, it wouldn't last ten seconds. Since no one was guarding the outside, I circled wide around it to the east exterior wall and used an application of scrying to confirm my position against the room I wanted to enter and that it was empty.

Taking the mana from the storage crystals was painless and quick. The only hiccup was when I tried to use the channeling locks and found they did such a poor job at limiting transference loss that I could do it better without their help. Even that was a minor setback. I was happy to trade a few extra seconds per storage crystal in order to retain another fifteen percent of the mana they held.

Karad had set himself up in a parlor near the middle of the house, and if my spying was accurate, he would be met by Solidaire, the head of the Barrier Wardens; Melmir, who oversaw the Collectors; and Shel, who directed the Arborists. I did not miss the fact that none of them thought it was important to invite any of the foremen who kept the field workers organized. Really, that said all that I needed to know about where the power was centered in the village.

The other three were supposed to meet Karad at the manor, and I'd decided that I was going to crash that meeting after I spied on it. With the amount of mana I'd just taken from the village, I was more than confident in my ability to handle four adults. Even if everyone brought a second-in-command, eight was still within my limit. The size of the parlor itself limited them, so unless they moved their meeting over to that dusty town hall section of the manor, I felt safe confronting them.

I just needed people to clear out of the manor, hopefully without anyone stumbling over me first. It wouldn't be the end of the world if I was discovered, but it wasn't how I wanted things to play out. They'd already long since finished their examination of Noctra's suite, really Iskara's. And if anyone did come in, I'd hear them in the main room and have plenty of time to hide or escape.

I settled back to wait for the appropriate time.

CHAPTER
FIFTY

My sole concession while I regenerated mana was a single telepathic message to my parents that said nothing more than, *I'm working on a way to get you out of there. One way or another, you'll be free tonight. Just hold on.*

I did not try to have a conversation, since even that simple message cost me over an hour's worth of mana production. Really, it was sentimental and foolish of me to do even that much. That was one spell I could have cast to save myself in the event that things went sideways when I crashed the meeting wasted on reassurances instead.

As the day moved towards evening, people started filtering out of the manor without being replaced. Eventually, it was just Karad, two other people from the Garrison, and the guy who ran the Collectors, Melmir.

I'd snuck around and figured out which servant's room shared a wall with the parlor. Their voices were muted, but I could hear the conversation through the wood and plaster.

"What's taking those two so long?" Melmir asked.

"Work to be done. They'll be here soon," Karad said.

"They should have already been here."

"What do you want me to do, go out and drag them in by their ears?" Karad asked.

"You could send your two men there to go find them and escort them here," Melmir said.

"I could, yes. Let me ask, though: do you know who or what killed Lord Noctra? Are you confident that you can defend yourself if they come back?"

"I..." Melmir faltered. "Fine, we'll continue to waste time. It's not like I have anything better to do, right?"

"Melmir, I've seen how little you do. You oversee seven people and none of them need it. Iskara isn't even here right now, ancestors only know where she's gotten off to."

Minutes ticked by and eventually, the parlor opened. A new voice joined the group, saying, "I'm not the last one here? I thought for sure I would be."

"If only," Melmir grumbled. "I'm sure you have a good excuse."

"I take my job seriously," the newcomer said. "And seeing as to how something from outside the barrier may have gotten in and murdered Lord Noctra, it's been quite a day organizing my Wardens to account for extra shifts and overlapping patrol routes. We can't all sit around doing nothing like you, Melmir."

"I don't just sit around all day," Melmir sputtered while the other two men laughed.

The laughter was short-lived, and Karad asked, "Have you found anything out there?"

The third man, who I assumed to be Solidaire, said, "Other than Sellis and his family returning to the village? No. If the story one of my men told me is true, they've got some magic to them now. He was going to bring them in, and the next thing he knew, he woke up from a long nap near dawn with them nowhere to be found."

"That's troubling. When did Sellis become a mage?" Karad asked. "Just what happened to him out in the wastes?"

"Please, there's no way that man learned how to do magic in secret," Melmir said. "It's been twenty-five years since the last time a spirit blessed someone that way. Sellis was barely a baby."

"Isn't Lord Noctra's assistant able to do some spells despite not being a mage?" Karad asked.

"Well... yes, technically," Melmir admitted reluctantly.

The sheer ignorance in this village was astounding. Even in a mana desert, people shouldn't have so little knowledge of how magic operated. What had happened to this island that had isolated it so badly from the rest of the world that even the knowledge of how magic worked had disappeared? The map I'd seen had clearly marked a passage off the island on its northern shores, so there must have been trade with the mainland at some point in their history.

Maybe it was just the lack of ambient mana pushing down the importance of learning even the basics of how magic worked over the years. Not for the first time and certainly not for the last, I cursed my misfortune to be born in a place with so little mana that what should have taken me weeks to accomplish ended up costing me years.

I couldn't fathom why people would even settle here in the first place. Maybe once, back before whatever disaster had befallen the region, but to come back and build civilization anew? Why? Were the original settlers running from something that needed magic to survive, some great beastly monster that couldn't reach them here? Anything so powerful that it could chase thousands of people into the sea and only be stymied by a magical dead spot would certainly have been killed by one great power or another.

When I finally got out of this place, I was going to devote some real effort to figuring out exactly how so much had gone completely wrong in one specific location. There had to be an explanation, but I could not for the life of me guess what it was.

Eventually, the last person invited to their meeting showed up. She was a middle-aged woman named Shel, one of the few people living in the village whose voice I didn't recognize at all. The Arborists had their own homes in the woods north of town they'd cultivated, practically had their own separate society, including a Collector who dealt with them specifically. That was how valuable their work cultivating a source of mana, fruit, and timber was to the village.

"Alright, I'm here. Let's get this over with," Shel announced as she swept through the door. It smacked closed behind her, and conversation died down at her appearance.

"So nice of you to join us," Melmir said snidely.

"Go fuck yourself," she said, her voice perfectly pleasant.

I let out a startled snort, then clamped my hand over my mouth. Hopefully no one had heard me. Considering how heated Melmir's response sounded, I was probably safe. There were no less than three different people yelling and I heard furniture clattering as they surged to their feet.

"Enough," Karad bellowed, cutting through everyone else. "You two, out. The rest of you, sit down and let's get this over with. We don't have time for your bickering and sniping."

I heard footsteps and the parlor door closing, then the sound of multiple people sitting down. "Alright," Solidaire said. "We're all here now. Start us off, Karad."

"It's simple," the leader of the Garrison said. "Lord Noctra is dead and Iskara is missing. Someone needs to run the village. You all have your responsibilities already, and the Garrison is in the best position to step in and make sure things keep moving smoothly. It'll be less disruptive for everyone if I handle enforcement of the laws just like I've always done.

"The problem is the magic. The closest we have to a mage to defend the village from monster attacks and keep the barrier functioning is sitting in a jail cell right now," Karad said. "So, what do we do about this?"

"I maintain that there's no way Sellis learned magic," Melmir said.

"Why not?" Solidaire argued. "He was Lord Emeto's student all those years ago. Who's to say that he hasn't figured out a few tricks on his own?"

"With what mana?" Melmir asked. "He's not a mage. If he was, the Testing would have shown that."

"He's something," Karad said. "The night he and his family disappeared, Lord Noctra summoned him to the manor, and then sent a few more of my people to get the rest of his family, all of whom vanished, and my guys reported something similar to what that Barrier Warden kid mentioned."

"Mmm, yes, we had two people that were similarly asleep and unable to be woken that night," Melmir said. "And all the mana held in the draw stones vanished as well. But it definitely wasn't Sellis."

"Who else would it be?" Shel asked. "I can promise it was none of my people, but you know I don't keep tabs on what's happening down here."

"That's just it. There's no one else it could be. I assure you, we keep careful track of the tithe, and everyone contributes every night," Melmir said.

"Well, it has to be someone!" Karad said. He paused and added, "Doesn't it?"

"I know of no such monster that sneaks around putting random people to sleep, if that's what you're asking," Solidaire said. "Are we so sure this is related to Lord Noctra's death?"

"Hell of a coincidence if it's not," Karad said. "What if Sellis stole something from the manor the night Lord Noctra summoned him, something that he could just point at a person and make them fall asleep?"

"Did Lord Noctra possess something like that?" Shel asked.

"I have no idea, truthfully. Cherok was up here trying to help us figure out what all these things here do, but he didn't even have a guess on half of them." Karad paused a beat, then added, "And I don't trust half of what he did tell me."

"What does Sellis himself have to say about this?" Solidaire asked. "Have you tried questioning him yet?"

"He and his wife both gave me a story about Lord Noctra kidnapping Sellis, shipping him out in the middle of the night, bound-and-gagged in a cart, and the rest of his family going after him to rescue him."

"Was there any way to verify or disprove that story?" Solidaire asked.

"Sure, just go ask Nermet what happened. He disappeared along with him and showed back up in the same group."

"I somehow doubt the village simpleton is going to give me a clear story."

"I tried anyway," Karad said. "Didn't get much out of him. He seems even more out of it than usual."

"I never did understand why he was part of the Garrison to begin with," Solidaire said.

"Big and strong, and as long as he has someone else with him to tell him what to do, he's reliable," Karad said.

"Plus he's Karad's nephew," Melmir added.

"Ah. I see."

"Let's move this conversation back to the direction it needs to go," Shel said. "Lord Noctra is dead. The barrier will fall soon if it hasn't already, and there will be nobody to reactivate it. We should cease tithing immediately. People will need all their mana to defend themselves, and we'll need volunteers to double or even triple the Barrier Wardens numbers."

"Agreed," Solidaire said. "What we're doing now is only going to work for a week or two before my men are too tired to keep going. They're going to start making mistakes and missing things."

"I can get some Garrison people worked into your patrol schedules as a stop-gap measure," Karad said. "Maybe we can get the Collectors trained up and folded into the Wardens for the time being."

"But—" Melmir started to say before Shel cut him off.

"What are the odds that we can get a new mage sent here from Derro? How did that go last time?"

"It was two years between Lord Emeto's death to Lord Noctra's arrival," Solidaire said. "A group of six of our best villagers braved the wastes to get to Derro and get help. Only four of them came back. It will almost certainly be some of mine that make the trip this time, and spirits blessing, another mage will be willing to relocate to the village. It's best to proceed as if we're on our own for the time being. Otherwise, Alkerist might cease to exist by the time anyone arrives to defend it."

If there was ever a line custom-made for me to step into the conversation, that was it. I put together a phantasmal step spell and passed through the wall into the parlor to see the four of them seated around a table, their faces cast in dancing shadows from the light of several flicking candles and a single lantern hung from the ceiling.

"About that," I said, announcing my presence and causing both Karad and Solidaire to recoil and jump to their feet. Melmir sat there, his jaw hanging low, and Shel looked at me with something that I thought might be curiosity. "I have some ideas if you've got a bit of time to hear me out."

FIFTY-ONE

S olidaire advanced forward to grab me, but stopped at Karad's outraised hand.

"Sellis's boy?" Karad asked. "How'd you get in here?"

"Magic," I said dryly.

"Don't get smart with me," Karad said harshly.

"Or what? You'll throw me in a cell with my parents?" I asked.

"That's exactly where you're going," Karad told me.

"No, it's not. You want to know why?" I asked. Without waiting for an answer, I said, "It's because you want a mage for your village, and I'm the only mage you've got. Maybe you can send some people to Derro. Maybe they get there in one piece. Maybe they even convince a mage to come back with them. How long does it take? Two months? Three?"

"You're a child," Melmir said. "We haven't even had a ritual night since before you were born, let alone one that resulted in someone in the village being blessed."

"And yet, I'm a mage anyway," I said. I held up a hand and spun mana into a cheap light spell. Instantly, it engulfed the flickering lights from the candles and bathed the meeting in cool blue highlights. A moment later, the light shifted to a warmer white color, then to a soft green. I left it on a yellow-white that mimicked sunlight and sent it up to hover near the lantern after extinguishing all the open flame with a bit of elemental manipulation.

"Some kind of monster from the wastes," Solidaire declared. "It killed the boy and took on his form."

He drew his sword and made to lunge at me. My first thought was to put him to sleep like I'd done to the others, but I wanted him awake to hear this. I blasted him in the face with a burst of elemental air to disorient him, clamped down on his foot with minor telekinesis to make him trip and stumble, and as he staggered forward, I moved past his outstretched blade to touch him just once on the forehead. That was all I needed to channel paralyzing grasp into his body.

Solidaire hit the floor with a thump and didn't get back up. I held up a hand to stop Karad from attacking and said, "He's fine. He just won't be able to move for the next fifteen minutes or so. He can listen from the floor while the more reasonable people have a conversation. And no, I'm not a monster from the wastes, though I suppose it would be fair to call me a monster. I am the same Gravin that I've been my whole life... just... awake now."

"What is he talking about?" Karad asked, throwing a glance back at Melmir and Shel.

"I don't have a clue," Shel said calmly. "But it seems interesting."

"It sounds like a pack of lies. So a little boy got his hands on some trinkets and his daddy showed him how to channel mana into him. Bravo on learning at such a young age. That really is impressive, but no one's buying—"

Melmir's mouth kept moving for another few seconds as I cast silence on him, but he quickly stopped when he realized there was no sound coming out. Karad and Shel both stared at him for a moment, then Karad started laughing.

"What I wouldn't give to be able to do that at some of my meetings," he said.

"As I was saying, you're all familiar with the concept of reincarnation?" I asked. Karad shrugged, but Shel nodded. I continued, "Imagine, if you will, that when you die, your soul is born anew as a baby to live another life, and again, and again and again, but you never remember your old lives. It's a fresh start every time. Now imagine a mage so powerful and skilled that he found a way to keep his memories the next time he was born. Imagine he's walking around, remembering every single bit of magic he's ever known, capable of doing so much, if only he had the mana he needed to do so. That's me."

"That does not seem like the most likely explanation to this scenario," Shel said.

I raised an eyebrow and gestured toward first Solidaire, who remained paralyzed on the floor, then Melmir, who was silently glaring daggers at me. I then looked up at the ball of light I was maintaining in the air, then to the candles, and finally glanced over at my shoulder to the solid wall behind me. "How many demonstrations do you need?" I asked.

"Oh, I'm not doubting you know your fair share of spells," Shel told me. "You're obviously not a normal child. I'm not sure I believe your explanation for how you know this magic, but that's not really relevant, is it?"

"It's not?" Karad asked.

"No. This child is offering to step into Lord Noctra's place and maintain the magic we rely on to keep us safe. I'm not suggesting we hand him control of the village, but if we were to monitor him and make sure he is doing as he says he can, it would certainly solve the current issue."

"Well, funny story there," I said. "That whole story you think my dad is trying to feed you, that's all true. Noctra was in debt to a cabal of mages in Derro. The ward stone powering your barrier has been broken for a long time, probably since that incident that killed the previous governor, if the stories I've heard are at all accurate. It looks like somebody tried to fix it but didn't have a clue how to. I can fix it for you, though. Probably take about twenty minutes. Honestly, I'm not sure it's really necessary. You've been barrier-free for well over a decade and things seem to be working out fine."

Melmir rose from his seat and jabbed a finger my way. His mouth moved like he was screaming at me and his face was starting to turn red, but my magic stopped any sound from coming from him. I waited, a smile on my face, as he tired himself out. Karad and Shel exchanged a look, and she started laughing softly.

"The opportunity to learn that spell alone would be enough to keep me listening," she said.

"That's on the table," I told her seriously. "I ignited Father's core to save Nermet's mind, but he's sadly not interested in becoming a true mage. I was thinking I'd find two or three people who do have an interest to take on as apprentices, at least so far as learning the basics go. I'll show you what your group ritual is trying to accomplish randomly and how to make it happen on purpose, and you can 'bless' as many people as you want with an ignited mana core."

Everyone froze there. "Impossible," Shel whispered.

"But Sellis can use magic now," Karad argued.

I snorted. "Barely. I taught him one spell. I'm the one who put all those people to sleep. I'm also the one who killed Noctra, just to clear the air on that one. It wasn't some monster that snuck in. It wasn't my father. Iskara is dead too, by the way."

Karad bristled at that declaration, right up until a force blast shot out from my finger and cut one of the candles on the table in two. "Let me make myself clear," I told him. "I am more than capable of defending myself. Noctra used this town for his own ends the entire time he was here. Iskara was his keeper, a representative of the cabal he was indebted to. The best that could be said for him was that he killed the occasional monster that came around, and that was the action of a shepherd protecting his sheep from the wolves.

"I'm not interested in being your shepherd. What I am offering is to teach you enough magic to protect yourselves in exchange for a safe haven for me to exist in for the next ten to fifteen years and the release of my family. I'll ignite a few cores for you and teach you how to do the same, repair your ward stone, and defend the village from external threats until you're strong enough to do it without me."

"Let's say we believe your claims," Karad said tentatively. "That makes you a murderer. You've admitted to killing two people. How are we supposed to trust you to keep your word?"

I shrugged. "Iskara was trying to kill me, and Noctra was trying to sell my father. I suppose if you can refrain from doing things like that, we'll get along fine. I'm not in the habit of murdering people who annoy me." I shot a glance at Melmir and added, "No matter how much they do so."

"We... we need a few minutes to discuss this," Karad said.

"Certainly."

I walked through the room and paused at the parlor door. Purely for dramatic effect, I snapped my fingers as I released Solidaire and Melmir from the enchantments. "I'll be right outside when you're ready. Take as much time as you need."

Then I pushed through the door and closed it behind me even as

Melmir's voice rose in pitch. I smiled and walked across the hall to a sunroom of some sorts, where I pulled a chair over so that I'd be visible from the parlor once someone walked out, then settled down to try to replace some of my mana.

I'd used up more than I'd wanted to, but it was important to make a strong impression. I already had my age working against me. I needed them to take this seriously, to treat me like I legitimately had something to offer. I didn't care what lie they spun out to the rest of the village to hide the fact that a three-year-old was bullying them into doing what he wanted, just so long as they accepted the bullying.

If I had to go live off by myself in the wastes, I was going to squander too much time, effort, and mana just surviving. It would make the process of building my lattice go from taking two months to a year. Here, I'd probably lose a month, maybe two training some apprentices up to the bare minimum, but I'd be relatively safe.

Besides, it appealed to me to take this muddy little village and transform it into a bastion of arcane power. If everyone had an ignited core and knew a few spells, this place would change from one that was on the brink of disaster to an oasis in the desert. I didn't know if it would compare to Derro, but assuming they suffered the same lack of ambient mana, which seemed a safe bet given Noctra's relationship and mana debt to the cabal there, those people weren't any more magically gifted than the locals.

Magic made the world a better place, and while there were plenty of counterexamples of dark, evil spells that would never see the light of day again if I had my way, at its fundamental level, magic was a net positive. This island that lacked it truly was a wasteland in so many ways. If I could get it started on a better course, I'd be happy that I'd done my part.

Of course, I was still going to figure out what cataclysmic event had scarred it so bad that it had been cut off from the world's mana core. It had to be something that happened in the last few hundred years, else the land would have healed, and ambient mana returned. But it was so unlikely that something this world-breaking would have occurred without me noticing it. I'd gotten more reclusive in my old age, rarely leaving the Night Vale in the last few hundred years, but it wasn't like I didn't still know what had been going on in the world.

The door to the parlor opened and Solidaire looked out. He spotted me immediately and scowled, but didn't make any aggressive moves. "We have a few questions if you'd like to join us again," he said shortly.

"Of course. I'd be happy to answer them," I told him. I ignored the ungracious frown on his face as he held the door open so I could walk past him.

FIFTY-TWO

I'd half expected someone to be waiting to jump on me as I walked through the door, but they must have thought better of it. They were sitting in the same formation they'd been when I'd made my first appearance, and Solidaire took his seat wordlessly after letting me in.

"What would you like to know?" I asked as I looked around.

"How sure are you that you can fix the barrier?" Karad asked.

"Completely. I've already looked over the ward stone prior to any of you getting here. Assuming no one has taken a hammer to it between then and now, there's no reason I can't fix it as soon as this conversation is over, provided we can reach an agreement."

"This is ridiculous," Melmir muttered, his voice so soft that I doubted I was meant to hear him. Nobody else reacted, at least.

"And you can really invoke the blessing of the spirits to make new mages?" Shel asked.

"I don't know about any spiritual blessing, but yes, I know the conditions required for a person's mana core to ignite and start producing up to twenty times as much mana as it otherwise would. It's not that hard to do. And yes, I am willing to do it for a few people and teach them how to do it as well. Within six months, the entire village could have ignited mana cores."

Shel settled into her chair, a satisfied smile on her face. Given the mana requirements it took to tend to a bunch of trees, I had no doubt that the Arborists struggled more than anyone else to do their jobs on a limited mana budget. The idea of having half a dozen mages, even apprentice mages, probably appealed to Shel immensely. I would be very surprised if my initial batch of volunteers didn't include at least one Arborist, possibly even Shel herself.

"How do we know any of this is true?" Melmir asked. "Yes, you can do magic. I acknowledge that. As preposterous as it seems, you truly do appear to be a mage. But so what? Lord Noctra was a mage. He couldn't grant a spiritual blessing. How are you going to do what a capable, experienced, adult mage couldn't?"

"I'm going to be blunt here," I said. "Noctra was an amateur. He was in his forties and still working with a stage one core. You saw his experiment with the dust jackals, didn't you? He was trying to figure out how to advance his core to stage two, something that would be considered an end-of-year project for your average second-year student at any major academy. I've met fourteen-year-olds with fully functional stage two cores. I will complete my own mana core's transformation to stage two in the next few months. There are a million things I can do that that hack couldn't."

That caused some bristling around the table, but no one responded. After a moment, Karad cleared his throat and said, "Yes, well, there's still the matter of Lord Noctra's demise. Regardless of whether he was in fact a traitor, we can't condone wanton murder. You're asking us to not only look the other way, but to give you a position of power as a reward for killing not one but two people, and to take your word that it's okay because they deserved it. You can understand why that's an issue, I hope."

"I get it, yes. But you've made a mistake. I'm not interested in a position of power. In fact, I want the opposite of that. I do not want to replace Noctra. I don't want to run your village. I don't want to do any administrative work, and I don't want to make any decisions that don't relate to the use of magic. I am more than happy with being placed under house arrest, if you'd like to do so. You can send students to me for regular magic lessons, and as long as I've got a bare minimum of comfort, I won't object to staying in one place for the next few years."

"You can walk through walls," Solidaire pointed out. "How are we supposed to confine you to house arrest?"

I shrugged. "Look, you need to accept that whatever you decide to do, you don't have any power over me. I could give you another demonstration, if you like?"

Solidaire and Melmir both glared at me, but neither said anything. I continued, "I see two ways this can go. One, you work with me. I help keep your town safe and bring you some much-needed knowledge on the fine art of magic. Two, you refuse to work with me. I leave. I take my family with me. You'll never see any of us again, and whatever comes in the future will be on your heads to deal with."

Shel was the most accepting of my words, possibly because she was the most disconnected from everyday life in Alkerist and also had the most to gain from a partnership with me. Solidaire was harder to read, but I thought I'd at least partially won him over with my promise that I could fix the barrier. That would make his life significantly easier if I could actually pull it off, and if not, he wasn't in any worse of a position than he was now.

Melmir and Karad were the two holdouts, Melmir both because I was threatening to make his organization redundant and just through plain obstinacy, and Karad because I represented a very real security risk. If I'd been a normal person, I'd be arrested immediately and probably executed. He was absolutely right that normal people didn't get away with murder.

As the de facto chief of the village's police force and the person most likely to assume control of the day-to-day operations, it was his job to capture me. And he knew he couldn't do it. I could see it in his eyes. He was measuring steps, trying to think of how many seconds he'd need to reach me, wondering if he could do it before my magic caught him.

He'd seen what I'd done to stop Solidaire mere minutes ago. I could do the same to him, or maybe worse. Karad had no leverage to make me do what he wanted, and it galled him. He didn't want to say yes to me or let me walk away, but he didn't think he could stop me. Oh, maybe he could pretend to play along, gather his whole group up, shoot me in the back, or kill me in my sleep. But what if he tried and failed? What would I do to him?

I didn't need mind reading to know his thoughts. I'd seen them before, many times. It had been early on in my career as a mage during my first life, but I still vividly remembered that exact look in the eyes of many lords and rulers until I'd advanced so far in power that even the thought of challenging me seemed to disappear.

Karad wasn't stupid. He knew my offer had too much value to turn down. He'd accept it, and he'd hate me for it. He'd probably try to add some stipulations, which I might or might not agree with, but if I turned him down, he'd have no choice but to agree anyway. And then, sometime in the next few weeks if he thought he could get away with it, he'd try to kill me. If that didn't work, or if he lost his nerve, he'd tell himself he could wait until he'd exhausted all my value, and kill me then. After all, I wouldn't be expecting it years down the road.

That had never worked out for anyone who'd tried it on me in the past. Even the ones who'd sent mercenary assassins hadn't been safe from my retribution. The longer the chain between the man with the knife and the man with the coin, the more bodies there ended up being, but no one had ever tried to kill me by proxy and survived the attempt.

I'd have to replace Karad with someone more pliable to my will if I was going to stay in the village long term, or else I'd have to impress on Karad that his schemes would accomplish nothing but his own death to thoroughly cow him over the next decade. I expected my mana core to be full-sized by age sixteen, eighteen at the most. At that point I could advance to stage three and then stage four in quick order. I'd have more than enough time to save up the mana I needed. Having a core that could hold over thirty times as much mana as my current one and produce it almost a thousand times faster would make everything that came after easy.

"You will be escorted to the cell your family occupies," Karad said after he finished his internal debate. "You will remain there while we announce Lord Noctra's death. Your family will be released, as by your own confession they were not responsible for the murders of Lord Noctra or Iskara. We will place you in a small home with slotted windows too narrow to crawl through and a locked door that you will be confined to except by special permission, and all instructional sessions will be closely supervised."

I rolled my eyes, and Karad paused to glower at me. "Go on," I prompted him.

"I realize that none of this can actually stop you from leaving, but it's going to be hard enough to sell the idea that a child murdered an adult mage."

"I did it in his sleep," I said. "Maybe throw that detail in there."

Melmir was looking at me with disgust now, but Shel didn't seem to care much. Then again, she hadn't shown interest in anything except the idea of igniting a mana core. It was abundantly clear to me that she only cared about gaining more power, though whether that was to help with her work or for personal reasons, I wasn't yet sure.

"Yes, well... there is that. As to whether we'll reveal Noctra's crimes, I haven't decided. We'll have a meeting tomorrow to determine that," Karad said.

"No."

"Excuse me?"

"No, you're not covering up his crimes. My parents are already going to be treated like dirt because of this. You're not going to hide Noctra's scummy behavior and let everyone think it was Father's fault. You'll tell them the truth of what I did and why I did it. This isn't going to be some closed-door deal that you get to cover up and pretend never happened until you're in a good position to tie up the loose ends."

"Just what are you implying?" Melmir asked.

"That you'll either try to kill me within the next week or sometime in the next few years after you feel you've gotten all the usefulness you can out of me. I'm not going to make it easier for you to do your dirty work. Speaking of, I'll be needing Nermet with me until I can finish unraveling the spell Noctra put on his mind. He might never be the same, but he'll be a lot better than he was."

Karad rubbed a hand across his face and glanced around at the other three people in the room. When no one objected, he let out a frustrated sigh and nodded. "It's going to cause problems if we draw attention to this, but if that's what you want."

"I cannot believe we're just caving in to this child's demands," Melmir said.

"If he can do even half of what he claims, it'll be well worth it," Shel told him. She turned to focus on me and said, "All of these conditions are of course contingent on you being able to live up to our expectations. We'll expect you to repair the ward stone immediately and grant the spirits' blessing to someone as soon as we have a candidate."

"I can repair the ward stone now," I said. "I'll need more mana to 'grant the spirit's blessing,' as you call it. By myself, it would take at least a week to gather that much mana. If the whole village wants to continue with the nightly tithes, perhaps two or three days. I will also need at minimum a few weeks to teach your candidate proper mana manipulation techniques. Depending on how quick a study that person is, it may take more. Their progress will be measurable, and you are free to check in with them as often as you like."

They didn't look happy, but no one objected to my terms. That was good, since there was no changing them. I did need time to collect the mana, and whoever they sent forth would need to learn a few mana manipulation techniques. There was no getting around those facts, at least not as I currently was.

"I can't believe I'm saying this, but..." Karad shook his head. "I believe we have an agreement."

CHAPTER

FIFTY-THREE

Fixing the ward stone was just about as easy as I'd expected it to be. Someone got me a bucket of dirt to use as raw materials, which I quickly poured into the cracks and transmuted into new stone to fill the holes. That took a bit more mana than I wanted, but it only took a few minutes before I had a smooth, unblemished surface.

Removing all the problems Noctra had caused with his own attempts to modify the rune structure so it would work again took a lot longer. I ended up filling in almost a third of the runes with a mud paste that I then transmuted to make fresh, new stone.

Luckily, stone shape was a versatile spell. It wasn't meant to be used to carve runes, but if the caster knew exactly how the whole structure would look and could envision it all at once, it was possible. It still took me six casts to finish carving the new runes, but when I was done, the ward stone was whole and operational again.

"That took closer to an hour," Shel said. She'd been standing in the corner observing the entire process.

"I underestimated the amount of damage Noctra did that I would need to repair," I told her. "But it's done. I've triple checked for any errors, and while you can never be certain until you've turned it on, I'm fairly confident this should work without issues."

Considering that the wards the stone generated were barely better than basic level spells, it would be an embarrassment if I'd messed something up. Truthfully, I was more concerned with interference caused by my stone shape patches not adhering properly than I was by miscut runes. It probably would have been easier to junk the ward stone completely and carve a new one, had I the spare mana to devote to the task.

This was for the best. The villagers might not understand exactly what I'd done, but they knew what it looked like before and what it looked like now. The visible damage was gone, and new runes had been carved to fill in those blank spots. Their minds could comprehend that it was repaired, that this ward stone, which had supposedly protected them for many years before it broke, would once again function the way it had for their parents.

"Alright, this is done. Just needs some mana to power it."

"Are you going to do that?" Shel asked.

"No way. This is a communal project. If you want it going at full power without interruption, you'd need, hmm... five or six apprentice mages devoting all their mana to it. Figure half the village powering it directly. It'll take the entire village if you're going through draw stones and the person handling them knows what they're doing. Transference loss will probably cause you problems. Better to train a dozen people with ignited cores on how to keep the ward stone going."

"How long will that take?" Karad asked from the door.

"Two or three months. Depends on how smart the people are. Some people pick things up quicker than others."

"And in the meantime?"

I shrugged. "Hasn't worked in years. What's another few months? If a monster does wander in, let me know and I'll kill it for you."

Karad grunted and looked back out of the room where the others were waiting. I didn't hear either of them say anything, but they must have been satisfied, because he turned back to me and said, "Alright, let's get you to your parents. I'll make the announcement in an hour when everyone comes to the square for the tithe."

It wasn't hard to hear Karad from the Garrison cell. He'd given the order to release my family, and after filling them in on our deal, we waited with our Garrison soldier escort whose name I was almost certain was Wilbur.

"Hey Thavin, how long do we have to wait here?" Father asked.

Thavin? Where had I gotten Wilbur from?

"Until Karad says to let you go," Thavin said.

That wouldn't happen until after the speech, but since I was back to pretending to be a normal kid, I'd kept my mouth shut while being escorted to the Garrison headquarters. While we waited, I caught snippets of Karad's speech.

"—betrayed us all from the start. The draw stones—"

The outrage from the crowd drowned out the next section, and I could tell I wasn't the only one here annoyed by that.

"—ward stone is cracked like someone smacked it with a hammer. I don't think it's worked since—"

Karad hit all the relevant points, exposing what we knew of Noctra's plans. He didn't go into details about Iskara's role, other than to say that evidence suggested she was in on the whole thing. Not once was my theft of mana from the draw stones mentioned, possibly because it wasn't public knowledge to begin with.

Then, at the end, he went off script. I wasn't particularly surprised, and honestly, it was probably a clever bit of improvisation, but it also served to tell me that Karad still thought of himself as in charge. We'd made a deal, and he was making executive decisions without consulting me first.

"—in what I can only describe as a true miracle, our ancestors have blessed a child with the gift of magic and knowledge of its ways. He uncovered these nefarious schemes and confronted—"

Then again, from Karad's perspective, maybe he really did consider it a miracle. Either way, he wasn't sticking to the facts. He knew damn well where my skills came from, but he was spinning it like I was some sort of gift from the spirits sent to protect the village. Maybe that would be easier for the villagers to swallow, but it was going to be hard to sell me as being under house arrest if I was an avenging angel instead of a murderer.

The speech wound down, leaving the villagers with mixed reactions. Some people were upset to find out what Noctra had been doing, others that their illusion of security had been stripped away from them. A few times, I caught Father's name coming from people, but even using sharpened senses, it was impossible to really sort out all the conversations going on at the same time.

A few minutes later, Karad walked through the door and glanced over at me. "That went about as well as we could have hoped," he said.

"Interesting twist you added there. If I'm the savior of our people, protecting us from the evil machinations of that scoundrel Noctra, how am I supposed to be under house arrest?"

Karad waved my question away with a quick answer. "You're in seclusion instead. Same thing, different name."

It was theoretically better for my family. Despite the grumblings and the unavoidable connection between Father and Noctra, this explanation gave the impression that the whole thing was more than the murder of an enemy. I didn't know how heavily religion factored into the village's overall mindset, but Karad would hardly be the first person to use excuses like "the spirits decreed it should happen" to justify killing someone.

I doubted any spirit had manifested anywhere on this island since it had turned into a mana desert, nor did I find it likely that the ancestors of anyone living in this village had ever been magically gifted enough to form a sapient spirit upon their death. All of them together merged into some sort of gestalt entity wouldn't have the mana needed to form a spiritual presence.

"Where's this house of mine supposed to be, anyway?" I asked.

"Shel said there is an extra house at the Arbor we can use for now. Come with me."

We filed out of the building with Karad in the lead and Thavin following up behind us. Senica and I were in the middle with our parents bracketing us. Two more people I thought might be Arborists were waiting for us on the street.

"You're still doing a tithe?" I asked when I spotted the tables set up. Most of the village had already left the square, but there were still about twenty people in lines waiting for their turns.

"You said we needed the mana to power the ward stone," Karad told me. "Besides, if you let people stop doing something they don't like, it's a nightmare forcing them to start again later."

"You won't get enough even from the whole village," I said.

"If you can make it work at night, that's a good start. Everyone's already used to that idea. It'll be nice that it's true."

"There are going to be people who can feel the difference," I warned. "Not everyone, but some people like my father."

"All the better. It'll lend credence to the idea that Lord Noctra was lying to us about the barrier. We all assumed it felt different because it had been broken and repaired. Foolish of us to just believe him, but how were we supposed to know the difference?"

"He had us all fooled," Mother said. "Did anyone suspect him, in all these years?"

"I think a few of us might have," Karad said. "Knowing what he did to my nephew, and what you've told me a few other of my people have been subjected to, I can't help but look back and wonder how many times someone who died 'accidentally' over the years just got too close to figuring out what was going on."

"Belthin," Father said.

"Exactly," Karad agreed with a nod. "That one never sat right with me. Belthin was a creature of habit. Work, a beer, then home. Every day. It was rare to see him go anywhere else if he didn't have to. And then one day he just doesn't show up and we find the body torn to shreds a mile out past the fields?"

"Was he the one that kept the braids in his beard?" Mother asked.

"That's him," Karad said.

"Shame what happened," Father said. "More so if he had just stumbled across Noctra doing something evil and ended up dead over it."

"Speaking of Noctra's victims, I'll need Nermet nearby so I can work on the subjugation enchantment," I said. "It'll be a delicate process, but I think I can get rid of the enchantment without causing any additional brain damage."

Karad blinked a few times and cleared his throat. "That... That would be nice."

I got the feeling that my father's insistence on saving the man might have been the thing that really convinced Karad to side with me. He'd probably gone back over his nephew's behavior and identified all the signs he'd dismissed over the years as things had gotten worse.

"Father is supplying the mana that Nermet needs right now to keep the spell from catastrophically collapsing. That means Nermet will listen to anything Father says as a side effect," I explained. "He should be the one to bring Nermet to me if you want to avoid causing a scene."

"I understand," Karad told me. "I'll get it taken care of tonight."

"Mom," Senica whispered beside me, "what are they talking about?"

"Oh, all sorts of boring grown up stuff," she told my sister. "Life's going to be a little different now, but we'll be alright. You were so brave for all of this; I think I'll need to find a way to reward you. What do you think?"

"I want to learn magic too," Senica said immediately.

Mother glanced at me, and I shrugged back. "We'll have a long discussion about what spells she is and isn't allowed to learn if you want her core ignited," I told her.

"That'll have to wait," Karad said. He stopped at the tree line we'd been steadily approaching and said, "You've got a few people of our choice to train first."

I waved away his concern. "It won't hurt anything for her to sit in on the basic lessons. Father can supply the mana I'll need to ignite her core if she reaches that stage."

I didn't expect her to. The average six-year-old didn't have the discipline needed to master mana manipulation to the degree necessary to complete the ritual. It happened, but rarely, and Senica hadn't even been able to pay attention to more than one of Father's lessons when there was literally nothing else to do.

"A topic for tomorrow anyway," Shel said. "Let's get you settled into your new home first."

"Lead on," I said as we walked into the trees.

CHAPTER

FIFTY-FOUR

I t turned out the Arborists didn't live much better than the rest of us. Their homes were made from the same mud-and-clay bricks, had the same thatch roofs, and were about the same size. Their houses were arranged in a circle with a dozen buildings in the middle of the Arbor, which took a bit of looking around to understand the logic of.

It was a giant circle with the Arborists in the center. There were six sections, all accessible from the center. One part contained fruit trees. Another had only trees that grew straight, good for timber. A third section had the thickest canopy, and a number of herbs with medicinal uses grew under those boughs.

A second ring of buildings containing greenhouses circled the houses, something I was extremely surprised to find. There'd been very little glass in the village, and we had no glass blower. What windows there were had obviously been created with magic. Finding not one but three long green-houses was highly unexpected, and I immediately started eyeing them up. It would be expensive in terms of mana spent, but I might just be able to grow a few specialty herbs to do a bit of alchemy with.

As we got closer, I realized that more than a few of the panes had been replaced with pieces of wood. Shel noticed me looking and said, "A few bad storms over the years. Lord Emeto built these many years ago, but since he's been gone, there's no one left to replace them. We used to have five green-houses, but we've scavenged so many panes of glass that we tore down two of them. About three years ago, we ran out of spares and had to make do with the patch jobs."

"And you're hoping I can help with that," I said.

"Among other things."

"I know the spell to transmute sand to glass," I said. "I could probably be persuaded to make some new panes in exchange for some space to grow a few herbs for my own projects."

I'd need to make some glassworks as well, but I'd hold off on that until I finished my mana lattice and confirmed the plants I had in mind would actually grow here. Even in a magically controlled glass box, some plants just couldn't thrive. That was a problem for later, though. It'd be months before I was ready to make an attempt at alchemy.

"There's a spell for that?" Shel asked, surprised. "Lord Emeto used to just glass a section of the desert with some fireballs and we'd cut the panes out after it cooled."

"Did he?" I laughed. "What an incredibly inefficient way to go about that. I suppose if it works, it works. I wonder why Noctra never replaced the panes if that was how you were all going about doing it."

"Too expensive," Shel told me. "He needed the mana for other things. At least, that's what he told us."

There was a hint of bitterness in her voice, well-masked and only detectable because I was listening for it. Nobody was happy about Noctra bilking the village out of years of mana. On the bright side, he'd made it extraordinarily easy for me to take his place, since I was actually capable and willing to spend mana on the village's behalf. If they wanted to continue the tithe, I'd happily make them glass panes and keep their barrier going and whatever else they liked, though I'd be keeping a fraction of the mana for my own use as a labor cost.

It was better than the last guy. He'd kept all of their mana and done none of the work.

We made our way past the greenhouses and into the circle of houses. Some of them were occupied, others were dark. One major difference between these houses and the ones back in the village was the presence of doors and shutters. It wasn't hard to guess why. This cluster of homes was surrounded by trees, and there were more than a few small animals living in them. Nobody wanted to come home to find raccoons and squirrels had raided the larder.

"This is the house you'll be staying in," Shel said, stopping in front of what was undoubtedly the most run-down building of the lot. "It's been empty for a while and we've been using it as storage, but I let everyone know to clean their things out, so it should be ready for you."

"You don't sound very sure about that," Father said.

Shel pushed the door open, revealing a dark interior that had nothing but dust in it. There was a lot of dust, so much so that I decided it was worth a bit of mana to use elemental manipulation to collect it all. "Step back for a second," I said.

I cast the spell, summoning all the dust into one clump of dirt and sending it flying out into the trees to break apart. It wasn't a substitute for a thorough cleaning, but for a five-second job, it would suffice. Unfortunately, I had another problem.

"There's no furniture," I pointed out.

"Uh, yeah. This was all kind of last notice."

I turned to Father. "When you go back to fetch Nermet, could you bring my pallet out for me?"

"I'll have some of my guys bring Nermet's stuff over from my place as well," Karad added.

"Some food would be nice, too." I hadn't eaten all day and only the trickle of mana energizing my body was keeping me going at this point. I wasn't willing to show weakness to my new allies, who were still potential enemies, so I'd kept myself upright and energetic.

"So, this is where you'll live for the time being. You aren't allowed to leave this house without an escort, and I'll have somebody guarding you at all times," Karad said. "You'll teach other people at a designated location to be decided later. We'll bring a few candidates by in the next day or two for you to get started with. Once a day, I will personally escort you to collect mana for the ward stone."

I managed to hold back a laugh. Karad was deadly serious, but everyone here knew there was nothing he could do to stop me if I decided to leave. His only recourse would be to turn the village against me and make it impossible to live here peacefully. To an outside observer, it must have looked ridiculous to have a grown man in his forties threatening a small child like this. I wondered if Karad felt a bit foolish about the whole thing.

"I understand," I told him. "I'll stay right here and wait until you're ready for me to do some work."

That earned me a suspicious glare, and not just from Karad, either. Both my parents and Shel hit me with it. The de facto governor of the community watched me wordlessly for a moment before he shook his head, turned to Shel, and said, "Keep an eye on him like you said you would."

Then he grabbed my father, said, "Let's go," and walked off.

"Well, that was fun," I told everyone. "What should we do while we wait?"

<hr />

"Please stop asking me questions now," I said, exhaustion in my voice.

Shel was relentless. I'd spent two hours fielding questions that basically amounted to a staggering variety of issues the Arbor had, and her wanting to know if there were magical solutions for all of them. The answer was usually "Yes, but…"

I had a suspicion I knew where the bulk of the mana the Arborists produced once they'd ignited their cores was going to go, and it was going to be some spectacularly boring chores like warding trees against burrowing insects and increasing the yields when they harvested fruit.

"But I had a follow up question about magically reinforced panes of glass," Shel said. She flipped through the notebook she'd produced until she got back to the page where she'd recorded what I'd told her about enchanting the green-houses and asked, "So you told me that we can set up an enchantment that will power itself with ambient mana, or we could if there was any here. I scrapped that idea before, but what if we hooked the trees up to the enchantments directly? It wouldn't be mana in the air, but it would still be mana, right?"

"It would kill the trees," I said. "Yes, it would work for a year or two if we kept the draw low enough, but eventually everything would wither. I don't think most of these trees could even grow in such a dry environment without mana to fortify them."

"We already have a watering rotation," Shel said. "Maybe if we increased the frequency on that, it would work."

"Maybe. But most likely they'd die."

It was about then that a group of men stepped out of the trees and approached. Father had my pallet carried in a bundle in his arms along with a familiar basket with some food, Karad was carrying another significantly larger pallet, and Nermet had a pair of chairs and a small table.

"Hey there, Gravin," Father said. "I hope I'm not interrupting."

"No, you're fine," I said. Shel let out a huff that was half annoyance and half amusement, but didn't say anything.

"Got you a few things for your first night. We'll bring you some more stuff tomorrow. Everyone's pretty tired from this whole ordeal," Father said. I held the door open for him to carry everything in.

As we were setting things up, he leaned over and said in a low voice, "Has she really been going for hours?"

"Yes," I groaned.

"Best to just tell her you're tired and call it a night," Father said. "Is Nermet going to be alright here? It's not too much distance or anything?"

"No, it's fine. It'll draw a bit harder on your mana reserves than normal, but this is only a mile or so. I'm going to make removing his subjugation a priority."

Karad, who'd been listening without participating, glanced over at his nephew, then gave me a nod. "Thank you," he said softly. "Have a good night, you two. Gravin, do not leave this house."

Father left soon after, leaving me with Nermet, who'd been instructed to get some rest, and two Garrison members positioned outside. Neither seemed happy about that arrangement, and I suspected there would soon be some new construction to build something that more closely resembled a prison with multiple rooms.

Shel, thankfully, left me alone at that point. I spent an hour or so thoroughly going over the subjugation enchantment in Nermet's mind again, and began making plans for what order I'd need to cut pieces of it and where I'd need to place my own temporary enchantments to hold pieces of the spell in place until I'd fully disconnected a section. It was going to be a delicate job, that was for sure.

All in all, this hadn't been a total disaster of a day. More people knew my secret than I was happy with, but I was in a position to rapidly advance my core to stage two thanks to not only my own mana, but the village reserves I could skim from. I was technically a prisoner, but nobody was really under the illusion that I'd stay here. At some point, Karad would try to get rid of me, but that was a way down the road still, and I'd only grow stronger between now and then.

Things weren't perfect, but this was a good start.

CHAPTER
FIFTY-FIVE

I was up before dawn and working on Nermet's condition. I wanted to get that fixed as soon as possible to relieve the burden on Father's mana core, and because I thought it would go a long way towards improving my relationship with Karad. Unless I missed my guess, Shel was already on my side since my knowledge was so useful to her job, Solidaire would come around now that the barrier was properly functioning, and Melmir just hated me for reasons unknown. I was unlikely to sway, him since I was likely going to put the Collectors out of work entirely in the next few months.

Maybe the reasons weren't so unknown after all.

Karad could still go either way. Right now, he was tolerating me as a temporary solution, but that didn't mean he might not try to find an alternative. His job was also going to become more difficult as more and more people ignited their cores and began to learn magic. I was fully expecting a meeting with him in the next month or so, sharply limiting what spells I was and wasn't allowed to teach people. Since I planned to ignore any such order, that would probably be when he switched over from reluctant ally to hostile element.

By that point, I'd have either built up enough good will that he couldn't do anything about me, or he'd start actively working to sabotage me. I wasn't sure if he'd isolated me now to diminish my involvement with the rest of the village to protect me from the backlash of killing Noctra, or as groundwork to keep me from gaining too much influence and authority later on, but he seemed smart enough to have thought up both reasons.

It truly was impossible to escape politics, no matter where I went. The only answer was to become an iron-fisted tyrant who ruled unchallenged by virtue of unassailable power. Even then, there would be problems like insurrections and rebellions. I'd learned my lesson a long time ago: don't play politics, just be strong enough to prevent anyone else from dragging me into their games. I wasn't at that point again yet, and I likely wouldn't be before Karad made his move.

The next few years were going to be annoying. This was exactly why I'd wanted to remain hidden, so I could build my strength back up without interference or interruptions. The only silver lining was that the village was so isolated that I didn't have much to fear about any rumors reaching the ears of some of my old enemies who were still kicking around. By the time any of them caught wind of my reincarnation, I'd be strong enough to return to the world stage as a power to be reckoned with.

I'd just finished fashioning the first of six shims I would use to hold the framework of Nermet's subjugation spell stable while I severed it piece by piece when someone knocked at the door. "One moment," I called as I slid the shim into the spell right behind the cutting blade of my will in one smooth motion, then withdrew from Nermet's mind.

He would need an hour or two to adjust to that new splinter of my magic before it was safe to put in another one, so now was a good time to stop anyway. Over the next week or two, depending on his recovery rate, I'd eventually isolate the subjugation magic completely and be able to remove it in one whole chunk without causing any damage to his mind.

It was something like cutting down twenty or thirty trees all tangled together as opposed to ripping them out of the ground, except in this case, all the displaced dirt would be chunks of Nermet's brain. I couldn't just cut down one tree, or it would put stress on the others. They might hold for two or three, but eventually there'd be so much weight that they'd drag the whole twisted knot out of the ground and kill Nermet. Instead, I needed to saw through each one in such a way that they remained upright and in place until I'd cut them all loose.

I opened the door to find Shel standing there, blinking as she looked down at me. "Good morning," she said.

"Is it?"

"Is it what?" she asked.

"Good?"

"I think so. It's the dawn of a brand-new age for us," she told me. "Sorry to wake you so early, but there's a lot to get done."

"You didn't wake me," I said. "Who are these people?"

There were three other people standing behind Shel, not including a pair of Garrison guards flanking the door. The only one I knew was Ayaka, the Collector who was friends with my father. I was guessing the other two were Arborists, just based on process of elimination. They were the ones who most rarely came into town, so it was a good bet that if I didn't at least recognize them, they were connected to the Arbor in some way.

"Your first class of apprentices," Shel said. She turned and pointed towards one of the people I didn't know. "Talik. Vhan. Ayaka. She's from the Collectors. Talik and Vhan are two of my people."

"I remember you," I said to Ayaka. "Good to see you again."

"I'm really only here to spy on this whole process and report back to my boss," Ayaka said. "But he's been a jerk lately, so..."

She spread her hands in a helpless gesture, and Talik started laughing. "That's my cousin," he said. "And you're wrong. Being a jerk isn't something that started lately. He's been that way since we were kids."

"Melmir is a deeply unpleasant person and we'd all be better off without him," Shel said pleasantly. "But that's not the reality of our lives, and we're not here to talk about him. Gravin, this is your class to teach. What would you like us to do?"

It looked like we were just glossing over Ayaka's confession—not that it was a surprise to me. If anything, I thought she might have volunteered for it. She'd seemed close with my parents when I first met her. It was possible she'd taken the job out of a sense of loyalty to them that extended to me. Or maybe she just liked the idea of becoming a mage and learning magic. I was admittedly pretty biased about the whole thing, but I couldn't imagine a better career.

"Where are we having this class?" I asked. Karad had mentioned a place to be designated later, but we'd never actually discussed where the place would be.

"Right here is fine, unless you think we need to go somewhere else."

I glanced around at the open space between the homes. There was no reason I couldn't teach here, at least for the time being. Once the apprentices had ignited cores and needed to practice blowing things up, we'd have to relocate.

"This will work," I said. "The first thing we need to do is to figure out what you all know how to do already and where you need work. So, I'm going to do a bit of testing, first to check your ability to sense external mana, then on how well you can manipulate it. Depending on the results, we might move on."

I doubted we'd be getting any farther than that today. Most likely, we would still be working on the exercises I planned to show them for the next week, which was fine by me. I needed to create a few storage crystals anyway. Mine had cracked when I'd ignited my own core, and I hadn't bothered to repair or replace it. Mana crystals were far more efficient anyway, but I wanted something that could be passed around.

I'd been tempted to use the storage crystals I'd found in Iskara's little workshop, just to save myself some effort, but they were so poorly made that I couldn't bring myself to inflict that level of transference loss on anyone. I was only planning on making three storage crystals of my own, but they'd be as high grade as I could get them with my limited tools.

"Alright, let's get started. Everyone line up over here. I'm going to unshield my mana core and start walking towards you. When you can feel my mana, say something. The goal is to train you to be sensitive enough to mana to feel it at a range of thirty feet. If anyone currently has a range better than ten feet, I'll be surprised, so don't worry if your range is much lower. Everyone ready?"

With my new students lined up, I let go off the shroud I'd pulled over my mana and started taking slow, steady steps forward.

My expectations had been practically non-existent, and somehow, I was still disappointed. I spent the entire morning and most of the afternoon working with four adults, some of whom were much better at taking instructions and criticisms than others, and by the time we were done, Shel was the only person who could reliably sense mana at all outside of her own body. Her maximum range was just short of two feet, and she had no ability to discern anything other than the presence or absence of mana.

I'd thought that this would be easier for them to learn due to the lack of ambient mana anywhere, but these people were all adults in their twenties or thirties. This was something they should have developed naturally just from being around other people. I'd been planning on showing them how to hone this sense, how to extend its range, and how to differentiate between a simple blob of mana and the complex weave of a spell.

That would be a lesson for another day. The group dispersed to attend to other responsibilities shortly after lunch with my instructions on how to continue training their ability to sense mana from a distance. Shortly after that, Shel reappeared with six bags of sand someone had scrounged up.

"You got the mana to make some glass panes?" she asked. "I'd like to swap out all the wood ones as soon as possible."

"I can do three," I said. "Do you have a frame for me to size them with?"

"We don't," Shel said. "Give me half an hour and I'll get someone to put one together."

Three panes used up more than I'd liked out of what I'd generated today, but I was keeping a mental tally, and I'd get that back when Karad came around to escort me through all the draw stone storage in the evening. I'd see how many hours the remainder could power the ward stone, but I doubted it would last all night, at least not at full power.

I spent the rest of the day doing miscellaneous chores while I worked to generate as much mana as possible. Shel got her glass, and I watched four Arborists work together to replace one of the wooden patches in the greenhouse. Once evening hit, the Arborists gathered together, and a draw stone was brought out of what I suspected was Shel's house. If I didn't miss my guess, it had been a former resident of my new home.

"Wait," I said as they all gathered around to perform their tithe. I walked over, watched closely by a Garrison member, and produced the first of the storage crystals I'd made. "This is a storage crystal. It stores mana like a draw stone, but it does so much more efficiently. The catch is that it's not automatic. You need at least a little bit of mana control to make it work.

"Think of a Testing, of how you had to push your mana into the device. This works under the same principles. If you are able to pour mana into this successfully, it will be a bit more efficient than using a draw stone directly."

The drawback was, of course, that the draw stone took everything whether the donor was willing or not, as long as they didn't have enough control over their mana to resist its pull. A storage crystal would be on the donor's honor for anyone who couldn't sense mana in others, which was why I put it in Shel's hand.

"Use your mana sense to feel each person's mana as they donate to the storage crystal," I instructed her. "You should be able to feel it dwindling from them."

"You heard the kid, people. Same deal as always, but we're going to use this tonight instead," the leader of the Arborists said.

One after another, each person gave their mana to the storage crystal. By the time they were done, there was enough mana in there for another sand to glass spell. I let Shel know, and she said, "Excellent! Can you make that for us right now?"

"I can," I said.

"Maybe we should see about standardizing this for the whole village," the Garrison guard said. "I'll mention the idea to Karad when I see him later."

"If you want," I told him. "I'll have to make a few more. Storage crystals only have a fraction of the capacity that a normal draw stone does, but if it's all going into the ward stone every night, it shouldn't be a big deal."

It was a small first step, but it was a step. Things were improving.

CHAPTER

FIFTY-SIX

Over the next week, I settled into a routine. I'd start the morning with Nermet, and periodically throughout the day, I'd come back to check on his recovery before I moved onto the next step. Then my new students would show up, with somebody bringing breakfast. I never quite deciphered how they decided whose turn it was, but it never ended up being mine, so I didn't complain.

Then it was lessons and instruction until lunch, with each of my students slowly growing more competent. Shel led the class for range of mana sense, but Vhan beat her in being able to sort through what he was sensing, even if he couldn't feel it from as far away. He tied with Ayaka when it came to actually manipulating mana.

Talik got further behind each day, and I got the sense that Shel was watching him and judging. She was probably planning on cutting him soon since he was falling behind, and I spent some time thinking about what I wanted to do about that. On the one hand, it wasn't really any of my business and I didn't care if he dropped out. On the other, this was my class, and I was in control of it. Letting Shel decide to cut someone who wasn't progressing fast enough would undercut my authority.

"Shel, do you have a moment?" I called out as everyone dispersed at the end of the afternoon lesson.

She paused in the middle of speaking to one of the Arborists who wasn't part of my class, glanced over at me, and said, "Just a second."

Oh, how far I'd fallen. No apprentice would have dared disrespect their master like that back when I'd been learning how to do magic. I'd been primarily self-taught, but on those rare occasions when I could convince a real mage to impart some wisdom to me, I'd made sure to present myself respectfully. I'd known the value of the secrets that were being shared with me.

Shel finished her conversation and dismissed the Arborist she'd been speaking with, a full three minutes later. I reined in the temptation to light her hair on fire. She wasn't a teenager with nothing better to do. She had responsibilities and subordinates.

That was all perfectly rational, but was still my time to teach, and it was an exercise in willpower to keep myself from tweaking her nose. I'd done my best to be pleasant and accommodating, perhaps to my own detriment. Maybe it was time to limit exactly how helpful I was going to be.

"What do you need?" Shel asked.

I set those thoughts aside and refocused on why I wanted to talk to Shel in the first place. "It's about Talik," I said. "He's struggling to keep up."

"Yes," she agreed. "I've let him know he's going to have to spend some of his time outside the lessons practicing if he wants to hold his spot."

"Yes, that's what I want to talk to you about. This is my class. Talik is my student. I will decide whether he's falling too far behind and what to do about it."

One thing I'd noticed about Shel was that she never lost her temper. She always had a smile on her face and a pleasant tone in her voice. "It may be your class, but this is my arbor, these are my buildings, and Talik works for me. I'd say that gives me the authority to do what I want with him."

"I disagree. If you want to work him to the bone until late into the night trimming trees or poisoning insects, that's your business. From breakfast to lunch, he's mine. Unless he comes to me himself and says he wants to drop out, he'll follow my instructions and you will not interfere."

"Gravin, your great magical talent aside, you are a murderer who is lucky to still be part of this community at all. If you don't like the rules you have to live by, we can always revisit your situation. I promise that the outcome will not be as favorable to you as the current arrangement."

She said it all like we were having a chat over afternoon tea. I could almost admire her ability to keep any heat out of her voice—almost, but not quite. Instead, I grabbed hold of her throat with greater telekinesis and dragged her down onto her hands and knees so we'd be eye level.

"You seem to be under the mistaken impression that you have the power in our relationship. Let me correct that for you. If I decide I'm not happy, I will take steps to correct that. I didn't kill Noctra because he was an evil person. I killed him because he was a threat to my family. If you become a threat... well, use your imagination. Me living here is a convenience, not a necessity. Put some thought into making sure you don't become inconvenient, Shel."

I released the spell, allowing her to suck in a ragged, gasping lungful of air. The pleasant smile was gone from her face now. Instead, she looked scared. Good.

"I don't go out of my way to cause problems," I said. "This can be a beneficial relationship to both sides as long as you don't start thinking you control me. Now, as I was saying, I will decide if and when Talik no longer meets my expectations, not you. Until that time, I expect him here every morning. You understand?"

"Yes," Shel said shortly. "If there's nothing else, I've got work to do."

"That will be all the lessons I have for today," I said. "Have a good afternoon."

Karad was a lot more wary than usual that evening when he came to escort me to the village to harvest the daily tithe. He didn't mention the incident with Shel, but I noticed he kept a bit more distance than usual and he didn't have much to say. He asked for an update on Nermet's progress, but otherwise didn't engage in conversation.

That suited me just fine. This nightly chore was a burden I was looking forward to offloading on one of my new apprentices as soon as they were capable of handling it. That was the goal for just about everything I did, really. My first-generation apprentices would take over much of the work I was doing for the village while I taught the second generation. Soon, they'd be igniting the cores of new villagers, and there'd be nothing left for me to do.

I was working myself out of a job, but by the time that happened, I'd be too strong for it to matter. By the time I was done pretending to be a Collector, I'd have built up enough reserves in my mana crystal to start constructing my lattice. At that point, I'd turn my efforts towards creating new tools, maybe a nice staff or a scrying mirror.

That night, Father came to visit me. The Garrison guard stationed outside the door let him through with a scowl, which Father ignored as he greeted me.

"How are you doing out here?" he asked.

"Everything is going according to plan," I said. "Well, the new apprentices are considerably behind where I hoped they'd be, so I'm expecting to need an extra month now before any of them are ready for a core ignition ritual. But otherwise, things are proceeding as I expected. How are things for you?"

"The same, just with a bit more fear than normal. Your mother has been hard at work getting our garden back up to her standards. You'd have thought that friend of hers from next door might have done something to preserve it, but no. I've been helping her in the evening now that I have so much extra mana."

"I'm sure it'll be flourishing in no time," I said. "What about you?"

"Nobody wants to work in tandem with me, but it doesn't matter much. I have the extra mana now to do the work of two men, so I still finish my section faster than anyone else. I think it's driving the overseer crazy, but everyone knows I'm blessed now."

Father paused and let out a chuckle. "You should see Cherok. He's practically choking on it. I overheard a few of the other fieldhands talking about how he was agitating the Garrison to get me taken back into custody—said he was afraid for his safety now. Karad laughed him out of the building."

"He's not taking it out on Senica, is he?" I asked.

"No, no. At least, she hasn't said anything. And I think she would, at least if she talked about anything besides mana. I guess that little bit you taught her went to her head, and now she's the school's 'mana expert,' which is also driving Cherok crazy. She's better at sensing mana and manipulating it than he is."

That surprised me. I'd thought she'd lost interest. She'd never come around during any of my lessons, but then again, I supposed she was in school while they were going on. "She's still practicing?"

Father nodded. "She's been bugging me for a few days to come out here so she can show off, not that she'll admit that's why she wants to visit. But, uh, your mother and I talked, and we think it's best that Senica waits until she's older to ignite her core, alright?"

"I agree completely. It would be irresponsible to give a child that age access to that much mana." I paused and thought of my own new students. Being shown up by a six-year-old might motivate them to try a bit harder. "She could join my morning lesson one day if she wants."

"I'll discuss it with your mother before I agree to anything," Father said wisely. He reached into his pocket and pulled out a book. "By the way, I finally managed to get ahold of a book for you."

"Oh, perfect!" I said as I accepted it.

It turned out that everybody could read the written language in those books, and they just accepted it as the written version of what we were all speaking. Apparently, they thought their language was pictographic, and everyone just memorized the symbols for individual words instead of learning an alphabet. That made sense since it was a completely different language, but I was at a loss as to how to explain how it had happened. Never in two thousand years had I come across such a strange phenomenon.

It had to be deliberate, but a knowledge suppression spell on that scale was hard to imagine. The Enotian language was one of the most common ones in the world, so erasing the written version of it would not be an easy undertaking. That was the kind of magic that required a celestial convergence to pull off.

I'd already tested my own knowledge of written Enotian and found it to be intact. Something about my reincarnation had insulated me from whatever had happened to it. But now, if I wanted to read anything written down here, I needed to figure out this new language. On the bright side, it definitely had an alphabet, and that meant I could ask what words meant and start decoding it. But it was just one more project I didn't need making demands on my time.

I'd work on it when I had some free moments, but it wasn't a priority. Chances were good that the books available here wouldn't give me any clues about what had happened to the world while I was gone anyway. Between this linguistic phenomenon and one of the moons going missing, it sure seemed like something had gone wrong.

If it weren't for all the other similarities and the fact that I'd already reviewed the invocations I'd tied to my soul to ensure they were working, I'd have thought I'd been reborn into some sort of mirror world. I'd already confirmed that wasn't the case, but it still bothered me.

One more mystery to solve someday after everything else. I set the book aside and put it out of my mind.

FIFTY-SEVEN

W alking with Karad to do the nightly charging for the ward stone was annoying mostly because my legs were much, much shorter than his. I had to practically jog to keep up with him, which looked entirely ridiculous. From a practical standpoint, it also wasted mana, which was what ultimately made me put my foot down about the issue after a few days. Karad had just grunted and slowed down a bit every time I fell behind.

At least he hadn't offered to carry me. More than a few people had thought nothing of reaching down and picking me up like they would any other child. One of the Arborists who had a son the same age as me was especially bad about that, to the point where I'd had to give her a mild shock on three separate occasions now.

There were spells to speed up growth, and if possible, I'd take advantage of them later. Reaching stage two took priority, and besides, it was a huge mana investment to essentially shave a year off each decade. I was still going to be a child for far longer than I wanted, but there was no escaping that. It would have been far more tolerable if I'd had access to an unlimited amount of mana to make up for my physiological deficiencies.

Near the end of the second week, as we walked through the arbor towards the village, he asked me, "How are the candidates coming along?"

"Not as well as I'd like, but they're still making progress. I'm hopeful that Vhan will be ready in the next two weeks. Shel probably won't be far behind."

"And the other two?"

"Talik is catching up. He hit a few stumbling blocks at the beginning, but now that he's figured things out, he's doing fine. Ayaka will probably be ready about the same time Shel is, but... politics."

"Because Melmir insisted he have someone in the initial class," Karad said. "You don't want her to have a blessing?"

"I don't much care one way or another," I told the captain of the Garrison. "I'm just expecting interference before she reaches that point. Despite my best efforts to retain control of my class, politics always has to have its say."

Karad chuckled and said, "It does. Sometimes I think it would be easier to just run a sword through anyone who disagrees with me, but no. We're civilized. We don't do that kind of thing here."

"I have been strongly tempted to set Shel's hair on fire more than once," I admitted.

"Hah! I would like to see that! She can be insufferable at times."

"I imagine we'll be having a group meeting soon to determine which spells will be approved for general use," I said. "I'm sure you don't want the average farmer learning spells like sleep or flame lance."

Karad paused mid-stride and glanced down at me. "No, that would not be ideal," he said after a moment. "If you are close to the point where your students are ready to start learning things like that, we should probably discuss what spells you are teaching. I had not considered this, but I will get back with you about a council meeting time."

"We're a council now?" I asked, surprised. Nobody had told me that.

"Not you. With Noctra's death and nobody to replace him as governor, it seemed like the best way to proceed for the time being," Karad said. His brow furrowed and he added, "At least, it did two weeks ago. I am regretting the decision now."

Finding out that I had severely overestimated Karad's political savviness initially had been a happy surprise. He was by no means stupid, but he also wasn't accustomed to considering the hidden agendas of his peers and that they might make alliances against him. I'd initially suspected he was going to be the most difficult of the four to handle. Melmir was more hostile towards me, but Karad had more power in the community. I was starting to think I'd been mistaken about that assumption.

That, or Karad was a devious mastermind who was playing us all for suckers. What were the chances of that, though?

"You should come to the arbor tomorrow afternoon after lunch," I said, changing the subject.

"Why's that?"

"I'm almost ready to remove the subjugation spell from Nermet. I'll do the final preparations tomorrow morning, and then after class, I'll remove the spell." That had only taken about a month thanks to the ample mana I was siphoning out of the storage crystals each night.

At first, I didn't think Karad would reply, but after a few more steps, he said, "Thank you. I will be there."

"I feel like I should warn you that there's no guarantee that he'll be able to think and act like a normal person once I'm done," I said. "My understanding is that he'd had some sort of accident as a child, long before Noctra took over his mind."

"Yes, when he was a boy. Nermet was climbing a cliff face. He slipped and fell, hit his head. Lord Emeto was able to heal him enough to keep him alive, but... he was never the same after. It was my fault. I was teaching him to climb. I should have stopped him when he snuck off. I knew he was going to practice to impress me. I didn't think that he'd go so high."

Human beings, young or old, were delicate, fragile creatures. A simple accident could leave someone dead or maimed, to say nothing of what happened to those who fell prey to the many monsters lurking in the hidden corners of the world. Magic was the great equalizer, the tool we wielded that put us on the same level as the greatest of monsters. I would never understand those who sought power, yet shunned the arcane arts.

"He'll likely still be that way after I'm done," I said. "I'm only trying to reverse the damage Noctra did."

Karad nodded along with my words. "Still," he said. "Thank you."

I wasn't a very altruistic person. I looked out for my family, avoided using people for petty gain, and otherwise ignored the problems of others. If not for my father's intervention, I would have put Nermet out of his misery all those weeks ago. Perhaps it was for the best that he continued to live.

Well, it was still a net loss with all the time and mana I'd spent working on him, but it certainly helped my position with Karad. So it had turned out better than it otherwise could have. And I supposed it righted one of Noctra's many wrongs. The types of mages who used magic like that were inevitably people the world was better off without.

"Yes, well, as I said, you should be able to take him home tomorrow afternoon," I said.

"I'll be there," Karad promised.

After I finished my nightly ward stone duty, I detoured to my family's hut to check up on them. Karad assigned someone from the Garrison to watch me, but he otherwise ignored me except to remind me that I needed to return to my new home in the arbor soon.

They'd replaced the curtain I'd used as a sail during our escape from the village all those weeks ago, though the new one was somewhat more frayed and patchier than the original. It did the job, but it didn't match the window curtains. That must have bothered Mother to no end.

"Hello," I called out from in front of the curtain. A few moments later, a hand reached out and pulled it aside. Mother grabbed me with both arms and pulled me into a hug that lifted me off the ground.

"My little boy! I've missed you," she said, still holding me tightly.

I put up with it for another moment before squirming my way loose. Reluctantly, my mother let me go and ushered me inside. The interior was pretty much what I remembered except for the missing pallet and a few chairs. There was only one by the table now. All of our visits over the last month had been them coming to me, so this was the first chance I'd gotten to see the hut I'd lived in again since returning to the village.

Mother saw me looking and said, "Some of our neighbors decided we weren't coming back, and it was better to take what they wanted now. Only one returned a chair after we got home."

The only surprising part of that was that even a single person brought anything back. At least they'd left the bedding alone. I supposed nobody wanted a used bed, but plenty of people had no problem taking an extra chair. Though I would have thought it would be easy to track everything down. Perhaps our return home wasn't as welcoming as it could have been.

"Are people giving you problems?" I asked. "Treating you differently?"

"We knew it was going to be different. As soon as Noctra singled your father out, it didn't matter what we did. Nothing was ever going to be the same."

"Treating you poorly," I clarified.

Mother shrugged and said, "It doesn't matter."

"It does to me."

She gestured to where Senica was sleeping and said, "Not where it counts. I made sure no one's trying to take anything out on her. If some people want to be jerks to your father and me, well, it's nothing we haven't dealt with before."

"Speaking of Father, where is he?" I asked.

"Out doing some late work," she said unhappily. "They're trying to push the limits of his new core, and tonight's experiment is how well he can work after a tithe."

Considering that Father could generate as much mana in thirty minutes as he used to with a full night's sleep, I imagined just the time he spent walking back to the field from the village square was enough to recover. I wasn't sure I liked the idea of them taking advantage of him to do more work like that, though.

"Is this voluntary?"

"He could have refused the work," Mother said.

"Without consequence?"

"Probably not."

I sighed. "Maybe we would have been better off not returning here after all."

My ears picked up the sound of the Garrison escort shifting in place outside the hut. He was clearly listening to the conversation and ready to report anything I said back to Karad. That had been part of the point of coming here, though. I wanted to check up on my family and make sure they were being treated properly, and I wanted Karad to know I was doing that. If there was a problem like this field work thing, I was going to put pressure on him to fix it.

By the time Karad came around for Nermet's recovery tomorrow, I suspected an overseer or two would have been spoken to about this. If not, I'd make sure it happened before the end of the day. It might not be possible to make everyone act like nothing had ever happened—not without resorting to some fairly nefarious mental manipulations—but I could at least keep people from taking advantage of Father's ignited mana core.

"This is our home," Mother said. "Where else would we go?"

"Anywhere we wanted," I told her. "We still could. There are plenty of other villages and towns out there. It's a big world."

"Maybe," Mother said, but she shook her head. "But after disposing of Noctra, we'd be leaving the village in a lurch if you didn't stay to help them."

"I only help because it's mutually beneficial. If things are growing worse for you instead of better, why should I waste my time helping these people?" I asked candidly. The guard outside shifted in place again.

"Because it's the right thing to do," Mother told me.

"And I'm happy to do it, as long as they do right by us as well."

"Life's not always fair like that."

"If life's not fair, it's going to be unfair in my favor," I told her bluntly. "Otherwise, what's the point of having power to begin with?"

The conversation died off there, both of us sitting in silence for a bit. After a few minutes, I made my excuses, promised to visit again another night, and left. There was no sign of Father coming home and it was well after dark. I wondered how many more hours he'd spend working under the light of the moons.

CHAPTER
FIFTY-EIGHT

"We're going to end today's lesson a bit early," I said as I noticed Karad approaching us through the trees. "Vhan, keep practicing gauging individual mana levels. Tomorrow I'm going to have you cold-reading other people's mana and helping Talik do the same."

The other three wandered off as soon as I dismissed them, but Shel stuck around. "Today is the day?" she asked, having noticed Karad.

"It is. It's going to take about an hour, and it'll probably be very boring to an outside observer."

"I'd like to stay as well. I know my ability to sense mana isn't developed enough to follow what you do, but it can't hurt to observe."

"As long as you can refrain from distracting me," I said. Truthfully, short of attacking me, I doubted there was anything she could do to disrupt my work, but it would be less annoying to not have them in the background chattering or pestering me with questions. Plus, it would be a good test to see if anyone was going to make a move against me when they thought I was vulnerable. I expected Karad would move to intercept them since it was his nephew I was working on, but either way, it'd be a nice little experiment to see if anyone was going to try.

The most likely result was that Karad and Shel watched me closely, with neither doing anything. I was still too valuable a resource right now. Once the first few apprentices went through their ignition rituals, they'd reevaluate, but there was a reason I'd been putting that off. It wasn't because I wanted their skills honed so that their cores would be as strong as possible. It was because I was collecting mana for my own upgrade and things were moving along quite quickly.

It turned out about a quarter of the town was capable of putting mana in a storage crystal without any instruction at all, and that fact alone had increased the amount of extra mana available immensely, even if it had resulted in me spending three extra days making a dozen more storage crystals. The Collectors, other than Ayaka, didn't have a way to tell if anyone was holding anything back, but even if people were, the sheer increase in efficiency made it so we were bringing in more mana than ever before.

I'd taken my cut, of course. The barrier was actually working for about eight hours a day, an utter waste of resources if ever there was one, and I'd heard that the Barrier Wardens had confirmed they could feel a tangible difference when they were near it. Individual people had made the trip across the fields at night when it was turned on to experience the difference for themselves, and there was no longer any doubt that Noctra had lied to everyone.

What this meant for me personally was that as the storage crystals helped cut off a huge chunk of transference loss from the draw stone system, I got a larger and larger portion of the mana the village tithed. At the rate I was going, my next big project was going to be building my mana lattice. I'd have a stage two core inside a month.

For the moment, it was well worth the hassle of pouring mana into the ward stones; creating new panes of glass for the greenhouses, including the new one that was under construction; casting occasional healing spells; and remaining under 'house arrest,' if it could even be called that. I rarely wanted to go anywhere, and when I did, I just went while one of Karad's people followed me around.

I imagined that as time went on and more villagers ignited their mana cores, our fields would begin to flourish, and they'd turn towards improving their general living conditions. Amenities such as chilled or heated water would be in their grasp. There was a lot of empty room inside the radius of the barrier near the manor, and I suspected new constructions of larger houses built out of better material would start popping up within a year or so. People would move into them, and the space their former homes occupied would likely be cannibalized as everything spread out.

That was all assuming that we survived the confrontation when the Wolf Pack finally sent someone out to check on Noctra and Iskara. If we were lucky, it'd be just one mage. A more likely scenario was a mage plus a group of warriors supporting him. The worst case was the entire cabal showing up, but I suspected they were too firmly entrenched in Derro for everyone to leave all at once.

While I considered the future of the village, I called Nermet out and got to work. As I'd told Shel, there wasn't much to see for anyone who hadn't refined their ability to sense mana. From her perspective, I was clearly doing something, but the details were all fuzzy. Karad just saw me sitting there staring at Nermet's head.

In reality, I was double checking every support structure I'd built into the subjugation spell as I'd slowly removed the hooks it had dug into Nermet's brain. All of the ancillary connections had been broken, one by one, until there was nothing but the main control loop left. Normally, tampering with this would cause the spell to tear into Nermet's mind and destroy him. Now, I had all its flailing tendrils safely detached and tucked away.

It was time to cut the main loop, restrain it, and pull the spell completely free. There were a lot of spells, countless varieties that did almost the exact same thing, but sometimes, some tasks just had to be done freehand by a master who was skilled enough in raw mana manipulation to pull it off. This was one of those times.

My mana was a scalpel wielded by my will, held steady by centuries of practice and discipline. Other, lesser mages might have been able to replicate what I was doing, removing the spell without killing its host, but I doubted there was anyone who could do it without causing additional damage to Nermet.

It took me the better part of an hour to make those final incisions in the spell's structure without flaying Nermet's brain. The entire time, he sat there unmoving while Karad and Shel hovered in the background. Finally, the last thread tethering the magic and Nermet together let go. The spell was now completely entangled in what was essentially a fake mind, happy and whole and doing what Noctra had designed it to do.

Shel saw it, even if she didn't know what it was. Her eyes followed it as it rose into the air and away from its victim. Then I released my own mana, let it flash into ambience, and the subjugation spell went wild. No longer anchored to anything, it lashed out in every direction in one last futile gesture before it dissolved.

Nermet blinked twice and fell forward. His arm shot out to brace himself against the ground before anyone else could reach him. With a low groan, he looked around, his eyes bright for the first time since I met him.

"Uncle Karad?" he asked, focusing on the Garrison captain. "What happened?"

"Nermet?" Karad's voice was hesitant. "You're alright?"

"I'm good," Nermet said.

This was the first time I'd heard him speak. There was a slur to his words, like he had trouble forming them properly and wasn't sure quite when to cut the sound, but he was easy to understand. I had no trouble believing he'd suffered a head injury as a child, but it could have been a lot worse.

Karad helped his nephew to his feet and embraced the man in a hug. "You're back," he said. "You're you again."

"I'm me," Nermet agreed.

"Yeah, you are," Karad said, laughing. "I missed you."

Nermet just looked at him, silent and patient.

"Come on," Karad told him. "Say thank you to this boy here. He's the one who saved you and brought you back to us."

"Thank you," Nermet said, but it had the feel of a child following instructions without really understanding why.

"You're welcome," I told him. "Have a good day."

"I can't believe it really worked. I owe you one, kid," Karad said before leading Nermet away.

Shel and I watched them go. It was one of the rare times I'd seen her lose her pleasantly bored expression. It was hard to place what exactly was going through her head, but if I had to guess, I'd say she was just starting to realize exactly how much of a gulf there was between the two of us. I'd just done something she couldn't even see, let alone replicate.

Shel knew that I wasn't really a child. I was an adult in a child's body, but it seemed like she'd expected to catch up easily enough. Maybe she'd thought she'd replace me within a year once she'd learned everything I could teach her. If so, this might have served as a demonstration that she had a long way to go.

"Something on your mind?" I asked.

"No, just... it's good to see Karad happy, and it's kind of weird to have Nermet talking again. It's been years since he really said anything. I'm kind of surprised he remembers how."

"Hmm, yes, well... my father is the one who fed that spell mana for the last month to keep Nermet alive while I worked on him."

"I believe you mentioned that," Shel said. "What will he do now that he has his full mana generation available to him? Should I expect to see him in class tomorrow?"

"I doubt it. Father has expressed almost no interest in learning how to cast spells. He's still spending his mana on unstructured invocations to do field labor."

And he was filling up a storage crystal I'd given him on the side for me. It wasn't much, but every little bit helped. I'd need to visit home again to empty that, and also to discuss whether they'd made a decision about igniting Mother's core as well. At the moment, I was hesitant to do it since the last two ignitions I'd performed had drawn mana sniffers in, though maybe that would be a good thing. It might help keep this new council a bit more tractable if they got to watch me fry a few monsters with fire blasts.

It would be something that I coordinated with the Barrier Wardens before I did it, if for no other reason than to foist off watching for incoming trouble to them. Now that I thought about it, I should probably mention that before this group I was teaching reached that point. Maybe I'd attend one of these council meetings they were having.

"When's your next meeting with the others?" I asked.

"Why?"

"Because I need to talk to Solidaire and Karad about you, so we might as well do it when you're all in the same room. We can uninvite Melmir if that makes it easier."

Shel burst into laughter. "No, no, he has to be there too, at least until we can dissolve the Collectors as an organization. If we ever can, I mean. People seem to like the new storage crystals, though. I'm hoping we can replace all the draw stones with those."

"That is one of my goals," I said. "And train someone else to transfer the mana over to the ward stone so I don't have to do it every night."

By then, I'd be stage two and generating more mana than half the village combined anyway. I'd rather have the time back in my day to work on other projects than the extra mana in my budget, and if the village wanted me to do something, they could just hand me a fully charged storage crystal or two. Now I just needed to keep them on board with my plans so we could get that far.

CHAPTER
FIFTY-NINE

Learning how to modify a mana core was a key part of being a mage. The ignition itself was only the first step, and that didn't really do anything but wake up the core so that the entire thing started producing mana instead of just the terminus point. Depending on how well it was handled, the average mage could expect to see their mana generation increase tenfold. My technique was a bit more thorough, and I'd managed to double that number.

With Father, he'd been my only student and I'd been able to work closely to guide him, but there had also been outside situations necessitating shortcuts. We'd still managed a respectable sixteen times baseline increase, confirmed once I'd had a few days to get accurate measurements, but I would not have said I was satisfied with it. Given the time to do it right, I was sure he could have managed to do better.

Now I had four students and a dozen other projects all making demands at my time. Freeing Nermet had been my top priority, and with that finished, I'd turned my attention to making more storage crystals, faster. My current models were a little bit better than the one I'd made for myself a year ago, but there was really only so much I could realistically do to improve them. Every one I made was a net gain for the total mana the village produced, especially now that people had a working barrier and were easy to convince to make the effort to learn to use a storage crystal.

I'd ended up scrapping the set Iskara had owned. They were so ineffi-cient that they were barely better than a draw stone. Recycling them to serve as the base units for a new set of storage crystals saved me a bit of time, but not much else. Fortunately, all the mana used in their creation was being supplied by the rest of the village, so time was the deciding factor for when I was deciding how to proceed.

My personal mana crystal was also getting close to max capacity, a sight that would have pleased me greatly under other circumstances. Unfortu-nately, finding the time to work on my own lattice was difficult with all the demands of the village. Shel wanted more glass every day, both for their new construction and to stockpile spares. I was trying to stay on top of this project since I planned on claiming a portion of the new greenhouse, and it was fortunately the least time-consuming of my ongoing projects.

Training the new students took up about half my waking hours. The walk to town to clear out the draw stones and storage crystals, then to the manor to empower the ward stone before returning home, cost me another two hours. Storage crystal manufacturing was an ongoing project that I prioritized since it was resulting in good mana returns and it provided a way for the entire village to work on basic mana manipulation, but it would still be weeks before I'd made enough of them that I didn't need to do daily laps to harvest the mana.

Between all of that and various odd jobs, I only had a few hours a day to work on myself, and those hours were regularly consumed with visits to or from my family. It was only now, finally, with my work on Nermet completed, that I was able to start tapping into all the mana I'd saved up to begin constructing my lattice, which brought me back around to my orig-inal thought: learning how to modify a mana core was integral to being a successful mage.

The theory was simple. A mana core was the part of a person that touched on mana, drew it from the Astral Realm, and collected it for use here in the physical world. A normal person's core only touched the Astral Realm at a single point, but a mage with an ignited core touched the Astral Realm in a much larger space. How much larger was dependent on a few factors, one of which was just the size of the person.

Mana cores grew with age, the same way bones and organs did. All other things being equal, an adult might generate three or four times as much mana as a child just by virtue of being bigger. That was also why certain species of monsters grew to such large proportions, because when it came to mana generation, it was an inarguable fact that bigger was better. There were no downsides to going big if the only concern was the sheer amount of mana generated.

For us reasoning, sapient beings who possessed the ability to modify our mana cores, bigger cores were harder to work on. It was more than possible to take a smaller, person-sized core and change it in such a way that it generated mana more rapidly than a giant's. Of course, it was just as possible for that giant to modify his own core to maintain his superiority, but it was more difficult, and it became less and less likely to see monsters with cores beyond stage three or four.

This was why giant, sapient creatures were the apex predators of Manoch. Monsters like dragons with both sheer size and the ability to modify their cores were among the most dangerous beings in existence. There were a few deep-sea leviathans that might rival them in power, but fortunately, their territories rarely had any overlap.

All of that was far beyond what I was trying to achieve in my almost-four-year-old body. Right now, I had a stage one core, fully ignited and touching on mana. What I needed to do in order to advance to stage two was to form my lattice, which was done in a process similar to growing a mana crystal, except I had to do it inside my core. The lattice was visualized somewhat like runes that had been laid down in lines on the inner walls of my core, creating new points of contact with the Astral Realm.

Having bits of crystallized mana floating in my core while I manipulated them was not a comfortable experience, but it would be worth it when I was done. There were a million variations on the patterns used, and the one I'd selected was balanced to give me short-term power without sacrificing long-term flexibility. I wanted to be able to add onto and replace parts of my lattice as I grew and my mana core got bigger.

Eventually, when I was an adult, my lattice would be three-dimensional and resemble a sort of spiderweb of interconnected runes that filled the inside of my core. For now, that wasn't really possible without constant, weekly maintenance. If I tried it as I currently was, the anchor points would separate from the walls, and the whole thing would collapse. Using stronger anchors would inhibit the growth of my mana core, so the only realistic option was to create something modular that didn't attempt to bridge the interior of my core, but instead crawled all over the walls like creeping ivy.

Or at least, that was what I would do if I could find the time to work on it. It had been four days since I'd sent Nermet on his way, and it seemed like Shel had made it her mission to make it impossible for me to get more than half an hour of uninterrupted time.

I didn't even need to check to know it was her knocking on my door twenty minutes after I'd settled in place on my bed to turn my attention to my mana core. She had this irritating habit of knocking in a pattern, two beats, pause, three beats, repeat.

Annoyed, I cracked open one eye and glared at the door. As tempting as it was to just ignore her, the problem with being on house arrest was that she knew I was there. Otherwise, there wouldn't be a guard standing outside the door. They were getting real sick of that, too, especially since it turned out that a new construction with multiple rooms wasn't in the plan after all.

With great reluctance, I stood up and crossed the hut to open the door. "Hello, Shel," I said.

"Gravin. Hi. The next council meeting is in an hour. Time to go."

I would have liked a little bit more warning than that. She'd seen me a few hours ago for our regular class. Showing up at my door and dragging me there unexpectedly made it feel more like I was being summoned to appear before the council rather than meeting them on my terms. There was a time when I would have summoned an entire council at my convenience, sometimes literally pulling them from wherever they were to attend to me.

Admittedly, I hadn't done it much in the last few centuries of my life. At that point, I was old and too tired to be bothered. I had spent most of my time alone, uninterested in the world or its problems. In a way, it was nice to become involved again on such a limited scale. There weren't so many players that it became hard to keep track of them, and none of them were so powerful that I had to worry about them suborning any of the other ones.

It was easy and safe. I was the only one with any magic at all, even. On the other hand, I lacked the significant advantages I normally had, so I suppose it evened out somewhat. Otherwise, I never would have been summoned to a council meeting with no notice like this.

I followed along at a moderate pace, slightly faster than a walk but not quite a jog. It was nothing new when walking with an adult, and even though I was extremely aware of how silly I must look, I'd grown accustomed to it. It wasn't worth the horrendous mana expense something more dignified would run me.

"What's tonight's meeting for?" I asked as we cut out through the southeast side of the forest to travel directly to the manor.

"General reports and coordination with a bit of time set aside for you to update us on everything you're responsible for. I told them you wanted to talk specifically about our upcoming ignitions as well."

"Everyone going to be there?"

"Melmir sends someone else half the time. Solidaire usually shows up but is always late," Shel said. "Karad is there the whole time, but he's so distracted with other things that he's not paying close attention."

"It doesn't sound very productive," I said.

Shel shrugged. "It's not. Such is the price of bureaucracy."

I resisted the urge to roll my eyes. Alkerist didn't even have two hundred people. They knew nothing of the burdens of a functional bureaucracy, where progress through the system was measured in weeks or months, not hours. Just getting a request seen could be an ordeal in and of itself, and a project that should have taken two weeks from start to finish could easily drag on for an entire season, only to end up cancelled barely halfway done.

When considered from an efficiency standpoint, there was something to be said for an iron-fisted tyrant's rule. Of course, benevolent tyrants were a rarity, and they'd eventually be replaced by someone who wanted all of the power, but lacked any sort of empathy for the citizens they ruled over.

We were a long way away from that, though perhaps not so far from a petty tyrant in the form of someone like Noctra. If his cabal did what I expected, they'd be sending people soon to retake control of the village, only this time, they'd have to do it by force if they wanted to return to the output Noctra had gotten from them. Nobody was going to believe lies like his again.

I made a mental note to discuss what preparations they'd made on that front in addition to the business of igniting a few cores in the near future as we entered the manor. Somebody had taken the time to clean up the meeting hall on the west side of the building, even though the meetings were still closed to only the council members.

I settled into a chair near Shel, traded a nod with Karad, and waited for everyone else to arrive.

CHAPTER
SIXTY

Council meetings were, unsurprisingly, boring. Karad had reports from the field overseers—food was still growing at the same rate it always did—and Solidaire had reports on movement sights out in the wastes—none—while Shel had reports on the arbor, which at least had something of substance thanks to all the work I'd been doing.

Melmir did decide to attend personally, much to my disappointment. It turned out the reason he'd done so was that he knew I was going to be there —probably before I knew, which again annoyed me that I'd been given no advance notice—and he wanted to level some accusations against me.

"I have here in my hand reports on all the mana tithed over the last two weeks," he said, brandishing a dozen or so papers, "and the numbers aren't adding up. That's because this monster in disguise right there is stealing from us. He's no better than Noctra was."

Everyone turned to look at me while Melmir shot me a triumphant smirk. Without waiting for a response, he went on. "I've had my people carefully monitoring how much mana we've been taking in with this shyster's scheme, and while I'll admit that the new crystals have been more efficient than the draw stones, and people have been amenable to donating what mana they have, the barrier's up time hasn't increased to match. Where has all the extra mana been going, hmm? Tell me that!"

Well, the truth was that I *was* skimming some mana off the top, but that didn't make Melmir less of an idiot. "Did you account for all the mana I've used helping the arbor? I must have made a hundred panes of glass in the last few weeks," I asked.

"I did! According to your own statements for how much you need for that work, that still doesn't account for even half of what we've taken in."

I nodded along. He was right about that. Probably about half of the mana I collected went into the ward stone. But it was their mana, and if that made the villagers feel safe at night, far be it from me to point out that they'd been without a barrier for fifteen years and had been fine.

"How do you think I'm making those storage crystals?" I asked Melmir. The smirk slipped off his face and he glanced around the room. "Forgot to account for that in your calculations?"

He scowled down at me and dropped back into his seat, his face red. Solidaire and Karad weren't quite laughing, but I could see amusement on their faces. Shel, on the other hand, was openly snickering without making a single effort to hide it. I wasn't laughing, though. I'd seen the look he'd given me when he'd sat back down, and I had a sudden suspicion that he was thinking if murder was good enough to solve my problems, it might just be good enough to solve his as well.

"Those storage crystals aside, you are correct," I said. "I have been keeping mana back, which leads into the topic I am here to discuss. Within the next few weeks, I will be putting the four candidates through their ignition rituals. This will consume some mana, which I've already stored, and more importantly, it may draw in monsters that are sensitive to large mana workings. An ignition ritual uses at minimum seven times as much mana as the subject can hold in their core.

"For that reason, I would like to coordinate with the Barrier Wardens to keep watch and schedule the ritual for a time when the barrier is active. After completing the ignitions, I will be available to handle any monsters that notice."

"Now hold on a minute," Solidaire said. "You never told us anything about monsters coming to the village when you sold us on this plan."

"It's not a real issue," I replied. "It's just something to be aware of. The risks are negligible, and I am taking steps right now, in this very meeting, to mitigate them down to nothing."

"What if they breach the barrier somehow?" Karad asked, turning to Solidaire. "Could your men handle them?"

"Depends what it is and for how long. Our job is really more about detecting monsters soon enough to give Lord Noctra time to respond. That's not going to work for obvious reasons. I guess the real question is, how well can we rely on a child to protect us?"

"Perhaps a demonstration is in order," I said. It would be a waste of mana, but it might help get them to take me more seriously. Part of the problem was that they were still under the impression that I was asking for permission. I wasn't. I was informing them what I was doing and requesting that they coordinate with me. If they refused, I would still go ahead with my plans. It would just be more inconvenient for them to deal with the aftermath.

I hopped out of my seat and walked over to the door. After pushing it open, I made sure everyone was watching, then I pointed to a big, round rock so large that I would have had to climb to get on top of it, and wide enough for me to lay down on. I used stone shape on it to split it down the middle and into multiple chunks.

A resounding crack echoed out from where the rock split, followed by a series of thumps as individual chunks hit the ground. "Monsters are much less resilient to damage," I said, leaving the door open as I returned to my seat.

The demonstration was ridiculous. The spell I'd used wouldn't even work on a living monster, not unless it was some sort of earth elemental, and even then, the monster would resist such a weak spell. A flesh-and-blood creature would require a completely different type of magic, but none of them knew that. The split stone would serve its purpose of verifying my offensive magical capabilities in their eyes, even if what I'd done was a simple transmutation.

"Now, as I was saying, it's possible that the ignition rituals will draw monsters hunting mana towards the village. I will let you all know in advance so we can coordinate extra Barrier Wardens to watch for incoming threats. When one is identified, I will... handle it."

"Is there anything else we need to do to prepare beforehand?" Karad asked, his eyes lingering on the split boulder outside the house.

"No, no. I'll take care of everything else."

"When do you think I'll be ready?" Shel asked, cutting Melmir off just as he opened his mouth to speak.

"Probably within the next three weeks, but we'll see," I told her. "Vhan might beat you there."

None of them would be undergoing the ignition ritual until I finished my own lattice and upgraded my core to stage two, regardless of whether they were ready or not. I still had my own safety and wellbeing to consider, plus I wanted the increase to my mana generation before I worried about fighting off hostile invaders. Speaking of which...

"Another topic I wanted to go over is your preparations for dealing with whoever comes to investigate Noctra's disappearance," I said.

"I don't think that will be an issue," Karad told me. "It's been weeks, and no one's shown up."

"So?" I asked.

"So, what makes you so sure they will?" Melmir asked.

"Because he was in contact with a cabal and has been sending them your stolen mana for over a decade," I said. "What makes you think they won't send anybody?"

"Well," Solidaire said slowly, dragging the word out, "It's not so much that we don't think there's a chance it'll happen as it is that what are we supposed to do if it does?"

"Defend yourself, maybe?" I suggested.

"Sure, and we're doing that. All of my people have swords, and we're practicing with them more," Karad said. "But you just split a rock in half like it was nothing. How do I parry that? You didn't even have to touch it. We don't know how to fight against someone who can kill us just by looking at us."

That was a fair point. I hadn't gone out of my way to teach them how to hunt mages specifically because I didn't want them hunting me. For the time being, it was very likely that whoever showed up would be stronger than I was. If I started teaching people basic invocations like mana shielding that they could do without an ignited core, I was teaching them how to defend against me, too. It wasn't that I couldn't break through a simple mana shield, but I couldn't do it fast enough to overcome a few dozen people using it at the same time.

"So you're relying on me to... what, win a duel against this theoretical mystery mage?" I asked. "It's not that I mind fighting, but it would have been nice to be asked first."

"Yes, well, as I said, it's been weeks, and no one's shown up. It might never come to that," Karad told me.

"I suppose this brings me to my next point. We'll need to discuss what spells I teach our newly minted mages, and in light of your defense preparations, it would seem prudent to add at least a few combat-oriented spells to their repertoires."

"If I'd known we were doing that, I'd have chosen different people," Shel said. "None of the Arborists are interested in fighting. Perhaps someone from the Garrison or Barrier Wardens should be added to the class."

"The next class, maybe," I said. "We don't know how much time we have left. You'll have to learn how to cast a basic fire blast and hope you never have cause to use it."

"I don't know—" Karad started to say.

"Fire blast, mana shield. Sleep, perhaps. Sharpened senses will be a must. Healing touch, if we have time. Unfortunately, the most useful spells are not novice ranked, so we'll have to work up to them. I suppose elemental manipulation would be a good starter spell. Perhaps light, though that's not particularly useful except on those rare nights with mostly new moons."

"How long is this going to take?" Solidaire asked.

"That will depend entirely on them. My father grasped a novice tier spell in less than two days, but that was with me exclusively focusing my attention on him and assisting him. This is a different set of circumstances."

I didn't go out of my way to give this council much more than the basics for what spells I planned on teaching. I didn't want or need their approval for my curriculum, and besides, every apprentice was different. Conjuration was by far the best discipline to draw from when looking for combat magic, but some apprentices just didn't have any talent for it. I wasn't going to force someone who wanted to be a diviner to become a conjurer instead.

I would insist on a well-rounded assortment of novice tier spells, though. The whole point of novice tier spells was to get a chance to find out what a new student was good at, to find their strengths so they could lean into them and identify their weaknesses so they could fix them. In all likelihood, it would be me who fought off any cabal spies or assassins anyway, so while I wanted to impress on the council the need to take the threat seriously, I wasn't overly concerned if their preparations didn't measure up.

"I think that's about all I have to say on the subject for now," I told them. "Oh, but a bit of news to make Melmir happy. Once this first batch is ready, I plan on handing over mana collection duties to Ayaka. You're all handling the storage crystals anyway, so one of you can charge up the ward stone. It's not hard. I'll show her how and make sure she can handle it on her own, but then I'm clearing that job out of my schedule."

"You can't just make decisions like that!" Melmir objected.

Funny. I'd have thought he'd be happy to have a bit of responsibility come back under his control. There was just no pleasing some people.

CHAPTER
SIXTY-ONE

I sat in a chair I'd made using stone shape on a big rock I'd relocated to my new home and watched my four apprentices play a game of catch. Instead of a ball, they were using an unrefined sphere of mana that held its shape only by the will of whoever was holding onto it. Every time one of them slipped, the sphere shrank a bit as streamers of mana escaped from it. It had only been ten minutes, and already the sphere was less than half the size it had been when they started.

The game served two purposes. First, it was a way for them to practice both their ability to sense mana, necessary in order to even see the otherwise-invisible ball, and their control of external mana to shift it back and forth. Second, it gave me a way to gauge their progress. Ayaka had taken the lead in the category of mana sensing, and I could see her track the sphere's progress as it moved back and forth, not just when it was near her. She also had the best ranged control, and the sphere lost the least amount of mana during her hand-offs.

All four of them were ready for the ignition ritual. In my estimation, Vhan's internal mana control would likely mean he had the best results, but all of them would pass well beyond the minimal threshold. Even if I held back from helping them, I suspected only Talik might have some problems keeping his mana in motion long enough to complete the ignition ritual. His early issues put him a week or so behind everyone else, a miniscule amount in the long-term, but a significant disadvantage when they had less than a month's training.

Things were going relatively well. I had all the mana I needed and was almost finished forming my lattice. Soon, the first generation of apprentice mages would be unleashed on the village, though I'd still be responsible for teaching them some specific spells. Depending on how things went, they'd all likely cap out at basic spells. That was fine for brute force magical solutions, which was honestly all the village needed to survive as long as their ward stone didn't break again.

Though it wasn't like that had been all that useful any time in the recent past. I did have some concerns that an entire village of over a hundred mages might just generate enough magic to look appetizing to various monsters, but by the time they reached that point, twenty or so villagers would be able to keep their barrier running every second of every day without stressing themselves.

The mana sphere flashed into nothingness, and the game ended. Without needing me to prompt them, they immediately started tallying up who'd lost the most mana and who'd lost the least. Getting an accurate summary of the results was also part of their training, with the idea being both to notice what everyone else was doing with their mana and to be able to multitask well enough to handle the sphere and keep four separate running totals in their heads.

None of them got it exactly right, but between the four of them, they got the shape of things well enough to determine who had actually won. Once they were done arguing about it, they turned to me in unison to get my official ruling.

"Don't look at me," I said. "You were supposed to be keeping track yourselves. Do you think you're right?"

"Yes," Ayaka said. The others echoed their agreement, though with less confidence.

"Then I guess you're right," I told them. "Have a little faith in yourselves."

"That must mean we're ready to receive our blessings," Shel said.

"Probably, yes," I agreed.

"Wait, really? Why haven't we done it yet?" Vhan asked.

"Mostly because I have other demands on my time," I said. "And because you don't get a second chance to do this. Yes, you could do well enough to ignite your core a week ago, but you'll do a better job of it today than you would have then, and next week, you'll do even better. Isn't it worth an extra week or two of practice to have a properly ignited core?"

"How much of a difference would it make?" Ayaka said. Always practical, that one. I was starting to think if there was anyone in the group I'd take on as a true apprentice beyond the ignition ritual and some instruction on novice spells, it was her.

"Last week, unaided, I would have said your ignition would increase your mana generation speed by six-fold. This week, I think you would have an eight-fold increase instead. If you keep working this hard, in another month, that'll be eleven-fold."

"At some point, it's got to stop being worth the diminishing returns," Vhan said.

"This is the foundation for the rest of your relationship with mana. The closer to perfect your ignition is, the more that power will multiply as you advance."

That wasn't really true for this particular group. I had my doubts that more than a handful of people in the village would advance past a stage one core. Of those dozen or so that made it to stage two, I doubted anyone would reach stage three without assistance. Even then, only two or three people at most would have the discipline and skill needed, assuming I provided the knowledge.

"What about your core?" Shel asked.

"Hmm. A somewhat personal question," I said. Only Shel knew my origins as I'd laid them out for the village council, but in societies where many people were mages and knowledge was much more readily available, giving away that kind of information could be dangerous. It allowed mages to more accurately gauge the strength of their enemies. Here, my only magic-wielding enemies were already dead, but there was always the possibility of a cabal member interrogating someone for information on me when they did finally arrive.

"Let's just say you'll need a lot more practice if you want to match me," I said. I didn't tell them that I'd be helping their ignition rituals along to smooth out any flaws in their techniques. There was no sense in letting them know that they could slack off and expect to receive similar results. Besides, I still needed another day or two to finish my lattice.

The group started up another game while I continued my painstakingly slow work and enjoyed the view of the arbor. It was no Night Vale, but considering the village was located in a wasteland and none of the Arborists had any real magical capabilities, they'd built something impressive. If the trees were a bit scraggly and the underbrush was thin enough to see the occasional wildlife scampering through, well, I imagined the place was going to look very different within a year.

For now, the black-barred hawk perched on one of the trees got to enjoy an easy view of its potential meals. I'd noticed that one particular raptor had claimed most of the arbor as its territory and I rarely saw any other birds.

"Admiring the hawk?" my guard asked, nodding up towards where it was perched on the north side of the clearing where the Arborists lived.

"Hah. Yes, I am. I should be watching my students, though," I confessed.

"No harm in it," the guard said. "Standing out here makes me think I went into the wrong line of work. Don't get me wrong, I don't have a problem being part of the Garrison, but there's a lot of beauty in the arbor."

If only he knew what he was missing. The arbor was something special, but only because the Arborists tended to it and kept it thriving despite the harsh conditions here. There were some truly awe-inspiring views in this world that only a select few were lucky enough to behold. I doubted the arbor would ever be one of them, but I might help it along a bit once things settled down here.

"We're lucky to be here right now, too," the guard went on, oblivious to my inner musings. "I was talking to Luthra—that's my cousin who works here in the arbor—and he told me that it just showed up a few days ago. He's been an Arborist for nine years now and he's never seen that species of hawk before."

I froze in place for a moment before turning my gaze from the hawk to the guard. "Is that so?" I asked, doing my best to sound casual. "Has anyone else seen a hawk like that before this week?"

"I wouldn't know. Why?"

Maybe it was just a coincidence. Animals did exist, after all, and not all of them were man-eaters. The arbor was the perfect place for regular, non-threatening species to make their homes, at least compared to the waste-land of rolling hills full of nothing but scrub grass and the occasional muddy stream winding its way down from the mountains.

Then again, I had been waiting for Noctra's cabal to show up. An animal familiar spying on the village was a reasonable opening move. It was too bad there was no way for me to tell without capturing the hawk to inspect it, and if it was a familiar, that would be tipping my hand. I was already preparing for an encounter, and letting them know I was onto them wouldn't do me any favors.

"No reason," I said. "Just wondering how lucky we really are."

There were a few people who needed to know so they could prepare, but putting the Garrison or the Barrier Wardens on high alert would just give the game away. Another two weeks would have been about perfect, just enough time to prepare some weapons and defenses for myself. I'd thought I'd have more time than this, and in hindsight, some useful equipment might have been a higher priority than reaching stage two.

If the hawk was a familiar, and if the mage bonded with it was here, that meant an attack could come anytime between an hour from now and another week. If I was wrong, and the bird was just a bird after all, then I had an unknown amount of time to finish my lattice and construct myself a few defensive trinkets.

No matter how I looked at it, the more time I had, the better off I'd be. My first group of students were only just now reaching the point where I could work on other projects while they practiced, and my personal growth had stagnated because of the time I'd spent tutoring them. Unfortunately, any variance in the routine could alert the unknown mage that he'd been detected. I would need to continue as I had been.

It looked like I was going to be in for a sleepless night finishing up my lattice, and I'd need to carefully consider what I worked on next. It would be foolish to construct any sort of weapon while letting my opponent spy on me. Nor was a weapon the best use of my time. A reactive defense to save me from an unexpected ambush was more important. As long as I had mana at my disposal, I was confident I could beat any other mage in a duel.

The lattice came first, then a shield ward of some kind, then some sort of scrying amplifier to help me find the enemy mage. It was tempting to flip that order, to find and strike first, but in terms of time and mana spent, the shield ward would be the work of an afternoon once I had enough mana generation to keep it powered, while a scrying amplifier would take days at minimum to put together and had no guarantee of success.

All of this might still be a false alarm. "Shel," I said as the students wrapped up their game. "I need you to do something for me."

"What's that?" she asked.

"Find out if that type of hawk sitting up there in the trees is natural to this area, and if so, how long it's been here," I said in a low voice to prevent anyone else from overhearing.

"May I ask why?"

"I'm probably just being paranoid, but mages can bond with animals and use them to spy. I think we have more time before Noctra's friends come looking, but I want to be sure that hawk showing up is just a coincidence. Don't spread this around. If it *is* a familiar, we don't need to alert its mage that we're onto him."

"Got it," Shel said. "I'll have an answer for you in a few hours."

CHAPTER
SIXTY-TWO

When I was a young man, full of a burning hatred for the rich and powerful, I killed some nobleman's son. I remembered it, not because of how important the man was, but because it was the first time I'd ever seen a pocket watch. I never did quite manage to put it back together correctly, but in my defense, I had bludgeoned him to death using several telekinetically propelled rocks and damaged the pocket watch in the process.

Putting my lattice together once I finished forming the last piece sometime just before pre-dawn light started brightening the sky was a similar process to playing with that watch. The pieces were tiny and required a great degree of delicacy and precision to handle. They also required a significant understanding of how things fit together, as so many of the pieces looked similar but did not function properly if switched around.

I might not have been able to repair that watch, no matter how many different fabrication spells I'd utilized, but I was an expert at constructing lattices. I'd seen all kinds and spent considerable time researching them. I knew the benefits and drawbacks to basic lattices; I knew how to adapt and modify designs for individuals.

And I'd given over endless hours to researching my own particular path back to power prior to my reincarnation. I could put this lattice together in my sleep, which was good because I couldn't use the mana in my core for anything else while I was integrating the lattice. Three-year-olds were not built to pull all-nighters, and without mana to keep my energy levels up, I was beyond exhausted.

I finished putting the last piece of the lattice into place and felt a rush of mana cycle through it as it activated. Immediately, new mana started pouring into my core off the lattice. I spent the first minute of my lattice being active calculating my new rate of mana generation, then the next five minutes going over it and confirming it repeatedly.

I'd expected to boost my mana generation from twenty times normal to fifty, with some slight accommodations made for a minute loss in maximum core capacity. My lattice was extremely thin and fragile, thus why it was so time consuming to make and put together, so the capacity loss was barely a single percent of my total.

My output, confirmed by quadruple checking, was closer to seventy times normal generation, even accounting for the slightly smaller core space. I wasn't inclined to complain about it, but it shouldn't have happened. I was immediately concerned that what seemed like a boon now would come back around as a problem down the road.

My lattice's modular design was a compromise forced on me by my accelerated timeline, and I was concerned that in my sleep-deprived state, I'd done irreparable harm to my potential by incorrectly slotting all the pieces together. If I couldn't disassemble the lattice to make modifications to it later, I might find myself stalled out at stage nine again, just like in my previous life.

As many times as I went through it, everything looked perfect. I redid my calculations for the hundredth time since being reborn and confirmed they were correct. By everything I knew, I should be generating fifty times my unignited rate, not seventy. Either I'd made some serious mistake that I'd never caught in all the years I'd spent working on my reincarnation plan, or being born here in a mana desert had introduced an unanticipated variable.

The level of ambient mana should not have made a difference. It certainly hadn't mattered when I was igniting my core. My mana core functioned precisely as planned at that step. The only difference I could see was that at that point, I'd been entirely dependent on my own mana, barring a sliver I'd taken from Senica. Now, I was using mana accumulated by the village that had been at least partially filtered through draw stones. There was no reason that should matter, but I couldn't think of anything else that had changed.

Perhaps it was something on a global scale that had thrown off my calculations. I did have a missing moon and a missing written language as of yet unaccounted for. I couldn't see how that would affect my mana lattice, not at this stage. It wasn't until stage six that a mage needed to link to a genius loci, and I was years away from that point. Prior to that, celestial anomalies would be irrelevant.

I was strongly tempted to tear the lattice back down so I could go over it piece by piece, but given the situation I was in with an unknown number of hostile mages potentially trying to kill or enslave me, reducing my own power right now was a terrible idea. I would just have to accept that I'd miscalculated something, move forward as best I could, and research it later when time permitted.

At least the error was in my favor for the moment. I officially had a stage two core, strong enough to refill from empty to full in a bit over two hours. It wouldn't be all that helpful in a combat situation—that was where stage three shone—since those kind of fights tended to end in seconds or minutes at most, but it would greatly accelerate my prep work, which included keeping the reserves in my mana crystal close to full in addition to having the resources needed to produce enchanted items.

Before any of that, I wanted a nap. I'd be relying heavily on body reinforcement invocations to function today, but at least an hour of sleep wouldn't go amiss. I'd be lucky to get that before people started showing up, but I'd do what I could. The mystery of my mana lattice would keep for another day.

I ended up getting two hours of sleep, thanks to my sympathetic guard. He'd known I'd been up all night and had turned away my students when they'd arrived. Instead of insisting, they'd set up nearby and begun practicing without my oversight.

Bless that man.

I dragged myself back to consciousness through gritty eyes and a head stuffed with fuzzy cotton, took a few moments to sort myself out and get upright, then sent a burst of mana through my body to chase off my fatigue.

Another quick check of my lattice confirmed that everything was working properly, if not to my specifications. There was no sign of any degradation or imbalance. My core was just sitting there, full and starting to leak mana into the atmosphere.

The desert, thirsty beast that it was, soaked up the ambient mana instantly. I couldn't even begin to guess how much mana it would take to heal the scar on this land, but it would probably be the work of generations to fix it if it was left to heal naturally. Someday, when I'd recovered the full breadth of my powers, I might come study the problem in detail and see if I could devise a solution.

It turned out that reincarnating in a new, young body had rejuvenated my decayed motivation to go out into the world and have an effect on it. I wanted to change things, to make them better, to see new places and meet new people. For most of the last three centuries of my life, I'd remained cloistered in the Night Vale and rarely accepted visitors. I couldn't imagine spending so many decades of my new life just sitting still, watching the world pass me by.

I shook myself out of my thoughts, got dressed, and opened the door. I already knew what my students were up to, having felt the mana moving around as soon as I woke up. Not wanting to interrupt them, I settled into my seat to observe while occasionally glancing around for any feathered spies that might be nearby.

"Everything okay?" Shel asked when she noticed me a few minutes later. I couldn't blame her for her inattentiveness considering how engrossed they all were in the training. "You seem... different."

Did I? Damn, I was leaking. It wasn't a secret among my trainees that I could hide my mana core from their senses, but I hadn't properly accounted for just how much more mana I was producing now than I'd been a few hours ago. I adjusted my mana shroud to compensate, but it was likely too late.

"I was making modifications to my mana core last night," I said. "It was a long process. I'm fine, just tired now."

I ignored the worry I saw in their faces. For all that I was their teacher here, and I'd demonstrated my capabilities in that arena quite thoroughly, I was still a child. Sometimes that fact overwrote that I was 'blessed by the spirits' or whatever. Shel was probably the best about treating me like an adult, if only because she knew that I was mentally much, much older than her. I hadn't told the council exactly how many years I'd been practicing the art of magic, but they got the point.

To the rest of the village, I was a miracle child blessed by all their ancestors and then some, sent to free them from Noctra's predations and guide them to an age of prosperity. Or something like that. I should have paid closer attention to Karad's speech. I hadn't realized he was going to go that far off script like that.

"Now then, as to the four of you, I think you've gotten the hang of this particular exercise," I said. "So let's make it harder."

The four exchanged glances while I once again lamented my lack of training tools. I couldn't justify the frivolous waste of mana on various transmutation spells to manufacture what I needed, but I could and had asked my guard from last night to fetch me a set of blindfolds.

"Tinzo, did you get them?" I asked.

"Sure did," he said, opening a pouch on his belt and pulling them out. He handed them over to Ayaka, who distributed them to everyone else. "Even switched to have back-to-back shifts just so I could watch this."

"And... what are we doing with these?" Talik asked, a trace of nervousness in his voice.

"This exercise has three components," I explained. "You'll take positions across from each other, put on the blindfolds, and then use your mana sense to keep track of each other. Whenever you feel that you are ready, you may throw a ball of mana at your opponent. Your task will be to not only track each other, but the mana being sent at you, while simultaneously forming your own ammunition and sending it at your target."

"Why do we need to be blindfolded?" Shel asked.

"Because it's a lot funnier that way," I said, which earned me glares from everyone except the Garrison guard. "Okay, fine. It's because it's easier to sense mana when you can block out other distractions, but it can be more difficult to move when you can't see what you're doing. The blindfolds will help you see an attack coming while making it harder for you to dodge it. The earlier you sense it, the more time you'll have to adjust your own position."

"This training is necessary in order to receive a blessing from the spirits?" Vhan asked. It was easy to see just from his expression that he didn't believe me.

"If by 'spirits' you mean 'me,' then yes, it's necessary," I told him. "I don't know what any spirits might want, but I want you to do this. Anything and everything you can do to increase your ability to sense fine amounts of mana and control it is going to be useful when it comes time to complete the ignition ritual.

"Now, go ahead and get into position. Two people over here, two over there. And blindfolds on... Ready? Begin."

I shared a smirk with Tinzo and my students flailed around, stumbling over uneven patches of ground where I subtly altered things with elemental manipulation. Sometimes, training was good for the teacher as well as the student.

The smirk fell from my face when I glanced over and saw a familiar hawk watching us from high up in one of the trees. It reminded me that, tired as I was, I needed to use these next few hours to start constructing that shield ward. Hopefully my own work wouldn't distract my students, but if so, I'd just call it an extra challenge to keep them on their toes.

I had a feeling they were going to need to be able to defend themselves sooner rather than later. The enemy might not even wait for me to ignite their cores. Or maybe that's exactly what he was waiting to see. Just how much did they know already, anyway?

CHAPTER
SIXTY-THREE

Enchantment and inscription were two disciplines that accomplished similar purposes through radically different methods. Enchantment was great in that it was much easier to practice since it didn't require any raw materials, and that enchanted objects could be used by non-mages. The drawback was that eventually, the mana would run out unless consideration was given to recharge it with ambient mana. In that case, the enchantment needed to remain in an area of high saturation, lest it risk running dry and breaking.

In short, it wasn't really suitable for life in Alkerist, at least not for any long-term effects I wanted to utilize. There were plenty of spells that used the principles of enchantment to create temporary effects lasting anywhere from minutes to hours. The sleep spell was an excellent example of that, and would be one of the spells I introduced to future students who were part of the Garrison despite Karad's hesitation.

But for making long-term enchantments, I would need to structure them in such a way that I could continually pour more and more mana into them. It wasn't impossible, but it also wasn't practical. If I was busy doing something else, I didn't want to have to enchant the piece all over again because I didn't have the spare mana for it that week.

There was a reason the ward stone had runes inscribed on it. Inscriptions didn't have that problem. They were more like a guide for mana, telling it how to act in order to produce the effect. Anybody, even a village full of non-mages with dormant cores, could give an inscribed object the requisite mana, and it would produce whatever spell it needed to, no matter how long it had been sitting there.

There were downsides, of course. For one, inscription needed a physical medium, and if the runes were damaged, the inscription no longer functioned. For another, inscribed objects tended to be big because a lot of runes were needed to describe the magic, and while the size of the rune itself wasn't relevant, they did all need to be uniform. Of course, it was harder to carve smaller runes.

When I considered how I wanted to make my shield ward, I put a lot of thought into whether I should enchant something to get me through the next few weeks or inscribe something that would last longer. I even considered doing a core invocation, which merged some principles of enchantment with inner-body magics to create effects that were a continual drain directly on my mana core, but since I still wasn't sure what I'd miscalculated with my mana lattice, I decided to go in a different direction.

That led me to my current project. I'd used stone shape to create a flat oval of stone with a hole on one end and then transmuted it to alabaster since I was going to be making tiny, precise cuts. Alabaster was one of the easiest types of stone to work with for this kind of project, so I'd grimaced and spent more mana than it would take to form an entire wall of glass to make it.

Since I lacked all of the tools needed to carve runes, and because I'd never much understood mages who claimed the art of it all was relaxing and meditative, I cheated and used stone shape to add the runes that way. It was still a slow process, but I preferred it this way. Even the best stone carver could make mistakes, and I was pressed for time. Being able to smooth over imperfect runes to try again allowed me to rush the work so that I could finish it in a single day instead of spending weeks on the piece.

There was a knock on the door just as I finished my final inspection and threaded the shard of rune-carved stone with a strip of soft, supple leather. A quick glance out the window confirmed the time for me. Karad had come to collect me for his nightly round and likely talk to me about the suspicious feathered spy lurking in the area.

I paused for a second while I tried to remember if hawks had excellent hearing as well as eyesight. Everyone who knew anything about predatory birds knew their eyesight was unrivaled, so much so that some spells used to enhance vision were named after them. There was significantly less information commonly available on their hearing, but I vaguely remembered a conversation at a roadside tavern many years ago with an inebriated druid who'd rambled about several animals whose hearing was underestimated due to them being famous for other senses.

It was probably best to assume at least a human-level of natural hearing, and that wasn't even getting into what invocations the hawk might be able to use if it truly was a mage's familiar. I hadn't sensed any mana coming from it, but it wasn't inconceivable that the other mages in Noctra's cabal could shroud their mana and extend that ability to a familiar.

Karad knocked again. I dropped the loop of leather over my head and tucked the amulet under my shirt, then walked across the hut to answer the door. "Time to do the nightly rounds?" I asked.

"And discuss that other thing," he said with a nod.

As soon as we were away from the Arborists' homes, he started to speak, but I cut him off. "Not here. Wait until we get out of the trees."

I got an annoyed glance and a grunt in reply, but he followed my instructions. A few minutes later, when we were out in the open, I cast a quick scrying spell to check for animals, then said, "Shel told you about my familiar theory."

"She did. It sounds... Well, it sounds ridiculous, if I'm being honest. But you're the expert in magic, not me. How likely do you think it is?"

"It's certainly possible," I said. "It could just be a coincidence. There's no way to know without actually capturing the bird so I can get a good look at it. If it is a familiar, I'll be able to see the mana in it forming a bond to its mage. But if I do that and I'm right, we're letting the mage know we've discovered him."

"So we have to assume that any visible preparations we make are compromised," Karad said.

"It gets worse, I'm afraid. There are some limits to what kinds of animals can be bonded as familiars, but I've seen plenty of examples of mice, rats, spiders, and the like being used. I have no proof the hawk is a familiar, but I also don't have any proof that it's not or that it's the only one. Mages who specialize in familiar bonds can easily keep an entire stable of animals to use as extensions of their own magic."

"If that's the case, I don't see how we can expect any sort of defense to succeed," Karad said.

"I agree. We're either completely fine if there are no familiars, or entirely exposed if there's a mage out there spying on us. Answering that question is going to be my next project. If I can confirm the existence of an enemy mage, I might be able to take them out and end the threat before it reaches the village."

"How long will it take, though? They could attack tonight."

"Or not for another week. Or not at all," I said. "I don't know. Maybe I'm just being paranoid. I think someone will show up eventually, if only to find out why the guy who owed them a bunch of mana stopped making his payments. That ledger indicated that Noctra was nowhere near paying off his debt. But is there a mage staring at the village through the eyes of a hawk he bonded as a familiar right now? I just don't know. Yet."

"That's not a lot to go on, Gravin," Karad said. "I've given you a lot of leeway despite all the crap I'm catching for letting a little kid run around doing whatever he wants. I need something better than this."

"I'm working on it," I told him. "Unlike you, I don't have ten other people to take care of problems for me. For example, right now I'm walking around collecting mana when I could be building a scrying amplifier to look for the hypothetical mage lurking around out in the wastelands. If I had a subordinate, I could save myself all this time. Instead, I have four trainees who are also taking up more of my time. I can only do so much with the hours I have in my day, and until some of those trainees can pick up the slack, you're going to have to be patient."

The conversation fell off as we entered the village and didn't really resume until I'd finished emptying the draw stones. Those were seeing less and less use, and I had high hopes that the whole village would convert over to storage crystals if they decided to keep this structure. The more likely outcome in my mind was that they'd do away with it entirely once enough of them had ignited cores and this sort of communal collection was no longer necessary.

"How long until you've got your scrying thing ready to go, and how much mana are you going to need to power it?" Karad asked. He paused a second, then added, "In terms of how many hours we're not going to be able to power the ward stone, please."

"Just to construct it, a day. That shouldn't use up enough mana to be noticeable. It'll be like doing a few extra panes of glass for Shel. To power it and actually find someone? Well, it mostly comes down to luck. Will the mage be in the first place I look or the fifth? Is there one there at all? What if there is, but they move from a place I haven't yet looked to one I already checked and I miss them completely?"

"You're not reassuring me here," Karad said.

"I'm not trying to. I'm telling you what I'm going to do and what difficulties I'll face. You're a grown man in his forties; you shouldn't need reassurances from me, not if you plan on running this village."

"You know, sometimes you can be a jerk."

"I've been called worse," I said. "Sorry, but I don't have the time or energy to coddle anyone. I'm trying to work with all of you here, and I appreciate that you've been willing to look past my appearance and take me seriously. I also appreciate that I have yet to hear any rumors about me that even come close to approaching the truth. I was sure Melmir would spread it around out of spite, if nothing else."

Karad snorted. "He probably would if he believed it himself."

"Be that as it may, I think I'm doing a lot of good for the village. I have confidence that we'll survive the fallout of Noctra's schemes."

"Maybe they'll look around, confirm he's dead, and leave us alone," Karad said.

I snorted, but didn't say anything. I didn't have to.

"Our official position remains that we're unlikely to be bothered by hostile mages," Karad told me. "Unofficially, I'd appreciate it if you could speed up your work. If you need a bit of extra mana to make it happen, that's fine by me."

"Unfortunately, the resource I'm short on is time," I said. "That's not something you can help me with."

"Once you do the blessing ritual on the first group, that'll help, right?"

"Yes and no. They'll need even more of my time to actually learn any magic, but if Ayaka can take over ward stone maintenance, that'll help even things out. Most of the magic I spend my day doing is too advanced to expect any of them to replicate in the next six months. Even the basic tier spells like fire blast aren't something they're going to be able to do any time soon. If I had my way, they'd have another two months of training before we even ignited their cores."

"That long?" Karad asked.

"I won't actually spend that much time working with them before we do the ritual, but it would be better if I did. It's a problem of needing the short-term gains now. We're giving up long-term potential for it."

"They know that?"

"They do," I confirmed. "In their heads, at least. I don't think they really grasp the difference yet."

Karad let out a frustrated sigh and raked his hand through his hair. "Do what you think is best. Let me know if you need anything."

Mutely, I nodded. It was good that we were in agreement.

CHAPTER

SIXTY-FOUR

After I got back, I had tonight's door guard help me test my new shield ward by throwing things at me. Maintaining something like a mana shield at all times was far too expensive, but wards had the advantage of being extremely cheap to power. At least, they did if they weren't designed to create a miles-wide barrier. For a single person, a personal defense ward was far more manageable.

The key to a good ward was that it relied heavily on divinations to detect the conditions under which it should activate another spell. Most of what made my amulet complicated was defining what those conditions were. Any physical object coming at me with significant speed and mass would cause the runes to activate a mana shield. The ward did its best to automatically regulate how much mana needed to go into it to keep me safe, so it needed additional runes to judge factors like weight and pointiness.

If a spell came my way, the ward would do its best to disrupt it. Failing that, the amulet would try to slow the attack down so that I could react to the magic. At its heart, that was the shield ward's purpose: to give me enough time to evaluate the threat and prevent an ambush from taking me out. I had to sacrifice flexibility to keep it portable, but it worked.

I did have to imbue a significant chunk of mana into it to keep the wards active and to give it the resources necessary to repel an attack. Once every few days, I'd want to top it off, but if all the mana did get drained out—such as if I was attacked—the inscription wouldn't break like an enchantment would.

For my next project, I created a piece of glass shaped to be about three feet by one foot in dimensions. That was the easy part. Scrying mirrors didn't work if they weren't mirrors. Unlike a regular mirror that used silver paint as a backing, a scrying mirror needed liquid mana infused into it in order to serve as a lens for the spell. Unfortunately for me, the easiest way to collect liquid mana was through various plant life that thrived in mana-rich environments.

That didn't mean it was impossible to get my hands on, just that I'd have to do the conversions myself. I borrowed a wooden bowl from one of my new neighbors and was in the process of slowly dripping beads of liqui-fied mana off my fingertip into the bowl when someone knocked on my door.

"Come in," I called out, not looking up from my work. Mana didn't like to exist in physical form, and it rapidly converted through states until it crystallized. Keeping it in that medium state of liquid was an exercise in concentration and stamina.

"Gravvy!" my sister said as she rushed across the room to tackle me with a hug. The drop of liquid mana that had been about to drop off my finger went flying into the air, where it flashed apart back into its natural state. Her eyes wide, Senica watched it disappear while she ignored my glare.

"What was that?" she asked.

"Just a magic thing. Don't worry about it," I said as I looked past her to see Father standing in the door frame.

"Sorry to visit so late," he said. "Senica wanted to come see you. She was not happy that she was asleep when you came to visit us."

"I don't see why you have to live out here anyway," she complained.

"Well, partially it's because I use my magic to help the Arborists. We're fixing up all the greenhouses and building a new one, and making the trees grow healthier so there's more fruit for everyone. And partially it's because they're afraid I'll blow something up in the middle of the village and people will get hurt. This was a compromise as a place to live that's not too close to the middle of everything."

"They're still working on a new home for you on the east side where there are no fields," Father said.

"Are they? No one has mentioned it to me since it was floated as an idea before I ended up here."

"There were a few guys working on it, but it's a slow process. We'll probably have another harvest in before it's done."

"I'm sure the Arborists will appreciate it," I said as I extracted myself from Senica's hug so that I could relocate the bowl to a safer spot on a shelf. "They haven't said anything, but I get the sense this place was being used for storage, and none of them are thrilled about giving up a corner in their own homes for all the things that used to be in here."

"What have you been doing here?" Senica asked.

"Mostly teaching people how to use magic," I said. "Making glass for the greenhouses. Preventing insects from getting into the trees."

I wasn't about to tell anyone that I'd brought my core up to stage two. Noctra's experiments told me that the concept of a mana lattice wasn't unknown to the local mages. He might not have known exactly what the best lattice for himself was, but he was smart enough to have tried to figure it out. It was safe to assume the other mages in his cabal might have the same knowledge.

I could be facing several mages with stage three cores. If that was the case, I needed every advantage I could get, which right now meant stockpiling as much mana as I possibly could. My next piece of equipment might need to be a larger mana crystal at the rate I was going.

My current mana crystal would give me everything I needed to handle one stage three mage. If I got lucky, I could take on two. I would have to catch them completely off guard in order to kill three mages.

"Insects? That sounds boring and gross," Senica said.

"It can be both of those things," I agreed. "And not all insects are bad, but these ones were."

"Maybe I should learn how to do this," Senica said, a thoughtful frown on her face. "Would it help Mom in the garden?"

I glanced over at Father and asked, "She needs help in the garden? It looked fine to me."

"No, no. I've been giving the full tithe amount for the whole family so your mother can get the garden back in order and your sister can practice."

That explained why Senica still had mana in her core less than an hour after the tithing. She should have been running on empty and exhausted enough to already be asleep.

"And I've been practicing a lot!" Senica announced. "Father showed me how to do the stuff you taught him."

"Really? Can I see?" I asked.

I wasn't expecting much. I'd already taken a measure of Senica's talents and while she was good for a child, that wasn't that same as just being good. I was sure that if she kept at it, one day she'd be a prime candidate to learn magic, but that day was still years down the road.

Mana swirled in Senica's core, slowly at first, but faster and faster as she concentrated on it. I shot Father a look, knowing he could also feel Senica's mana move, and he nodded back. "Huh," I said. "How about that."

The mana jumped out of her core, flashing down her limbs and back again, just like she'd done back in the wastes, except much faster now. Then an orb of it manifested in her hand. She threw it up into the air, where it perfectly maintained its shape without leaking a single bit out, before she caught it in her other hand and absorbed it back into her core.

The entire time she was doing that, her mana kept spinning, faster and faster. She wasn't quite up to the point where I'd let her complete an ignition ritual on her own, but she could probably do it if she was given enough mana. Against any expectations I had, she was inexplicably ready to move her core to stage one right now, at least if I helped her.

"That's... very impressive," I said.

"Like I said, I've been practicing a lot," she told me smugly.

"Father, how much time have you spent on practice with her?" I asked.

"Not too much. They'd been working me pretty late up until last week. I went over what you taught me and made sure she was doing it right, and she's just been going at it on her own every night."

"I bet I'm better than you now," Senica told me.

"Maybe not quite yet," I said. "Give it a few more weeks to practice and I'm sure you'll catch up. I can teach you some other exercises if you'd like."

It took me less than twenty minutes to figure out that Senica was better than any of my current four candidates. Maybe it was the free time, or how much energy she had to goof around and mana was a shiny new toy, or maybe it was just that our family line was talented. It was hard for me to say what Gravin would have been capable of if I hadn't awakened my past life's memories.

I gave brief consideration to performing the ignition ritual on her, but ultimately decided against offering it. Despite her apparent talents, she was still a child, and soon there would be spells circulating through the village. It wasn't impossible to imagine her getting her hands on instructions to cast dangerous magic. Of course, a dormant core by itself wouldn't be enough to stop her, but it would mitigate her ability to practice it to such a degree that she was unlikely to catch anything on fire in the next year or two.

All the same, I made a note to talk to our parents about her progress when she wasn't around. Perhaps finding out that his daughter was so talented would convince Father to reconsider wasting his own mana as a field hand. It also might just get Mother to accept her own ignition, even if all she ever learned were gardening spells.

The pair stayed an hour or so, just long enough to catch up on everything. Mother had come down sick and decided to stay home and rest. Father's duties were more in line with everyone else's now. Senica wasn't necessarily enjoying school, but Cherok hadn't tried to pull any new tricks on our family using her as a weak point.

Other than resolving to stop by sometime in the near future to check on Mother and see if she needed magical healing, it was a good visit. It gave me time to relax, to disengage from work for just a little while. I'd been so focused on creating new tools, training new mages, and piecing together my mana lattice that I'd barely taken time to breathe. Every night, I slept less and less, and I'd begun pulling all-nighters.

"Thank you for visiting," I said. "I didn't realize how much I missed you."

Father gave me a hug on his way out, but didn't linger at my doorway. Senica was already racing ahead, mana faintly coursing through her body to give her more strength and speed. "You should come home more often," he offered as his parting words. "It's not like we're that far away."

"I will," I promised, though it was a lot more complicated than that. I found that I meant that, too. As soon as my preparations were complete, I was going to make more time to see my family, Karad's house arrest be damned.

My temporary home empty once more, I turned back to my bowl of liquid mana. The sooner I finished this step, the sooner I'd have the scrying mirror operational. Then we'd see just how much danger we were really in.

CHAPTER
SIXTY-FIVE

S hel and Karad sat on either side of me and watched my new scrying mirror as it followed after the black-barred hawk. For the last hour, it had flown in a rough circle around the arbor, stopping frequently to rest and scan the ground for prey.

"Are you really sure this is the best use of your time?" the Garrison commander asked. "This bird is... This is nothing."

"This is the only lead I've got," I said. "It's this or just randomly look around the wastelands and hope to spot something. If there is a mage out there and they're smart, they won't be in the open anyway. It would take far more mana than we've got to effectively find them through magic alone."

The hawk lifted off suddenly and all three of us leaned forward. Usually it took short flights of a few seconds here and there, but this time it was rising up into the air and not showing any signs of coming back down. I sat back, a satisfied grin on my face, and said, "Now let's see where you go when you're not here."

The fact that the hawk wasn't wheeling around through the sky, circling endlessly in search of food, gave me hope. It was on a mostly straight course west and north of the village and would arrive at the mountains in minutes. While it was possible it had a nest there and I'd find nothing of interest or importance at the end of its journey, I didn't think that was going to be the case.

Sure enough, the hawk entered a cave halfway up the side of the mountain and I willed my scrying sensor to follow it. Inside, a sort of rough home had been set up, with a bedroll for sleeping on, a rug, and a small workbench. The owner of those supplies was sitting near a campfire that clearly burned only through the power of magic since it lacked any wood.

He was a man, probably fifty or so years old by the looks of him, but possibly much older if he was using magic to prolong his life. For all the wrinkles on his face and his gnarled hands, he certainly moved like a man half his age. He lifted an arm for the hawk to settle on, completely ungloved, and it landed gracefully enough that the man didn't even flinch as its talons circled around his arm.

"That's either a very, very well-trained bird, or there's magic involved," I said. "I think we can safely assume we've found a mage who's interested in the village. I suppose it could be a coincidence and this person has nothing to do with the cabal, but that's stretching things."

"Can your spell let us hear him?" Shel asked as she leaned closer to study the man's appearance.

"Not through the mirror, unfortunately. I'd need another day to modify it for that."

"It's real, then. There really are hostile mages watching the village. What do they want?" Karad asked.

"My guess would be the mana that's going into the ward stone," I said. "They obviously know about it. The real question is whether they'll be reasonable and accept that Noctra's dead, or if they'll try to take over and resume his operation."

"I got the impression that he wasn't here voluntarily," Karad said.

"Iskara was his keeper," I agreed. "She was the one handling all the draw stones. To me, that says not only was he not here by choice, but he wasn't even trusted by the cabal to hand over the mana he harvested. That doesn't sound like an organization that's interested in taking 'no' for an answer. What I really wonder about was if the governor before Noctra was also associated with them."

"I don't see how he could have been. The ward stone worked back then and there was no tithe. What mana was there to give them?" Karad asked.

That was a good point. It was far more likely that the Wolf Pack was aware of our little village and wanted Emeto to join their cabal, but he'd refused. They'd eventually learned about his death and sent one of their junior members who was in trouble with the cabal out to manage the place and turn it into a mana farm. I had no proof, of course, but everything in my theory made sense.

"So what now? Do we wait for this mage to come to us or go attack him first?" Shel said.

"*We* don't do anything," I told her. "I am going to continue to investigate before I make a move. It looks like this mage is here by himself, and he is most likely part of Noctra's cabal, but we don't know for sure. I can't imagine there being another person living in this camp with him, but there could be other camps."

"Why would they come separately?" Karad asked. "That doesn't make sense."

"Only if they're part of the same group. Whoever this mage is, he's been observing us for over a week and hasn't made a move. What is his goal? Is he going to just gather information and then leave? Is he even part of the Wolf Pack?"

"You think he might not be?" Karad asked, a look of confusion on his face.

"No, I'm sure he is. But there's a possibility that I'm wrong, and I'd rather not attack an innocent man who's just looking around. Taking someone's life just because he's acting suspicious without any proof isn't the way I want to go about handling this situation."

There'd been a time when I would have already killed the man, back when I was paranoid that everyone was out to get me. Considering the awful things I'd done, it was an entirely justified paranoia, but it had led me down an even darker road that resulted in a lot more death and destruction, most of which could have been avoided.

"I would say that I applaud your restraint if the situation were different," Karad said, "but can we afford to continue to let this mage set up whatever plans he's working on? We should at the very least capture and secure him while you investigate."

"How do you plan to do that?" I asked. Even if the mage's core was only at stage one, I'd need to stand guard over him constantly to keep his mana drained below a usable level. There were other ways to do it, but they were mildly torturous and included things like driving spikes made of draw stone into the man's body.

Even incapacitating spells like sleep didn't tend to work well on mages.

Anyone who knew what they were doing would absorb the artificial enchantment core even if they were unconscious. The spell might even fail to take hold at all if they were aware it was coming and good enough to fight it off. It wasn't impossible to make it work, but it would require a huge investment of mana to overcome a mage's natural resistance.

That was just for a mage with a stage one core. At stage three, it would take the entirety of my mana crystal to put that mage down even for a few minutes, and I'd need to take him by surprise. Since my scrying mirror didn't let me sense mana, I had no way to tell what kind of fight I'd be walking into right now. I needed to plan for the worst and hope I'd be pleasantly surprised.

"We could use the draw stones," Karad said.

"No," Shel told him. "Even I can resist those easily now. Anyone with a bit of practice can figure it out. I've actually been wondering how many people have been doing it all along with the nightly tithe. Ayaka has been telling me that the Collectors keep records and have suspected some people figured out how years ago and just kept it quiet."

"What a mess."

"It's temporary," I said absently as I leaned closer to the mirror. The mage in question had finished feeding his hawk scraps of meat and it had flapped over to a perch set up for it. Now he was writing something down in a journal, but I was wary about getting the scrying sensor closer to him so I could read it. I'd taken measures to keep it shrouded and undetected, but the closer I got, the more likely it was that he'd notice it anyway.

"How long is temporary?" Karad asked.

"I don't know," I said.

I hadn't seen evidence of wards, but if there were any, they'd be set up at the mouth of the cave. Sending my scrying spell deeper in would risk alerting the mage, no matter how well I'd hidden my magic. I just couldn't quite make out what he was writing from my current angle. If he would turn just a little bit...

The bird must have made some noise, because the mage shifted, turning at the waist to look at it. I saw his mouth move, but I didn't bother to try to read his lips, not with the page finally visible to me. I might only have moments to skim its contents.

Names. It was dozens of the villagers, most crossed out. Ayaka was on there, with an underline. So was my sister, though she had a question mark next to her name. Father and Mother were listed right next to her. Mother also had a question mark, but Father was underlined.

"He's trying to figure out who can use magic," I said. "That's what the spying is for."

Noctra had done the same thing, now that I thought about it. He'd singled Father out based on our Testing results as someone with unusual talent, kidnapped him, and had been in process of sending him to Derro, presumably to his associates there. I wasn't sure what the cabal was going to use them for exactly, but Noctra had made it obvious he didn't care about Father's wishes, only that by delivering what he saw as a magic-capable person, he'd clear some of his own debt.

The mage turned again and blocked my view of the journal he was writing in. He flipped to the back, noted something else down, then tore out a strip of paper. With a practiced motion and likely a bit of mana to seal the paper, he tied it to the hawk's leg. It immediately flew off, and I pulled the scrying sensor back to keep an eye on it.

"He's in contact with somebody," I said. "It would almost have to be someone close by if he's using his familiar to pass notes. Derro is too far away for a hawk to fly there and back in one day, and it's been hanging around the village every day."

I ignored Karad and Shel as they debated what the mage we'd found was up to and what it meant for the village while I chased the familiar through the sky with my scrying sensor. About fifteen minutes later, it dove into some rocky crags southwest of town. There, with their camp hidden by walls of stone, were another six men.

Four of them were dressed in something similar enough that I took it as a uniform: baggy black canvas pants tucked into calf-high boots with sleeveless green tunic belted at the waist. Each was armed with a one-handed ax on their belts, and I spotted unstrung bows with quivers of arrows near their tents. Of the other two, one of them was wearing an outfit that had the same general color scheme, but with a lot more ornamentation on the belt, thick leather bracers, and a band of what looked like rune-etched copper wrapped around one bicep. I mentally pegged him as a commander to the other four.

The last one, the one the hawk had delivered the message to, was obviously a mage. It wasn't the elaborately braided pale-blond hair or the half-dozen rings on his fingers that gave it away. It wasn't even the expensive cloak dyed a dark purple, or the pendant with an amethyst two inches wide on it. No, the real tell was the staff that floated upright next to him while he read the message. It was six feet in height, and I counted no less than four mana crystals studding its surface in a band around the top.

"At least two mages working together and what looks like five hunters," I said. "This is going to be trouble."

CHAPTER

SIXTY-SIX

"I think we can safely presume hostile intent at this point," Karad said. "Just look at all those weapons."

"They would need them just to cross the wastelands. They could be for monsters, not to use on us," Shel argued.

"They're manhunters," I said. "My guess is Noctra's cabal thinks he's fled, and this hunting party was sent to run him down and remind him of his obligations. But then they got here and found out he's actually just dead."

They certainly hadn't wasted any time in arriving. If anything, they'd have had to have left almost before I killed Noctra to get here so quickly. It made me wonder if it was Iskara's death that had triggered this expedition. I hadn't noticed a Dead Man's Seal on her prior to killing her, but it wasn't outside the range of possibility. They were easy enough to break, and it was possible I'd just missed the flash of mana when it detected that its host had expired, especially since she'd died down on the ground below us.

I could easily picture a candle flaring to life in some room miles and miles from here. A shadowy figure hidden in thick robes would note it, report Iskara's death, and the cabal would immediately dispatch their hunters after the most likely culprit: Noctra himself trying to slip his leash. Only, their tracker would arrive at the village and quickly learn that Noctra was dead. He'd delay taking action to report back to Derro, receive new orders to investigate the sudden revival of the barrier and new sources of magic showing up.

It was all entirely plausible in my mind. The only question left was what orders they'd been given. Would they attack and try to capture us? Were they waiting for me to ignite more cores so they could harvest those people as resources to be captured and drained? Was it a recruitment pitch? If so, did we actually have the option to say no? 'Serve willingly or be a slave' was not that unusual a stand for people with power to take, stupid as it was. That was an excellent way to get assassinated by a subordinate looking to obtain their freedom.

"There are some positives here. We've got five people who presumably aren't mages and should be relatively easy to capture and hold onto if needed. Of the two who definitely are mages, they're working together but don't have a means of instantaneous communication. If we go after one of them, we'll retain the element of surprise to use against the other one."

If I had to pick a target, it was going to be the mage with the familiar. He was the one gathering information; without him, the others wouldn't know what was going on. Taking out one mage while effectively blinding the other was about as good an opener as I could manage with my limited resources. Even getting to that cave was going to be expensive, let alone fighting.

With my mana crystal completely full, I could manage a teleport there and back, but that would be it. Every spell I cast in that fight would be time I spent waiting to generate more mana before I returned back to the village. Flying would be cheaper, but it carried the risk of being seen on the approach unless I mixed in invisibility, which would easily push the mana cost up past teleportation, even if I only used it for ten or twenty seconds.

Teleportation was better. In. Attack. Out. If I did it right, I'd only be there for ten minutes. All I needed to do was catch the mage off-guard, overpower him long enough to ask some questions, and then, depending on the answers, possibly kill him before I teleported back. It would take something like ten or eleven days to recover all the mana that few minutes cost me on my own, but it was workable if I relied on the village to supplement my reserves.

In my mirror, the mage had finished reading the message his associate had sent him and was speaking to the hunting party. Even without sound, it was easy to tell he was describing people. Lip reading wasn't something I'd set out to learn, nor was it a skill I'd used in a long, long time. It had been well over a thousand years since I was so unskilled that I couldn't weave sound into my scrying. And never had I been as mana starved as I was now, not even as a child in my previous life.

Despite my lack of proficiency, I caught enough words to get the general gist of it, and him holding his hand up at certain heights as he described new targets made it easy to confirm. That combined with the fact that I recognized the underlined names in the other mage's journal told me everything I needed to know.

"They've got targets picked out," I said. "Probably planning an abduction."

"Me and the other students," Shel said. "Who else?"

"My family," I told her. "I didn't get a long look at the paper, but the obvious connection was anyone doing magic or associated with it in some way. I wouldn't be surprised if there was another list of important people, like the rest of the council. They might also go after the Barrier Wardens individually to prevent any sort of alarms."

"We'll be ready for them," Karad said. "I'll go speak with Solidaire right now and get messages out to everybody. Those crags are miles away. By the time they get here, we'll be in place to stop them."

This left me with a bit of a dilemma. I could go after the familiar-using mage and expend all of my mana in a sneak attack that would leave the enemy blinded and likely unable to get a message back to Derro, though killing the mage might also activate a hidden Dead Man's Seal. If I did that, I'd need to rely on the Garrison and Barrier Wardens to defend us from that other group, and if their mage was in any way competent, that would result in people dying.

The worst part of this was that I still didn't know their true goals. I was predicating my entire strategy on assumptions I was making, admittedly ones that were looking more and more likely to be correct by the minute. I needed more time, and it didn't look like I was going to get it. If it came down to people in the village getting hurt or people invading it with a capture or kill list, I knew what I'd choose.

"Do either of you know if we've got any spare mana in storage?" I asked. "Anything at all that wasn't fed into the ward stone this evening?"

Curse my thoroughness, I'd already cleaned up every bit of mana I could find. The emitters used for Testing were spotless now, as was every single bit of the manor. I'd gone out of my way to hunt it all down, even to the point of consuming all of Noctra's stockpiled, if subpar, resources.

"Well, there's a draw stone here," Shel said. "I'm not sure how much mana it's got in it. Nobody's used it in weeks."

Even if it was at capacity, that wasn't going to be nearly enough. I'd need a different strategy if I wanted to address the incoming threat and the mage acting as a scout. And I'd need to come up with it right away, since it looked like we'd gotten lucky enough to get warning of an imminent attack just before it happened. The hunters were gathering up their gear, but only the stuff they'd need for a fight. It looked like they were planning a raid that ended with a retreat from the village once their goals were met.

Its mission complete, the hawk went back on the wing. I took a moment to study the angle and confirm that it was coming back to the village, probably to scout for the approaching hunters. That settled the attack order for me. I needed to take out the mage bonded to that familiar first.

"Could you pull the mana back out of the barrier?" Karad asked. "It's not going to do us a lot of good against other humans, anyway."

"Theoretically, I could drain it, but that would almost certainly damage the ward stone itself."

It would do for a last resort tactic, but I had another idea. With a thought, I shifted the scrying mirror back to the mage hiding in the cave up in the mountains north of the village. "There's enough mana in this mirror for it to hold this view for another ten minutes," I said. "If something goes wrong and I don't come back, well, adjust your plans accordingly."

"Wait, what are you doing?"

"Taking a piece off the board," I said. "Now stop distracting me. This isn't as easy as I make it look."

Teleportation was a master tier spell. Even in my prime, there had been few mages capable of casting it. It required mastery of both the conjuration and divination disciplines and, unless the caster had reached at least stage five, it was so mana hungry that it was impossible to cast directly from internal mana reserves. That forced the mage to rely on channeling mana from an external source while trying to weave together a spell at the absolute highest ranking for difficulty.

It took me about five minutes to weave the whole thing together, and by the time I finished, my mana crystal was down to around forty percent. I'd either slightly overestimated how much I had available or I'd underestimated the transference loss. It was a good thing I wasn't planning on teleporting back when I was finished, or that plan would be completely shot. It would take hours to amass enough mana to pull off a second teleportation now.

The spell took hold, and I was hurled through the Astral Realm to land just outside the cave, where I immediately noticed two things. First: I hadn't eaten in a while and that meat smelled really good. Second, and more importantly: the enemy mage only had a stage one core. It held three times as much mana as mine, but that was a function of his age, not any advancements he'd made.

I'd shrouded my own mana usage as much as possible, but there was still a slight chance that he'd noticed me. If he was anything like Noctra, I didn't need to be concerned. I was expecting a higher level of skill since presumably these mages were in good standing with their cabal and hadn't spent a significant portion of their life running a backwater mana farm. That probably translated into more time spent training and more access to the kinds of resources mages consumed to grow stronger.

It wouldn't make a difference to this mage, in the end. The only thing he could affect was just how much mana it took to take him out and whether I was forced to kill him. Life sense gave me his position and told me he was facing away from me. Weight reduction reduced my already soft footsteps to practically nothing, and shadow cloak let me slip into the darkness hanging around the outside walls of the cave.

The mage had a trio of candles lit on his writing desk where his journal lay open. He was using ink that I detected as faintly magical, probably imbued with standard enchantments to aid in longevity and keep it from fading. I could sense a mana crystal hidden under his clothes over his chest, perhaps strung on a necklace, and he had a wand in an arm sheath on his left forearm, ready to be drawn and have deadly magic channeled through it at a moment's notice.

None of that mattered, since I wasn't intending to give him that notice. I ghosted forward through the dark, cloaked in magic specifically designed to make me functionally impossible to see, and prepared to attack.

CHAPTER
SIXTY-SEVEN

I knew the force bolt was a mistake the instant I let it fly. It wasn't that the enemy mage had spotted me or that his reflexes were so great that he was going to twist out of the way. No, it was the light welling up from under his shirt. The shield ward snapped into existence and shattered my force bolt an instant before it would have taken the mage in the back of the head.

Without getting a look at the inscriptions, I couldn't know for sure what the shield ward was designed to defend against, but I judged from the light patterns coming through the shirt that it looked like the runes had been etched across the surface of an extra-wide leather belt. I was betting they were about fourteen times bigger than mine, so if I assumed both sides of the belt were being used—a terrible idea, since the runes would get worn down on the inside length, but which would make the shield ward twice as strong while it lasted—there wouldn't be enough surface area for the inscription to have more than two or three possible triggers.

The most likely probability was that it deflected only magic, and that it would have at most enough mana for five or six spells. I doubted I'd over-power the shield ward before the mage got a chance to fight back, and while my own shield ward was fully charged and sophisticated enough that there probably wasn't anything he could throw at me to actually break through it, there were far more efficient ways to take him out.

The mage was already spinning toward me as I cast my next spell. He had just enough time for his face to screw up incredulously and start to say, "What the—"

I cast gravity twist onto the ceiling above the mage. Chunks of rock immediately broke apart under their own weight and crashed down on him, propelled entirely by nothing but their own magically bloated weight. Even if his shield ward dispelled the extra weight, they were still heavy and numerous. The mage was half buried under them before he had a chance to react.

Environmental effects were a big weakness in shield wards. It was easy to find ways around their triggers that still relied on magic when a ward could shield its bearer from direct attacks. Far too many mages had met their ends thinking they were invincible because they had a piece of jewelry that would prevent a fire blast from igniting in their faces or an arrow from perforating their lungs. That was one of the main reasons my own shield ward spent so much space defining different trigger conditions, so that it was likely to activate in almost all scenarios.

Of course, there was only so much it could do. If I'd been in that mage's position, my shield ward would have deflected the first ten or twelve stones, mostly dependent on weight, and then failed. It would have given me a second to react and not much else, but that was the whole point, after all.

I wasn't happy with the situation, mostly because I suspected I'd killed the mage. It didn't help that using gravity twist had cost me more than three times as much mana as a simple force bolt, but I hadn't had a lot of time to weigh my options between discovering his shield ward and giving him time to attack me. I should have predicted something like this and prepared accordingly, but I'd underestimated him.

It was funny, in a macabre sort of way. I'd devoted so much effort to considering scenarios and how to effectively combat them, then missed a simple, basic, obvious one. Worse, it was one I myself had prepared as a defense, and hadn't thought that someone else might have as well. I could say that it wasn't reasonable to expect such a defense, that thus far, every spell caster I'd met had been about as skilled as a second-year apprentice and only half as well equipped.

Reality didn't care about excuses. The simple fact was that I'd slipped up and accidentally killed a mage I was trying to capture alive. If I'd had time to think, I would have prepared something that could have overwhelmed the shield ward and allowed me to hit the mage with a mana drain. I could have restrained him and asked a few questions.

But no, I'd gone into the fight jittery, acted reflexively when I'd encountered an unexpected obstacle, and failed to accomplish half of my objectives. The mage was dead, and I fully planned on looting his body, but I didn't get the chance to ask him a single question. I hadn't even stolen his mana; that had all dissipated with his expiration.

Greater telekinesis shifted the rocks that had bludgeoned the mage to death aside, revealing a bloody mess. His face was unrecognizable, and his skull had been split open. Unfortunately for me, the wand had been snapped by an unlucky strike directly to its length. I wasn't terribly upset by the loss, if for no other reason than it was worthless to me and there were no other mages to pass it on to in the village. I'd craft something better for my would-be apprentices later. The mage's mana crystal had also been damaged by the collapsing stone to the point where it wasn't worth salvaging, so I left it on the body.

The man's belt was still intact. I used telekinesis to pull it off of him for examination later, then gave the body a once-over to see if I'd missed anything. Two pieces caught my eye. One was a wristband made of leather, something that I probably wouldn't have given a second thought to except I remembered the mage's familiar landing on the same arm the wristband was on. Tugging it off revealed a string of runes carved on the inside that, at first glance, looked to be a simple spell that sheathed the forearm in protective force magic.

That and the belt would both be useful, since anyone able to manipulate their mana well enough could channel some into the items to generate the spell effects. I had half a dozen people back at the village who could manage that, including my sister. Someone would find a use for these items.

The last thing I noticed on the body was a signet ring on one hand. It wasn't enchanted in any way, and since precious metals lacked value to a master transmuter, I wasn't inclined to steal it to sell, but when I noticed the insignia, I had to get a closer look. It was a stylized wolf's head with one eye closed and a line drawn through it.

I'd already known it was likely these mages were part of the same cabal Noctra had ties with. This served as a simple reinforcement of that, but it was nice to have a bit more proof that I hadn't murdered a nosy but ultimately harmless recluse. I hadn't been inclined to believe that even before

I'd found the ring, not with the hawk serving to send messages to that group of hunters, but every little bit of proof that I was correct in my thinking helped.

It was far too easy to kill because it was convenient, and I knew first-hand that the more I saw murder as the first resort to my problems, the worse they'd get in the long run. I wasn't about to slide back into that dark pit again, but it did highlight one simple fact: it was a lot harder to find alternate solutions when I was so weak. Power normally gave me a breadth of options I was now lacking.

I turned the ring over a few times to look at it from all angles before slipping it into my pocket. Mostly, I was trying to remember if Iskara had one like it on her finger. If so, I hadn't noticed it before her body was tossed over the cliff to the scavengers. Noctra definitely hadn't had such a ring, but from everything I'd learned, he was in bad standing with the cabal. I wasn't even entirely sure if he'd been part of it originally, or just a rogue mage who owed them a lot of mana for some reason, though I suspected the former.

With the mage's body as thoroughly looted as it was going to get, I took a few minutes to rifle through everything else. I didn't want to waste mana coming back out here later, and I knew I had at least half an hour before the other mage with his hunting party reached the village. Other than the journal detailing the results of his spying on the village, there was nothing really worth the effort of taking. I certainly didn't need a rug or a dead man's bed roll.

I'd regained some mana, but not enough to teleport back home. That was all part of the plan. Now that I didn't need to worry about a mage who specialized in spying seeing me, I simply walked back outside the cave, made sure I had everything secured, and cast a flight spell. True flight was much different than the trick I'd done combining elemental manipulation with weight reduction to drift along on a sustained gust of air. That had let me move two or three times faster than walking, and it was fine for how much mana it used when circumstances allowed it.

An actual flight spell hurled me through the air so fast that one of the components of it was an actual shield of force shaped something like in a curved dome in front of my body to prevent damage from the wind as it streamed by. Flight made without it was uncomfortable at best, and could result in actual injuries.

I burst into the air, mana draining out of me far, far faster than I could replace it and quickly devouring the reserves in my mana crystal. I clutched my prizes close to my body as I flew face first to reduce the size of the shield I needed. The wastes stretched out below me, looking like nothing so much as a sandbox someone had scattered a handful of rocks in. As I approached the village, the trees of the arbor were a brown smear in the distance.

It was only in the last mile or so that I began my descent directly into the arbor. As I dropped low, I noticed a hawk in the sky, circling the village. Bereft of its connection to its master, it would soon revert back to a normal bird. There existed the possibility that another mage could form a bond with it to try to salvage any new information it had acquired, but such bonds were permanent, and breaking them was damaging to the mage and the familiar both.

I could have killed it easily then, but it was nothing more than a relatively harmless hawk now. Other than being a scourge on the local rodent population, it couldn't affect the fate of the village, and I suspected it was only here at this point because this was where its last job had taken it before I'd killed its master. Other than using sharpened senses to confirm it didn't have a return message from the blond-haired mage tied to its leg, I left it alone.

One thing about flight spells that took a bit of getting used to was the descent. Going up wasn't a problem, and maintaining altitude was easy as long as the caster wasn't afraid of falling, and wasn't stupid enough to run out of mana, but coming back down was a different story. There were two ways to do it: the easy way and the fast way. Given how badly I needed to manage my mana these days, I chose the fast way.

It felt like my stomach was doing backflips for about ten seconds as I plummeted in what was close to a free fall, only for the flight magic to catch hold and slow me down in short order. That was somehow an even more nauseating sensation, but it resulted in both of my feet on the ground in the clearing outside my home.

I took a moment to breathe and reflect that it hadn't been as bad as the last few times I'd been flying, no doubt a perk of my new, young body. Then I ran back to my house to get my scrying mirror retargeted. I'd taken care of one problem, but another, arguably much bigger, threat still loomed.

CHAPTER
SIXTY-EIGHT

K arad and Shel were both waiting for me, the former looking upset and the latter looking ill. "What was that?" Karad demanded as soon as I walked through the door, one of his fingers jabbed in the general direction of the scrying mirror. "I thought you said you weren't going to kill him."

"I wasn't planning on it. I didn't expect him to have a shield ward and I didn't have a lot of time to come up with an alternate solution before he started throwing spells back at me. Yes, I could have used a different spell that would probably have subdued him without killing him. If I'd been able to think of one in the second I had, I'd have used it. I wasn't, and I'm not going to apologize for valuing my own life over an enemy, one that is spying on us and reporting that information back to an armed, hostile force that's probably even now heading towards us unprovoked."

"There was so much blood," Shel said with a shudder. She glanced at me once and then closed her eyes. "And you just started taking things off a dead body."

Her squeamishness was a bit of a surprise, but some people were just like that. Additionally, the village was itself relatively peaceful. There were occasional fights that ended with punches being thrown and farmers spending a night in the only jail cell in the entire village to cool off, or getting publicly caned in the square, but even those were rare. The village just didn't have enough people to have a lot of what I considered to be crime. It was too easy to get caught doing something here.

I wouldn't be at all surprised to learn that Noctra's death was the only murder in living memory and that most villagers were squeamish about death. Not even the farmers were immune, especially since so many of them were field workers growing crops. The village's supply of livestock was rather pathetic, with most of what they kept being chickens. There wasn't a lot of slaughtering going on here, and besides, killing a chicken and killing a man were not the same at all.

"Believe it or not, most places aren't as nice and friendly as we are here," I said. "The spoils of war are a very real thing, and I'm not just talking about pretty jewelry and metal cookware. I haven't flipped through this whole book yet, but I think it's safe to assume this is going to be a slave raid. This team is here to capture whoever they can, with valuable targets having already been located in advance, kill whoever's left, and loot whatever's valuable."

"With six people?" Karad scoffed.

"At least one of those people is a mage," I said. "Don't think for a second that I couldn't kill every single person in this village in less than ten minutes if I wanted to. If that mage is in any way worthy of that staff he has floating next to him, he'll be able to do the same. I'm going to be spending most of my remaining mana trying to stop him from burning down homes and fields."

In truth, I was slightly regretting killing the other mage first. I didn't want either reporting back to the cabal and he seemed far more likely to get away, plus he was the easier target, but it had taken a huge toll on my mana reserves. I would need a week of doing nothing else but rebuilding them to recover to full capacity, which was a mental calculation I was heartily sick of doing.

My old stage nine core generated mana close to fifty times faster than my current stage two core did, or roughly three thousand times faster than my core when it had still been dormant. I had very rarely had to worry about conserving mana then, and had plenty of tricks to speed up my recovery by using ambient mana if it became necessary. Compared to back then, I was constantly frustrated at how slow and weak my new body was.

But my back and my knees didn't hurt anymore, so that was something.

"Have you started making preparations to defend the village?" I asked.

"I sent one of my people to go round up the Garrison for him," Shel said. "We were waiting for you to get back so we can check on the other group before Karad leaves to give orders."

That wasn't the worst plan I'd ever heard, assuming whatever runner they'd sent did their job. It did have one big hole, though. "What about the Barrier Wardens?"

"Solidaire's got the patrol schedule. I'll need to get with him to even figure out where everyone is," Karad said. "Just hoping there's enough time."

At least he was aware of the flaw in his plan. I activated the scrying mirror and studied it for a second, then said, "It appears we're in luck. They've stopped for some reason."

All six men were grouped closely together. The five hunters were in a loose circle facing outwards with the mage in the center. I could see a bit of tension in their stances, but none of them looked overly worried. They were ready for trouble and confident that they'd handle it when it came.

"What are they doing?" Shel asked as she looked over my shoulder.

"Probably encountered a monster," Karad said. "Maybe we'll get lucky and it'll take care of our problem for us."

"I wouldn't bet on it," I said. "Not with that mage there."

One of the men pointed at something, and the mage turned to face that direction. I could see his mouth moving as if he was shouting his incantation as he made some vague gestures with his staff in the direction the hunter had indicated. A few seconds later, a pillar of stone thicker than a man at its base and tapered to a delicate point at the end erupted out of the dirt. Hanging from it, bloody and thrashing, was a monster that looked somewhat like a turtle, if they were vaguely bipedal and nine feet tall.

The stone pillar had punctured its underside and come out at an angle through one of the leg holes in its shell. At the mage's command, three of the hunters started filling it with arrows while the rest continued to scan the environment.

That scene repeated itself two more times before the group allowed themselves to relax. The hunters went about recovering what arrows they could while the mage took a moment to collect himself. I couldn't feel his mana expenditure through the scrying mirror, but I knew how much it would cost me to cast a stone spear spell like that. It was about twice the maximum amount my mana core could even hold right now. A normal adult without a stage three core would be able to cast that precisely once before they needed to recover mana in some way.

"Spirits protect us," Karad said. "How are we supposed to fight against someone who can do that?"

"You're not. That's my job," I told him. "Your job is to protect the targets the hunting party will be looking for."

I didn't mention that I'd be doing their job as well, at least for my own family. It wasn't that I didn't trust the Garrison to try its hardest. I just didn't think they'd win. I needed to find and stop the enemy mage before doing anything else, but I also needed to keep an eye on my family so I could defend them. In fact, it might just be better to round up all the priority targets and put them somewhere safe.

Where would that safe place be, though? It couldn't be somewhere obvious from their spying. That eliminated the arbor as an option. Noctra's former home was too big to effectively defend and was another obvious place to check. But we *could* evacuate the entire village there. If we concentrated every member of the Garrison and Barrier Wardens in one place, it might work.

It was too bad the barrier itself couldn't be altered to help us right now. Once it powered down in a few hours, I could make alterations to the ward stone, but not while it was active. One of the biggest drawbacks to inscriptions was that they ran until they were out of mana. Enchantments could be deactivated at will, but an inscription, once fed mana, would do whatever it was designed to do for as long as it could. Trying to change that while it was running could have disastrous results.

"What do you think about pulling the entire village back to the manor?" I asked.

"If you can take care of the mage, it's a good idea. We can lock and barricade the doors," Karad said. "But if you can't... well, it puts everyone together in a nice convenient box to be killed."

"If I can't stop the mage, it's not going to matter much," I mused out loud. "It boils down to where we want to stand our ground. We got a lucky break catching onto this whole scheme just before it came down on us, but it doesn't leave us with a lot of time to set up defenses or lay traps. Our choice is whether to fight them in the village, or rush out to meet them in the wastelands."

"If we don't have cover, those hunters are going to pick us apart with their bows when we approach," Karad said.

The best option wasn't realistic. If I'd had the mana, I'd have gone out myself and ambushed them out in the wastes. I just didn't have enough left to get more than a mile outside of the village before I ran into them, not if I wanted to still be able to fight after. Plus, leaving the village potentially meant dealing with monsters. The odds were slim, but as we'd just seen, there were a few of them still roaming around.

"We've got a few bows, right? A couple of the Barrier Wardens are hunters?"

Karad and Shel exchanged uncertain looks, and he replied, "Maybe one or two? Not enough to match them either way."

This village sure wasn't going out of its way to make it easy to save them. Every plan I thought of failed immediately because there wasn't enough time, manpower, or mana. Sad as it was to say, the most likely role the villagers could play in the upcoming battle was that of a distraction. If that was all they were good for, we might as well lean into it.

I fed a bit more of my precious mana into the mirror and pulled it away from the hunting party just as they got moving again to scan the path between them and the village. For the most part, it was open wastes with a few rocky hills here and there. Usually, the ground was baked and cracked earth, but sometimes it was sand. There were always ways around the sandy patches, and I didn't think having a bit more footwork to do would make a lot of difference in slowing them down, anyway.

I scried all the way to the edge of the fields without finding what I was looking for. Well, if it didn't exist, I'd just have to make it. There was a small hill near the south edge of the fields that I could modify to suit my purposes.

"Alright, this is where we'll make our stand," I said.

"That's wide open! They'll pick us off easily," Karad objected. "And even if they don't, there's nothing stopping them from going around and ignoring us."

"I'll make you some cover, and keeping their attention is why we have bows of our own. I need you to get at least a dozen men, as many bows as you can, and meet me at this hill. We've got at best half an hour before they get here," I said. When Karad didn't move, I dismissed the image in the mirror and said, "Well? Go!"

CHAPTER

SIXTY-NINE

I 'd picked this particular hill for two reasons. First, I was making an educated guess about what path the hunting party would take on its arrival, assuming they moved in a relatively straight line. Second, it was the only possible defensive point anywhere near the projected route our enemies would take.

As we moved, I explained my plan to Karad. "Essentially, I'm going to hollow out the crown of the hill. Your men will be able to kneel down in there and have total cover. The idea is that if the enemy wants to progress through that way, they'll have to go through your bow range. If they go around, it'll take them more time and allow you to chase after them."

"Which we don't want to do, since we'll be in the open, too, and they're going to have a lot more bows than us," Karad said.

"Right. Unfortunately, there's not a lot of cover out there, so I don't see a better option. Besides, how many ranged weapons do we have?"

"Just bows? One or two. Most of the Barrier Wardens also carry slings. I'll spread them around the outskirts of the village so they can use the homes as cover after we get everyone to the manor."

I nodded. "I'll take care of the mage. The hunters are up to you guys. Try not to shoot me."

"How are you going to do that?" Karad asked.

That was a good question. The primary hurdle was going to be getting the man in range without being spotted. My initial thought was to hide somewhere and wait for them to pass by, but that relied on correctly guessing their route and their incompetency. Presumably, these men were expert hunters and trackers. Absent any magical camouflage, there was every possibility that they'd notice me hiding well before they reached me.

Banking on a plan that relied entirely on an enemy to make a mistake was a terrible idea. I would need to be more active in creating openings, ideally ones where the hunters were preoccupied with Garrison and Barrier Warden forces, leaving me free to take out the mage without interference. At the same time, I couldn't burn all my mana creating that scenario, not if I wanted to have any left for the fight itself.

I wasn't happy about the circumstances I'd been faced with. The only other feasible option I could see was to fight in the village itself, but we'd have to spread our people thin to cover all the different approaches, too thin to effectively fight back. At least this way, if the hunters wanted to circle around the hill, they'd have to go wide and they'd leave themselves open to being harassed from the back.

"It'll depend on how well you guys distract them," I said. "I'd like to sneak up on him, but I'm not going to manage it with all six of them wary and looking around for trouble."

Karad peeled off to go round up his men and get them started on evacuating the villagers to Noctra's manor house. At least, I assumed that was where he was sending everybody. It didn't really matter, so long as they weren't in the way of the invading group. I wouldn't be terribly surprised if the huts closest to the fighting got damaged in some way.

It took four casts of stone shape to hollow out the top of the hill like I wanted. By the time I was done, a pair of Barrier Wardens were climbing the north slope to join me. Soon enough, there were twelve people up there. Contrary to Karad's expectations, they had four bows and six slings between them.

Karad himself showed up with the last group and quickly set about giving his people their orders. That wasn't anything complicated, he just told them to keep their heads down and challenge the group approaching the village. They expected, at best case, to get into a long-ranged fight and hoped to keep the enemies at bay with their superior numbers. The most likely result was that they'd force the enemies to go the long way around, and that the village defenders might give chase depending on how that played out. They had additional Garrison and Barrier Warden members stationed in three groups in the village itself, but I didn't think anyone was under the illusion that a group of ten amateur villagers was going to over-power five well-equipped mercenaries and a mage.

"Our blessed child here is going to conjure up some magic to help us, though what exactly that magic does will depend on how this confronta-tion plays out," Karad said with a gesture towards me. "I can't give you any orders regarding him now other than to watch out not to hit him when you're shooting. He'll be out there somewhere doing his best to neutralize the other mage."

"Ridiculous," someone muttered. "He's barely older than a baby."

Karad either didn't hear that or chose to ignore it. My talents might not be well known on an individual basis to the villagers, but they all knew who had fixed the barrier and produced the storage crystals that allowed the village's mana to be stretched much farther.

Explanations and orders finished, Karad turned to me and asked, "How long do we have?"

"I'm not sure. I need to conserve my mana now, but you'll see them as they approach. There's not a lot of cover out here," I said. "I'll be low to the ground in that field over there, so try to do all your shooting before they get that far."

The whole group watched me climb back down the hill and disappear into the two-foot-high stalks of bean sprouts, where I barely even had to hunch down to keep my head from poking up too high. I went in about ten feet, then shifted around until I found a place to lay on my stomach and peer through the stalks to get a good view of the open wasteland.

It wouldn't be long now—just a few minutes.

They arrived in much the same formation we'd seen them use in my scrying mirror, with the hunters in a ring around the mage. I felt his mana long before I saw any of them, and I gave silent thanks that they were mostly taking the path I'd predicted. They were a little bit farther off to the side of the hill than I'd expected, but still well within range of a bowshot. If anything, this trajectory would be even more likely to force them to enter the fields near my hiding place.

I wanted to groan when Karad challenged the approaching group with shouted words instead of unleashed arrows. They certainly didn't waste any time on their entirely predictable response; three of the men pulled their bows off their shoulders and sent some arrows his way. With a surprised yelp that was clearly audible from my position, he ducked back down.

The hunters eyed the hill warily. I doubted they were any sort of surprised when the village's own archers popped into view and let fly a few shafts tipped with hunters' broadheads. Other than noting that the battle had begun, I did my best to ignore the exchange. My focus was on the enemy mage.

My first impression of him was that he was by far the most competent mage I'd met since my reincarnation. His core was shrouded well enough that I could tell he had mana, but not how much. The mana crystals set into the top of his staff were equally hidden. I could pierce the shroud and get an accurate read on his reserves, but not without him noticing.

There was another mana crystal on a ring on his left hand, though once I took a moment to study it, I realized it was actually a low-grade storage crystal being used to power an enchantment in the ring itself. Without getting closer to the mage, I couldn't tell what the enchantment was designed to do, but it looked familiar. I also spotted a belt that looked suspiciously similar to the one I'd taken off the mage with the familiar. Unfortunately for me, there were no stone ceilings to collapse on this guy's head out in the open wastes.

I didn't have so much mana left over that I wanted to waste it tearing through a shield ward, but I could if I needed to. It would have to be fast enough to put the mage down before he was able to pump more mana into it, which wasn't necessarily a problem, but it certainly wouldn't be efficient. It would be far better to circumvent the ward altogether.

That was easier said than done. I was making assumptions about how it worked. My tried-and-true ward testing spells would cost far too much mana to use and, frankly, be massive overkill. I sincerely doubted this mage's wards extended to his astral body, and if they did, I was dead either way. No mage who'd reached that point in their career was going to be beaten by a fresh stage two with limited access to mana, no matter how much they knew.

If I operated under the assumption that I could win this fight, the shield ward probably defended against direct conjurations and possibly physical attacks. It might also ward off enchantments, but I already knew it didn't stop divinations, and I doubted it would contest transmutations, either.

My scouting was interrupted by a stirring in the mage's mana. He was backing up his hunters and, unsurprisingly, casting some sort of earth-based conjuration. Breaking the villagers' cover apart so his hunters could pick them off was an excellent mana-conserving strategy. Magic might be flashier and more impressive when it came to dispensing death, but an arrow through the eye would kill just as quickly.

The spell was actually a good sign. It started at his feet and raced forward through the ground, directly on course to strike the hill. Just the fact that he'd chosen himself as his origin point told me that he probably lacked the skill to manipulate his spell structures in real time to change that. Some spells, like fire blast, had their origin points built in as the target, but the mage was using a spell that would fracture the ground and force the villagers to either flee or be crushed as they fell in, and that started as a thin crack at the mage's feet.

The spell made it about halfway to its target before my own counter spell hit it. Threads of mana unfolded and engulfed the spell, each one doing its best to worm into the rune structure and distort it until it broke. Within moments, the mage's spell fractured and fell apart, leaving nothing but a long, narrow crack in the ground.

Counter spelling was an interesting technique. It wasn't a spell so much as a way to directly manipulate mana. I favored a style I thought of as tentacle dueling, wherein I sent my own mana out in a tightly packed ball of individual appendages that collided with the target spell, then tried to overwhelm it as the tendrils unfolded. It was more useful against stationary, long-term effects like wards and traps, but if the enemy mage was going to throw magic that moved that slowly, I'd easily counter it.

The counter spell wasn't free, of course. But it was flexible in terms of how much mana I could put into it, and I'd definitely used significantly less to break that earth shatter spell than my opponent had poured into forming it. If the spell was close enough to me, I could even recover that mana. In this case, unfortunately, both the earth shatter and my counter spell dissipated into the environment well before I could regain control of it.

I glanced over at the mage, who was standing there with a look of shock on his face. Anger quickly replaced that, and he started weaving a new spell.

Whatever I might have to say about his magical capabilities, I couldn't accuse him of being stupid. That new spell was divination, probably designed to find fellow mages, and he cast it fast enough that I couldn't get a new counter spell in his way before it went off.

The mana washed out in every direction from the mage, invisible filaments searching for anything that met the spell's criteria. Before I could react, the first one settled on me.

CHAPTER
SEVENTY

There was no way I was going to stop that thread of divination-driven mana from touching me. If I'd had more time and set up some wards around the area, I could have deflected it without the mage becoming aware of that, but that was a tricky proposition. It wasn't something I was going to accomplish in the half a second I had before the divination swept over me.

What I could do was give it misleading information. The spell was a basic divination that functioned to detect mana in the area. It wasn't all that reliable in my time, but here, with no background mana to sift through, it would do an excellent job of telling the caster exactly where anybody with a core was. Even hiding my mana with a shroud wouldn't stop the divination from finding me.

It would also find every bit of mana I sent out to brush up against the many other filaments weaving through the area. I sent out two dozen mana threads of my own, each one deftly weaving around the divination and touching it at various points in the field. To the mage, it would seem as if there were a hundred mages hiding in the field.

The drawback to that kind of spell was that it didn't give good feedback. It simply told the caster whether there was mana there, not how strong or what kind. To that mage, there were either dozens of people or dozens of mana crystals in the field. I didn't think for a second that he'd believe either were true, but my hope was that I'd effectively stopped him from narrowing my hiding spot down any further than just somewhere in the field.

My opponent had an obvious solution to that. Mana stirred around him, this time much quicker than his earth shatter spell. The mage held up his staff, all four mana crystals gleaming, and a line of fire shot out into the air over the field, where it broke apart into hundreds of falling sparks that ignited the crops.

Shouts of protest came from the hill, and a hailstorm of stones rained down on the outsiders attacking our village, but the hunters put their bows to good use and quickly forced all the Garrison and Barrier Warden members back behind cover. Their brief salvo provided me with an opening, though, one I wasn't planning on passing up.

While the hunters had their eyes on the hill, I sent out my own spell. Wind burst was strong enough to knock a child to the ground and even stagger a grown man if he wasn't prepared for it, and in this environment, it was strong enough to pick up dust and sand to blind people—and that was exactly what it did. With just a lick of elemental manipulation to keep the sand in the air, it lasted more than long enough for me to cast my next spell.

The mage's shield ward had activated, proving that hostile conjurations were one of the triggers. With the number of mana crystals his staff held, I wasn't keen to fight a battle of attrition against him, so it was time to try something new. Rather than hurl fire or ice his way, I shaped a spell that I wasn't entirely sure would slip past his defenses.

Mind spike was a spell grounded entirely in the divination discipline. I was gambling that his shield ward wouldn't cover it, but if I was right, I might disable him early on in the fight. The spell coalesced in my vision, a single wire of mana connecting it to the mage before a black shard of pain sped away to strike the man at the end of that path.

There was a flare of mana at the final moment, not from the shield ward, but something the mage did himself. He cried out in pain, surprising the hunters that accompanied him, but I couldn't tell how effective my attack had been while the sandstorm was still going around them. I figured I had a few seconds, and I spent that time using elemental manipulation to pull air away from the fires starting to spread through the field. It wouldn't matter if we won today only to have people starve later. The village was nowhere near the point where it had the margins to afford an entire field going up in flames.

A sharp slash of wind cut through my sandstorm, scattering it to reveal a handful of men with faces and arms abraded by the sand, and one mage clutching at his head while angrily glaring in my general direction.

"Enough!" he bellowed. "Come out and face me, you coward."

I certainly wouldn't be doing that. This guy was proving to be surprisingly resilient compared to the other mages I'd killed, and while I would have loved nothing more than to crush him with a single spell, those magics were beyond me for the moment. I wouldn't have been able to use something like aura crash even if my mana crystal had been full. It would have been overkill for this fight anyway, and most of its impact would have been wasted since its primary purpose was to prevent them from generating new mana. It *would* have messed with the mage's ability to draw mana through those crystals, though, limiting him to whatever spells were inscribed on his staff.

While the mage was puffing himself up and striding towards the field, his minions were advancing on our fortified hill. They were working in unison, carefully timing their shots to keep an arrow going every second or so. At that rate, it seemed like they'd run out soon, but they looked more than willing to engage in melee combat.

I needed to end this fight before the hunters reached the villagers, or at least distract the mage long enough to help them. Otherwise, it was practically guaranteed that there would be fatalities in our ranks. It wasn't that I had a problem with a few people dying off, but they were ostensibly my allies, and I had gotten myself deep into a mindset of resource conservation.

"Whoever you are, you can choose to face me willingly, or I will flush you out," the mage declared as he strode forward to face the field.

Mana flared through his staff again and three more lines of flames burst forth, one after another. The whole field was ablaze now, and there was no way I was going to save it without devoting a significant amount of mana to the process. Worse, the mage was steadily burning away my cover. I was almost surprised that he was willing to waste so much of his own mana, but from his perspective, it wasn't wasted if he forced his opponent out of hiding.

With a heavy sigh, I stood up and pushed my way through the stalks to stand at the edge of the field. The mage's jaw worked silently for a moment when I appeared, then he composed himself and said with a slight bow and a flourish of his staff, "I am Ebalnat, Magician of Conjuration and Transmutation."

I blinked in surprise at that. It had been many, many years since any rivals had spoken to me like that. Ebalnat's actions were those of a duelist at the beginning of a match. After a certain point, mages didn't fight duels. If they wanted to kill another mage, they did so as efficiently and skillfully as possible. In fact, it hadn't even been legal in most countries for mages who reached the master rank to duel. There always ended up being too much collateral damage.

My surprise was less that Ebalnat would challenge me to a duel and more that the customs I was so familiar with were present here as well. It forced me to once again ask the question of just where I was. So many things were different from what I expected, but every now and then, something like this cropped up and reminded me that I was still on Manoch after all.

With a sigh, I pulled myself into a proper duelist's stance and gave my own bow. "I am Keiran, Mage."

Back in my youth, it was considered somewhat offensive to give so little information. Judging by the look on Ebalnat's face, that hadn't changed. He gave me a sneer and said, "Lying about your skills won't save you. I'll test them for myself."

Without another word, he cast his first spell at me. This close, I could almost hear him muttering the incantation, and with a slight application of sharpened senses, his words became clear. "*Utrach demios falrit,*" he said, finishing the spell that would char my flesh from my bones.

Except it didn't. My own mana snaked in and ripped it apart as the structure was forming. Ebalnat blinked at me, surprised that his spell had fizzled. I started walking forward. With every step I took, I was able to utilize my counter spell technique faster, and at this distance, he wouldn't get off any spell that took more than two seconds to cast. For him, I was betting that was most of them. Ebalnat must have realized the same thing, because his next spell was a single word.

"*Fring,*" he snapped as he flung a hand out and a blade of ice flashed into existence. Ice blade was a novice spell, notable for training because it combined elements of conjuration and enchantment. It was a good practice spell for new apprentices trying to learn how to join disparate disciplines into a single style.

That did not mean it couldn't kill me if I let it. As simple as it was, it could still slice through my skin. Properly aimed, it could tear my throat open with ease and leave me flat on my back, gasping out my last breaths.

Ebalnat did not properly aim his ice blade. Even if I made no effort to defend myself, it would slice into my arm as it passed by instead of hitting anything vital. I wasn't sure if he was expecting to spook me with the attack and trying to compensate for the direction he guessed I would dodge or if his aim really was that bad, but a single step to the side was enough to let the spell pass harmlessly by. In less than two seconds, it burned through the artificial mana core keeping it solid, and the spell vanished.

Really, I didn't even need to do that much. This was exactly the kind of spell a shield ward was designed to stop. That was why I hadn't bothered to throw basic conjurations back at him. I was almost positive his own shield ward would stop conjurations and ranged physical attacks. I'd already proven he wasn't immune to mind spikes, but he'd shown a surprising amount of resourcefulness in deflecting most, if not all, of the attack using his own mana.

If that was the case, I wondered how he'd do against a physical attack. I cast a quick transmutation to draw a thin blade of stone from the ground and presented it to him while turning my body to the side.

Ebalnat sneered at me and said, "What could you possibly do with that, pretend mage?"

Despite how small it was, it was still stone, and thus quite heavy for my child's body. That was easy enough to fix. Villagers all over were able to increase their strength and stamina just by flushing mana through their body in unstructured invocations. I was aiming to be a bit more efficient than that.

"This spell is called empower," I told Ebalnat.

"That's a stupid name for what is obviously a very mediocre transmutation spell."

The invocation came to life in my body, sending strength and speed through my limbs. The stone blade felt light as air, and I dashed forward, covering the forty feet between us in a few seconds while Ebalnat flailed in surprise and tried to cast some sort of spell.

He didn't manage it before I was inside his shield ward.

CHAPTER
SEVENTY-ONE

I was not an expert swordsman, nor was my body conditioned for combat. I was wielding a rock I'd shaped into the form of a sharp stick. It was an awkward, unbalanced weapon that I was only able to swing around because of the mana coursing through my muscles. Against anybody with some martial training, it would have been an attack doomed to fail.

I stabbed Ebalnat in the leg while he gawked at my approach. He cried out in surprise and tried to club me with his staff, but he didn't have the coordination to strike across his body while simultaneously shifting his weight to flinch back from my strike, even though a mana shield flashed into existence just as the blade struck him.

It was easy to dodge his attack, and now I was inside his shield ward. I could sense the mana flickering in the air behind me, looking for triggers to activate its full defensive potential. That ward was behind my back, and I could already tell that it hadn't been designed with a melee brawl in mind. I swung my fake sword at Ebalnat again, mostly just to keep him off balance, and slapped my free hand onto his leg.

A basic mana shield was good for stopping kinetic strikes and not much else. It was an excellent defense against my haphazardly formed sword. It would even work against conjurations that created solid matter to throw at him. Stabbing or clubbing him was right out. But a mana shield did almost nothing against anything that wasn't some sort of physical attack.

Shocking touch sparked between my fingers and raced through his muscles. Ebalnat's whole body arched as lightning raced through him, and he cried out in pain. He staggered back and tried to put some space between us, but at this point, I was literally close enough to touch him. Any spell that took even a second to cast was fair game to be countered.

I saw him start to weave together a transmutation to reshape the ground, likely to form some sort of wall to split us apart, but I broke it before he could finish the spell. Ebalnat responded by lashing out with his staff, far too quickly for me to parry. My own shield ward flared to life and repelled the blow, causing him to stumble a few steps back.

I chased after him and put another shocking touch into his other leg. Things were getting messy now, our shield wards overlapping, his mana shield flickering as he tried to modify it on the fly to stop my spells, and us circling around each other in some odd game of tag, each trying to touch the other without being hit in return.

Melee brawling had never been a specialty of mine. Prior to my original ignition, I'd preferred to avoid fighting at all, if possible, or to strike from an ambush and end a battle in a single decisive blow otherwise. An enemy who didn't know he was in a fight did not do a good job of defending himself. Once I'd started using magic, I'd kept the same strategies, fighting only when I had to, and always from an advantageous position if I could.

This fight was too much of an uphill battle for me to do that. I had Ebalnat outclassed in skill, but he had me beat in raw mana reserves, and his defenses had been in place well before I'd laid eyes on him. He'd come to the village expecting a fight, one he had no plans on losing. I'd been forced to get in close in order to effectively use any of the spells that had a chance of working, and while he might not have expected that, getting into a fist fight with a grown adult when I didn't even come up to his waist wasn't a great strategy.

It seemed he'd figured out that he wasn't going to get off a spell that took him longer than a single word to cast. He raised his staff, shouted, "*Abratus! Abratus! Abratus,*" and sent three bursts of flame at me. Each one exploded against my shield ward, but rather than dissipating, they lingered on, draining more and more mana from it.

I had a combination of spells that I was confident would get me through that mana shield, but they came with two downsides. First, they would be fatal. There would be no chance to capture Ebalnat and question him. Second, they'd tap me out for mana, so I'd only get one chance, and I'd have almost nothing left to help the villagers or defend myself if the hunters turned on me.

The lethal attack I could live with. Considering the amount of damage Ebalnat had already done, I doubted anyone would hold it against me if I had to kill the mage. The other part, I wasn't happy about. The easy solution might end up getting me killed in the long run if the hunters turned on me. My shield ward wouldn't hold up to concentrated fire from five guys with bows, and I wasn't keen on the idea of leaving my fate in the hands of Karad and his underlings.

Brute force was out, and spells like mind spike and shocking touch weren't getting the job done. By the time I battered down Ebalnat's mana shield, I'd be running on empty. I needed to do something else. Fortunately, I already knew what was going to bypass this shield.

I rushed forward, already weaving the spell in my mind. Ebalnat had grown wary of my touch and was quick to shove his staff between us. I dodged around the tip, trusting my own shield ward to keep me safe. Unlike the other mage's belt, my ward's trigger range started at my skin and radiated outward in every direction. It cost a bit more mana, but I made up for it with conservations in other parts of the spell.

I leaped upward and slapped a hand onto Ebalnat's chest. He was quick to grab hold of me, but not quick enough to prevent me from discharging the transmutation spell I'd cast into his body. The ring in his finger came to life, and now that I was up close, I recognized the spell it contained as a mana drain. It was horrendously inefficient, but that wasn't the point. Ebalnat wouldn't gain any mana from the attack, but draining me completely dry would leave me defenseless.

It would have, if I hadn't just transmuted his heart from living organ tissue to a lump of granite. Ebalnat grunted, gave me a puzzled look, and staggered a single step forward. His staff fell out of his grasp and drifted off to the side, where it floated in the air. The mage grabbed at his chest for just a moment, then his eyes rolled upwards, and he collapsed to the ground.

I missed the finer details of his death while I was busy fighting off his ring's mana drain attack. By the time I'd pried myself loose from his grasp, the only thing keeping him from lying face down in the dirt was my own grip on his wrist. I let go and took a step back, letting him finish his descent to the ground. He'd be dead in seconds, and he was already unconscious.

There was no point in wasting the mana, and since I had a few seconds still, I threw out a mana drain of my own to help replenish my own reserves. I didn't get much out of him—no surprise there. Most of his mana was held in his staff's mana crystals, the same as my own structure. But it was a slight gain, and the mana otherwise would have been wasted upon his death.

It would have been nice to stop right there, but unfortunately, Ebalnat's death did not mean my troubles were over. I still had a field burning behind me, one which I needed to save as much as I could if I wanted the village to have food in the coming months. There were also still five other hostile men attacking us. Even if I had forgotten that fact, one of them reminded me a moment later when an arrow deflected off my shield ward.

I didn't know exactly how many more hits I could block before the ward ran out of mana, and I wasn't eager to find out. Sadly for them, with Ebalnat defeated, there was no one to distract me and no one to protect them. I sent out a round of mind spikes as the quickest way to incapacitate them, and almost as one, four of them collapsed. The last one, the man I had pegged as their leader, had some sort of defensive talisman that allowed him to resist the spell, but without the rest of his crew to back him up, he was quickly overpowered by the village defenders.

"Leave the others alive for questioning," I yelled over at the men before turning my attention to the field itself.

There were thirty or forty fires already spreading, and it would have been worse if I hadn't already worked to mitigate the damage. Elemental manipulation wasn't terribly expensive as far as channeled spells went, but it did take me almost two minutes to finish snuffing out the fires. Someone else would have to go through and assess how much was salvageable.

By the time I'd turned my attention back from the field, Ebalnat had finished dying of a heart literally turned to stone, and the village defenders had killed three of the five hunters. I was guessing the last two had surrendered, and it was only Karad or some other person with a cool head who'd managed to get everyone else calmed down enough to accept it.

There were four bodies on the ground that I recognized. Two were Garrison, two were Barrier Wardens. I couldn't tell from over here if they were dead, but on the off chance that it was possible to save someone, I hurried over. My mana was nearly empty, but I could probably triage a stab wound or three and maybe save someone's life.

I gave Ebalnat's corpse one last glance as I rushed past. His staff, its connection broken with its owner, was laying in the dirt. Later, when I had time, I'd collect the various magical trinkets and study them to see if anything was worth refurbishing. I somehow doubted the mana crystals would be high-quality enough to make it worth claiming the staff as my own, not to mention it would look ridiculous to walk around with a staff that was three feet taller than I was. Maybe if he'd had a nice cane...

By the time I'd reached the hill, both of the enemy hunters who'd surrendered had their hands bound behind their backs using a pair of belts donated by two Garrison men. Each was holding the top of his pants with one hand, a sight that should have looked ridiculous, but the grim looks and the amount of blood everyone had on them killed any amusement I might have had.

Only one of the four from our side who were down needed help, and he probably would have made it without my assistance. He'd taken an arrow in his hip, and when he'd fallen, he'd landed in a bad way that had jammed it through the bone. Extracting it was a work of magic by itself, and while healing the wound wasn't beyond my abilities, it was beyond my means. The man had to settle for a spell to numb the pain and stop the bleeding for now, along with my promise to help him get back on his feet once I had some more mana to work with.

"I think we're done here," Karad said to me soon after I finished working.

I glanced at the two prisoners, already being led back to the village to be placed in the jail. "Somehow, I think we've got a lot more work ahead of us."

"Yes, but not right now. We're safe, aren't we?" he asked.

"For today, probably. What are you going to do with the bodies?"

"Burn them. They were enemies of the village, and I could see it causing issues putting them in the cemetery."

Karad was adapting well to the political lifestyle. "Strip their gear before you burn them," I said. "There are a few magical trinkets in there, and every bit of information helps. Let me know if you find anything interesting on the corpses themselves. Tattoos, ritual scarring, anything like that."

"... Yeah, sure."

SEVENTY-TWO

O ther than examining the prisoners to confirm that their mana cores were dormant and empty, I spent the night recovering and going over the various pieces of enchanted or inscribed gear the party had been carrying. The axes and bows the hunters had were nothing special. Karad would be happy to add them to the village's armory, but I had no interest in them.

Ebalnat's outfit took me longer to go through. Only one of the rings was magic—the mana drain spell he'd tried to hit me with right as I was transmuting his heart into a lump of rock—but I did find another signet ring with a one-eyed wolf's head on it. Idly, I wondered what the story was with the missing eye. It was probably related to the cabal's history in some way.

The mana drain ring itself was a mixed bag. For some reason, Ebalnat had fashioned it with a mana crystal attuned to him, not a storage crystal like I'd first thought. It powered the enchantment that allowed anyone wearing the ring to activate its mana-draining properties. The stolen mana would be siphoned directly into the mana crystal, so there was no real reason to attune it to Ebalnat other than paranoia about it being stolen. Even with him gone, the ring would continue to function until it ran out of mana, which it would unless someone started using it, since no one would be able to recharge an attuned mana crystal.

The amethyst pendant was Ebalnat's primary mana crystal, surprisingly empty and subpar to my own. It reminded me of every other mana crystal I'd seen on a member of the Wolf pack. They obviously had some sort of shared method of growing their crystals, and it did not yield great results. It was serviceable, but this thing was eight times bigger than my own mana crystal and yet its reservoir was half the size. I tossed it to the side to be stored away with the mana crystal bracelet I'd taken off Iskara. Cracking the attunements on them would be good practice for my hypothetical future apprentice someday.

I gave the belt he'd been wearing a cursory examination, but I could tell it was the same as the one that other mage with the familiar had used. Apparently, they were standard issue for Wolf Pack mages. Too bad Noctra hadn't owned one; it would have saved his life. Iskara's status as an adept must not have warranted one, either.

There were only two other objects of interest. Ebalnat's staff was the most complicated piece by far, and I set that aside to examine the copper band the leader of the hunters had been wearing around his left bicep. It was an interesting piece, actually four different inscriptions all on one loop of metal. Each was an invocation, which in my mind was a bit of an odd choice since those were internal spells and the whole point was that they saved in efficiency by being generated inside the mana core itself.

I supposed for a person who couldn't be bothered to learn those basic level invocations, it made sense. There were invocations for sharpened senses, basic body empowerment, muffled sound, and masked scent. They'd be of limited use to a hunter with a dormant core, but I supposed it was possible the man had also been an adept and regularly bought stored mana from mages or was supplied by the cabal he'd apparently worked for.

Much like the mana crystals, it was something for my future apprentices to play with. It wasn't badly designed or anything, but its purpose was redundant. Nobody did inscriptions for basic tier invocations. They were supposed to be for difficult spells that the average person lacked the skill to perform, or for something like a ward that needed to run constantly, even when the mage wasn't going to be around.

Finally, the staff. I couldn't see myself using it, but I had high hopes that this particular piece of gear would be worth breaking the attunements on the mana crystals. Ebalnat had declared himself to be a magician of conjuration and transmutation, meaning he was able to cast intermediate tier spells in those two disciplines and presumably basic spells in all the others. If he'd mastered one more discipline to the intermediate tier, he would have been able to call himself a full mage.

If it turned out that the inscriptions were any good, this staff might become integral to the village's defenses soon. It would probably become the property of the first apprentice I took on who was interested in fighting off monsters or, in some cases, men. If no one came along with that mindset, I'd replace the mana crystals with storage crystals, and they could pull it out of their armory when the need arose.

The staff itself looked like four branches that had been softened to allow them to be braided together, then returned to their former strength. More likely, they'd been deliberately coaxed to grow that way. There were eight spells inscribed on its length, two on each branch. Of the four mana crystals, those were equally divided among the inscriptions instead of being chained together. That was a poor design in my opinion, since it meant the user could have three completely full mana crystals but be locked out of using two of the inscriptions if the fourth crystal that was linked to them was empty.

That problem was mitigated somewhat by the use of mana crystals, since Ebalnat had been able to draw mana from one crystal and put it in the other, albeit at a transference loss. But the more I studied the staff, the less impressed I was. Everything I'd taken from the mages of this area was the work of apprentices or possibly inept magicians. I was aware that my own standards were exacting, even for an archmage, but I'd taught enough apprentices to have a good idea of what they were capable of producing on their own, and these trinkets did not measure up.

The staff had fire blast, flame lance, rain of fire, force bolt, and earth shatter for conjurations in it. The three transmutations were stone wall, earth to water, and earth spear. It wasn't an impressive or diverse collection, but it did cover most of the major points needed to survive wandering in the wastes. All Ebalnat had needed to carry with him was food. With his staff, he could dispatch enemies from a distance as well as create shelter and water.

Other than the float enchantment worked into the top of the staff that was almost out of mana, there wasn't anything else to it. Ebalnat hadn't even included any sort of focusing enchantments to increase his range or accuracy. I tossed the staff onto the pile with the other pieces and let out a frustrated groan. "Why is it that everything these people have is junk?" I asked out loud, though there was no one else there to hear me.

At least it made them easy to fight. If they'd been well-equipped, that whole battle would have been a lot more difficult. The after-battle report was a bleak thing, though. I finished jotting down the information in this bastardized written excuse for a language that everyone thought was Enotian, left the papers with the loot in a secured room in the manor, and dragged myself back home to my own bed.

As much as I would have liked to go straight to bed, I forced myself to spend the next two hours scrying all over the wastelands looking for threats. I had no doubt that I missed hundreds of hiding places despite seeing a few dozen monsters or beasts in my scouting. I didn't find any other people, though, and that was the whole point of my search. Only after I'd done my best to confirm there were no stragglers out there within twenty miles did I finally collapse onto my bed to let my poor, abused mana core start to recover.

It was a restless night, one where I kept waking up every few hours. I took advantage of that to keep refilling my mana crystal over and over, with the results being that when I got up for good the next morning, I felt awful, but had added enough spare mana to cast a good four spells—or eight or nine cheap ones. It was far from enough to make me feel any sort of safe, but it was a start.

Classes were canceled that morning, for obvious reasons. Though none of my students had taken part in the fighting, I was too busy to instruct them. When I got up for good, I felt their mana outside anyway, but it looked like they were doing some exercises we'd already reviewed. As long as they weren't expecting me to referee, that was fine by me.

Today, my house arrest guard was Ganor, the man I'd mentally dominated to get him to deliver the message and key-turned-scry-beacon to Cherok. I stopped next to him when I walked outside, then looked up and said, "Karad leave any messages for me?"

"Uh, no?"

"Anything about our new prisoners?"

"Nope," Ganor said.

Much as I didn't want to do it, I supposed my first stop would be the Garrison jailhouse, all one cell of it. I had questions that I needed answers to, even if it wasn't likely that the two men there had them. I would much rather go back to bed, but it was too important to find out if there were more people coming.

"Alright, let's go," I said.

"Go?" Ganor echoed. "You can't go anywhere. You're supposed to remain here."

I supposed there had been a reason Ganor hadn't been my escort before today, and that all the injuries had limited who they had to spare today. This was the first time any of them had tried to enforce my house arrest on me.

"I need to go to the Garrison," I told Ganor. "Come on, walk with me."

"You're staying right here," Ganor said. "Technically, you shouldn't be allowed outside."

There were probably better ways to handle it. Shel wasn't even thirty feet away, and all I needed to do to get her involved was raise my voice. Even if she didn't have direct authority over Garrison members, she could likely have found a way to resolve things peacefully.

But I was tired and in a bad mood. I'd literally fought and risked my life for the village not twelve hours earlier. I was done with this game of pretend to make them feel better. My already foul mood was plummeting at the thought of dealing with this idiot, and all of a sudden, what little patience I had left was gone.

Of all the ways I could have resolved this issue, casting sleep on Ganor stretched the limits of my restraint. I wanted to do something much more painful, but I settled for a small smile at the satisfying thump his unconscious body made as it hit the ground. The movement caught the attention of my students, who stopped their training to look over at me.

"Everything alright there?" Talik called over to me.

"Just fine," I told him. "I've got to go over to the Garrison building and take care of some business. I'll be back soon."

"Before you go, we were wondering if you were claiming that staff," Ayaka said.

I kept myself from snorting. I wouldn't be caught dead with that piece of junk. "Nope. All yours. Is that what you're playing for today?"

"Winner gets first dibs on any loot you're not keeping," Shel said. "I think we can all agree that we want the staff."

"Heh. Well, best of luck to the four of you then. I'll be back in an hour or two. Let me know who ends up winning it."

With a single look back at Ganor, face down and snoring into the dirt, I walked through the arbor toward the village square.

SEVENTY-THREE

There were four people guarding the cell, but Karad was not among them. That was understandable, in light of everything that had happened yesterday. Other than the one scorched field, the village had escaped the conflict undamaged. As far as people went, the Garrison would be shorthanded, and the Barrier Wardens would likely be divvying up a few extra shifts over the next few weeks.

Karad himself had taken on a bunch of extra responsibilities in his bid to take Noctra's position. Even with me picking up the slack on all magic-related duties, that still left the actual running of the village in addition to his normal duties as the leader of the Garrison itself. I was no bureaucro-mancer, but I understood that it was quite time-consuming to keep the wheels of civilization well-greased. Apparently, even in a village as small as this one, that theory applied.

One of the cardinal rules of interrogation was to question prisoners separately. It was more time-consuming, but also much easier to sniff out possible lies that way. Unfortunately for me, the village only had the one cell. It wasn't so much an insurmountable problem as it was a petty annoy-ance. I was significantly less frugal with my mana now that I'd completed my mana lattice.

"What are you doing here?" Trusai asked.

"Questioning the prisoners," I said.

The guards exchanged glances. "Is... is he allowed to do that?" one of them asked.

"He's not even supposed to be here!" another one said.

"Look, if you want to go get Karad and drag him over here, go ahead. I can wait a bit, but the longer we delay, the longer it takes me to get around to doing the healing on your friends."

"Why not just do that first?"

I shrugged. "More important to find out if there's anyone else out there."

"Don't waste your time," one of the prisoners announced. "We're not going to tell you anything."

"Stupid kid. Ridiculous that anyone is listening to you," the other prisoner added.

"Now, you say that, but..." I mind spiked both of them. Cries of pain as they grabbed at their heads filled the inside of the building, but they quickly faded away. "I'm not above a little torture to get the information I need out of you, not if it saves the lives of my people."

The Garrison members looked torn between placing themselves between me and the prisoners and standing off to one side. They were having a huddled debate in whispers that would soon boil down to sending someone to go fetch Karad, but it hadn't quite reached that point yet.

"Which one of you wants to go first?" I asked. I was standing about three feet from the cell, far enough back that they wouldn't be able to reach me through the bars even if they pressed their bodies right up into them. It wouldn't matter if they tried; my shield ward was more than strong enough to deflect any clumsy attempt at a grab, but it was better to not give them any false hope that might end up wasting some of my mana.

"Do your worst," the first prisoner said.

I mentally divided them into blond hair and big nose, for obvious reasons. Blond was the chatty one, and Nose was the sullen one hunched up and glaring at me. Perhaps he was less resilient than his friend when it came to recovering from mental attacks. That was as good a reason as any to start with him.

"Very well," I said as I cast a sleep spell on him. Blond's eyes rolled up into his head and he dropped like a sack of potatoes.

"What'd you do?!" Nose yelled, leaping at me. He rebounded off the bars, well short of grabbing hold.

"Nothing permanent, and nothing painful. Yet."

There was fear in his eyes, fear that hadn't been there a moment ago. I didn't know what these two had been expecting to happen to them prior to my arrival, but I was starting to suspect they'd had dealings with mages before. Perhaps the Wolf Pack had a fearsome reputation back home.

My small stature had worked against me, but magic didn't care about the age of the practitioner, only the mana. If I could trade on a ruthless reputation other mages had cultivated, I was more than happy to do so. I raised my left hand and pointed a finger straight up. At its tip, I conjured an illusion of a jagged shard of black crystal, a physical representation of a mind spike.

"I'm going to ask you questions now. Every time you don't answer, I'll shove one of these in your brain. If I think you're lying to me, same thing. This won't kill you, no matter how many I hit you with. You'll just wish you were dead."

That wasn't strictly true. Mind spike wasn't fatal, and one or two shots wouldn't cause permanent damage, but a dozen or so over the span of half an hour was a different story. If it came down to that, I'd have to mercy kill Nose, but I'd wait until I'd woken Blond up and asked him my questions again first. Hopefully, it wouldn't come to that.

"First question. Are there any other groups out there getting ready to attack us?" I asked.

Nose's eyes flicked down to where Blond was passed out on the floor next to him. He licked his lips and said, "N-no."

"You're sure about that?"

"Just us," he said.

"I see." I cast mind spike and waited for him to stop writhing around. Once I had his attention, I said, "Sometimes I'm going to ask you questions I already know the answer to, just to keep you honest. What you should have said there was, 'Yes, there's another mage, and Ebalnat has been communicating with him via messages carried back and forth by a hawk.' I won't hold it against you if you don't understand all the intricacies of the magic, but I watched you receive a message with my magic, so I know you knew about it."

Nose glared at me through hands clutching at his face. "You're a devil child," he said.

Behind me, the three Garrison members looked queasy. None made a move to stop me. The fourth had, presumably, left to fetch Karad. I suspected I had less than half an hour left before I had to stop questioning the two prisoners.

"Let's try again. Any other groups out there in the wastelands besides yours and that other mage who was spying on us with the bird?"

This time Nose didn't hesitate. "No."

I nodded. It was possible he was lying, but my own scrying hadn't turned anything up. "Tell me about who hired your group to come out this way. You're from Derro, right?"

"Yes," Nose said. "You killed the mage who hired us. Both mages, I guess."

"What did you know about them?"

"The one with the bird didn't like to talk. His partner gave all the orders. My team is part of the monster hunter's guild in Derro. They contacted us using guild channels and hired us for protection during travel."

More and more I wondered how Noctra had planned to actually have Father carted all the way to Derro with nothing but Nermet to ward off an attack. Was Nermet some sort of idiot savant with the blade and no one had told me? Or maybe he was only supposed to go so far before meeting someone else who'd take possession of Father.

"Are there any camps or waystations between here and Derro?" I asked.

"Yes," Nose said, surprised at the question. "We made stops at Falling Wall and Blighter's Hole on our way here."

"And how far away are those?"

"Uh, Falling Wall's about a day's walk from Derro. Blighter's Hole is another two days, then two days to this village."

So, it had been a risk transporting Father out like that, but not as much as it seemed at first glance. "Tell me about them," I said.

Nose described a satellite village near Derro that sounded much like my own, except it had walls around it, and most of the food grown there was used to feed the citizens of Derro itself. I could only speculate that the land was much more arable there, or that they had significantly more mana to devote to growing produce. The second stop on their journey was little more than a guarded trading post hunters used when they wanted a drink, somewhere to offload pelts and the like, and a safe place to sleep for the night. Its population fluctuated anywhere between five people and fifty.

Neither sounded like places I had any interest in visiting.

I grilled Nose for another twenty minutes, asking him anything I could think of regarding the mage cabal operating out of Derro, the two mages who'd traveled out here with the monster hunters who'd taken a stab at being human hunters and found themselves lacking, Derro itself, and everything Nose knew about magic.

It wasn't that Nose was eager to talk, but after he earned himself a third mind spike when he tried to clam up about his friends, he didn't give me any more trouble. Once I was satisfied, I put him to sleep and prepared to wake up Blond.

"Why were you asking him so many questions about that other place's magic?" one of the Garrison guards asked.

"Trying to get a feel for how advanced their mages are. This guy didn't describe anything too sophisticated, which doesn't mean much. He could be oblivious, or the cabal based in this city might not operate in the public eye. I got the impression that they had power and influence, but not direct control of Derro."

"Why does it matter, though?" the guard pressed. "It only matters that they leave us alone. You already confirmed there was no one else coming."

"No, I confirmed there was no one else here now, as far as he knows. He could be wrong about both of those points. I doubt this cabal will be willing to just give up after losing so many of their mages to me."

The door burst open and Karad strode in. "What in the hell is going on in here?" he demanded.

"Interrogation," I said. "I was just about to wake Blond over here up."

"No one gave you permission to do this," Karad told me. "And if they did, they didn't have the authority."

"I acted on my own authority," I said. "It was granted to me when I turned a man's heart into a lump of stone while it was still inside his chest."

"You can't just go around doing whatever you want!"

"Yes, I can. I've done my best to be polite and patient and helpful, but let me be perfectly clear. This village needs me. I do not need it. I am living here as a matter of convenience, and I am investing my time and mana into it in return. I would be more than happy to relocate somewhere else if you can't accept that."

"Maybe you should," Karad said.

I leaned back a bit and studied his face. "Well then, maybe I will."

Or maybe I'd wipe that sneer off Karad's face with a well-placed shock lance. I'd seethe about this conversation later, but for now, I needed to question the second prisoner to look for inconsistencies in their stories.

"I'm going to question the blond guy now. You can stay and ask questions if you want."

"What kind of questions?"

"If there's anyone else out there getting ready to attack us, or back in Derro where they came from. How strong the mages there are. That kind of stuff."

Karad glowered at me, but gave me a sharp nod and stood there, arms crossed while he watched. I turned back to the prisoners, both of whom were caught in enchanted slumber, and reached out for the artificial mana core I'd placed in Blond to power the spell. Draining it gave me back a little under half what I'd used to make and implant it, but it was more than I would have had otherwise.

Blond groaned as his eyes opened, and I once again held up my illusion of a mind spike. "I'm going to ask you some questions," I told him. "Let me tell you the rules about how you answer them."

SEVENTY-FOUR

I sat in my home-turned-prison and watched another 'secret' meeting between the four adults who ran the town in my scrying mirror. Shel made no effort to hide why she was leaving the arbor any time they had one, and after my argument with Karad earlier, I'd expected an emergency session to be called.

"He was torturing them?" Melmir asked, his face trying to convey far more disgust than he actually felt. If there was anything I'd learned about the head of the Collectors over the last month, it was that he was the kind of kid who'd pulled the legs off of spiders just to watch them struggle. It was a good thing for the world he'd never amount to anything more than a petty tyrant making a handful of people miserable in a backwater village no one had ever heard of.

"I didn't catch the first one, but from what my men described, yes. He had some kind of spell that didn't do anything but cause pain that he used repeatedly to force them to answer questions," Karad said.

"And you just stood there and let him," Solidaire pointed out. "Some might say that makes you every bit as culpable."

"What did you want me to do, club him over the head and drag him out of there? That child is too dangerous. If I'd attacked him, I'd have had to kill him."

"That would get you exiled or executed," Shel said. "Dangerous he might be, but he's also undeniably useful. We're trying to punish him for the whole Noctra thing, but the fact of the matter is he was right. He was right about the mana, he was right about the debtors, he was right about the barrier. Gravin is always right. And, for now, he's still willing to help us."

"I threatened him with exile today," Karad admitted. "He didn't seem to care. Gravin truly thinks he'd survive just fine out in the wastelands. Maybe he would."

"You know what your problem is, Karad?" Melmir asked.

"I'm sure you're about to tell me," the Garrison leader muttered.

Melmir talked right over him. "It's that you can't decide if he's a child or an adult. You keep trying to treat him like a kid, but then if something happens, and you need a mage to sort it out, well then he's an adult. But only for a few hours until you don't need him anymore. Then it's back to pretending he's a normal boy. You can't have it both ways."

Well, that was a surprising bit of insight from an unlikely source. My respect for Melmir rose just a notch. I still didn't like the guy and wouldn't trust him with any real measure of power, but he'd apparently been paying enough attention from the sidelines that he'd called Karad's issue perfectly.

"So which is he, then?" Karad asked.

"He behaves like an adult. He thinks like an adult. If that outlandish story of his is true, he's older than the entire village combined. So treat him like an adult. He's supposed to be under house arrest, but he comes and goes as he pleases. Stop letting him. That soft spot in your heart you've got for him because he helped out your nephew? Grow some calluses over it and start treating him like the criminal he is."

That was not the direction I wanted the conversation to go, but I couldn't really have expected any better considering the source. It looked like my time in Alkerist might soon be up, and if so, I needed to take care of a few things before I left.

"And what do we do the first time we try to tell him he can't do something and he refuses to cooperate?" Solidaire asked. "It seems like every day he shows us some new magic that we have no defense against. He could be watching this meeting right now, just sitting there laughing at the thought that we have any control over him. Or worse, maybe he sees us as threats and we're about to go the same way Noctra did."

He was half right. I wasn't going to kill any of them, but at the same time, I wasn't going to let them run my life. I had my own goals to achieve, and while I had invested some time and mana into the village, it wasn't anything I wasn't willing to walk away from. Having a relatively secure place to sleep and ready source of food and water was convenient, but nothing I couldn't manage myself.

I'd really thought I'd have more time to consolidate my power before I left. The Wolf Pack's quick reaction to my assassination of their assets in the village had completely screwed up my timeline. I wasn't ready, but I could make do, and it sounded like it might be time. Things had escalated far too quickly, perhaps in part because I'd misjudged just how threatened they all were by me. If I tried to dig in and hold a place here, it would end in bloodshed, and my family would likely end up paying part of the price.

"The way I see it, we've got two options. We either let Gravin run wild, doing whatever he wants, and hope the spirits protect us, or we treat him like anyone else. He's not above the rules, despite what he seems to think," Melmir said. "He doesn't just get to decide he's going to ignore being placed under house arrest, not that that was an appropriate punishment for committing murder. He should have brought us proof so we could act on it instead of taking it into his own hands."

"And if he doesn't agree?" Shel asked, cutting Melmir's rambling.

"The same as anyone else, obviously. Exile or execution."

"You want to kill a child? What is he, four? How do you think the village will react to that?"

"I don't see where we have a choice," Melmir said. "Either we get control of him, or he's won."

"We could try working with him instead," Shel said dryly. "He's actually pretty reasonable about requests."

"That's the same as letting him do whatever he wants," Solidaire said.

"So, what, it's about your egos? You need to know that you can crush him with the weight of your laws, and just as important, he needs to know it? It's no wonder none of you can get along with him."

"Shel," Karad said. "He tortured two men today. No one told him to do it. No one authorized it. He didn't even bother to inform us that he was going to do it. You can't do stuff like that on a whim. And it's not the first time he's gone off to do whatever he wanted. He's not supposed to leave that house. That was the whole reason we put him out of the way. I've been letting it slide, and that was a mistake.

"He looks like a child, but he's not. You didn't see him fighting that other mage. He didn't even flinch when bursts of fire were exploding in his face. He's not new to violence, and he's not afraid to murder someone. Knowing he killed Lord Noctra was one thing. Even watching him ambush that mage in the cave was disturbing for all it looked like an accident, but he killed that last mage without hesitation. He's a man trapped in a child's body who is far too comfortable with removing problems using lethal force. I am afraid of what's going to happen to this village when he decides we've become a problem to be handled."

The meeting went around in circles for another hour. Shel tried to defend me, but it was painfully obvious that she was more interested in what I could do as an asset for the village—and herself, since she was still working on igniting her core—than she was in my personal wellbeing. That didn't offend me, but it did mean that I would only have her support for as long as I was useful. Melmir and Solidaire were against letting me stay, though Solidaire was surprisingly bloodthirsty about it. His proposal was that they kill me in my sleep once I'd shown Shel how to ignite more cores.

Karad and Melmir advocated for exile, the former as a softer solution to the problem, and the latter because he was too afraid of retribution if they tried to kill me and failed. To be fair, he was right. I was willing to work with the village council, but the second they moved against me or my family, I'd slay them without hesitation.

The thought that I might object just as lethally to being exiled as I would to attempted assassination apparently hadn't entered Melmir's mind. In all fairness, I was planning on just leaving after I finished my preparations and made my final threats, so in a way, he was right.

After ensuring the village council had no plans to move before the morning, I let the thin thread of mana I'd been running into my mirror's inscriptions snap. I had a lot of work to do tonight, and not a lot of time to do it. By this time tomorrow, I would be gone. Ensuring my family's safety after I left was my top priority.

To that end, I had some modifications to make before morning. The mirror needed two beacons added to it, and I planned to strengthen the durability enchantments on it. It would be the core of my family's defense, after all. I couldn't have it being shattered by someone like Karad or Solidaire. Since completing these tasks before anyone thought to try to stop me would make everything easier, it was going to be a long night.

I arrived at my family's hut about two hours before dawn. It had been trivial to slip out of my own prison without alerting the now-three Garrison guards sitting outside of it simply by walking through the back wall. Carrying my mirror with me through the arbor had been more of a challenge, mostly because it was almost as tall as I was and twice as wide.

Nobody was awake when I arrived, which suited my purposes just fine. I pushed the curtain aside, cast a light spell that had just enough mana to give dim illumination to the interior of my parents' hut, and took a seat at the table. The mirror itself was left leaning up against a wall.

My family lived in a hovel, no better or worse than the dozens of other hovels that surrounded them. Things could be so much better with access to better resources and knowledge, even here in the middle of a desert with no mana. But the leaders of Alkerist had made it quite clear that they valued control over progress, so the current state was how things would stay.

Father sat up in bed and blinked up at the light I'd hung in the air. "Gravin, what are you doing here?" he asked in a bleary voice. "How early is it?"

"Earlier than you'd like to get up, or later than I'd like to stay up, depending on how you want to look at it," I told him. "I need to teach you how to use this mirror I made, and I don't have a lot of time to do it. Some things have happened, and I'll need to leave the village for a while, so this will be the only way we'll have to communicate."

"What?" Father asked, all traces of sleepiness gone from him.

That woke Mother, which was fine. Senica's snores continued uninterrupted from her tiny pallet off behind my parents. I'd wanted to talk to them first anyway. My sister didn't need to know all the details, like that a quarter of the council wanted to murder me in my sleep and another half was willing to settle for just exiling me.

"Come here, let me show you how to make this mirror work," I said. "I'll explain everything while you practice."

CHAPTER

SEVENTY-FIVE

I 'd been digging through Noctra's books for about three hours before Karad finally caught up with me. He barged into the room, a deep scowl on his face and anger in every jerky movement he made. "By the spirits, what do you think you're doing?" he snarled at me as he came to a stop opposite the desk I was sitting at.

"Looking through these books for information," I said. "I'd planned on doing it earlier, but there was always something in the way. By the time I'd finished teaching myself this blasphemous written language—which does not in any way match our spoken one—I was busy dealing with our uninvited guests."

"You are under house arrest. You can't just sneak out. This was the deal you agreed to," Karad said.

"I'm altering our agreement," I told him without bothering to look up as I flipped another page. The effect was somewhat spoiled by the fact that I'd placed several books on the chair to boost me up to a height where I could use the desk. "Or rather, since you plan to run me out of town or kill me, whichever is easiest, I am inclined to say the agreement no longer applies."

Karad gave a rueful laugh. "Solidaire was right. You were spying on us."

"It seemed prudent," I said. "Don't you worry, though. I'll be leaving today. You won't even have to fight me. Once I'm done skimming through these and I decide which ones I'll be taking with me, I'll just gather a bit of food and be on my way."

"You know, you wouldn't have to go if you just stopped doing things like this," Karad said. There was still a lot of anger in his tone, but he was doing an admirable job of controlling himself. The twitching in his hands had stopped, at least. That had to count for something.

"No. I'm not going to let you control what I do. You don't get to tell me where I can go or when. I'll do as I always have: whatever I want to, whenever I feel like doing it. I was willing to go along with that farce of a deal and assist the village in growing because it was convenient for me to do so, but it seems you all thought you had some method of enforcing it on me. That was a mistake on your part."

"What about the barrier? And the people you were going to give the spirits' blessings too?"

"Not really my problem now that I'm an exile, is it?"

Karad didn't have an answer to that. I flipped another page and kept reading.

"You're still not allowed to be here," he said finally, just to fill the silence.

"Then do something about it, if you can."

I glanced up and saw him standing there with his fists clenched at his side and fire burning in his eyes. With some visible effort, he controlled himself, said stiffly, "See that you're beyond the barrier's range by sundown," and spun on his heel to march back out of the room.

"Karad," I said just as he reached the door. He froze in place without looking back. "I'm leaving my scrying mirror with my family. It will remain in their care. I will be speaking to them regularly to ensure they do not suffer in any way over your issues with me. Rest assured that I can return at a moment's notice if I feel a need to. I am... very protective of them. It would be in your best interest to ensure nobody tries to take out any frustrations they might have on them."

I'd placed a scrying beacon and a teleportation beacon enchantment on the mirror itself in addition to modifying it to allow Father to communicate with me directly through it and showed him how to keep both charged. I could check in on them for a fraction of the mana I would otherwise need, and, if necessary, teleport back to the village. Short of remaining here myself to watch over them, it was the best I could do on such short notice with limited resources.

"I understand," he said.

The door closed behind him, leaving me alone to sort through more books. Karad hadn't even contested the idea of me taking any with me. Judging by how much dust had been layered in the room when I'd arrived, no one here valued the knowledge of a world beyond their village. Typical.

Shel was the next to find me. I didn't know who exactly had told her, but she walked into the room just as I was finishing up sorting through the various tools Noctra and Iskara had used in their experiments. Much as it pained me to leave it all behind, especially in the hands of people who didn't have the first clue what any of it did, my current mana constraints demanded I pick and choose what to take, and the only value I was likely to get from any of the instruments here was a small amount of coin from selling them when I reached Derro.

"I'm surprised you're leaving," she said. "I really figured you'd kill Mclmir, maybe Solidaire, too."

"There's nothing here worth fighting over," I said. "You all needed me far more than I needed you."

"Well, that's the truth. I don't suppose you have any plans on igniting any cores on your way out?"

"Is that the only reason you're here, Shel?"

"What do you want me to say, Gravin? It was a transactional relationship, and we all knew we were getting the better end of the deal. Why do you think no one at the arbor objected to your coming and going, even though we all knew you weren't supposed to leave? I don't care if you want to stay or go, but I'd hoped you would at least finish what you started with your students."

"I'll make you a deal," I said. "That corner of the new greenhouse that was supposed to go to me, you'll plant what I tell you there. I don't know how often I'll stop by to harvest it, but I will, and you'll keep growing whatever I want. You promise that, and bring me three full storage crystals before I leave in a few hours, and I'll help you ignite your core."

"Three full crystals?" Shel said. She paused to think about that, then nodded. "I think I can manage that."

No doubt Ayaka would be receiving a visit soon, as I couldn't imagine an easier way for Shel to get what I wanted. In a sense, she'd be stealing the mana from the village, but I found it difficult to make myself care. Their mana had been stolen from them for so long anyway, what was one more day? Besides, without me to power that ward stone for them every night, they didn't have much they could do with it anyway.

Technically, Father could do that. In teaching him how to activate the scrying mirror, I'd inadvertently given him enough knowledge to get the ward stone working. I'd made sure he knew that, but left it up to him to decide whether or not he wanted to offer that service.

"I trust you'll be able to find me once I leave the manor," I said.

"I'm sure I'll manage somehow," Shel agreed.

"If not, the offer will remain open. I'll be back to visit my family from time to time."

"They can't even exile you properly," Shel said with a laugh. "Bunch of idiots, anyway. They couldn't just leave well enough alone."

"Luckily for them, it's not worth the headaches that would come with killing them," I said. "You'd better hurry or I'll leave before you get what you need."

Shel left, and a few minutes later, I followed her out of the manor. Despite wasting all afternoon there, my total haul was two books and a map. It wasn't that I wasn't interested in a few other books, but I didn't want them bad enough to carry them a hundred miles or more while I walked through the wastelands.

I stuffed my loot into a satchel I'd absconded with and left to go find some food for my journey.

"You can't go!" Senica wailed as she squeezed me in her arms.

I shot an exasperated look at my mother, but there was no support there. I'd gotten a similar hug from her moments earlier, even though she'd already known my plans. "I'm not leaving forever," I said. "Just for a little while. I'll be back to visit."

"Why Derro?" Mother asked.

"That's where the cabal that's harassing the village is located. Presumably, that means they've got some knowledge about what's going on. They're just a stop on the road, though. The world isn't supposed to be like all of... this," I said with a vague gesture. "I've never seen such a large scar. Normally, mana would fill the air, more than anyone could ever use. Here, it's more precious than water. One day, I'll show you what I mean."

I hoped to, at least. The more I learned, the more I was starting to suspect something catastrophic had happened between my death and rebirth. I had a moon missing from the sky, some sort of global language curse, and a mana desert covering well over ten thousand square miles. Finding some explanations to these mysteries was the real reason I was going to Derro, though I might just break the Wolf Pack's power while I was there.

My plan was to wrap up my goodbyes here, talk to my father in the fields on my way out, and begin my journey. That plan was currently being interrupted by Senica crying and refusing to stop hugging me. Just as I'd managed to extract myself by promising to bring her to wherever I ended up so she could see the world outside the village, Shel appeared in the doorway.

"Gravin? Good, I was starting to worry," she said. "I've got the storage crystals you needed."

"Excellent," I said. "Let's go ahead and take care of this right now then."

I took the mana out of all three crystals, almost twice what I needed to make the ritual work. One crystal was my payment, the others were for Shel herself. Under my instruction, she got her mana spinning. It only took a few minutes, especially with me aiding her, before she reached the critical state needed to ignite her core. As soon as it was over, she looked at me with wonder in her eyes.

"That's it? That's all it takes?" she asked. "It's so simple. How did we... for so many years..."

"Blame that on the tithe. Nobody ever had enough mana to fill their core," I told her. "Now, I've got one last stop to make, and then I'm off to begin my exile."

"Ah, yes. I'll walk with you, if you don't mind," Shel said.

"You mean escort me out of the village."

"Something like that," she agreed.

Karad, Melmir, and Solidaire were waiting for us out on the street. I walked past them without a word, and they silently fell into step behind me. I quickly located Father in the west field and made my way to him while my entourage of councilors trailed behind me. I pretended not to see the Barrier Wardens with suspiciously familiar bows lurking behind buildings or pillars of stone. My shield ward was fully charged, and if they tried anything, I'd fry the lot of them.

For a nice change of pace, no one made a move against me. I walked up to Father, who looked past me toward the councilors and shook his head. "You're going through with it?" he said.

"I am."

Father pulled me into a hug, one that squished my satchel—now full of food—into my side. "Good luck, son. Be safe, and be careful. I know, I know, I don't have to tell you that."

"I'll check in soon," I said. "A few days at most. I love you, Father."

"I love you, too. I'm sorry things didn't turn out the way you wanted."

"I was always going to leave eventually. This is just a bit sooner than we expected," I said. "It's fine. I accomplished everything I needed to before I set off on my own."

"You're too young to be so grown up," Father told me.

"Sorry."

"Don't be. You're still my son. You're just also... Keiran, too."

"I am, and that's how you know I'll be fine. Goodbye. You'll hear from me soon."

"Safe journey, Gravin," Father said.

I adjusted my satchel and walked toward the setting sun while my father, four village councilors, a handful of Barrier Wardens, and a dozen or so farmers watched me leave.

End of Book 1

ABOUT THE AUTHOR

D.E. Sherman, also known as EmergencyComplaints on the internet, grew up reading fantasy and tried his hand at writing his first novel on an old MS-DOS text editor program when he was seven years old. That story didn't pan out; maximum character limits were a thing back then.

Undeterred, he kept writing on other platforms, reading full-time, devouring JRPGs, and playing D&D. He is now the author of several series, including Keiran, The God Machine, and Ascendant.

Author website:

ABOUT TIMELESS WIND PUBLISHING

Founded in late 2020 by Lorne Ryburn and Silas Sontag, Timeless Wind Publishing is an up-and-coming indie publishing house. We love sci-fi and fantasy—progression fantasy, power fantasy, LitRPG, time loops, cultivation, system apocalypse—genre fiction of all kinds! We're prolific readers within these genres and endeavor to bring awesome books into the limelight.

We look forward to helping authors (aspiring and published alike) develop and expand an audience of readers who believe in their vision.

Our logo is an exotic cat from a Palmyrene ruin. The word along its back roughly translates to, "Alas!" or "What a shame!" This word is present on all gravestones in Palmyra. It's a recognition that all things come to an end... even the best people and stories. Alas!

We hope our readers will have "alas" moments when they finish our books.

Connect with Timeless Wind Publishing

TimelessWind.com
Facebook.com/timelesswind
Twitter.com/timeless_wind
Instagram.com/timelesswindpub

www.ingramcontent.com/pod-product-compliance
Lightning Source LLC
Chambersburg PA
CBHW020250030726

47499CB00001B/140